BLACK MAPS

BLACK MAPS

PETER SPIEGELMAN

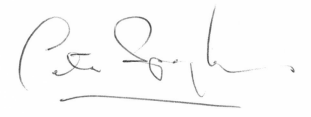

ALFRED A. KNOPF · NEW YORK 2003

THIS IS A BORZOI BOOK
PUBLISHED BY ALFRED A. KNOPF

Grateful acknowledgment is made to Alfred A. Knopf for
permission to reprint an excerpt from the poem "Black Maps"
from *Selected Poems* by Mark Strand. Copyright © 1979, 1980
by Mark Strand. Reprinted by permission of Alfred A. Knopf,
a division of Random House, Inc.

ISBN 1-4000-4075-2

Manufactured in the United States of America
First Edition

For Alice

The present is always dark.
Its maps are black,
rising from nothing,
describing,

in their slow ascent
into themselves,
their own voyage,
its emptiness,

the bleak, temperate
necessity of its completion.

—Mark Strand, "Black Maps"

BLACK MAPS

Prologue

In the dream we've swum straight out from shore. The ridged, sandy bottom has fallen away below us, and the beach has vanished behind ranks of glassy waves. The sky is cloudless and the sunlight so bright off the faceted ocean that my eyes are squinted and bleary. The wind throws scraps of the Atlantic in our faces. Anne and I are drifting in the chop. I know this place. This is Nantucket. This is our honeymoon.

Anne is giddy and breathing hard. The water has made her cropped, blond hair a sleek cap, and has made her hazel eyes pure green. Her forehead, nose, and cheeks are tanned, and her teeth are very white. She floats on her back, tilts her head to the sun, and lets the water toss her.

I am breathing hard too, in short, audible bursts. Anne is laughing and speaking, but in the wind and the chop and the sound of my own breath, her words are lost to me.

Her shoulders and arms and the tops of her breasts are brown and smooth. I see the muscles shift in her forearms and wrists as she treads water. Her swimsuit is green, and through it I see the shape of her nipples, the lines of her ribs, and the rounded muscles of her belly. We have rested, and now we turn toward shore.

In life I am a strong swimmer, but here I am tired. Anne swims ahead of me, the soles of her feet, her long legs, her elbows and hands, flashing in water and sunlight. Her strokes are fluid and perfectly timed and she pulls farther and farther ahead. I beat through the waves behind her in short, arm-weary strokes. My legs feel heavy, and cold patches spread across my shoulders and back. Saltwater washes through my mouth and eyes, and the wind grows louder in my ears.

Anne swims on, beautifully and with great intent. She is so far ahead now that I only glimpse her, through moving alleys and corridors of waves. My belly and groin are cold, and I am less swimming now than punching and kicking the water.

Suddenly, the sky clots up with thick cloud. The ocean goes gray all about me, and the waves become falling slabs of slate. A heavy sadness washes over me, and I realize that I am crying, and that with every breath I am calling her name.

As the rain begins, I am lifted up high on a wave, and I hang there, caught. Below me, the beach is gone. Instead there is a rocky shore and a narrow, wooden dock running over flat water. Pines rise steeply from the water's edge; low clouds are caught in their jagged tops. Beyond the dock, among the trees, I see part of a house—a gravel path to wooden steps, a deep porch, a stone chimney, green clapboards, black shutters. I know this place too. This is the lakefront. This is our home. This is the swim that Anne takes every morning, from June to September.

She has reached the dock, and climbs the small metal ladder at the end. Water streams from her brown shoulders and legs, and I see the muscles working in her calves and thighs as she steps onto the dark planks. Her swimsuit is cut high on her slim hips, and has ridden up over her rear. She stands on the dock and hooks her fingers in the seat and tugs it down. She combs her fingers through her hair and shakes the water out. It falls from her hands in gleaming drops. She bends and reaches for the towel folded by the ladder.

Now Anne turns to look out over the lake. Of course she cannot see me, or see the wave that has pitched me up so high. But she sees a cloud rolling in from the far shore and a wind coming with it across the wide expanse of water. She sees the surface ripple and darken, like goose-bumps, she thinks, and feels a chill herself. She wraps the towel about her shoulders. Her dark brows furrow. She looks for something out on the lake. Me? Not me. I am at work by now—no, still at work from the day before. She does not see me because I am not there. Neither does she see the figure cross behind her from woods to house, scale the porch railing, and crouch in the shadows, waiting. I try to call to her but I am choked by sadness and fear and I cannot make a sound or even take a breath.

And now this wave is breaking and I am pitched headlong under a solid sheet of gray water. The ocean rushes through my nose and ears. I cannot shut my mouth to it. I welcome it. I am tumbling now, not sure of where the surface lies, caught in some cold undertow and headed out to sea.

I washed up across my bed like a castaway, tangled in sheets like seaweed, gripping pillows like an oar. I rolled on my back and stared at the ceiling and the shadows sketched there by the thin morning light. The phone was ringing far away, at the other end of the house, but even at a distance it made my eyes shake in my head. I lay there, waiting for the spinning to stop and for the answering machine to pick up. But neither would happen. I was still drunk, and I'd shot the machine last week.

Chapter One

Everyone was in a bad mood. It was a palpable thing in midtown, as pungent as the bus exhaust on the cold evening air and as loud as the traffic. The streets were awash in it. Cars and trucks and taxicabs were locked in mortal combat, surging forward by inches, then rocking to a halt, their drivers cursing and leaning on their horns, their passengers fuming. Surly streams of people poured from office towers and washed into the gridlock, adding their own fulminations to the angry grind. Sharp elbows and rude gestures were everywhere.

Maybe it was the season that brought it on—a week before Thanksgiving, the cusp of the holidays. Maybe it was the prospect of Christmas shopping, or of all that family time, bearing down like a freight train. Maybe it was the gnawing obsession with this year's bonus—assuming there was one—or the corrosive dwelling on the next round of layoffs. Maybe everyone was battle fatigued—edgy from the latest terror alerts, strung-out from life in the crosshairs. Or maybe it was just another hellish rush hour. Whatever, it was some nasty karma.

At seven p.m. I was threading my way through these wretches, headed up Park Avenue toward 52nd Street. The intersection was a particular mess. Sawhorses and traffic cones were scattered across it, and in the middle of the street was a trench that belched steam. Steel plates only partly covered the excavation, and I wondered if anyone had yet disappeared into its depths. I crossed 52nd, threading between two taxis, and pushed against a wave of people into the lobby of Mike's building. I crossed the marble floor to the guard station, produced half a dozen pieces of ID, waited while they called upstairs, signed in, and got on an elevator. I pressed 30, and the doors closed silently.

Michael Metz is a partner at the law firm of Paley, Clay and Quick, and the firm's biggest rainmaker. He's also my friend, and has been since college, from the day we first chased each other around a squash court, vying for a spot on the team ladder. For the last couple of years, he's also been my most regular employer. Mike's got an eclectic practice—corporate work, entertainment, matrimonial, every now and then some criminal work. And I've done lots of different things for him—background checks, find-the-girlfriend, find-the-boyfriend, find-the-assets. But tonight, he'd said, was something different.

The elevator doors opened with a sigh, and I stepped into Paley, Clay's reception area. At this hour, in this season, it was dark and quiet. The front desk sat in a pool of light and looked like a mahogany toll-booth. It dwarfed the old guard dozing behind it. He yawned and rubbed his eyes as I approached.

"John March to see Mike Metz," I told him. He flipped slowly through the wrinkled papers on his clipboard and punched some numbers into the phone. He whispered into the handset, and told me in a voice I could barely hear to go in.

I pushed through glass doors and walked down a broad corridor lined on one side by shelves of law books, and on the other by offices. The offices were mostly dark, though here and there I spotted some luckless associates and scowling paralegals. I turned a corner and passed a vacant conference room, an empty kitchen, and a small clutch of people staring anxiously at a copy machine. I walked through another set of glass doors into a region of larger offices, Oriental rugs, and dark wood paneling. Partner country.

Mike stood at the end of the hallway, outside the double doors of his office. He was bent over his secretary's desk, pen in hand, leafing through a thick file. He was, as always, impeccably turned out. He wore a navy suit, expertly cut to his lanky frame, a brilliant white shirt, and a tightly knotted tie, patterned with green and gold dolphins leaping on a field of royal blue. His cuff links were enamel hexagons in a blue that matched his tie. His cap-toed shoes were gleaming black. As a concession to the late hour, he had unbuttoned his jacket.

He pulled a sheaf of papers from the file, set them on top of the folder, scrawled something on the top page, and put the whole pile in the center of his secretary's spotless desk. He straightened to his full six-foot-four height and ran a hand through his sparse, dark hair. Mike is in his middle thirties, just a couple of years older than me, but he looks forty-something. The price of partnership, I guess. He still plays competitive squash, though, and the impenetrable calm and arctic patience that drove me nuts in college still carry him into the late rounds of every tournament he enters. They make him pure hell to face in a courtroom, too. He eyed my clothes.

"You sort of dressed for the occasion," he said. "Thanks." Unlike Mike, I was not always impeccably turned out. According to him, several of his partners were sure I was a bicycle messenger. But now, in gray flannels, a black wool polo shirt, and a black leather jacket, I was well within the bounds of appropriate.

"No visible tattoos, no piercings, and I unscrewed the bolts in my neck. What more could you ask?" I said. "Where's your guy?"

"In the conference room, but let's talk a little first." Mike leaned against the desk.

"That would be good," I said, "since you've told me exactly nothing about this." I sat in his secretary's chair.

"There's a reason. The guy is shaken up right now, and based on what he's told me, he's probably right to be. I've known him a long time, and he's not usually a jumpy guy. But right now he's scared and paranoid."

"Okay, he's scared and paranoid, no different from most clients. But what's his problem? And does he have a name?" Mike looked at me. A rueful grin came across his lean, sharp-featured face.

"He does," Mike answered, "but he'd rather I didn't tell you what it is—or anything more about him—until he's had a chance to size you up." My eyebrows went up. "He wants to look you over. He wants to get a sense of you before he starts talking about his problems. Like I said, he's scared. You have to bear with him."

"He understand that I'd actually be working for you on this?"

"He understands. And I told him I've had a lot of experience with you, and that you're smart and thorough and stubborn, and that you run faster and jump higher and have healthy teeth and a shiny coat, and probably some other lies too. But he's jumpy." Mike shrugged.

"Let's go," I said, sighing, and I followed him into the conference room.

The room was dim, lit only by the small ceiling lights that shone on the architectural prints ranged around the walls, and by the city lights that glowed through the bank of windows opposite the door. In the center of the room was an oval table in dark wood. A man was sitting at it, facing the door. On the table, next to him, was a small filing box. The man didn't look scared and he didn't look jumpy. He looked rich.

He was in his early forties, with olive skin and black hair brushed straight back from a wide forehead. He had a broad chest and thick neck, and thick shoulders and wrists. His wide face was clean-shaven, with dark, deep-set eyes and a nose that looked like it might once have been broken. He had the start of a double chin and a slight blurriness to his jawline that might some day ripen into jowls. But it hadn't happened yet. Now he was like a sleek, well-fed bear. And a well-dressed bear, too. He wore a shirt striped in several shades of blue, and a silk tie in a dark, solid red. At his cuffs were intricate gold knots. A gray suit jacket was slung over the chair next to him. He stared at me but said nothing.

I sat down across the table from him. Mike shut the door, drifted over to the window, and stared out at the nighttime city. The man sat back, propped his elbows on the arms of his chair, and looked at me over the top of his steepled fingers. Then he rubbed his eyes with his fingertips and took a deep breath. And then we were all quiet for a while. Still looking out the window, Mike prompted him.

"You had some questions for John."

"Yeah," he answered after some thought. He slipped a thick silver pen from his shirt pocket and began to twirl it in his right hand. "Yeah. My first question is how long have you been doing this? Investigating." His voice was surprisingly soft and had a trace of an accent. Brooklyn or Long Island.

"Just over two years," I answered. "I was a cop for seven years before that."

"In the city?" I shook my head.

"Upstate."

"Albany?"

"Farther north. Burr County. It's in the Adirondacks." He was quiet and looked at me some more.

"You from up there?" he asked.

"No." I didn't offer any more. He thought about that a little and then went on.

"You were a detective?"

"I was a sheriff's investigator for five years. I spent the first two in uniform."

"Homicide investigator?"

"We weren't set up that way. We were a small department, so investigators covered everything. Property crime, domestic, drugs, vice. And homicide," I added.

"Not much white-collar crime up there, I guess," he observed. I laughed a little.

"Not much."

"How old are you?" I glanced at Mike, who gazed like a lighthouse keeper out over the city.

"Thirty-two."

"You go to college?"

"Yes."

"You start with the sheriff right after?"

"Yes."

He pulled the cap off his pen and then slipped it back on, again and again. He looked down at his large, well-kept hands while he did it, like they were someone else's hands. He looked up at me again.

"Were you good at it?"

I glanced at Mike. No help there. He could have been working out his tax returns or figuring the age of the universe or reminiscing fondly about his last meal at Le Bernardin.

"I was good at it."

"Why'd you stop doing it?" I saw Mike's shoulders stiffen. The man stopped playing with his pen. I took a deep breath.

"Personal reasons," I said. He was quiet for a while.

"It was your choice? They didn't ask you to leave?"

"It was my choice."

The man leaned back in his chair. "And the private investigating, are you good at that, too?" I paused. This was getting old.

"No, not really. Mostly I hang out at home watching TV, faking my time reports, and padding my expenses." The man sat up. He held his pen in his fist, looking at me, the first stirrings of anger on his brow. Mike turned around, his face in neutral. I went on, speaking evenly, matter-of-factly.

"What do you expect me to say? Of course I'm going to say I'm good. And that could be true or it could be a load of crap. And there's not much we can talk about here that will tell you one way or the other. I can understand your position. You've got a problem, and it must be a bad one if you need to hire someone like me. I imagine the last thing you want is to make it worse by involving some clown who's incompetent, indiscreet, greedy, or worse. I'm not that clown, but you've got to take Mike's word on that. Or not."

He sat perfectly still in his chair, looking across at me. Mike sighed and said, "Well, I think we're done for the moment, yes?" The man slipped his pen back into his pocket and nodded his head very slightly.

"John, could you wait outside?" Mike asked.

I shut the door behind me.

Chapter Two

I sat at the secretary's desk, and after about two minutes Mike opened the conference-room door.

"Come in and have a seat, John," he said.

"I passed?" Mike rolled his eyes.

"It's your winning personality. Come on in." I came.

"John, this is Rick Pierro. Rick, this is John March." Mike walked around the table and sat down. Pierro rose, and we shook hands. He was about my height—just over six feet. I tossed my jacket on the table and sat.

"Sorry for making you jump through hoops, but this thing has got me wound up pretty tight." Pierro's palms were on the edge of the table, and he leaned forward slightly as he spoke. "What you said about trusting Mike was dead on. I trust him absolutely, and he tells me only good things about you. And you seem like a no-bullshit guy to me—so let's go." The accent was Long Island.

"Not a problem," I replied. "What are we here to talk about?" Pierro glanced at Mike, then took a deep breath and dove in.

"You know much about Wall Street?" he asked.

"Some," I replied. A smile flickered across Mike's face.

"I'm at French Samuelson. You hear of it?" he asked.

"The investment bank," I said. Pierro nodded.

"That's what we are now—for better or for worse. When I started there, twenty years ago, we were a meat-and-potatoes commercial bank—deposits, loans, checking accounts, all the basics. Now we do it all—everything from traditional banking to mergers and acquisitions, IPOs, even venture capital. And we're market makers in cash, fixed income, and derivatives, in every major trading center." He said it with an odd mix of pride and irony.

"I've seen the change firsthand. I joined French straight out of college, went into the training program and then into corporate lending. I did well there. For three years I was the top loan producer, and in the meantime I'd gotten through b-school at night. Then I made the switch over to investment banking, and I did even better. I started as a junior associate in mergers and acquisitions. In two years I was running a team. Then I did a stint in London and another in Singapore. And in both places I brought in big deals, and big fees. I got management responsibility, too. From Sing I came back to the States, and ran a couple of different industry groups in M&A. And for the last three years—until six months ago—I ran all of M&A in North America. Six months ago I took over our venture capital unit." He paused.

"Nice career," I observed. I didn't know what else to say. Pierro slipped his pen out of his pocket again. He twirled it in his thick fingers and nodded.

"I've done alright—despite what's happened in the markets," he said. "And, you know, I'm not an old guy. I got some miles in me yet. Two months ago, I find out I'm up for a spot on the executive committee. That's the group of about a dozen senior managers that actually runs the whole place; you can't go much farther at French." Pierro paused again and looked at Mike, who moved his head minutely. Pierro continued. "A week ago, I get this." He reached over to his suit jacket and took a thick envelope from a pocket. He slid it across the table.

Inside was a fax. The cover sheet bore only Pierro's name in bold type, along with the message, "We'll talk soon." Vague, but ominous. The fax itself was comprised of five different documents: two letters and a memo, each dated eighteen years ago, and each concerning a company called Textiles Pan-Europa; a two-page list of what appeared to be funds transfers; and a copy of a year-old magazine article. One of the letters was on French Samuelson stationery; the other one, and the memo, were on the letterhead of a firm called Merchant's Worldwide Bank. I leafed through the fax a couple of times, but I didn't get it. Mike and Pierro watched me.

"This needs some explaining," Mike said. "Have you read about Merchant's, John? It got a lot of press a few years ago, and there's a story on it every so often because the case is still going on." The name was familiar, but I couldn't place it and I told him so. "Maybe you know it by another name," he said. " 'Money Washing Bank.' "

"The money-laundering thing," I said. Mike nodded.

"I'll give you the *Reader's Digest* version; the details are in the file." He pushed the filing box over to me and began.

"Merchant's Worldwide Bank was the largest of several dozen institutions owned by a Luxembourg holding company called the Merchants Group. And, according to federal prosecutors, it was the largest criminally controlled financial services firm that anyone's ever heard of. It had a lot of legitimate customers and did a lot of legitimate business, but that was basically window dressing. MWB's real business was servicing a clientele that ran the gamut from bad to worse: drug dealers, arms merchants, dictators, terrorists—bad, bad guys.

"Money laundering was their leading service, and they were top-of-the-line providers. This wasn't retail smurfing—no mom-and-pop operation passing a few million a day on the street. This was a wholesale business. They maintained hundreds of corporate shells—anyplace in the world you might need one—ready and waiting to funnel cash by the tens of millions, even the hundreds of millions, daily. These were entities with structures so twisted you'd need an army of accountants just to draw the org charts. And they controlled real companies too—legitimate businesses with offices and employees and products and everything. They'd buy into them, usually secretly, and turn them into cash conduits. Behind it all, to move the money around for them, they had a massive network of correspondent banks that included some of the biggest firms in the world." Mike leaned back in his chair, his hands clasped behind his head.

"It was unique in terms of scale and scope, a beautiful thing, in its own way," Mike continued, a hint of admiration in his voice. "But it started coming apart just over three years ago, when the number two guy at a regional bank called Southern States Trust tried to buy drugs from a DEA agent in San Diego. They got him dead to rights, video and all, so he did a lot of talking. One of the things he talked about was who really owned Southern States. A hungry assistant U.S. attorney in San Diego started pulling, and it all started to unravel. He documented a chain of secret ownership for Southern States through over a dozen proxies, in six different countries, leading back finally to MWB. The roof really caved in a short while after, when the head guy at MWB, a Pakistani named Zahed, was a no-show for a meeting with the U.K. authorities. Two weeks later he turned up in Kuwait, dead.

"That's the condensed version. I didn't even get to the investigation of the thing, which is a soap opera in itself. The number of agencies involved in this country alone is staggering. Add in the players from all the other countries MWB operated in, and you get a zoo. It's all in the file." I was quiet for a moment, letting the story sink in, recalling some of what I had read about MWB over the last couple of years.

"Mike, you know I always like the business, but this kind of forensic accounting thing is really not my line," I said. "There are firms that specialize in this." I knew he understood; this was for Pierro's benefit. But Mike went on.

"MWB is the background, John, but this case isn't money laundering. Take a closer look at the fax."

I picked up the fax again, and went through the five documents in it. The first was a letter on MWB stationery, from an MWB managing director named Gerard Nassouli to Emilio Dias, who had apparently been the treasurer and CFO of Textiles Pan-Europa. It was dated February 14, eighteen years ago. Valentine's Day. In the letter, Nassouli reports that he has been dealing with a "sympathetic" and "flexible" banker at French Samuelson, who will help to establish a credit facility for Textiles' U.S. subsidiary, Europa Mills U.S.A. In the letter, he names the banker: Rick Pierro.

Next was an internal MWB memo, dated a week after the letter, written from Nassouli to "The Files," and describing a meeting between him and Pierro. At this meeting, according to the memo, Nassouli and Pierro filled out the French Samuelson credit facility application for Textiles, and they prepared the Textiles corporate documentation, required to establish an account at French.

This was followed about three weeks later by a letter from Pierro to Dias, confirming that a revolving credit facility would be established for Europa Mills. The next document was the list of funds transfers. Each entry consisted of a date, an amount, an ordering party, and a beneficiary. There were well over a hundred of them, listed on two pages, and they spanned a six-year period that began eighteen years ago. Given the context, and the parties involved in the transfers, they seemed to represent drawdowns by Europa Mills U.S.A. against its credit facility at French, and subsequent repayments of the loans, with interest, by Europa Mills' parent company, Textiles Pan-Europa. If that's what they were, then in a six-year period, something over $120 million had flowed back and forth between French, Europa Mills, and Textiles.

The final document in the fax was an article from the *Economist*, an issue late the previous year. It was a piece about the aftermath of the MWB collapse, or one aspect of it. It focused on four different European companies. According to the article, they had all at one time been vital, expanding concerns, but were now just so much twisted metal in the larger train wreck of MWB. They were a few of the many companies secretly controlled by MWB, the story went, which had turned them all into conduits for money laundering. One of the firms listed, its name underlined in the fax, was Textiles Pan-Europa. According to the article, many of the executives of these now defunct companies were missing. Some, like the Textiles senior executive team, had turned up dead.

Pierro moved restlessly around the room while I read, for a while reading over my shoulder. Then he wandered into the hallway, to pace. Mike went to the window again and stood there motionless and silent, his head nearly touching the glass. When I finished, I stacked the papers into a pile.

"So?" Mike asked, without turning around.

"The implication, I guess, is that Textiles was an MWB front, and that they were using the loans from French to wash money—pumping clean dollars from the loans into Textiles' U.S. subsidiary, and paying off the loans with dirty money from the parent company in Europe." Mike nodded, still staring into the night. I leafed through the first few pages of the fax again.

"And I guess this memo from Nassouli to 'The Files' is meant to be the smoking gun. The credit application and the corporate documents should have been prepared and signed by executives from Textiles, not by the salesman making the loan." Mike nodded again. The dark glass reflected the smile on his face. I continued. "But there doesn't seem to be anything conclusive here. Nassouli's memo is the most damning, but you can't tell from this if it's accurate, or even genuine. And there's nothing that tells us if the loans were arranged before or after MWB came into control of Textiles." Pierro came back into the room as I was speaking and sat down across from me.

"That's right," he said, softly. "Nothing concrete, just the suggestion that I was working with these bastards, and that I was a party to fraud." I looked again at the message on the cover sheet.

"You think this is blackmail?" I asked them both.

Pierro answered. "Mike's a lawyer, so he'll say he's not sure. Me—I don't know what the hell else it could be." Mike still had not said anything, nor had he moved from the window. We were coming to a tricky part now.

"Assuming that's what this is, how much leverage do they actually have here?" I asked, looking across at Pierro. His chuckle surprised me.

"Hey, I like that. Much better than 'Are you a crook, Rick?' Very smooth. But the deal with Textiles was by the book. I did all the homework I was supposed to do on that deal, and on every other credit line and loan I produced. Textiles had everything in order. Did I do business with MWB? Absolutely—lots of it, and so did everybody else on the Street back then. They were big players. And clean players, as far as anyone knew at the time. I knew Gerry Nassouli, and I thought he was a smart, funny guy. He introduced us, and a lot of other firms, to a lot of deals. But that meeting in the memo, the one with Nassouli and the account forms, that didn't happen."

"So, what do you want to do about it?" I asked. Pierro answered quickly.

"I want to know who sent this. I want to know what he's after."

"If it is blackmail," I said, "you'll find out what he's after soon enough."

"Yeah, but he'll be a lot easier to negotiate with if I know who he is," Pierro replied. I was quiet for a while.

"I'm not sure I follow. Are you saying that you want to bargain with whoever sent this?"

"Yeah, exactly," Pierro answered. "I want to know what he wants, and if I can work him into something reasonable—and I have assurances that he won't be back for more—then I'm happy to pay him to go away." He said this as if it were the most natural, logical thing in the world. I looked over at Mike, who was still by the window, silent. I shook my head.

"Blackmail usually plays out in only a few ways," I said. "If the victim's guilty, and the bad guy's proof is for real, then the victim pays—and usually keeps on paying, because bad guys don't walk away from a meal ticket. Or else the victim decides to tough it out, and take the heat for whatever it is he's done, rather than be somebody's perpetual cash machine. In which case, the bad guy either follows through on his threats or figures it's too much trouble and goes away.

"If the victim's clean, then he tells the bad guy to take a hike and he calls the cops. What doesn't happen is an innocent guy paying up, and trying to make some sort of deal with the blackmailer. The payment alone looks like an admission of guilt. On top of that, you run a risk of pissing the guy off—which may cause him to up his price, or worse. If you're in the clear on this, my advice is to go to the cops." Mike turned from the window and came back to the conference table.

"Sound familiar?" he asked Pierro. Mike looked at me and shrugged resignedly. "I told him the same thing when he first came in with this."

Pierro smiled indulgently, like we were good guys, funny guys, but a little slow on the uptake. "I know what you're saying, but the fact is I have a lot invested at French, a lot on the table right now that I can't walk away from," he said. He turned to me, more serious now.

"That investment is important, John, because I've got a big family to take care of. My wife, Helene, and I, we've got three kids to raise. And we take care of my folks, down in Boca, too. We also help out Helene's family—her mom and her sister in North Carolina." He paused and looked down at the table for a moment. "These people depend on me, John. They look to me, and I'm not going to let them down."

"I'm not following, Rick," I said. "If this stuff is bullshit, then you should be fine at French. Your career there shouldn't be at risk." He laughed again, but this time there was an edge to it.

"My career there has *always* been at risk. Maybe you haven't noticed, but I'm not the typical French Samuelson investment banker. I dress the part now. I got rid of my polyester suits, and cleaned the dirt from under my fingernails, but I'm the odd man out there, and I always have been.

"You know what my old man did for a living? He worked in the yards at the Long Island Rail Road. The old lady was a receptionist, made minimum wage working at a chiropractor in Huntington. I was the first one in my family to go to college—much less get an MBA. There weren't too many guys with that pedigree when I was coming up at French. It might've been different if I'd stayed on the banking side, or gone to the trading floor. There, there were always a few guys like me, some who'd started as clerks or in the mailroom and worked their way up. But not in investment banking.

"It's been an uphill battle for me from day one, but I've gotten where I have because I've produced. Year in and year out, I put up the numbers—even the last couple years, when the M&A business dried up and blew away. If I hadn't, I would've been out on my ass. There are some people at French who think I'm basically a cleaned-up car salesman, and maybe they're right. But like it or not they live with me, because of my P&L.

"Now I'm up where the air is thin, John: the executive committee. There aren't many seats up this high, and the fighting is vicious. And the way things are these days—on the Street, and in the press—one whiff of something like this, whether it's true or not, would finish me. It'd be over for me at French and anywhere else."

There was no hint of self-pity in his voice, no chip on his shoulder. He spoke with a confident reasonableness that made everything he said seem self-evident and simple, and made what he was suggesting seem the obvious, practical course. I could see how he would be a devastating salesman. We were quiet for a while.

"I think this is a bad idea," I said finally. It seemed woefully inadequate in the face of Pierro's certitude. "Even if I can come up with something and you can strike a deal with the guy, you'll never be sure he won't come back someday."

"I don't need to be sure," Pierro answered. "I just need him to stay quiet until the executive committee meets and decides on new members. If this thing doesn't screw me up, I'll make it—believe me. And once I do, it's a different game. Then, I'll have a seat at the table. I'll be part of the most senior management of the firm, and any problem I have will be the firm's problem too. Certain people won't be able to flush me down the crapper based on rumor. When I say that the deal with Textiles was straight, people will hear me out."

"When does the committee meet?" I asked.

"Five weeks from now, just before Christmas," Pierro said.

"Not a whole lot of time," I said. I turned to Mike. "And what about the feds? The MWB case is still going on." Mike nodded. "Nothing good is going to happen if this takes us into their territory. Best case, they get really pissed off. Worst case, they take an interest. I don't need to tell you how ugly that could be." Mike nodded some more.

"I've discussed the dangers with Rick, at length," Mike said. "We'll have to be careful about coming to their attention, very careful. If we reach a point where you think that's becoming a possibility, you let us know. We'll decide then whether or not to take it any further."

"I only hope I recognize that point when I get to it, and not after I've passed it," I said. Mike and Pierro just looked at me.

"I'll read the file over," I said to Pierro. "That'll tell me better where we stand. And then I'll need to talk to you some more." Pierro stood, smiling.

"That's great, John, really. It's all I could ask for. Call me tomorrow and tell me what you need. Just let me know." Pierro pumped my hand and picked up his suit jacket. He squeezed Mike's shoulder. "Mike, thanks again. I know you think this is nuts, but I really appreciate your help." He looked at both of us, practically beaming. And then he was gone.

"So?" Mike asked.

"He's a good salesman," I answered. "But not the back-slapping type that makes my teeth hurt. He comes across as a regular guy from Long Island, somebody you'd have a beer with and argue with about the Mets' latest trade. Very much 'what you see is what you get.' "

Mike nodded. "It's what sets him apart from the rest of the M&A crowd. He's not just another smug prick with a spreadsheet."

"But what he wants doesn't make sense, assuming he's being straight with us."

"Doesn't it?" Mike shrugged. "In this environment, it's hard to argue that allegation alone isn't enough to kill a career. Just last month, a client of mine got blown out of the running for CFO at a public company. A background check turned up a twenty-year-old cheating charge—just a *charge*, mind you—from his undergrad days."

"Point taken. How long have you known Pierro?" I asked.

"About ten years. He was one of my first clients as an associate here. We've done real estate work for him, trusts, wills. And I know him a little socially. He and Helene used to have a place in the Hamptons; Paula and I ran into them a few times out there." Paula is Mike's wife.

"Do you think he's lying?" I asked.

"Clients lie. That's axiomatic."

"But this client, in this case?"

"I don't know," he said.

We sat in silence a while longer, then I picked up my jacket, the fax, and the file box. Mike walked me to the elevator. The old guard was still on duty, but if he noticed our passage, he made no sign. Mike pushed the button.

"You have Thanksgiving plans?" he asked. "We're going out to Water Mill and having some people over. Why don't you come?" I hemmed and hawed and started shaking my head, but Mike went on.

"What else are you going to do? Come on, come out and stay the weekend. Paula would love to see you."

"Thanks, Mike, and tell Paula thanks too, but I think my family has roped me into something," I lied. My sisters had tried to talk me into a family dinner, but I'd resisted so far, and planned to keep doing so. It satisfied Mike, though. The elevator came, and I rode down.

Chapter Three

The temperature had dropped and a raw wind had picked up. Rain was on the way. The streets had cleared a little, and I was able to get a cab downtown without bloodshed. It let me out on the corner of Sixteenth and Sixth, because traffic on my street was blocked, as it had been several times that week, by a moving van double-parked in front of my building. I was getting a new upstairs neighbor, who was arriving in stages. I looked up at the fifth floor, at the row of tall, arched windows that ran the width of the building. Light poured out of them, and several were open. I could hear music drifting down, something classical, but too faint to make out.

I climbed the short flight of iron stairs that led from the street to the building entrance. The movers had propped open the heavy glass and wrought iron door with a large cardboard box. Printed in neat, angular letters across the top was "J. Lu—Kitchen." I looked around. No movers, no one minding the truck. Almost nine at night—the perfect time for a lunch break. I put my toe against the box, shoved it into the entry vestibule, and stepped inside just ahead of the closing door. More boxes cluttered the small lobby and the narrow hallway that led to the elevator. I rang for the elevator and heard the bell clang somewhere up above, but heard nothing else. I rang again, but the elevator stayed where it was— on five, I guessed. I took the stairs.

I lived on the fourth floor, in my sister Lauren's apartment. She'd gotten married a few years ago, and as far as I knew was very happy in her digs on the Upper East Side, but she'd hung on to this place just in case. I was glad to keep it warm for her. The building is an old one, from the 1890s. For its first hundred or so years it was a factory. Then, in the 1990s, it was reborn as residential space. One big loft on each floor. The building still bore marks of its industrial roots in the oversized elevator and the sixteen-foot tin ceilings, but the individual lofts had been renovated in very different styles. I knew the advertising guy on six had done something with a lot of brushed aluminum that made his place look like the inside of a turbine, and the two women on the third floor had turned theirs into a Craftsman bungalow. Lauren's place, my place at the moment, was tame by those standards: white walls, bleached hardwood floors, a kitchen area in cherry wood and green granite, halogen lighting, sparse, comfortable furniture in soft leather and wood. I'd told Lauren that if the PI thing didn't work out, I might open a Banana Republic in there. She'd smiled sweetly and flipped me the bird.

I flicked on the main lights and set the file box on the kitchen counter. My plan was to go for a run, then eat something and read the file. While I wasn't quite sure what to make of Pierro or his story, I was eager to work. I try to keep the downtime between cases to a minimum. It's not a money thing. For me, downtime is dangerous. It's unfocused, disorderly, and open-ended, and too easily filled with memory. Work keeps all that at bay—work and running. They're cheaper than substance abuse, and ultimately less trouble. I listened to my voice mail on the speakerphone while I changed into my running clothes.

There was a message from Lauren, trying again to cajole me into a family Thanksgiving. "John, it's me. Call me about Thanksgiving. I promise it won't be horrible. Ned's at his best when he's carving up big pieces of meat, and Janine is sure to get shitfaced, which is always amusing. Seriously, you should come. Everyone wants to see you. We *do* worry, you know. Call me." Although she's just three years younger than I am, Lauren sounds like a breathless sixteen-year-old when she pleads. Ned is my eldest brother; Janine is his well-kempt wife. Maybe I could tell them that I was having Thanksgiving dinner with Mike.

Then there was a message from Clare, calling from a pay phone as always. "Hi. It's about six-thirty. Look, I'm sorry about Monday. You caught me off guard, and I wasn't sure if you were kidding or what. It's hard to tell with you. I'll try you later. Maybe we can get together tomorrow—I'm free in the morning, around ten." Clare was . . . I'm not sure what. A friend of mine? I couldn't claim to know her very well, and besides a certain cynical worldview, a high level of aerobic fitness, and intercourse, we didn't have much in common. Someone I was dating? Can you say that about a woman who's married to someone else? A woman I'd met a few months ago, running in Central Park, and began having sex with soon after—that, at least, is accurate.

And there was a message from Donald. He spoke slowly, and his deep, gravelly voice filled the room. "Just saying hello. Call when you can. Had a good deer season this year. Got some nice steaks, if you want 'em. Hope you're okay." Donald Stennis had been my boss—the Burr County sheriff—and my friend. He'd also been my father-in-law, back when I'd had a wife. I'd phone Donald when I had a long time to spend. It was always good to talk to him, but for the past three years it hadn't been easy.

I pulled on running tights and a shirt, a wind shell, a reflective vest, my shoes and gloves and hit the streets. It was maybe ten degrees above freezing now, with a nasty wind. Rain, mixed with the occasional snowflake, was being driven sideways. Nice weather for a run. I'd keep it to five miles or so.

I headed west to Ninth Avenue, worked my way south through the quieter streets of the West Village, and then west again to the highway and the piers. I was slapped around by gusts for a mile or two, and it was hard to find a rhythm, but the wind settled into a steady blow from the north as I came to the river and my pace steadied and quickened. For a while I ran along the edge of Ground Zero, and the wide gash of sky there was still disorienting, and somehow oppressive. Even after all this time, a charge of anger and sadness surged through me.

As they often do when I run, my thoughts sprinted away on their own. I thought about Clare, and the last time I'd seen her, on Monday. As always, we were at my place, it being a little awkward to go to hers. I'd fallen asleep and woken up groggy and disoriented at dusk. The last dregs of pale, cold daylight came in through the big windows. The apartment was dark otherwise. Clare had showered and was dressing. I'd watched her for a while in silence—her precise movements as she pulled jeans over her long legs, pulled on socks, laced her shoes, fastened her heavy steel watch, and brushed out her long, pale hair. And as I watched I felt, quite suddenly, as bleak and lonely as I had in a long time. Maybe it was because I was still half asleep, or maybe it was the fading

light that brought it on. Or maybe it was that, even watching her familiar ritual of dressing and departure, Clare seemed utterly a stranger.

She had paused to examine the profile of her small, bare breasts and
flat belly in the mirror, and saw that I was awake. She smiled and kept on
inspecting. When she was satisfied, she pulled on a black turtleneck,
bound her hair in a ponytail, and packed all her toiletries into the
leather duffle she always brought with her. Time to go.

She'd slipped on her coat and was bending to kiss me when I caught
her arm and pulled her down to sit. She'd looked puzzled. For no reason
I could think of, I'd asked her what she was doing for Thanksgiving and
if she wanted to spend it with me. At first she'd thought I was joking.
Maybe I had been. I wasn't sure why I'd asked her, or if I actually wanted
to spend the holiday with her at all. Then she'd gotten mad.

"What?" she'd sputtered. She'd pulled her arm away and stood.
"That's . . . what is this bullshit? That's not . . . I thought we had an
understanding here." She'd checked her watch, annoyed and impatient.
"I'm supposed to be somewhere. I can't do this now." And she'd left.

She was right to be mad, really. The rules, though unstated, were
clear nevertheless, from the time we'd started up months ago. We'd see
each other once or twice a week, most weeks. The sex was good, athletic
and inventive, and with the added frisson of the illicit. We didn't talk
about much, and what we did say mostly amounted to facile observa-
tions on current events and on the various urban types we both knew.
We most definitely did not talk about her husband or about the lives
either of us led outside the confines of my bed. She made small gestures—
she'd bring flowers or coffee, pastries or fresh orange juice—but they
were the habits of a well-mannered guest more than tokens of affection.
We were a convenience to each other, amusing, undemanding, needing
zero maintenance. She was right to be mad; I'd crossed a line. And even
a couple of days later I wasn't sure why.

And then I settled fully into my stride. My thoughts ran on to someplace I didn't follow, and all I knew was the rhythm of my own breathing
and the sound of my shoes on the pavement. The rain, the wind, the terrain, even the pumping of my arms and the pounding of my legs were
abstractions now. I didn't feel the cold, and the thinning traffic was
irrelevant. I could run all night.

I'd done over six miles by the time I'd completed the loop that
brought me home. The moving van was gone, and so were the boxes.
The elevator was back, too. Upstairs, I put on some coffee, and while it

brewed I stretched, peeled off my running clothes, and stood under a hot shower. Afterward, I pulled on jeans and a polo shirt, poured the coffee, and put on a Steely Dan disk—music to launder money by. Then I opened a can of tuna and started reading.

Mike's people do excellent research, and their work on MWB was no exception. The file was a compendium of the coverage MWB had received in both the mainstream and the financial press since the first stories had broken about three years ago. It included an overview of MWB's activities, a who's who of MWB executives, and a summary of the investigation, with a review of the indictments handed down so far.

I read through it, making notes as I went. Some of the pieces from the trade press were a little heavy going, but I actually know more about Wall Street than what I admitted to Pierro. For three summers while I was in college, I was an intern on the trading floor of a pretty big firm. When I wasn't too hungover, or busy chasing female interns, I learned a few things. But my exposure to the financial world predated this. It was the world I grew up in, the family business, at least on my mother's side. My two brothers work on Wall Street. So does my older sister, Liz. My uncles, my mother's brothers, had worked there too. And my maternal grandfather. And his two brothers. And a hoard of cousins, as well. All in the employ of the small merchant bank started by my great-grandfather: Klein & Sons.

Mike's briefing had hit the high points. The money-laundering operation was extensive, and the file described the wide variety of techniques that MWB had employed. Included in its repertoire was the kind of scam that the fax seemed to implicate Pierro in: arranging loans of clean money to companies controlled by bad guys, who then paid off the loans with dirty money. But MWB had gone beyond just the laundry business. It had leveraged its network of correspondent banks, its vast inventory of shell corporations, and its stable of bought and paid-for politicians and influence peddlers, to become a kind of superstore for shady financial services.

Say you were a hardworking drug lord, being unreasonably harassed by law-enforcement types in your home country. MWB could offer you not only the means to move your wealth offshore, they could provide a squeaky-clean corporate front for you to operate through, and solve your immigration problems, too. Or maybe you were a terrorist, with donations to collect from sympathizers worldwide, and operating cash to distribute to your cells. MWB could be your one-stop shop, aggregating and laundering the in-bound cash, and acting as paymaster virtually anywhere. Or perhaps you were a less-than-honest businessman, looking for help in sidestepping some annoying regulations or a bothersome government probe. MWB had cadres of sympathetic legislators ready and waiting, if the price was right.

That was maybe the scariest part. MWB's reach was broad, and every place it operated, it corrupted. Its U.S. activities were a good example. Through the firms it controlled, both directly and covertly, and its platoon of gray-haired, heavyweight shills, MWB was a huge donor to politicians at every level—local, state, and federal. Party affiliation was irrelevant; MWB was in the market for access, and it bought in bulk. MWB executives and their proxies were also big charitable contributors, which bought them social access, and influence of a different sort.

The review of the investigation started with MWB's front man at Southern States buying a couple of pounds of heroin in a San Diego parking lot. A little more than three years after that auspicious event, twenty-eight MWB executives and their proxies were either in jail, under indictment, under investigation, fighting extradition, or on the run. Gerard Nassouli was one of those executives. He had been the treasurer of MWB's New York branch; but his current title was Fugitive, Whereabouts Unknown. He had last been seen on March 7, three years before.

Mike was right about the investigation—it was a zoo, and a messy one at that. In this country alone, it involved several U.S. attorney offices, the FBI, the Treasury, the SEC, the CFTC, the OCC, the Federal Reserve, and several state banking boards. The DEA had chips in the game because of what MWB did for drug dealers. Likewise, the CIA had an interest because MWB counted terrorists and several heads of state among its clients. Ultimately, an interagency task force was created to tame this sack of snakes. An assistant U.S. attorney from San Diego, a guy named Chris Perez, shared the lead with an assistant U.S. attorney from the Southern District of New York, a woman named Shelly DiPaolo. They were rumored to be smart, ruthless, and politically ambitious—an ideal partnership.

I was surprised that in nearly three years, with a small army of investigators and what was no doubt a fat budget at its disposal, the task force had so far produced only modest results. There had been an initial spate of indictments, and some convictions—a few wins at trial, a few plea bargains—but not much else after these. Rumor had it that more indictments were on the way. With so much time and money down the drain, there were no doubt plenty of people in New York, San Diego, and Washington who were counting the days.

Running in parallel with the MWB investigation, and nearly as complicated, was the liquidation of the bank itself. MWB had gone under even before the first indictments were handed down, and its legitimate customers had been queued up for years trying to get even some of their assets back. Courts and regulators in several jurisdictions had agreed on a committee to oversee the liquidation, but because of the complexity of MWB's activities and the ongoing criminal investigation, the committee needed specialized help. They had brought in Brill Associates, a high-end corporate security and investigations firm, and Parsons and Perkins, the big accounting firm. I knew Parsons only by reputation, but I had run across Brill more than a few times. They had some good people, a lot of ex-feds. They had some real bastards, too. But I had a friend there, a guy I'd known since my days upstate. I made a note to call him.

By the time I finished, I had several pages of notes. I knew more about MWB than I had, but no more about who might be trying to squeeze Pierro. I hadn't expected to. That's where the investigating comes in. There were several places to start looking. People with access to the documents in the fax—that could include Nassouli, other MWB employees, people from Textiles, and maybe even people at French Samuelson. Pierro might have some ideas on that front. The list could also include people working on the MWB investigation, or on the liquidation team. My friend at Brill might give me a way in there, though I'd need to tread very lightly. And then there was the fax itself. It had been sent from somewhere, and there was a phone number printed on the top of each page. However thin, it was a thread to pull on.

I went to sleep at around two a.m., to the thump and slide of boxes being moved around upstairs.

Chapter Four

"I don't know a thing, and I don't want to know a thing," the bodega man said. He was a tall, thin Latino in his middle fifties. His salt-and-pepper hair was cut short, and his graying mustache was neatly trimmed. He wore pressed khakis, a gray sweater, and new-looking sneakers. And he was never still. Just then he was vigorously wiping down the small countertop near the checkout, where an earlier customer had spilled a little coffee. The counter, like the whole store, was clean but thick with merchandise. Combs and painkillers, condoms and CDs, lighter fluid and vitamins and an endless supply of batteries were crowded in dense but orderly displays around the register. His morning rush was over, and for the moment we were alone in the store.

"Look, you're not the police. I don't have to talk to you. Besides, who ever got into a hassle because they didn't talk to somebody?" I could think of a few people, but I didn't comment. He came around the counter and headed briskly down one of the narrow aisles. I followed, sure that I'd be swallowed in an avalanche of tampons and breakfast cereals.

"And besides, you know how many people come in here every day to make calls or send faxes?" Actually, I had no idea, but I suspected he'd tell me. For someone with nothing to say, he liked to talk. "I get sixty, seventy people in here some weeks, some weeks more. They got no phones, so they come in here and buy cards and make calls. They send faxes, and get them here too. That's a lot of business. How am I supposed to know anything?" I could appreciate the sentiment.

I followed him down more aisles to the back of the store, where his copier, phone, and fax were, in a little kiosk near the refrigerator section. There was a swinging door to a back room beside it. He pushed it open and reached in and rolled out a metal bucket and a mop. He started mopping the floor.

"I'm not interested in all the business you do in a week," I said. "I'm interested in somebody who sent a fax from here eight days ago. It was a twelve-page fax, to a local number. Is that longer than what your customers usually send? Do a lot of them send faxes locally? Do you remember who sent faxes eight days ago? Do you keep any records?" He stopped mopping and looked at me for the first time since I'd walked in.

"You're not a cop," he said, as if he hadn't already said it a half-dozen times.

"I'm not," I affirmed yet again. He mopped in silence for a while, and then stopped.

"Pay me," he said.

"Why should I pay you? You keep telling me you don't know anything," I pointed out. He chuckled a little at that.

"Yeah, yeah, but since you're not a cop, you can charge in some expenses, so you can pay me. Besides, maybe I know something." He went back to his mopping.

"Tell me something, and I'll pay you what it's worth," I suggested. I was smiling too.

"Okay, okay," he said, laughing, "but no less than a hundred."

"No less than fifty," I offered. He stopped working and leaned on the mop.

"Okay. First off, you'd be surprised what people send from here. Long letters, big documents, local numbers, long distance. They do all kinds of things. I don't keep records. But I remember about a week ago . . . maybe the day you're interested in . . . this bag lady comes in. She stinks to high heaven, got maybe fifty sweaters on, and these high-top sneakers that are five sizes too big. I'm thinking, she wants to sell me cans or something, and I'm about to ask her to leave. But she didn't have cans. She had a long fax to send. I'm pretty sure it was to a local number. See, that's different. I don't usually get street people in here sending faxes."

"You know who she is?" I asked. He wrinkled his brow elaborately, like I was crazy.

"You ever see her before? In the neighborhood?" I asked.

He thought about this. "Maybe yes," he said. "Maybe in the park, across from the hospital, over by the playground. I walk by there most every day. I could've seen her around there, or maybe it was a different bag lady."

"Besides the sweaters and the sneakers, what did she look like?"

He thought some more. "She was white. She was old. I mean, they all look old, but she really was old. Maybe sixty, older maybe. With a lot of frizzy gray hair sticking out." He gestured with his hands out by the sides of his head. "She was pretty short, five foot one or two, but round. I don't know how much of that was sweaters. What else? Her high-tops, they were blue . . . really dirty, but like electric blue."

I was impressed, and I told him so. I gave him two fifties, plus seventy-five cents for a cup of the strong coffee he had just brewed, and left him to his cleaning.

Finding the bodega on Madison and 98th Street had been easy. One of the reverse directories on the Internet had taken the phone number on Pierro's fax and given me an address on Madison. At nine a.m. I'd taken the Lexington Avenue subway up to 96th and walked west. It was a beautiful fall morning, clear and cold, yesterday's rain not even a memory. I saw the corner storefront, and the English and Spanish signs in the window, advertising phone, fax, and copying services, and figured that was the place. I hadn't expected much, really. Blackmailers don't typically give their phone numbers out too freely. On the other hand, I try never to overestimate anyone's intelligence, and it was a lead I had to follow.

Coffee in hand, I went around the corner to Fifth Avenue, walked north a couple of blocks to Mt. Sinai Hospital, crossed the street, and went into Central Park. I entered just above the East Meadow and near a small playground tucked up against Fifth. I was in a rectangle of the park that was bounded to the west by the Park Drive, to the north by the 102nd Street entrance to the drive, to the east by Fifth Avenue, and to the south by the 97th Street transverse. There were only a few miles of footpaths running through the area, but I was hoping not to have to cover them all. Based on what my friend at the bodega had said, I decided to work my way out from the playground.

Finding someone living on the streets is either pretty easy or nearly impossible. It's a question of habit. There are some street people who, regardless of how disturbed or detached from reality, follow routines. They travel in defined territories, along consistent routes. They sleep in the same places and eat in the same places; they go to the same spots to bathe, to find clothes, to find money, and to get medication. If you know one of the stations along their route, and you have enough time to wait, they will often come to you. There are others, though, who follow no discernible pattern. They roam widely, sleeping and eating wherever and whenever opportunity presents itself. These people are almost impossible for one person to find without some luck or divine intervention. I hoped that the blue-sneaker lady was a creature of habit.

At this hour, the playground was almost empty, just a few moms bundled against the morning chill, watching their preschool kids, who were oblivious to it. No street people in the playground or on the benches nearby. I walked north. On the path that wound its way to 102nd Street, I met some runners, many dog walkers, and some more mothers with strollers, but no blue-sneaker lady. I walked west along the Park Drive access road, and picked up another path headed south. This one was quieter and less traveled. The traffic sounds from Fifth and from the transverse were muted to a background susurrus. I could hear the bare tree limbs rubbing in the small breeze, and the mangy gray squirrels were loud as they bounded through the fallen leaves. A few tough sparrows hopped around on the path just ahead of me, looking to mug me for breadcrumbs, and even the sound of their tiny talons on the pavement was distinct. Beneath the soot and the exhaust fumes, I could even make out, faintly, the loamy smell of autumn. I finished my coffee and wished I had another.

I rounded a bend and came upon two men picking carefully through a trash can. They each wore many layers of wrinkled clothes, in shades of dust. One was tall, with a graying beard; the other wore a brown knit watch cap. They were sifting through the garbage for cans, bottles, and other recyclables that could be exchanged for cash. They worked efficiently, without talking. When they realized that I wasn't passing by, they paused and straightened up, looking me over warily. I was wearing jeans, a pair of beat-up paddock boots, and a leather jacket over a black turtleneck. I didn't think I looked particularly threatening, but they might've taken me for a cop, or somebody who wanted to take something from them. I stopped while I was still about ten feet away, so as not to make them more nervous.

"I don't want to bother you guys, but maybe you can help me. I'm looking for somebody. A woman who hangs out in the park around here. She might live on the street. Around sixty, short, kind of round. Has bright blue sneakers. You guys seen her around?" I asked.

The shorter guy stopped looking at me and bent to his work again. The taller one answered in a clipped, midwestern voice.

"We're up here working is all. Don't know anybody up here. Saw some people down that way. They might know." He pointed down the path, to where it forked off to the west, and went back to work also. I thanked them and headed west.

I followed the footpath as it curved through a wooded area and led up a rise. I heard whoops and shrieks as I neared the top. I looked down toward the East Meadow and the source of the noise.

"Shit," I said to myself.

About fifty yards down the path, near a curving row of benches, four teenage boys were hassling a group of street people. The street people were huddled together on a bench. There were five of them, and they all looked older. The boys circled and swooped around them, yelling, posturing, gesturing obscenely, and punctuating all this with kicks and tugs at the plastic bags and paper sacks that the older folks clung to desperately. A shopping cart was tipped on its side nearby, its cargo of can-filled plastic bags strewn around the benches. The largest of the boys was taking experimental jabs at the head of one of the old men, working himself up to something more serious. One of the old women wore dirty, electric blue high-tops.

"Shit." As a rule, I dislike teenage boys. It's a mean-spirited view, I know, and probably an artifact of being a cop. But too often they seem to come in only a few varieties: combinations of sullen, whiny, hostile, self-destructive, and whacked-out, or the ever-popular "all of the above." And too many of them are armed. Unfortunately, I was not.

It was best to do it quickly. I headed down the path. As I approached, I could see that all four of the kids were white. Two were blond, two were dark. The two blond kids were younger, sixteen or so; the other two might have been eighteen. But they were all good-sized. Three of them were just under six feet and meaty, though still a little gawky, as if not quite full grown. The fourth one had gotten there. He was about an inch taller than me and outweighed me by maybe twenty pounds. He looked heavy in the arms, shoulders, and chest.

They were an interesting brand of urban outlaw. Beneath their 'hood affectations—the baggy pants and skewed ball caps, the hand signals and the heavy street dialect—they were preppies. They were well scrubbed and well groomed, and their clothes were expensive and clean. They all wore button-down shirts. I caught a glimpse of a crested blazer under one parka, a school uniform, though I couldn't make out which school. One of them had a plaited fabric Nantucket bracelet on his wrist; two others wore rep ties and expensive watches. They were ridiculous wannabes, but I was still wary of weapons.

They paused when they saw me coming. They expected me either to turn back or hurry by, pretending not to notice. I did neither. I came down the path at a slow walk, looking directly at them. They were puzzled, and the three smaller ones looked to the big kid for a lead they could follow. He was closest to me, on my right, as I walked along. The others were arrayed behind him near the benches.

"Hey, ese, what the fuck you looking at, motherfucker?" the big one said. I stopped and stared at him. He was pumped up from beating on old people, so he didn't pause to think. He stepped toward me and started to raise his hands, maybe to push me, maybe just to get in my face. Whatever. I backhanded him across the mouth with my right hand, then pivoted and drove my left fist into his kidney as he staggered off the path. He went down on his knees, and I kicked him in the balls from behind. He went forward on his face with a hard thud. He made little rasping sounds and clawed at the dirt, but otherwise didn't move much. It happened so quickly that the other three kids just stood there. But I didn't. I stepped over the big one and came at them.

The two younger ones were smarter than they looked. They ran. It was the right move for them, and they were good at it—fast out of the blocks. The other one, a ferrety-looking kid with pale blue eyes, was stupid. He had a hunting knife with a six-inch blade in his hand, held low against his thigh, and though he had no idea what to do with it, he wanted to do something. I caught his wrist in my hand just as he began to raise the knife, and held it tight. Then I stepped in very close and put my thumb over his eye and pressed. Hard. He started to struggle and twist away and tried to hit me with his free hand, but I was too close and he didn't know how to do it. I pressed harder still. He screamed and dropped the knife. I pushed him away, and as he staggered back I slapped him openhanded on the face and head a half-dozen times. Then I grabbed him by the collar and threw him down next to his pal.

"Nice and quiet, ladies, while I see some ID," I said. The big one showed no ability to move much, but I kicked the ferrety kid lightly in his side and head to reinforce the message. I patted them down. I took wallets from both of them, and another knife from the ferrety kid. Nice. I stuck the weapons in my jacket.

I went through the wallets and between the two of them came up with five fake IDs, nearly three hundred dollars in cash, three condoms, four credit cards, and two cash cards. I also found a nickel bag of pot, two joints, and what might have been two tabs of blotter acid. Finally, I found some real ID—a driver's license and a learner's permit. I held on to the cash, the dope, the weapons, and the real IDs, and tossed the rest on the ground. Then I spoke to them.

"Let's see, we've got Cross, age eighteen, and Simms, age seventeen. You must be the baddest boys on the Upper East Side." Simms, the little ferrety one, tensed up like he was going to bolt, so I put my boot on the back of his head and pressed his face into the dirt a little. As much as I enjoyed terrorizing violent brats, I needed to end this before anyone else came down the path.

"You ladies know what a deep pocket is? Never heard the phrase? Well, it's a technical term lawyers use for the parents of assholes like you. And it's the place I'm going to take a big fucking pile of cash from, if you or your buddies come near these people again. On top of which, I'll personally hold you down so these folks can take a straight razor to your balls—assuming you've got any. You hearing me, girls?" I got something that was halfway between a sob and a sullen grunt from Cross; from Simms I got nothing.

"Off to school, now," I said, and gave each of them a sharp kick in the rear. They yelped and scrambled up, gathering their stuff. The older kid ran off, and when he'd gotten about twenty yards away, started shouting obscenities. Simms backed away from me slowly and spoke.

"Give me my money and the rest of my shit," he said, sullenly.

"I don't think so, homeboy. Now run along before you get hurt," I said. His eye was red and bleary, and he looked at me with a seething hatred that he had trouble putting into words. Finally he settled for "Fuck your mother," and turned and ran up the path. Such fine boys; their parents must be very proud.

During this time the street people had said not a word, and when I turned back to the benches, I saw why. They were gone. Or nearly gone. One woman remained. She'd righted the shopping cart and was collecting the cans scattered on the grass. Her blue high-tops flapped with every step she took. Sometimes it's better to be lucky than good.

"Can I help you?" I asked.

"I'm not pressing charges against those bastards. I don't want anything to do with 'em. I just hope they don't come around again next week looking for payback." She paused as she hoisted a large bag into the wagon. "I guess I should say thanks; so thanks. But you should've just shot 'em, the little pricks." She was round, indeed—built like a beer keg, in fact, and it wasn't all sweaters. Her crumpled, gnomish face was barely visible beneath a wild bush of gray hair. Her voice sounded much younger than she looked. She had some sort of accent, but I couldn't place it.

"I don't have a gun on me today," I said. "Maybe next time." She gave a little snort at this.

"Don't cops always have guns?" she asked.

"Yeah, but I'm not a cop."

"Just a good citizen, huh? We're just lucky you came by? You look like a cop to me." Everything she said was steeped in a deep cynicism. I liked her.

"I used to be a cop. And I didn't just come by. I was actually looking for you." She didn't like this. She stopped working, but did not look up at me. When she started again she was tense, ready to flee at any moment.

"Look, I'm not here to give you trouble, and I'll pay you for your time. I just want to ask you a couple of questions," I explained in my best sincere, nonthreatening manner. She was having none of it. She laughed derisively.

" 'I just want to ask you a couple of questions.' Nothing good ever started with that phrase, mister," she said.

"Here's almost three hundred bucks, for nothing—whether you talk to me or not." I held out the wad of cash I'd taken from the kids.

"Yeah, I see how much that cost you," she said, but she was looking at the money.

"I'll throw in a hundred more, for five minutes." She squinted at me and at the money, still suspicious.

"I hope they're easy questions. My mind's not what it used to be," she said, and took the cash.

"There's a bodega on Ninety-eighth and Madison, where you can make phone calls and send faxes. Did you send a fax from there eight days ago?" She knew what I was talking about, but she hesitated. Not nervous, just cautious.

"I know the place. And, yeah, I was in there with some stuff to send last week. Guy paid me fifty bucks to do it. Twenty-five up front, twenty-five when I brought him back the little slip that says it went through."

"Did you know the guy, ever see him before?" I asked.

"Nope. Just came up to me in the park. I was sitting over near the playground. He walks up and asks if I want to make some money," she answered.

"What did he look like?"

"He was like you," she said, as if that told me all I needed to know.

"What do you mean he was like me? He was my height? My age? My hair color? His face looked like mine?"

"No, no. He was taller than you, and older, maybe forty-five or fifty. Built like you, though, kind of lean and wiry, but bigger in the shoulders. And not so pretty," she said, and laughed a little.

"That's very nice, thank you. Then what did you mean when you said he was like me?"

"I mean he acted like you—he acted like a cop," she explained, as if I was a little slow.

I thought about this for a while. "What makes you say that? Did he say something? Did you see something?"

"You can just tell. Like with you and those shitheads. You smacked them around good, but you weren't mad or anything. It's like you didn't care one way or another about them, like they were just *things*. And the way you talked to them—you needled them, but mostly to show them you could. The fax guy, he acted the same way to this old juicer who was lying on the bench next to mine. The old wino hears this guy talking to me, so he shuffles on over, looking to make a buck. This guy just stares at him for a while, all cold and scary. Then he puts his hand on the wino's shoulder and does something that makes the old guy go white as a sheet, practically drops to his knees. Then he tells the old guy, real matter-of-fact, to get the fuck out of his sight before he gets his arm torn off. Like you with those kids, see?" I saw. It's always nice to hear that you come across like a psychopath.

She finished collecting the cans and bags, and I helped her push the cart back onto the footpath. She didn't have much else to tell me. The guy had approached her in the morning; he'd been alone. They'd walked to the store; she'd seen no sign of a car. He'd waited for her outside, around the corner. He was minimally polite, but said nothing that wasn't necessary to conduct their business. He'd paid her in tens and fives. He was wearing dark pants, dark shoes, some sort of short jacket in dark blue, zipped to the neck, a dark blue baseball cap—no insignia. What hair she could see was short and dark. No accent that she noticed. No scars, no birthmarks, no jewelry.

I asked her name and she hesitated, looking at me and looking away. Finally she told me. Faith Herman. I paid Faith the extra hundred, and gave her a card with my number on it. I told her to call if she thought of anything else or saw the guy again. She looked skeptical, like I'd told her to call when she'd won the lotto.

Chapter Five

I had lunch at a coffee shop on upper Madison. Afterward, I leaned in the sun outside the Cooper-Hewitt and made some calls. The first was to Tom Neary, my contact at Brill. Neary is ex-FBI, and I'd met him when I was a cop and he was working out of the resident agency in Utica. We'd gotten to know each other pretty well, at least professionally, well enough to do favors for each other every now and then. He'd joined Brill about the same time I'd moved back to the city, and not long ago had taken over their financial services group in the metro area. I called three different numbers, but the best I could do was his voice mail.

Then I called Pierro. I gave my name to his secretary and she told me, in hushed tones, that Mr. Pierro was working at home today, but had left instructions that I was to be given his number. She said it like he'd told her to give me his firstborn. I called him at home. He answered on the first ring, and said to come over any time that afternoon. He gave me an address on Park Avenue in the low 80s, a short walk from where I was.

The holiday tipping season was approaching, and all the buildings I passed were scrubbed, waxed, and polished to perfection. Their doormen were spit-shined too, and turned out like a bunch of Soviet admirals. Pierro's wore a long coat with big epaulets and lots of brass, and it probably outweighed him by ten pounds. He hauled open the door and pointed me across an acre of marble to the concierge, who announced me on the house phone. When he got the okay from above, he pointed me to the elevators.

"To the Pierros, Billy," he told the elevator man.

Billy closed the metal gate and worked the controls. We rose slowly. The old-fashioned elevator, the staff in full dress, the smells of wax and oil soap and brass polish, reminded me of the building that I'd grown up in. It was the same prewar vintage as Pierro's place, and just a few blocks south. It was my brother Ned's home now, and I hadn't set foot inside for months.

Billy pulled back the metal gate, and I stepped into a long, quiet hallway. It had pale gray walls and a high ceiling and thick gray carpet. It was lit softly and evenly from frosted glass sconces. At either end was a gleaming black door. Billy pointed to the right and waited silently while I knocked and was admitted.

Pierro answered. He was the country squire today, in a plaid flannel shirt, tan corduroys, and loafers. He smiled, and we shook hands.

"Hey, John, you made it," he said.

Pierro seemed relaxed and glad to see me, like I'd come over to drink a beer and watch the game. He closed the door behind me. We were in a high-ceilinged, rectangular foyer, maybe three hundred feet square. The walls were a buttery yellow, and they were hung all around with photographs in black wooden frames. The heavy cornice molding was painted a sage green, and a green and yellow carpet with an intricate floral pattern covered much of the hardwood floor. In the center of the room was an oval table in black wood. It was empty but for a vase of yellow roses, a stack of letters, and a set of keys on a silver ring. To the left, a doorway led to a short hall that widened into a butler's pantry. Beyond it I saw part of a large kitchen with black stone counters and cream-colored cabinets. On the long wall opposite us, the foyer opened onto a wide hallway that ran left and right. A child's laughter came from far off.

Pierro smiled more broadly. "That's my little guy. He's a wild man. Come on, we can talk in the study." He crossed the foyer and went down the hall to the right. I followed. "I wanted to work at home today, to get away from the phone," Pierro said, ahead of me. "So naturally, I've been on the phone all morning."

I glimpsed other rooms as we walked—dining room, living room, den. Beyond the apartment itself, which was easily worth a few million bucks, there was no aggressive show of wealth here, and none of the ugly fingerprints of professional good taste. The rooms were large and welcoming, with nice light and comfortable-looking furniture. The decor was tasteful but simple, almost spare.

Pierro led me to his study and shut the door. It was a small room, but large enough for an old rolltop desk, a swivel chair in green leather, a matching straight-backed chair, and a couple of brass floor lamps. The walls were lined with built-in shelves that were packed with books and family photos. Tacked above the desk were pieces of kid art: a smear of fingerpaints in yellow and red, a crayon jack-o'-lantern on a stone wall, a watercolor fish, a horse, nicely done in charcoal.

"So, where are we at, John?" he asked.

I told Pierro about my morning, and described the man who'd paid Faith Herman to send the fax. It rang no bells with him, but he was encouraged nonetheless. He seemed to believe that it was just a matter of time before I had it all figured out. I cautioned him against irrational exuberance.

"Let's not get ahead of ourselves, Rick," I told him. "We've got very little to work with here, not much time, and only one guy working on it. And what I found out today was not good news. Whoever sent the fax is not completely stupid. They may even have done this before. I want you to know, there is nothing encouraging here." Pierro looked deflated. I was glad; it meant I was getting through. I continued.

"I can try to get a line on people who had access to the documents in the fax, but that could turn out to be a very long list. We don't have time for that. Maybe you could help focus things a little more." Pierro shook his head.

"I've been going nuts ever since this started, trying to figure out who could have those documents . . . who would do this. And I just don't know. After all these years, it seems like anyone could have those papers." He rocked back in his chair, and last night's tension returned. He folded his arms on his chest and stared out over my head. "I just don't know," he said.

"We won't worry right now about how many hands the documents could've passed through over the years, okay? Let's focus on who had them originally, back when you first did the deal. Let's start there. Tell me about Textiles," I said. And he did.

It was, Pierro told me, one of several deals that Nassouli had brought to him. Textiles was a big MWB client in Europe. The company maintained a slew of cash accounts with the bank, to support its operations around the world. MWB also provided financing to Textiles. Textiles was planning a move into the United States and needed additional financing, in dollars, to support it. MWB couldn't take on any more exposure to the company, but French Samuelson, having no previous dealings with Textiles, could. Nassouli had made the match.

Pierro's main contact at MWB, on the Textiles deal and all the others that Nassouli brought to the table, was Nassouli himself. Pierro remembered working directly with only one other person from MWB: a guy named Al Burrows. Burrows worked for Nassouli, and ran MWB's correspondent banking department in New York. Pierro recalled him helping out on the Textiles deal, and on one or two others. He didn't know if Al was short for Albert or Alfred or Alvin, and he had no idea where the guy might be today. He spelled the name and gave me what he could of a description.

I took Pierro through the fax, looking not only for people who had access to each of the documents in it, but also for people who would've had the entire package. He wasn't much help. According to Pierro, the late Emilio Dias, the Textiles CFO, would have had most of the documents: Nassouli's letter to Dias, Pierro's own letter to him, and the list of drawdowns and repayments. But he also thought that Nassouli would've had the same stuff. Pierro, as a courtesy, had copied Nassouli on his letter to Dias; and all of Textiles' loan transactions moved through cash accounts at MWB.

I brought up Nassouli's memo to "The Files," the one alleging that he and Pierro had prepared Textiles' loan application. Pierro bristled.

"That thing is bullshit," he said, his face darkening. "There's no point wondering who had access to it, because nobody did. It was made up by the same asshole that sent the fax. End of story."

"So, the applications and the corporate documents—the Textiles people were responsible for those?" Pierro looked at me hard.

"I told you—yes. Is there another way I can say it?"

"How well did you know the company?" The muscles around Pierro's mouth clenched, then he closed his eyes for a moment and took a deep breath.

"I knew them as well as I was supposed to, John. The world was different then, I'll admit. The *know-your-customer* rules weren't as tight as they are today, and there was maybe less scrutiny on referrals that came from the private banking department or from another big firm—but we didn't just give the money away, for chrissakes. I kicked the damn tires, and as far as I knew Textiles was a legitimate concern."

"Okay, the allegations are bullshit, but what about the document itself? You're sure Nassouli couldn't have written this?" Pierro looked at me for a while and ran his hand over his forehead. When he spoke his voice was low and tight.

"Why the hell would he do that? Why would he implicate himself in something like this—especially since it never happened? Why would anyone do that?" It was a good question, and I had no answer to it. We were quiet for a couple of minutes, and Pierro's nascent anger seemed to fade. We moved on to the question of enemies.

Pierro readily admitted that in twenty years at French, he'd ruffled his share of feathers, perhaps more than his share. And he conceded that some of those birds might hold a grudge. But he thought it impossible that any of them would go to these lengths to get even. If the goal was to sink his career, he pointed out, there were easier and less risky ways to go about it. One could simply send the incriminating stuff to the French Samuelson executive committee and be done with it.

Nor did Pierro see any of them as potential blackmailers, for the simple reason that they were too damn rich already. I pointed out that we weren't yet certain this was blackmail, but in fact I agreed with Pierro's reasoning. The fax made more sense as the prelude to some sort of squeeze than as a warning of impending vengeance. Whichever it was, it was probably too risky a game for a senior investment banker to be playing.

Pierro considered all my questions carefully, and he was deliberate in his answers. And the talking seemed to relieve his tension. It often works that way with clients. Answering questions makes them feel like they're taking some action, like they're doing something. It's better than the feeling of waiting around for something to be done to you. But Pierro was astute enough to recognize that this was fleeting comfort.

"Is this really helping?" he asked.

"A little," I answered. "Right now, the documents are the only trail we have to follow. Textiles Pan-Europa is defunct, and so are the executives you dealt with back then, so working it from that side isn't promising. That leaves the MWB end of things, looking at the people who were there with Nassouli eighteen years ago, and the people who are there now. 'Burrows' is a new name; that might be helpful. But frankly, there's not a lot here." He nodded. I had more questions, but the phone interrupted us.

"Russell, hi. Yeah, I'm home today. No, I can talk, hang on a sec." Pierro put his hand over the mouthpiece and said, apologetically, "This is the one call I was actually waiting for today. Give me two minutes. Thanks." I nodded and left the study, closing the door behind me. I found my way back to the foyer.

The black-framed photos had caught my eye, and I walked slowly around the room now, taking a closer look. They were black-and-white pictures, and they all seemed to have been taken at fashion shoots. But they were not themselves fashion photos. Rather, they were candid pictures of the photographers, models, makeup people, and other assorted production types working on the shoots. And they were remarkable. The best of them caught petulance, vanity, pettiness, anger, frustration, and exhaustion all unawares. Even the less successful ones were arresting and beautifully composed. With their stark lighting and heavy contrasts they had the look of old crime-scene photos. Many of them had been taken outdoors, and I recognized streets in New York and London. They were superb, but I doubted that any of their subjects would have been pleased. In the bottom right corner of each frame, hand-printed on the matting paper, was the name "H. Barrie."

I heard footsteps approaching and a child's laughter, and I turned. A woman came into the foyer, pushing a small boy in a stroller.

"You must be John. Rick told me you'd be stopping by. I'm Helene." She smiled and put out her hand and I shook it. Her hand was smooth and warm, her grip firm.

Helene Pierro was somewhere in her thirties. She was nearly my height and slim, but no starving model. She had broad shoulders and a firm, athletic figure. Her glossy chestnut hair was gathered into a ponytail that came to her shoulders. There was red in it where it caught the light. Her slender brows arched over large, dark eyes. Her cheekbones were high and prominent, her nose long and straight, and her lips full. Her skin was fair but not unblemished. Fine laugh lines bracketed her eyes and mouth, and on her chin, like a comma, was a small white scar.

She wore gray wool pants and a green cashmere sweater and black loafers without socks, and I could see tendons shift in her slender ankles as she walked. Her jewelry was simple, but expensive—small hoops of braided gold at her ears, a matching chain at her neck, a thick wedding band. Her fingers were long and supple, her nails expertly manicured, with a clear polish.

She ran her hands through the little boy's hair. He wore jeans and sneakers and a red turtleneck with a sailboat on it. He had his mother's coloring and her big eyes too. He was smashing the pickup truck that he held in one hand into the dinosaur that he held in the other, and making dramatic explosion sounds that dissolved into wild laughter. He did this again and again, but for him it stayed fresh. He looked at me and gave me a little smile, but did not pause in his work. I was suddenly quite conscious of the knives and dope I was still carrying around.

"You haven't been waiting out here all this time, have you?" she asked. She had a gentle but distinct southern accent.

"No, just on a break. Rick had to take a call," I explained.

Helene rolled her eyes. "That man and the telephone, I swear," she said, smiling. "Do you want me to hurry him up?"

"That's alright," I said, "I can wait. I was just admiring these photos."

She grinned wryly and laughed. "Those? Yeah, they're kind of mean, but I like them too."

"I've never heard of H. Barrie. Did these fashion people bump him off when they saw the pictures?"

She laughed again. "H. Barrie isn't a he. H. Barrie is me. Barrie was my maiden name."

"You were a photographer?"

"That would be generous; I was strictly amateur. I was modeling back then, actually. Nothing big—catalogs mostly. I was working all those shoots, and took the pictures in my downtime. You're right, though, it did piss some people off," she said, laughing some more. "Not that I cared, mind you."

"You quit modeling when you got married?" I asked. She was aware that I was probing, now, but she didn't seem to mind.

"I'd more or less quit when I met Rick. I was working my last job, in London, and he'd just moved over from New York. Modeling was fun for a while, and I got to see more of the world than I would have from Asheville, North Carolina. But it's no kind of life, really."

"Do you still take pictures?"

"Just vacation snapshots now," she said, chuckling.

She knelt in front of her son and wrestled a coat on him. She zipped it to just under his chin, adjusted the small collar, ran her fingers through his thick hair again, and kissed his forehead. Then she pulled a knit cap on his head. This broke his concentration, and he focused on me for the first time.

"Hi," he said. I walked over and knelt down.

"Hi," I said.

"This is Alex. Alex, this is Mr. March," Helene said.

"Nice dinosaur," I said.

"T. rex," Alex replied, and with that he went back to his smashing. I stood.

"I heard he was a wild man. He doesn't seem so wild to me," I said.

Helene laughed ruefully. "Oh, he's just biding his time, believe me. We're going out to pick up his big sisters, and when those two get home they'll whip him into a frenzy." Helene pulled on her own coat, a chocolate brown shearling. She took the keys and envelopes from the table and slipped them into her pockets. "We've got to run. Are you sure I can't get him for you?" she asked.

"No, thanks, waiting is fine," I said

"Okay, then. . . . It was nice to meet you, and I'm sure we'll see you again." We shook hands, and she rolled Alex out the door.

The apartment was quiet. No traffic noise made it through the thick old walls, and the only sounds were my own slow footsteps around the foyer. I looked at Helene Pierro's pictures and thought about her. She struck me as more than just another trophy wife, though she seemed to be eminently qualified for that too. It was interesting that she'd asked me nothing about the case or what I was doing there, but it was hard to know what to make of that. It could mean that she didn't delve into her husband's affairs. It could mean that her husband had told her everything and she had no questions to ask. It could mean a bunch of other things too.

More footsteps, and Pierro was back. His cheerfulness had returned.

"Hey, John, sorry for the wait. Did Helene go out already?" he asked.

"Yes, she just left with Alex. He's a cute little guy," I said. Pierro smiled.

"Oh, yeah, but he's a handful. Come on, let's get back to it." We returned to the study.

"What else can I tell you?" he asked as we took our seats.

"Tell me about Nassouli." Pierro collected his thoughts for a moment.

"Gerry was a smart guy, charming too. He was a guy a lot of people did business with back then. He was a big schmoozer, and a big deal maker," Pierro said. "And he was very social. MWB entertained a lot. They sponsored events—concerts, sports, charity dinners, you name it. Gerry was their head guy in New York, so he'd be at all these things. Usually with a cigar and a brandy, and a model on his arm."

"It sounds like you knew him pretty well," I said.

"We were friendly. Like I said, MWB did a lot of entertaining. I was on their guest list, along with a lot of other people."

"When did you see him last?"

"It's been a long while. We lost touch when I went to London; that was around thirteen years ago. Nothing but company Christmas cards since then."

"I read in Mike's file that Nassouli was the treasurer of the New York branch. The kind of deal-brokering he did with you and Textiles, is that the kind of thing the treasurer usually does?" I asked.

Pierro smiled. "Not typically, no. But Gerry wasn't just the treasurer. He was MWB's head guy here—their main relationship guy with other banks, customers, regulators, you name it. So it was the kind of thing he did. And he loved it."

I had no more questions for the moment, and I told Pierro so.

"This was great, John," Pierro said, smiling. "Thanks for coming by. And thanks for your help on this." He was looking encouraged again.

"I haven't done much yet, and, as I keep telling you, there may not be much I can do," I said. "I'll poke around MWB, and try to stay away from the feds while I do it. And I'll try to get a line on Burrows. But our best bet may be to wait until someone contacts you again, and hope that gives us a little more to work with." Pierro nodded his agreement, but he still looked altogether too optimistic. He walked me to the elevator.

"I hear you, John, and I appreciate the straight talk. But I know if there's anything that can be done, you'll do it. I know you'll look out for us." He said good-bye as the door slid closed.

I thought about him on the ride down. He had seemed forthcoming in his answers, and sincere in his desire to help, but I knew that appearing guileless was his strong suit, and I was still uneasy. Pierro had come a very long way since night school, and I had no doubt that the distance was much on his mind.

It was colder outside but still clear. The low afternoon sun lit the east side of Park in a rich orange light, and cast the west side into shadow. I was in those shadows, looking for a cab downtown, when I saw Helene Pierro across the street, headed home with her three children. The girls had their mother's glossy hair, tied back in dark bows. They wore matching navy overcoats, and dark tights on their legs. Alex was still in his stroller, shrieking in delight each time his sister, walking beside him, pulled his knit cap over his eyes. The eldest daughter walked with Helene, who pushed the stroller. She was talking earnestly and at length to her mother, who listened and nodded gravely.

Chapter Six

The day had dwindled to cold, blue twilight by the time I got home. There were no moving vans out front or boxes in the hallways, no rumble of freight being hauled across the floor upstairs. I emptied my pockets of the contraband I'd taken off the kids in the park, flushing the drugs and tossing the knives in a drawer with my loose change. Then I checked my messages. There were two. One was from Clare. She'd called in the morning to say she couldn't make it, but would see me next week. She spoke hurriedly, and there was traffic noise in the background. Well, I hadn't exactly planned my day around her, either.

My older sister, Liz, had also phoned, to invite me to Thanksgiving with the family. She and Lauren had a good cop–bad cop thing going, and Liz was definitely the bad cop. The thrust of her argument, delivered in her tight-jawed, nasal drawl, was that if I didn't come I'd be running true to my usual asshole form, so why didn't I just surprise everyone and show up. She added at the end of her message that it had been too long since she'd seen me. That last bit must have been an effort for her. Liz is many things—smart, tough, acerbic—but nice is not one of them.

I had no call back from Tom Neary, so I left another message on his voice mail and went for a workout—a five-mile run and some weights at the gym on Fourteenth Street. I was back in less than two hours, just in time to miss Neary's call. He was having dinner at an Indian restaurant downtown at seven, his message said; I could join him there if I wanted. I showered, dressed, and walked to the subway.

Taking Tiger Mountain is a few blocks from city hall, and close to the Brill offices. It's a small, dimly lit place, with walls the color of paprika, and chairs and tables the color of saffron. I got there just after seven and it was still pretty empty, but even if it had been packed, it would have been hard to miss Tom Neary.

Neary is big—around six foot four and two hundred fifty pounds— like a refrigerator in a dark suit and tie. The feds who'd worked with him in Utica had called him Clark Kent. When I'd first heard it, I figured it was because of his looks—the dark, wavy hair, the chiseled features, the horn-rimmed specs—and the earnest, Eagle Scout quality he projects. As I'd gotten to know Neary better, I'd seen the subversive secret identity behind the mild exterior—the ironic sense of humor, the independent streak, the disdain for pompous authority—and I'd thought the nick- name even more apt. That independence, along with his smarts and his basic sense of fairness, had made it hard for him to find much peace with the FBI. I'd seen that firsthand, upstate. He had treated me decently at a time when it would've been easier for him not to, and he'd caught hell as a result.

In some respects I knew Neary well, but there was a lot I still didn't know. I knew he was married, but I didn't know his wife's name. I knew he had kids, but not how many, or how old, or what kind. I knew he lived in Jersey, but I didn't know the town. One thing I did know, from years back, was that he loved good food—foreign food especially. And after years in the culinary wilderness of Utica, Neary had come to the Prom- ised Land.

He was sitting alone at a table for four, poring over the menu like it was a holy text. His suit jacket was on the back of his chair, and his shirt- sleeves were rolled up over his big forearms. I took the seat across from him. He gave me a hand like a porterhouse and we shook. The waiter took my order for a cranberry juice. Neary was working on a ginger ale and ordered a backup.

"Cheap dates, huh?" he said, smiling. "But you're still living healthy, that's good."

"Have you ordered yet?" I asked.

"Just bread." He pointed to a basket of naan, plates of stuffed roti and puri and small bowls of various chutneys. "I'm thinking about a tan- doori," he said.

I took a piece of naan from the basket where it lay wrapped in a white cloth napkin, and bit into it. It was warm and a little spicy. Delicious. The warm bread and the riot of cooking smells coming from the kitchen spoke to my stomach, and my stomach answered back. I scanned the menu.

The waiter returned with our drinks and we ordered, then Neary sighed and turned his attention to me.

"Life still good in the private sector?" I asked.

"Life is busier than hell. It seems like every client I've got wants their security procedures overhauled, or their management vetted, or needs a few dozen investigators to help out on their shareholder lawsuits. Even with all the cops and feds jumping ship, I've still got more gigs than I've got people to fill 'em. But the money's good—we must be the only growth industry left these days. That's the upside," Neary said.

"And the downside?" I asked. He thought about it for a while.

"The gray areas are bigger, I guess, and there are more of them. The bureau was a political swamp, no question, and it had more than its share of professional assholes. But you always knew that you were one of the good guys, or that you were supposed to be. In the private sector, what you know mainly is who's paying the bill. For some people, that's enough. Me, I worry a little more. Must be the Jesuit schooling." He took a bite of potato-stuffed puri.

"You keeping busy?" he asked. I nodded, and we were quiet for a bit. Time to get to the point.

"I can count the number of times I've called you when I wasn't looking for a favor," I said.

"So can I. My tally is zero. Don't tell me you're going to screw up your stats now," Neary said, deadpan.

"No, I wouldn't disappoint you. I'm looking for a favor. But maybe I can do something for you, too." He raised his eyebrows, waiting.

Without using any names besides MWB's and Nassouli's, and staying vague about the dates, I laid out the bare bones of the case. It was blackmail, I explained, on account of some dealings my client had had almost twenty years ago, with Nassouli and another firm, an MWB client. I told him that my guy had gotten some documents, which might have come from MWB's files.

"If they did come from MWB, it could mean that the investigation is compromised, or that your liquidation work is. It could mean that somebody is doing a little freelancing." Neary stopped eating and stared at me as I spoke, his face empty. When I finished talking, he stared at me some more. Then he shook his head slowly.

"I must not be following," he said. "Your guy gets faxed a bunch of documents from a deal he did with MWB, twenty years back. Somebody wants to squeeze him. Now, you're trying to backtrack the documents. Okay, I'm with you up to there. It's after that I'm missing something— like the part where this has anything to do with me." Neary paused to tear off a mouthful of naan, and continued.

"These documents are twenty years old. You have no idea how many copies of these things were around back then, or who had them. And you have no clue where those copies could've got to in twenty years' time. But somehow you decide—I don't know why—that maybe they came out of my shop, or from the feds." He shook his head more vigorously. "I've got to tell you, this is the thinnest damn thing I've heard in a long time."

"It's pretty thin," I agreed. "But pretty thin is all I've got." Neary stared at me and shook his head some more. I continued. "I can't give you the details, but believe me, of the possible sources for these documents, MWB looks the best. Plus, I have reason to believe that a cop or an ex-cop might be involved." I figured it couldn't go much worse, so I told him about my chat in the park with Faith Herman, and how she pegged the guy who paid her as a cop. Some amusement mixed with his incredulity.

"This just gets better and better. Your solid lead is a bag lady who's probably off her meds and thinks everybody's a cop or a werewolf or a space alien. And based on this you figure it's got to be one of my guys, right?"

We paused as the waiter laid bowls of steaming soup before us. Neary regarded his with some reverence and tucked his tie inside his shirt. He had a few peppery spoonfuls and sighed heavily before he continued.

"Your star witness give you a description?" I gave him what I had. "Could be anybody," he said after a while. He had some more soup. "So, assuming I gave this an ounce of credence, which I don't, what's this favor you want?" he asked.

"I want to look around MWB, meet some of the people on the job, see how the records get handled, see who has access to what. See if I can find copies of the documents in the fax." Neary snorted.

"While we're at it, maybe I could put my whole staff in a lineup, for your bag lady to look over." Neary shook his head and had some more soup. "You want to tell me anything more about the documents, or your guy?" he asked. I looked at him, but said nothing. "But I'm supposed to just invite you in and hold your coat while you rifle the drawers. I guess client confidentiality only applies to your clients, huh?" He sat back in his chair and looked at me, expressionless again. He was skeptical of the trail I was following, and indignant at the suggestion that his operation might be compromised. But behind the sarcasm and the studied dismay, there was something else—a little worry.

"Look, I've got a very narrow set of interests here, Tom. I could give a shit about MWB, or how your people pad their time sheets or how the feds get tangled in their own underwear. I just want to know if these documents are in MWB's records and, if so, who might have got at them. Chaperone me if you're worried. You can slap my wrist if I step out of line." I paused to taste some soup. "But if you're really concerned about confidentiality, then you've got to be interested in whether one of your people has something going on the side." He turned this over in his head for a while, and then decided.

"Okay, you get the cheap tour. You can meet a couple of people, see how we manage the documents. And we'll have a look for your stuff. But unless we turn up more than the nothing you've got now, that's where it ends. And, trust me, I'll do more than slap your wrist if I think you're out of line." I believed him.

"Thanks, Tom," I said, and went back to my soup.

"You work closely with the feds on this?" I asked.

"Pretty close," he said. "I see them once a week, sometimes more."

"They hang around the office much?" I asked. Neary looked up.

"Not so much anymore. Why? You looking to avoid awkward encounters?" I nodded.

"I'd like to keep a low profile," I said.

"I bet you would," Neary said, nodding. But there was a knowing edge to his voice that I didn't understand.

"What?" I asked. Neary looked a little puzzled.

"Nothing," he said. "I'm just not surprised you'd want to keep clear of him." It was my turn to be confused.

"Keep clear of who?" I asked. Neary stared at me, an odd look in his eyes.

"Shit. You don't know, do you? You don't know who the special agent in charge on this thing is?" I shook my head. "It's Fred Pell, John." The waiter came to clear our soup bowls and lay out the main courses. But suddenly I wasn't so hungry.

Fred Pell, there was a name to conjure with. He was FBI, based in D.C. but posted to upstate New York when I'd met him, there to work the case with Neary and the rest of us—the state police, the Mounties, and the Burr County Sheriff's Department. Technically, he'd been Neary's boss, a fact Neary had all but ignored. It hadn't done much for their relationship, or for Neary's prospects in the bureau. But Neary had never actually hit the guy, and that was a claim I couldn't make. Of course, Pell had never threatened him with murder and conspiracy charges, or had him worked over in a holding cell, either, so maybe Neary just lacked the proper motivation.

Pell was all kinds of bad news. He was a career thug who saw everything through the lens of what was best for Freddy, and who divided his time between blatant self-promotion, vigorous ass-kissing, and plotting the downfall of his rivals. He was quick to lay claim to other people's successes, and quicker to run like hell from his own screwups, usually leaving some poor fool behind to hold the bag. And he was a bully, with an explosive temper and a wide violent streak. As Neary once observed, he was the guy most likely to be shot in the back by his own men.

But what made Pell really dangerous was that he was not a dumb guy. He wasn't as smart as he thought he was, and his ambition and malice often blinded him, but Pell had a certain animal cunning—like a mean, clever pig. When I'd last seen him, he believed that I had done just about the two worst things that anyone could to Freddy: loused up his shot at glory, and made him look stupid. So, he hated me. Knowing him, he'd nursed that hatred carefully for the past three years. Fred Pell. Small world.

"That's unfortunate," I said evenly.

Neary gave a grim little laugh. "Unfortunate, yeah, like a root canal with a wood chisel. He came on nearly two years ago. And in case you're wondering, he's the same asshole he's always been, only fatter now. All in all, a low profile is a good idea." He dug into his food. I did the same.

We worked our way through dinner, and as we did, Neary gave me some background. Brill and Parsons and Perkins, the accounting firm, were serving, in part, as high-priced librarians—sifting through the ocean of paper left behind when the bank was closed, and classifying and cataloging each document they found. And there were lots of them, dealing with everything from a multimillion-dollar bond issuance to an order for a thousand desk calendars—and a whole range of things in between. Loan applications, catering bills, deal tickets, expense reports, meeting minutes, account statements, car leases, letters to clients, and contracts for cleaning services. As Neary put it, it was like trying to alphabetize sand.

Taming the paper was only part of the job. Parsons used the documents to help evaluate creditor claims, sometimes reconstructing years of transactions to calculate what MWB owed to someone. Brill helped MWB's lawyers respond to the endless stream of subpoenas and discovery motions churned out by the task force and assorted defense counsel. Brill also provided physical security for the MWB offices around the world. In New York alone, Brill had twenty people at MWB, not including security guards. Parsons had over forty.

Neary echoed Mike's view that the investigation was a zoo, especially when it first got going. According to him, the first few months were classic interagency feeding frenzy, with everybody seeing MWB as a chance to make his or her bones. Things had settled down with the formation of the joint task force, though Neary thought there was still plenty of bad blood between DiPaolo and her counterpart in San Diego, Chris Perez.

"In a fair fight, I'd have to pick Shelly," Neary opined. "Perez has her on weight and reach, but she's got him hands down when it comes to just plain mean."

"She really that bad?" I asked.

"And getting worse," Neary said. "She made a good start on this case, got some convictions right off the bat. But now it's been a long time between wins. Rumor has it the folks in D.C. are getting a little antsy with Shelly. They're looking for some good news on the terror front, I guess, or to show how tough they are on white-collar crime. Apparently she's feeling the heat, and it's not helping her mood."

The waiter had cleared our dishes and brought the dessert menu. Neary ordered a flan and I went for the rice pudding and we both had coffee. We were quiet for a while, then Neary cleared his throat.

"You hear from the old guy?" he asked. I knew he meant Donald. I nodded, thinking about the call I hadn't yet returned.

"He doing alright?" Neary asked. His voice was low.

"He's still working, still fishing and hunting. And they still love him up there. He'll be sheriff as long as he wants. If he'd let them, they'd probably elect him to Congress," I said. But I wasn't answering his question. The answer to that question was no, Donald wasn't alright. He was light-years from alright, and he'd never get back there again, not any more than I would.

The waiter came by and topped off our coffees. I picked up the check, and we said our good-byes on the sidewalk. Neary would call me next week to set up a visit to MWB. He headed toward the Brill offices, and I caught a cab.

The sky had filled with bruise-colored clouds that promised rain or snow. On the ride uptown, it started to do both. I leaned my head against the cab window, and watched through half-closed eyes as it all came down. My head was full of upstate, memories of the case, of Pell, of Donald, and, inevitably, of Anne.

I shut my eyes completely and saw the dock, the gravel path and the porch steps, the blood and the fat, black flies. Suddenly, I was bone weary, and every breath was an effort. I'd intended to do some work that night, maybe start to look for Al Burrows, but when I got back home I lacked the energy even to turn on the lights. Still in my coat, I stood in the darkness, looking out at the night. My chest felt hollow and cold, empty except for a dull ache. I put my hands over my face.

It had snuck up on me. It had been so long since I'd felt like this, I'd gotten complacent and it had snuck up on me.

"Fuck this," I said softly.

And then I heard it. From upstairs. *Thump, thump—whump. Thump, thump—whump.* Rhythmically, and in rapid succession. Not boxes being moved. Not furniture. Probably not livestock. A pogo stick? Tennis? *Thump, thump—whump. Thump, thump—whump.* Enough was enough. I took the stairs up.

The fifth-floor corridor was just like the fourth—long and narrow, lit by hanging fixtures of thick, frosted glass. The stairwell was at one end, the elevator at the other, and the apartment door was in the middle. *Thump, thump—whump.* It came through the door, along with some music. Annie Lennox, it sounded like. A small, embossed card was taped above the doorbell. "J. Lu," it said, in thin black lettering on thick, cream-colored stock. I knocked—hard—and the noise stopped in mid-thump. Then the music got lower.

"Yes?" a woman's voice called from inside.

"It's John March. I'm your neighbor on the fourth floor. I don't know what you're banging on in there, but could you keep it down—just for tonight?" I sounded peevish, even to myself. I heard footsteps approaching the door, and someone opening the peephole. Then some locks slid back and the door opened.

"Oh, gosh. I'm sorry. Really. I couldn't find the box with the mats, and I didn't think sound would carry through these floors. Really, I'm very sorry," she said as she toweled off her forehead and neck. Her voice was a pleasant contralto. She wore a genuinely fretful look. But she made it look good.

She was Asian. Small, but not tiny, maybe five foot three or four, and slim, but not skinny. No, there was nice, compact muscle in her arms and thighs and calves. Her abs and obliques, too, from what I could see—which was a lot. She had on gray spandex shorts that came to mid-thigh and a matching tank top that left her flat midriff bare. Her hair was inky black, and cropped short—just to the stylish side of severe. She had a heart-shaped face, with delicate brows, large, brown—almost black—eyes, and high cheekbones. Her nose was small, with a nearly flat bridge. Her mouth was beautifully formed, her upper lip a perfect bow shape, her lower one full—almost pouting. She wore an emerald stud in each ear, and in her right ear, above the emerald, she wore a diamond stud as well. I guessed she was around thirty.

Her face and slender neck were flushed from exertion. Her tank top, between her small, round breasts, was dark with sweat, and so was the waistband of her shorts. Sweat glistened on her arms and on her belly too, and her hair was damp at the ends. Behind her, I could see the reason. In the center of the apartment, in a space cleared from a thicket of stacked boxes, a heavy bag swung from a metal stand. Her hands and wrists were taped like a boxer's, and so were her ankles and bare feet. I could see where some layers of tape, over the striking surfaces of her hands and feet, had been scuffed away by contact with the bag. Her elbows and knees were a little scraped up too.

She was looking at me, and I realized I was staring. I was also regretting my peevish tone. Her fretful look vanished, replaced by a little smile. "You're Lauren's brother, aren't you? You guys look alike." She stuck out her taped right hand. "I'm Jane Lu."

Chapter Seven

"Al Burrows? Yeah, that was my father. He died last year, at ninety-eight. But he never worked in no bank. The bastard barely worked at all." She paused to belch demurely. "What else you want to know?" Ada Burrows had a thick Long Island accent and sounded pretty old herself, but she was one of the more accommodating Burrowses that I'd spoken to all day.

"You know any other Al Burrows—any brothers or cousins or uncles by that name?"

"Nah, not too many Burrows men still alive. None named Al. I got a cousin Albert on Mom's side, but he's a Boyle, and I think he's dead anyway. What else?"

"Nothing else that I can think of," I said. She sounded disappointed. I was too. I crossed another name off my list.

Besides globalizing the market for junk in people's attics, and bringing joy to pornographers everywhere, the Internet has been a boon to private investigators, at least to the ones it hasn't put out of business. Thanks to the many search services available on the Web, the job of finding people, a staple of the PI trade, is vastly easier these days. Easy enough that a lot of folks dispense with PIs altogether and do it for themselves. The relentless march of progress, I guess.

Personally, I use the services all the time. Provide them with your subject's name, and you'll get back a list of people, complete with addresses and phone numbers, which just might contain the person that you want. The more data you can supply—a city, a state, maybe a date of birth—the better your results. And you can get more than just addresses and phone numbers. Many services provide information on criminal convictions, property ownership, bankruptcy filings, marriages, divorces—a whole range of public data. Much of it is available immediately, online. But while the services are big timesavers, they're not magic. If you've got nothing more to go on than a name, and that name isn't Rufus T. Firefly, or something equally distinctive, you may get back a very long list indeed. And then it's time for some old-fashioned legwork, or, as in this case, phone work.

By Monday afternoon, I'd been through nine A. Burrowses, Ada included. That was over half the number I'd turned up in a search restricted to the New York metropolitan area. Based on what Pierro had told me, the A-for-Al Burrows I was looking for was a white male, over six feet tall, and by now in his late forties or early fifties. Eighteen years ago he'd been heavyset and had thinning, dirty blond hair. By now he could be a bald blimp or, technology being what it is, a skinny redhead. No way to know until I found him.

Ada's father was my second dead A. Burrows, the other one having been run over crossing Queens Boulevard two years go, at age twenty-seven. His mother was inconsolable still, and I was sorry that I'd bothered her. I'd found Albert Burrows, out in Chatham, New Jersey, who might have been the right age, but who assured me, in barely civil tones, that he'd never worked in banking, and that eighteen years ago he'd been living in Capetown. Arthur Burrows, of Dobbs Ferry, was also about the right age, but his career had been in B&E and GTA, and eighteen years ago he'd been right in the middle of his second nickel bit upstate. Next to Ada, he was the chattiest Burrows I'd spoken with, and he told me more than I wanted to know about his personal relationship with God.

I'd found an Alexander in Katonah, who was in banking, but who'd been in junior high at the time in question. And I'd found Alberta, Arlene, Akeema, Amy, and Alyssa Burrows, scattered about the Bronx, Brooklyn, and Staten Island. Some were suspicious, some annoyed, others impatient, and a few downright surly, but none knew any man by the name of Al Burrows—or would tell me, if they did. I had just two Manhattan names on my list. Alfred Burrows had turned out to be a thirty-year-old black man; Alan Burrows was, so far, just a voice on an answering machine.

I shut down my laptop and pushed my chair back from the long oak table that serves as my desk. I stretched and worked the kinks out of my neck. Between dialing for Burrowses, checking in with Mike, and talking to Tom Neary, I'd been on the phone for most of the day. I'd told Mike about my walk in the park and about my meeting with our client. He'd already heard from Pierro.

"He called to thank me," Mike had said, "for bringing you in on this. He said it was a great move, and that you were a great guy, and that everything would be great."

"Great," I'd said.

Mike had chuckled. "He's a salesman—you've got to make allowances."

"Is he really as optimistic as he sounds about all this?" I'd asked.

"At some level. Mostly, I think he's boxed it up in his head and pushed it off to the side."

"It works, if you can keep it up," I'd said.

"It takes a lot of energy."

I'd told Mike about my meet with Neary, too. He went quiet at the mention of Fred Pell.

"Another reason to go carefully," he'd said after a while. I hadn't replied. "I'll interpret your silence as agreement," he'd said hopefully and rung off.

Neary's call came right after. I could have my tour today, he'd told me, if I could meet him at the MWB offices at three-thirty. I was surprised, and pleased, that he'd gotten back to me so soon, and said okay. I rubbed my eyes and checked my watch; it was one-thirty—just enough time for a run.

It had dried out over the weekend, but was still blustery, so I pulled on tights and a wind shell. I headed due west, toward the piers along the Hudson. I hadn't much time, and I'd done a long run on Sunday, so I was aiming for a quick four miles. I turned north at the river, toward Chelsea Piers. I was running into a steady wind now, and it was an effort to keep an eight-minute pace. The wind eased as I came up to 23rd Street, and I picked it up a little. As I ran, my thoughts turned, not for the first time, to my new neighbor.

I'd seen Jane Lu only once since knocking on her door, and then only briefly. She'd been leaving the building as I was coming back from my run on Sunday morning. She was with a clean-cut, frat-boy type with blond hair and lots of teeth. She was wearing jeans, an orange turtle-neck, and tiny, wire-rimmed sunglasses, and she'd given me a smile and a friendly hello. After fifteen fast miles, I wasn't sure that I'd said any-thing coherent in return.

She'd been nice as pie to me on Friday night—apologizing profusely for the noise, confessing her kickboxing mania, explaining that she'd been working with my sister, Lauren, for the past six months. She even offered me a Pepsi. And the nicer she was, the more ridiculous I'd felt for having been so irritated. At some point it had dawned on me that Jane recognized my discomfort, and so was being particularly gracious—the better to see me squirm. I'd found this interesting, if slightly annoying. There was a lot interesting about Jane—her considerable physical appeal, her rich, easy laugh, and the powerful intellect that gleamed in her dark eyes. I'd talked with her, with her doing most of the talking, for about twenty minutes before going downstairs, to bed.

I was back from my run in thirty-three minutes. I stretched and showered quickly, and dressed in gray trousers, a white shirt, a blue blazer, and a red paisley tie. And then I headed downtown.

I got off the subway at Wall and William, and walked south. Daylight had begun to fade, and the dark, narrow streets were growing darker. Soon the markets would close and the streets would fill with homeward pandemonium, but just now they were quiet. A few people stood at the entrances of buildings—smoking, talking, watching the traffic pass; a few others made for the subway—the first small trickle of the evening rush. A couple of TV news vans were parked near the old Morgan Guaranty building. Technicians snaked cables on the pavement out front, and bantered with the cops at the Exchange. A group of tourists rested on the worn steps of Federal Hall, studying their maps and debating their next destination. Some street vendors were shutting down for the day; others were setting up. Quiet for Wall Street. Quieter than it was those sum-mers, a century back, when I'd worked down here; quieter than just a couple of years ago—before the party ended, before the bubble burst, and the triumphal march of the imperial CEOs and celebrity analysts finished in a string of perp walks. Quieter than it was before the towers. Maybe it was my imagination, or something the neighborhood brings out in me, but the faces seemed paler, more tired, more worn and used up than I remembered. Maybe it was just a trick of the light.

I knew from Mike's file that, apart from its London headquarters,

New York had been MWB's largest office. The bank had been the marquis tenant in a prestigious tower at the bottom of Broad Street. It had occupied a quarter of the building, and its executive suites and dining rooms had boasted picture-postcard views. Now, whatever was left of the firm was relegated to two low floors, and there was nothing but a faded spot on the granite out front, where the MWB logo used to be. The lobby guard studied my documents and pointed me at an elevator and told me to get off at three. Neary was waiting for me, wearing a navy suit, a dark tie, and a white shirt.

"Tom," I said, extending my hand, "thanks again for this."

"Always happy to have you owe me another large favor. But I still think this is mostly a waste of time."

Neary led me through a glass door to a reception area. It was small, windowless, and unlovely, furnished only with a steel desk and a swivel chair. Set in the wall to the left of the desk was a gray metal door, and mounted beside it was a card-key reader. A uniformed guard manned the desk. He was a black man in his early fifties who, even sitting down and nearly motionless, managed to look tough, competent, and entirely humorless. He gave me the once-over with eyes like stones.

"Hi, Chet," Neary said, and flashed an ID card.

"Hello, Mr. Neary. This is your guest?" Chet asked.

"This is him," he answered. Neary wrote in the logbook and had me sign in too. He walked to the metal door and ran his ID card through the reader. The door gave a click, and he pulled it open.

We were in a corridor that extended to the right and left. Across from us, arranged end-on to the corridor, were row upon row of steel shelves. They reached almost to the ceiling, like library shelves. But the effect was more warehouse than library, as they were stacked not with books but with large, green filing boxes.

I followed Neary off to the left and around the corner. The floor was laid out like a square doughnut, and the four sides were mostly open space, given over to the rows of metal shelves. The aisles between the shelves were narrow, and as we walked past I saw windows at the other end, with dim views of buildings and airshafts. At each of the four corners was a cluster of offices, and in the central core were bathrooms, a kitchen, a room with copy machines, and access doors to the fire stairs and freight elevators. We passed maybe half a dozen people along the way, mostly young, mostly male, all casually dressed. They all knew Neary and greeted him.

The shelves aside, the floor was nicely fitted out. The carpets were coffee-colored and thick, and the walls were covered in a beige fabric. There was dark wood molding at the baseboards and the cornices. But the place had an abandoned, deserted feel nonetheless, and the ranks of high, metal shelves, stacked boxes, and narrow aisles made me slightly claustrophobic.

"We've got this floor and the one above," Neary explained. "They used to be MWB's back-office operations. We put in the security out front, pulled out the cubicles, and put in the shelves. Upstairs is set up just the same. Come on, I'll introduce you to someone."

"Any particular story you've told, about who I am and why I'm here?" I asked.

"I've been vague, and I intend to stay that way. Busman's holiday is all I've said. It's alright. My people are mostly ex-feds—they're used to not being told shit. And the Parsons people are all accountants—they expect even less."

Neary headed for one of the corners, and I followed. We walked into a small office that had been stripped down to the picture hooks. All that remained of furniture was a metal desk, two worn chairs in front of it, and a swivel chair behind it. A woman sat in the swivel chair, gazing at a computer screen. Her fingers were poised over the keyboard, and she had a pen between her teeth. She did not look up when we entered.

"Is now good?" Neary asked.

"Give me a sec," she answered, without moving. She had several windows opened on the screen. A browser was running in one, and she was reading a document displayed in it. She made some notes on a legal pad.

"There," she said to herself, and swiveled in her chair to face us. She stood and stuck out her hand. "Cheryl Compton," she said.

Cheryl Compton was an early thirty-something, maybe five feet tall on her tiptoes and one hundred pounds soaking wet. She had café au lait skin and thick, shoulder-length hair the color of dark chocolate. Her face was broad, and her features an attractive mix of African and Asian. Her eyes were large and pitch black, and they flashed with an impatient intelligence, despite the fatigue that lay over them just now. She had a small, square chin and a sharply etched jawline, marred by a little knot of muscle working on one side. Her full lips were pursed. Compton was casually dressed, in gray wool pants and a black sweater. Her only jewelry was a black plastic watch. She pushed a wave of hair behind her ear and sat. We sat too.

"Cheryl joined us about three years ago, from IRS," Neary began. "And most of her time with Brill has been on this account. Early on, she worked with the Parsons people and the technical guys, setting up the document management system, and now she's our senior investigator at MWB. And whatever we pay her, it's probably not enough, because she's the one who really knows what's going on around here." He smiled. Compton rolled her eyes elaborately, but some of the tension went out of her jaw. She turned to me.

"He tells me you're looking for some background stuff on what we're doing and how we do it. I can give you the ten-thousand-foot overview, and you can tell me where you want to go from there. I'm assuming you know the basics about MWB."

"I think so. I'll call out if you lose me," I said. She took a deep breath and began.

"Basically, there are three kinds of work going on here." She ticked them off on her fingers as she spoke. "There's liquidation analysis, litigation support, and document management. It sounds like consulting gobbledygook, I know, but it actually means something.

"Liquidation analysis is what the Parsons people are mostly engaged in, with some help from us. What they're doing, essentially, is reconstructing the bank's balance sheet—on the one hand determining what assets the bank still has, and on the other figuring out what it owes, and to whom. They'll take you through all the grim details.

"Litigation support is Brill's responsibility, and it's just a fancy name for sending documents to people. As you probably know, there are a bunch of criminal proceedings underway against former MWB employees, and more are coming. On top of that, a slew of civil actions are gearing up. That means that every day, day in and day out, the MWB liquidation committee gets requests—orders, really—to produce documents. Task force investigators, the U.S. attorney, defense counsel, civil plaintiffs, you name it—they all want documents—lots of them. If the liquidation committee agrees to the requests—and they don't usually have much choice in the matter—then we make sure that the orders get filled." Compton spoke quickly. She'd done this spiel before, and her delivery was practiced. She paused to see if I was still with her. I was.

"Central to these two activities is the third thing we do here: document management. It was the first task we had when we started, and none of the other work can go on without it. When we came on the job, it was like boarding one of those ghost ships in the Bermuda Triangle.

You know, where everything looks normal but all the people are missing. Senior management was in jail or on the run, and the people who actually did the work, the traders, operations people, and accountants, had all been let go. And we couldn't call any of them back, since they were all potential defendants. So we had an empty bank on our hands—a ghost ship. The only things that could tell us what the hell had been going on were the documents they'd left behind.

"But it was a huge mountain of paper, and organized filing was not MWB's strong suit. To get—and keep—control of the documents we use a set of procedures and a computer system. The procedures are straightforward, even if the work itself isn't. Every document we find on MWB premises is assigned a unique identification number, and is scanned in to a central documents database. Then, someone reviews it, classifies it, and writes an abstract of its contents, and all that goes into the database too. After that, the physical document goes offsite, to a warehouse out in Jersey we use as a storage center. From then on, any research we or the Parsons people need to do involving that document is done using the document database." A chiming sound came from her computer, and Compton paused to glance at the screen. She clicked something and continued.

"Say, for example, that Parsons needs to review all the correspondence that took place between MWB and some particular client. Using the system, they can look at it by date, by subject, by department, by a bunch of other criteria—all online. Or say we get a request for documents, maybe from the U.S. attorneys. We use the system to find what they've asked for, and we have the guys in the storage center ship the hard copy. And we also use the system to keep track of who has asked for what items, and to record what we send, and where and when we send it." She paused again, waiting for questions. This time I had some.

"Do only paper documents go into the database? What about e-mail? Or data from MWB's accounting systems?"

Compton began nodding before I'd finished my question. "Yep, yep—we use all that stuff. E-mail and any other electronic documents go in the database, the same as paper—only we don't have to scan them. We use their systems, too—their general ledger, their trading systems, their settlement systems—but that data doesn't go into the documents database."

"Is everything that's supposed to be in there actually on the database at this point?"

"Almost. We've got everything from the offices worldwide, but there are some documents from offsite storage that we haven't gotten to yet. That's a lot of what you see on the shelves out there."

"So you've got documents going back . . . how long?"

"Nearly thirty years, to when MWB first opened for business."

"And people need documents going back that far?"

"Well, not so much the feds. They're focused on more recent stuff, activity within the statute of limitations—the last seven years or so. But Parsons, for the liquidation work, they go back that far."

"All the work is done here? All the scanning and abstracting and the rest?"

"Yep. It needs to be controlled centrally. Once stuff is on the system, our teams in the overseas branches can access it. We're all hooked up to a wide area network."

"And once something's in there, how do you find it again? Do you need to know the ID number?" Compton grimaced a little at this.

"No. If you knew the number, you could get at it that way, sure, but nobody knows the numbers. Remember I said that part of what we do is classify? We use those classifications to find documents on the database. Every document gets labeled with information about its subject, its date, the person who authored it, and what department they were in, who it was sent to, who got copied on it, its source—meaning where we found it. And a bunch of other tags as well. We can search on any or all of those fields." Neary cleared his throat.

"Can you give him a demo, Cheryl?" he asked. Compton's jaw tightened again, and she glanced at her watch.

"I was going to turn him over to Mitch and Bobby for that, if it's okay," she said. Neary looked mildly surprised, but nodded.

"No problem," he said. "They're in their office?" She nodded. Neary and I got up, and I thanked Compton for her time. She gave me a quick, distracted handshake, and started clearing papers from her desk.

I followed Neary back down the main corridor, to an adjacent corner of the floor. We walked into another office, about the size of Compton's and nearly as bare, but outfitted with two desks. Two men were sitting at them.

"Mitch, Bobby, sorry to wake you. Cheryl nominated you guys to give a quick demo of the doc system," Neary said. The two men chuckled and stood to shake hands and introduce themselves.

Bobby Coe was a ruddy, balding guy, somewhere in his late twenties.

He was about my height, but stockier, with a round, open face, and large blue eyes behind wire-framed glasses. What little hair he had left was strawberry blond and short. He wore khakis and a red plaid shirt with the sleeves rolled up over his beefy, freckled forearms. Neary had said most of his guys were ex-feds, and maybe Coe was, but he looked more like an ex–park ranger.

His office mate, Mitch Vetter, was about the same age as Coe, but shorter, about five foot ten, and not as heavily built. He had dark, wavy hair, worn long in a vain attempt to hide the thinning patch on top. His face was pale and narrow, with thick brows and dark eyes set close around a prominent nose. He had a heavy beard, and his five o'clock shadow was barely lighter than his close-trimmed moustache and goatee. He wore black pants and a dark blue shirt, and he did look like an ex-fed—the kind you'd send to infiltrate a crew of Jersey wiseguys.

"Yeah, Cheryl told us," Vetter said. His voice was surprisingly high, and he had a heavy New York accent. "Step this way." Vetter sat down and spun his computer screen toward us. Neary and I pulled up chairs, and Coe came around and perched on the edge of the desk. Vetter had a browser running in a window on his screen.

"Cheryl gave us the basics, so you can cut to the chase, Mitch," Neary said. Vetter nodded.

"Cool. This is the search engine for our document database, and this is the main query screen," he explained. "With this you can filter through the whole database to find, for example, all the documents that were generated by the loan department on July 23, 1994."

His fingers flew over the keyboard as he spoke. He entered search criteria into several labeled fields that appeared on the screen. I could decipher the meanings of some of them, like "document date" and "author," but others, like "req loc ref," were gibberish to me.

"This isn't running on the Internet, is it?" I asked.

"No way," Coe answered, looking aghast. "It's running on an intranet we've set up. That's like a private Internet." Vetter clicked a button labeled "Search," and almost instantly the results appeared in the form of a list.

"See," Vetter pointed at the screen. "We got 124 items in all. We show the first twenty on this list. We can pick one and read the abstract." He highlighted an item and clicked another button. A new window opened, displaying a couple of paragraphs of text. "Or, we can see the original." He clicked another button and another window opened, this one containing the image of a document on MWB letterhead. It looked like a letter to a client.

"And if we want, we can then go and find any other documents that reference this same client," Coe said. Vetter demonstrated. The engine came back with 568 items, the first twenty of which were displayed on the screen.

"And if you need to find everything written by a particular person?" I asked.

"No problem," Vetter said, and he showed me.

"And for all of the items in the database, you keep track of where each one was found?" I asked.

"Yep," Coe answered. We were all quiet for a while.

"And you also use the system to keep track of who has requested which documents?" I asked.

"Oh, yeah. Everything gets logged—including who made a request, the date they made it, what they asked for, what we sent them in return, and when we sent it," Coe said.

"What about searches like the ones you just ran?"

"Online queries? Those get logged too—'everything' means everything," Coe said.

"Can you search for documents based on who has accessed them?" Vetter and Coe looked at each other for a while. Finally, Coe spoke.

"If you mean finding every document that, for example, Special Agent John Doe has requested—sure, that's easy. Like I said, if someone asks us to send something, we record who, what, where, and when on the system, and we can query on those things. If you mean finding everything that, say, I've accessed online, that's doable too, but not as easy. And not everybody could do it. It would mean searching through the log files, and this search engine doesn't look in those."

Vetter had swiveled around to look at me with the beginnings of curiosity. He drummed his fingers slowly on the desk, waiting for more questions and wondering. But before I could ask anything else, Neary suggested that we let them get back to work. He got up and thanked them and headed for the door.

Chapter Eight

"Too many questions?" I asked, when we were back in the hallway. Neary nodded.

"Vetter's antennas were starting to wiggle," he said.

"Sorry. I liked that system, though. Seems like it could tell me a lot about what I'm interested in. Documents written by Nassouli, documents found in his office, everyone who's asked to see them."

"We'll get there, don't worry. Besides, I can answer some of those questions, without any system," Neary said. "You want all the documents found in Nassouli's office? It's a real short list. Nothing, not a scrap of paper—not unless you count a yellow sticky pad and a box of tissues." I must have looked puzzled.

"We think he had himself a little shredding party before he hit the road," Neary explained. "Some of the other execs did the same, and it didn't make Shelly and her crew very happy when they figured it out. Speaking of which, you want to know who's been asking for Nassouli's documents? The feds will top that list. Until a few months ago, they were all over anything that had to do with him. They got copies of everything he wrote or was copied on or that made reference to him."

"And what happened a few months ago?"

Neary shrugged. "I don't know, exactly. Five, six months ago, it just stopped. No more requests. No more noise about him at all from the feds. And they get a little prickly on the topic. Not that I press."

"So . . . what, you think they found him?" I asked.

"You never know with those guys," Neary said, and raised his eyebrows. "Maybe we should call Freddy and ask. He'll be happy to share. Come on upstairs. You can have a look at the Parsons people, and then we'll poke around on the system." I followed him back through the metal door to the reception area and the elevators.

The fourth-floor reception area was identical to the third, except for the guard behind the desk. This one was a heavyset white guy in his middle fifties, with a florid face and reddish hair that was going fast to white.

"Hi, Tim," Neary said. "He's with me—signed him in downstairs." Tim nodded, and Neary opened the metal door with his card key. Four had the same square doughnut layout as three. It had the same forest of shelves and the same abandoned feel, too. I followed Neary to another corner, and another cluster of offices. He gave me some more background as we walked.

"Like Cheryl said, Parsons mainly does the liquidation work. The committee brought them on first thing, even before we got here. They've got forty-plus people here in New York, and probably another sixty or seventy in the other offices around the world. The partner running the engagement shows up here for an hour or two every month, and spends most of that time schmoozing the management committee. The real guy in charge is Evan Mills. Sort of an asshole, but a bright guy, once you get past the aging preppy thing." Neary gave a little laugh. "Hey—you two might have a lot in common. He should be around here somewhere."

We walked into a conference room. It was long and windowless, painted white and very brightly lit. Half a dozen computers had been set up on the metal and plastic conference table, and three men were gathered around one of them, peering at the monitor. They looked at us but gave no greeting.

"Mills?" Neary asked.

"Project office," one of the men answered and gestured with his thumb. The three heads bent again to the monitor.

I followed Neary next door, to a room that was more walk-in filing cabinet than office. It was about eight by ten feet and fluorescent-lit, and nearly all the wall space was covered by shelves. Most of the shelves were filled with big, white loose-leaf binders labeled "Time Sheets" and

"Expenses." Some bore the Brill logo, but most were stamped with the Parsons and Perkins chop. A small metal desk was jammed into the back of the room. Its top was crowded with a computer, a telephone, a fax, in and out trays, stacks of blank forms, and, just now, a pair of worn deck shoes.

The shoes belonged to a young man sprawled in the chair behind the desk. He had a telephone handset propped on his shoulder, and a big white binder in his lap. He was listening to someone, and he rolled his slightly bulging gray eyes at us in exaggerated boredom. He ran a hand over a broad forehead and through a tangle of blond hair. Then he smiled and made a "yackety-yak" hand gesture and shot Neary with a thumb and forefinger. Besides the deck shoes, he wore baggy khakis and a navy blue sweater over a blue striped shirt. His sleeves were pushed up over wiry forearms, and on his wrist was a thick metal watch that looked like it had been carved from the instrument panel of a fighter jet.

On closer inspection, the man aged a dozen years. There were streaks of gray in the blond hair, and a web of fine lines around his eyes and his wide, almost lipless mouth. The hint of color on his sharp nose was from broken capillaries, not sunburn. I put him at forty, plus or minus. He ran a hand through his hair again and spoke into the phone.

"Yes, Mrs. Cleaver, we'll get that over right away," he said with mock sincerity. "And then will you let the Beav come out and play?" He listened some more and sat up quickly. His hand tightened around the phone, and he answered back with venom, "You think this is a bad attitude? Come down here and talk to my people. They haven't had expenses reimbursed in over two months because you and your fucking bureaucrats can't get the paperwork right. My attitude is nothing compared to theirs. I'll resend the damn file, but—trust me—this is the last time we're going to have this conversation. The next time I'm taking it up with the engagement partner, and you can explain to him why you keep fucking this up." He slammed down the phone, and as soon as he did all traces of anger disappeared.

"What clowns. Trying to get accounts to process expenses, it's like dealing with the fucking IRS," he chuckled to himself. He put the binder on the desk and stood, stretching. He smiled at Neary and put out his hand. "It's J. Edgar himself. How're you doing, Hoov?" They shook. Hoov?

Neary smiled, with only a trace of strain, and made introductions. "Evan, this is John. John—Evan Mills. I'm giving John a little tour of the operation, and I was hoping you could give him a quick overview of what Parsons is doing." Mills gave me a surprisingly strong handshake.

"Anything for you, Hoov, you know that. You another fallen G-man?" Mills asked me. I smiled but said nothing.

"Not saying, huh? Eyes only, need to know, you could tell me, but then you'd have to kill me—I get it." He laughed and moved past us, into the corridor. Neary and I followed. Mills walked, and reeled off a practiced chatter as he went.

"I assume Hoov has given you the basics of who does what, right? So you know that Parsons is focused on the liquidation work. That's meat-and-potatoes forensic accounting. But what does that mean, really? I always say that forensic accounting is like archeology, but not as messy, and you don't get to camp out. They're both about collecting a million tiny, unremarkable pieces of dirt, to build a picture of something from the past. In this case, the thing we're rebuilding is MWB's balance sheet." Mills liked the sound of his own voice, and didn't pause or even glance back at us as he spoke.

"I'm guessing you have no accounting background. No one does, except accountants, and even they're not happy about it. So I'll keep the jargon to a minimum. A balance sheet is basically a tally of a firm's assets and liabilities. The assets are what it owns; the liabilities are what it owes. Creating this takes some sweat, but it's not usually rocket science. For a bank, tallying the assets is a matter of adding up the outstanding loans that it's made, plus cash or securities due to the bank from trading activity, plus whatever it has in its vaults—that could be cash, or stocks and bonds, or gold, or any number of things. And then you add in any cash or securities it has in accounts at other banks or custodians.

"Toting up the liabilities is the flip side. You look at any loans the bank has taken out, cash or securities it's holding for clients, bonds or commercial paper it's issued, whatever it owes from trading activity, and anything in its vaults that belongs to someone else. That's basically what we're doing here. Of course, with MWB there are complications." Mills led us to the kitchen alcove. He poured some poisonous-looking stuff from a glass coffee pot and leaned against the counter.

"You guys want? No? That's probably smart. Okay. The first and biggest complication in all of this work is the number of different legal entities—different financial institutions—that were under the holding company's umbrella. The sheer number of names whose activities we have to sift through makes things much more difficult. Also, the MWB people were lousy record-keepers. I don't know if that was by design or just incompetence, but it's amazing they were ever able to pass an audit." He drank some coffee and made a face.

"Those are the main problems, but we've had others to deal with. For example, the MWB traders were very active, so there were lots of deals still unsettled when their charter was yanked. We had to sort through all of those. Finding MWB's cash and securities accounts at other institutions was another pain. We had some statements to work from, but ultimately we had to canvass all the firms that provide those services, to see if they had any accounts for MWB. And then there were the vaults. You'd be amazed at what they had in there. And let's just say that a lot of it was of questionable provenance." Mills smiled to himself and shook his head.

"So, once we piece together the balance sheet, then what? What do we do with it? Well, all the liabilities are somebody else's assets. And no sooner had the regulators shut the doors on this place, than those folks started lining up with claims. To validate those claims, we're reconstructing MWB's activities with each of the claimants. It's excruciating work; the more complex cases go back years and involve thousands of transactions." Mills drained his cup.

"That's it. In a nutshell, that's what we're doing, here in New York and in the overseas offices too." He folded his arms across his chest and looked quizzically from one of us to the other. "I don't know what else there is to tell." I looked at Neary, and he looked back at me. Neither of us spoke.

"How do you do it?" I asked. "How do you go about putting the pieces together?"

"The mechanics of it?" Mills looked at me and shrugged. "One of my teams is down the hall. You can hear it from the horse's mouth." We followed Mills out of the alcove, back along the corridor, to the conference room Neary and I had peeked into before. The same three men were there. Mills spoke to all of them.

"Troops, let me tear you away from your labors for a moment. You all know Hoov, from Brill. This is his friend, John," Mills paused dramatically and looked at me, "Mysterious John. He has some general and very quick questions for you, and then you can get back to the salt mines." He turned to Neary and me. "Here you have Stan Greer," he pointed to a pale, thin, bespectacled man with straw-colored hair, wearing a blue plaid shirt, "Charlie Koch," a heavyset, freckled redhead wearing a Jets sweater, "and Vijay Desai," a slim, dark Indian man, wearing a bright red sweater over a black shirt. They looked slightly annoyed at the interruption and a little uneasy—in part, no doubt, due to Mills's introduction. "Mysterious John," indeed. Mills looked at me.

"Evan has described, generally, what kind of work you're doing here. But I'd like to get some idea of how you actually go about doing it. Maybe you can start with how you're organized—who does what?" They looked at Mills and then at each other, uncertain about who should talk. Mills looked bored and gave them no help. Finally, Desai jumped in.

"You know we're doing balance sheet reconstruction and claims evaluation?" he asked me. I nodded. "The balance sheet work is done by teams of people, all accountants with a lot of audit experience, usually three to six people on a team. We've split up the different MWB entities and assigned a set to each team. They work on the balance sheets for their assigned entities, plus they review the work from other teams as a quality check. We've got separate groups working the claims. Usually two to four people per team on those."

"And where do they start, what are they working with?" I asked.

Desai kept talking. "Mainly they're looking at data from the bank's general ledger systems and its other record-keeping systems. And at filings MWB made with regulators over the years, with the Fed, the State of New York, the Comptroller of the Currency, and so forth. Ultimately they go back to source documents—account applications, trade tickets, confirmations, loan agreements, statements, correspondence with clients, those sorts of things. We go to the document system for all of that."

Mills looked at his watch and then at Neary. "Hoov, if there's nothing else, I've got stuff to do, and so do these guys. Unless you want me to start billing you for consulting work." Subtle as it was, we took that as a hint to go.

Neary and I said our thanks and headed for the elevators. At the door that would take us to the guard station I looked back and saw Mills, standing motionless at the end of the long corridor, watching.

"Kind of an annoying bastard, isn't he?" I said, as we waited for the elevator.

"Yep," Neary agreed.

"Not much of a tour, either," I said.

"Not much," Neary agreed, "but then, we weren't paying for his time. Come on, we'll have a look for your documents."

It was after five o'clock when we returned to the third floor, and the dim views through the windows had darkened to night. Lights shone in the buildings nearby, and the floor seemed more deserted than ever. I followed Neary to a small office. The dark wood desk was bare except for a PC and a phone. Neary sat behind the desk, switched on the PC, and pulled the keyboard in front of him.

"Pull a chair around," he said, and I did. He typed quickly, logging into the network and bringing up the browser. When the search-engine page was in the browser window, he sat back and looked at me.

"So this is where we play 'I'll show you mine if you show me yours,'" he said. I looked back at him, silent. He continued, "I'm doing the driving here," he pointed to the keyboard, "and if you don't give me something to search for we're not going to get very far."

"You could always let me drive," I said.

Neary snorted, "That's not going to happen, John. I'm out on a limb just having you in here, so unless you open up a little, this is where we stop." We looked at each other in silence. Neary wasn't trying to strong-arm me, but he wasn't bullshitting me either. I had a choice to make. I nodded and pulled out my notebook.

"Everything I'm interested in is dated eighteen years ago. Let's start with letters from Nassouli, with dates in February of that year," I said. He nodded and started typing. The engine came back with twenty-one documents that met the criteria. I scanned down the results list. None of them were the ones I was looking for. The dates were wrong, and so were the topics. Neary looked at me, and I shook my head.

"We're zero-for-one," Neary said.

"Actually zero-for-two," I said. He shrugged.

"What's next?" he asked.

"How about letters to Nassouli dated . . ." I checked my notes again, "March eighth through March fifteenth that year." This time, the engine found eleven documents. And one of them jumped out at me. Neary saw me staring.

"Something?" he asked. I nodded.

"You going to tell me which one, or do I have to guess?"

"Show me the first five," I said. He clicked on each one, and each time he did a new window opened with an abstract of the document he'd picked, and an image of the original.

Mine was number three. It was the letter from Pierro to Dias, informing him of the establishment of the credit line. It was identical to the one in the fax. According to the abstract, the original had been found in offsite storage, in files from the correspondent banking department, specifically in the files of its former chief, Alan Burrows.

"Who else requested these?" I asked. Neary pointed and clicked a few times.

"Just the feds, about a year ago. I told you, they want anything involving Nassouli." We were quiet for a while.

"That it?" he asked. I nodded. "So, two of them we don't have, and no one besides the feds has accessed the third. Nothing here tells me that this shop was the source of your documents, John. I think you've got to look elsewhere." I put away my notebook and leaned back.

"You guys find documents from Nassouli's files in offsite storage?" I asked.

"Some, yeah," Neary answered warily.

"So he didn't call the offsite stuff back for shredding, huh?"

"No time, I'd guess," said Neary.

"The documents I'm asking about are pretty old—old enough to have gone to offsite storage. But you didn't find any of them there. How come?" Neary thought about this, not happy with where I was headed.

"Beats the hell out of me. Could be he never sent them offsite, and they got shredded with the rest of his shit. Could be he didn't give a damn about them, and tossed them years ago. The MWB people weren't that good at record-keeping."

"So I keep hearing. But it could also be the documents were here, and never made it into your system," I suggested.

"Bullshit," Neary said. He sighed heavily and shut down the PC. Then he leaned back in his chair and clasped his hands across his stomach and looked at me. "What else can I tell you?" he asked. I thought about it for a while, not really sure. The office was silent except for air coming through the ceiling vents in a conspiratorial whisper.

"This and the fourth floor—that's all that's left of MWB in New York?" I asked.

"Pretty much," Neary answered. "Nearly everything else has been cleaned out and sublet."

"Where was Nassouli's office?"

"On forty-four, one of the trading floors."

"Anything left there?"

"Not for long. They signed a sublease on it last week, and construction starts week after next. Equipment and files are long gone. There's not much left to see, but you can have a look if you want."

We went to the lobby, switched elevator banks, and rode up to forty-four. Another uniformed guard greeted Neary and buzzed us in. Neary took a big ring of keys from his desk as we passed. We went through a metal door and down a short corridor. This floor was the same shape as the lower ones, but had been built out very differently. A band of small offices ran around the doughnut's inner edge. They were windowless, but had glass walls that looked out on the rest of the floor. More, larger, offices ran around the outer edge. These also had glass walls, but they had windows as well, and sweeping views of the harbor and the uptown skyline. Sandwiched between the glass offices was the trading floor itself—five rows of long desks, separated by narrow aisles, running down each side of the doughnut.

If the lower floors had had an abandoned feel, this one seemed vandalized. The offices were nearly bare, with only some scarred furniture and the occasional moving box remaining. The blinds and drapes that had covered the glass walls lay in heaps in some offices, and in others hung twisted and askew. The carpeting was stained and torn in many places, and in many places was missing altogether. Rows of acoustical tile were missing from the dropped ceiling. The light fixtures that weren't mangled on the floor were mostly dark. The forest of technology—screens, keyboards, elaborate phone consoles—that usually covers any trading desk had been cut away from these, leaving behind a tangle of exposed cable and some cleaner patches on the filthy desktops. The trading desks themselves were like junked cars, gutted and left for scrap. The air was cold and stale and smelled vaguely like a bus station.

We picked our way across the trading floor to a big corner office. It had its own little waiting area and a glass-walled conference room adjoining it. Neary found a key on the ring and unlocked the door. This office was in better shape than the others. The drapes and carpets and light fixtures were intact, and the furniture that remained—a massive teak desk, topped in polished stone, two huge credenzas, and a set of teak bookshelves—looked undamaged. Neary stepped to the windows to take in the view.

It was spectacular. To the north, the Brooklyn Bridge, the Manhattan Bridge, the sweep of FDR Drive running along the East River, and a chunk of the Brooklyn waterfront—all glittered in the clear night. To the east there was more of Brooklyn, the shadowed mass of Governor's Island and the distant lights of the Verrazano, across a dark expanse of harbor. We looked out in silence.

"Nice views, but not much else," Neary said after a while. I looked around the office. A large moving box stood, unsealed, on one of the credenzas.

"What's in the box?" I asked.

"Stuff Nassouli left behind when he split. Desk doodads, those Lucite tombstones from some deals they'd done, and a bunch of pictures that were hanging on the walls, mostly of himself at parties." Neary reached into the box and took out an eight-by-ten color photo, nicely mounted between glass plates. It showed people at a party, a high-end one. The men were in black tie, the women in shimmering, gauzy things. I recognized the Temple of Dendur, at the Metropolitan, in the background. In the foreground was a man I took to be Gerard Nassouli.

He was handsome and, in that picture, could have been anything from thirty-five to fifty. The photo showed him from the waist up, and he seemed heavily built, but not fat. He had a broad face, with heavy-lidded, slightly almond-shaped eyes, a straight, prominent nose, and a wide mouth with full lips and lots of white teeth. His skin was dark, and his glossy, black hair and brows were thick. He wore a mustache and a Van Dyke beard, both closely cropped. He was smiling in the photo, and seemed to be speaking with someone outside the frame. In one hand he held a champagne flute aloft, his arm raised in mid-toast. His other arm was wrapped around a willowy blonde, slightly taller than he, who looked barely legal. She smiled faintly, her eyes closed and her head inclined toward his. His large, manicured hand rested proprietarily on her hip.

There was something sleek and ursine in Nassouli's immaculate hair and dark features and well-fed bulk, and I realized that he reminded me a bit of Rick Pierro. But where Pierro projected an open, what-you-see-is-what-you-get quality—a kind of friendly, regular-guy bear—there was something vaguely menacing and slightly leering about Nassouli— a piratical bear. A bear from the Hellfire Club.

"Here he is with an ex-mayor at a Knicks game. And here he's with a model at—what, the Belmont? And here he's with the girl from that game show, at some other black-tie thing." One by one, Neary took photos from the box and placed them on the tabletop. "Nassouli at some club; another black-tie party; here he's at Lincoln Center. At the Guggenheim. At the Garden."

The photos were identically mounted, between glass plates, and in all of them Nassouli was in the foreground. While he never looked directly into the camera, I got the sense he was always aware of its presence. The events in the photos spanned a couple of decades, and you could trace the passage of time through the changing fashions worn by the people in them. Only Nassouli himself seemed changeless. Perhaps slightly thicker, a bit fuller in the face in the more recent ones. Otherwise he seemed not to age. Dorian Gray bear.

"This looks like an old one . . . here he is at the Odeon." Neary laid another photo on the tabletop.

This one was black-and-white, and it was the only photo in which he seemed to have no awareness of the camera, the only truly candid picture in the bunch. It was a street scene, at night, taken from the backseat of a car, through a partially open window. It must have just rained, as the street was shiny and water was beaded on the window glass. Nassouli had just come out of the Odeon—part of the restaurant was visible behind him. He was coming toward the car and the camera. One hand was reaching out, as if to grasp the door handle. There were figures behind him, blurred, dark shapes, their faces white smears. Only Nassouli's face was in focus. And it was chilling.

The other pictures had hinted at something a little dangerous beneath the attractive, well-groomed facade. This photo left no doubt. This was no stylish rogue; this was evil—and all the scarier for its handsome packaging. In the photo Nassouli's broad face was infernal, his dark, hooded eyes gleaming, his thick lips pulled into a leering, satisfied grin. It was the look Torquemada might have worn after a busy day at work, or the smile the snake had worn, when he'd sold his first apple. It was a wonder he had hung it on his office wall.

The composition of the photo, its stark contrasts and heavy shadows, were familiar to me, and I didn't need to see the name, penned in tiny letters at the bottom right corner of the matte paper, to recognize the work of H. Barrie.

Chapter Nine

"You're gonna hurt yourself doing that, honey," called one of the girls, from the corner. She had a wobbly pile of orange hair, and legs that were bigger than mine. They were covered not at all by a leather skirt the size of a napkin.

"You're working way too hard," called another, laughing. "Come on over here, we'll relax you." Her eight-inch black stilettos and red vinyl jumpsuit glistened in the streetlight. She had the neck and shoulders of a wrestler.

"Morning, girls," I said. I waved and kept on running. "Girls" was neither politically nor anatomically correct, I knew, but it was what these guys aspired to, and who was I to argue. I was headed south on Eleventh Avenue in the predawn dark, on the last leg of a six-mile run. I passed the Javits Center and the trucks already lumbering around it, and went back on autopilot, one part of my brain on traffic and potholes, another trying to sort out exactly what I'd found at MWB. So far I had more questions than answers.

I'd seen something of the mess that Brill and Parsons faced at the bank, and how they went about cleaning it up. I'd seen their nifty document system. Slick as it was, it held only one of the items from Pierro's fax. Was that because the other documents simply hadn't been in the bank? From what I could tell, once something got into that system, it was hard to remove without leaving lots of footprints. But how hard was it to keep something out in the first place?

The people I'd met last night could've told me, no doubt. They seemed to know their business well, and also to know their way around banking, and MWB, and the document system. That kind of knowledge would come in handy if you were running a little side action in black-mail. Mike would call that wild speculation; so would Neary. They'd be right.

I had speculation to spare, and a lot of it was about Gerard Nassouli. His photography collection was an odd one. For the most part, it was vanity wall stuff—clichéd trophies that strained to paint the man as mover, shaker, and fashionable rake. All that was missing was the one of him in a smoking jacket and ascot, flanked by a couple of bunnies. Helene's picture hit the jarring note. Was that the real Nassouli she'd caught there, on that wet, nighttime street? And if it was, why did he advertise it? Did he like the way it recast the fluff photos, in a colder, more sinister light?

And what about Helene? She'd apparently known Nassouli, back in her salad days of modeling and amateur photography. But how had she known him? How well and for how long? And why had neither she nor her husband seen fit to mention it? True, I hadn't asked, so they hadn't lied, not exactly. But they hadn't offered, either. It bugged me, and I was going to talk to her about it.

I had come away from MWB with one hard piece of information: Al was short for Alan. Alan Burrows. There was only one Alan Burrows on my list—the one in Manhattan. I'd called him last night, as soon as I'd gotten home. He'd answered on the first ring.

My story to him was that I was doing background research for a writer who was considering a book project about MWB. It was a decent story, and Burrows hadn't questioned it. But neither was he eager to talk. His first response had been silence, and only the slight rasp of his breathing told me he was still on the line. Then he'd hemmed and hawed in a well-educated, soft bass about not having worked at the bank in nearly fifteen years, about having no contact with anyone from there since, about having gotten out of banking altogether. I'd pressed. I'd said that if it was more convenient, I could come to his office for a chat. He hadn't liked that idea at all. Finally, he'd relented. I'd be meeting him tonight, at his place.

Lots of pieces, and maybe not all to the same puzzle. I turned them over and over in my head as I ran, but no two fit together. A pale, pink light was rising in the sky as I headed east on Sixteenth Street.

I put coffee on and stretched while it brewed. I had my first cup standing at the kitchen counter. Then I showered and shaved and dressed, and had a few cups more with breakfast. When I was fully caffeinated, I called Mike and told him about my visit to MWB. He listened in silence until I got to the part about Nassouli and Helene. Then he blew out a long, slow breath.

"I take it Pierro didn't say anything to you, either," I said.

"Not word one."

"Anything to make of that?"

Mike thought about it. "I don't know," he said after a while.

We agreed that I would talk to Helene, and that we wouldn't mention the photo to Rick beforehand. I finished my update, telling him about Burrows and the meeting I'd arranged for tonight. He was about to ring off, but I stopped him, to share my rosy view on the state of this case.

"It's going nowhere," I said.

"Is it going that well?" He chuckled sourly.

"There's just nothing here to grab hold of. Some smoke, some lights in the sky maybe, some wild-assed guesses on my part, but nothing I can call remotely hopeful. If Burrows doesn't pan out, we'll need to have a talk with Pierro," I said.

"I agree," Mike said.

"How's he doing?" I asked.

"Fair to middling," he answered. "He's working same as usual—long hours, on the road a couple of days a week. And he's still got this penned up, off to one side. But I think the effort's getting to him."

"No more faxes?"

"No more faxes; no contact at all. Makes you wonder—why the wait?"

"To make him sweat, maybe. Soften him up for the squeeze." Mike thought about that.

"It's working," he said.

I spent the rest of the day on paperwork. It was slightly less compelling than watching paint dry, but it was unavoidable. I owed a final report to my last client, a big insurance company, and I needed to bring my case notes on this job up to date. There was no putting it off any longer. I switched off my phone, made more coffee, put Charlie Haden and Norah Jones and Macy Gray CDs in the changer, and opened my laptop.

With only a few breaks, I banged away on it till six o'clock, when the intercom buzzed to tell me that I had a visitor. Seconds later, a grainy image of a woman emerged on the small video unit mounted on the kitchen wall. My baby sister, Lauren. There was no point in not answering. It was her apartment, and she had a key. That's the way it is with my family; you can run, but you can't hide.

"You've given up on the phone altogether, have you?" she asked, even before she'd crossed the threshold. She hung an arm around my neck and kissed my cheek. At just under six feet, Lauren didn't need to stand on her toes to do it. Her face was cold from the evening air. She smelled like jasmine.

Jane Lu had been right about the resemblance. Lauren and I share our father's looks: tall, slim, pale, with the same straight, black hair, the same widow's peak, the same green eyes, set in an angular face, the same straight, prominent nose. Lauren's hair was parted down the middle and pulled into a loose ponytail that reached below her shoulder blades. She was wearing a cherry red turtleneck, black jeans, and black loafers. Her black coat was slung over her arm, and on her shoulder she lugged a beat-up gray knapsack. Her briefcase. It looked full, and I figured she'd come straight from the office.

"Checking up on your tenant? What's the matter, the rent check bounce?" I kissed her cheek.

"If you were just ordinarily rude, maybe ignored only three out of four phone calls, instead of every single one, you could save yourself these intrusions. Got a ginger ale?" She dumped her coat and knapsack, went to the fridge, and started rummaging.

"I'm working. In fact, I've got a meeting tonight and I need to go soon." Lauren found the soda. She popped the top and took a long pull.

"Don't worry, I'm not staying. I'm having dinner with Keith at that new place around the corner. I just stopped by to confirm," she pointed at me over the kitchen counter, jabbing the air with her long finger to punctuate each word, "that you are coming to Thanksgiving dinner at your brother's house." She took another swig of soda and smiled at me over the top of the can.

I heaved a big sigh and shook my head. "Lauren, look, I appreciate the concern, and the invitation, but I'm fine, really. I'd just prefer to have a low-key day, you know? Let the holiday slip by, fly under the radar." But Lauren wasn't having any.

"'Fly under the radar'? What the hell does that mean? You run fifty miles, eat some tuna from the can, and collapse on your bed? That was your last Thanksgiving, right? Sounds like a real blast."

"Yet somehow more appealing than a day of being lectured to, or treated like a live grenade, or like something the cat coughed up," I said.

"That's what you're expecting?"

"Because that's what always happens."

"Oh come on, Johnny—"

I cut her off. "You come on. I'm not in the mood to be improved just now, okay? So give it a rest." But Lauren was undaunted. Her green eyes flashed, and her voice sharpened.

"I'm your sister, asshole; I don't care if you're in the mood or not. Your family's worried about you, and we have a right to be. I mean, take a look at yourself. It's over three years since Anne died, and you live like some kind of freaking monk. You work; you run; you work; you run. You never see your family, and besides Mike, I don't know what you do for friends. And do you ever get laid anymore?" She shook her head. "I guess it's better than the drinking, but isn't there some middle ground?" I thought she was finished and I drew a breath to speak, but I was overly optimistic.

"And for the record," she said more softly, "I've never been interested in improving you. I don't give a shit what you do for a living, or where you do it. I just want you to be happy or, at least, accept the possibility of happiness."

"Laurie—" I said, but she stopped me again.

"No one's going to lecture, or look at you funny, I promise. We're your family, John; we want to see you. Your nephews want to see you." Lauren was relentless in the pursuit of her own way, willing to pull out all the stops. I saw where this was going and knew it was hopeless. I bowed to the inevitable.

"*No mas,*" I said. "Enough. I'll come." Lauren smiled. She liked nothing better than bending others to her will. I smiled back. "You think maybe that nephew business was a little over the top?" I asked.

"Hey, whatever works," she said. She took a long swallow of soda and looked at me slyly. "So, I hear you met my boss." It took me a moment to connect the dots.

"Jane Lu?" I asked. "She didn't mention being your boss. She just said you two worked together."

"That's typical Jane, very self-effacing. But she is definitely the boss. She's the hired gun the venture capital guys brought in, when they purged the old management team," Lauren explained. My sister ran marketing and sales for a dot-com that had survived a near-death experience.

"And we're damn lucky they did—she's some kind of management genius. We were all pretty burnt out after the market collapsed, those of us who were left, and when the VCs told us they were cleaning house and bringing in some rent-a-CEO, we didn't take it well, to say the least. Oh, they gave us this big song and dance about how great she was—MIT undergrad, one of the youngest ever out of Harvard B-School, cut her teeth at Goldman and McKinsey, brought a couple of biotech firms back from the brink, blah, blah, blah. We thought it was a bunch of crap. But six months later, there's actually light at the end of the tunnel, and we would all pretty much run through walls for her—me included. And you know how jaded I am."

"What did she do, put something in the water cooler?"

"Maybe. Or maybe it's that we've had our first profitable quarter ever, and we're on track to beat our year-end targets. Or that she rolls up her sleeves and puts in more hours than anybody else in the place. Or maybe it's that she's so fucking smart, it's scary."

"Wow. Tell me, are the T-shirt and decoder ring free when you join the fan club, or do you have to pay extra?" Lauren was not amused. She shook her head and grimaced, all to say, wordlessly, "I sometimes find it difficult to believe that an asshole like you is actually my brother." Then she looked at her watch and headed for the door.

"Enough of your low humor. I've got to meet the hubby. See you Thursday. It'll be just family, plus a couple of strays. I'll tell Liz and Ned and everybody." She slipped on her coat, shrugged her knapsack over one shoulder, and was gone.

By then it was time for me to get going, too, to meet Alan Burrows. I turned my phone back on before I left, and checked my voice mail. I had only one message, three hours old, from Clare. She wouldn't be able to see me this week. With the holiday and all, time had just gotten away. She'd call Monday. Sorry. Somehow, I doubted it, just as I doubted we'd get together next week. And, I found, I didn't much care. It was time to go.

Burrows lived in a skinny, brick-clad tower at the north end of York Avenue. Tiny cement balconies jutted from its upper floors like bad teeth, and the lobby was awash in veined mirrors and cheap marble. It was a rental building, the kind where the freshly graduated cram three or four to a one-bedroom apartment, and where the freshly divorced try to piece together new lives from the scraps of their old ones. A bored doorman pointed me to the elevators, even before he'd rung upstairs to announce me. I rode alone in a dim car that smelled like old food. Burrows stood in the open door of his apartment.

"This way, Mr. March."

Burrows was a handsome wreck. He was fiftyish and tall, six foot three or so, and broad shouldered, but thick through the middle—a college athlete fallen into disrepair. What once were stolid, John Wayne good looks had blurred and buckled, and now all the mileage showed. His fleshy face was deeply creased, and the skin around his spent brown eyes was dark, and shot through with a web of lines and veins. Broken capillaries had left a small purple stain, like a brushstroke, on his cheek, and another in a corner of his long, thin nose. His blond hair was mostly gray, and was thinning badly. It was brushed straight back, away from his high forehead, and looked damp, like he had just gotten out of the shower. The collar of his pink button-down shirt was damp too, and his sleeves were rolled back over hairless forearms. He wore soft-looking, brown leather slippers on his feet. His hands were thrust into the pockets of his khaki pants. He stood aside so I could enter, and did not shake my hand.

The apartment was small, low ceilinged, and sterile, like a very tidy waiting room. I stood in a short hallway. On my left was a pocket kitchen, on my right a bedroom and a bath. The living room was a white cube, dead ahead. The furnishings were sparse and cheap. A beige sofa, a matching chair, and a coffee table were arranged in a corner. A low bookcase ran along one wall; a dining table did double duty as a desk along another. An oatmeal-colored rug hid most of the badly laid parquet floor. Across the room, a glass door opened onto one of the balconies I'd seen from the street. It was no bigger from up here.

The walls were empty. The only picture in the place stood on the dining table: a faded, silver-framed photo of a young woman holding a baby. What books there were, were arranged by size on the shelves, so that biographies and histories were mixed with textbooks on real estate, and a thick, black bible with books on low-salt cooking and weight loss. His few knickknacks—a pair of silver candlesticks, a small carriage clock, a red lacquer box—looked out of place, as if they'd lost their way en route to another, better-appointed life.

Burrows motioned me toward the sofa, and I sat. He took a pair of gold, wire-rimmed glasses from his shirt pocket and put them on, wrapping the earpieces behind his ears. They made his eyes bigger, and gave him a scholarly look.

"Something to drink, Mr. March?" he asked. "I've got ice tea, juice, water. I could put up coffee if you'd prefer." His voice was deep and intimate sounding, but there was a stiff, almost formal quality to his speech and manner that made me think he wasn't used to having anyone in the apartment with him.

"Water is fine," I said.

He disappeared into the kitchen and reappeared with two glasses of water. He gave me one, along with a little paper napkin, and sat in the chair opposite me. He sighed heavily and looked down at his feet on the rug. He held his water glass with both hands and rested it in his lap. I noticed a gym bag and a pair of sneakers parked neatly in a corner by the door. I gestured toward them. "Just back from the gym?" I asked. The question seemed to surprise him, and he paused before answering.

"I am, yes. I go every night, after work."

"Disciplined," I said.

"I try to be."

"What kind of work are you doing, now that you're out of banking?" I asked.

He didn't hear my question, or chose to ignore it. "As I said on the phone, Mr. March, I don't know that I can be much help to you. I wasn't much help to the federal people when they came to see me, either," he said.

"When was that?"

"A long while ago. Two and a half years, maybe longer. But there wasn't much I could tell them." He took a slow drink from his glass. I smiled my best nonthreatening smile.

"Well, I'm starting with almost nothing on this, so whatever you can tell me I'm sure will help. And, as I mentioned on the phone, this is entirely confidential and off the record. The guy I'd like to talk to you about is Gerard Nassouli. I understand you worked for him."

Burrows kept looking down at his feet and shook his head a little. "Yes, that's who the federal people wanted to talk about, too. Where he might have gone to, who he might turn to if he was in trouble, had I heard from him, what did I know about his finances, did I know any of his friends, did I know of any property he kept overseas. They went on and on. I couldn't help much."

"They were interested in finding him, so they asked those kinds of questions. But finding him is not my problem. I'm more interested in what he was like. How he did business. How he made deals. I thought maybe you could take me through some that you worked on with him."

"I'm not sure there's much I can say." He took another hit from his glass.

"You did work for him."

"For seven years, the whole time I was at MWB. I was with the New York office, and Nassouli ran the office."

"And you ran the correspondent banking department?"

"For six years. The first year, I was the number two person in the department. Then my boss went back to London and I took over."

"And when you left MWB, you left banking altogether?"

Burrows looked up at me and straightened a bit in his chair. "I thought this was about Nassouli, not about me."

"It is. But all you say about him is that you have nothing to say. So I figured we could talk about things you can tell me. Like why you left MWB when you did, and why you left banking." I drank some water and continued. "I figure you must have been around thirty when you joined MWB. And you must've come in with a few years' experience, if they hired you as the number two guy in the department. Even allowing for a couple of years in b-school and my bad arithmetic, you walked away from at least ten years in banking when you quit. That's a big career investment to leave behind. Why'd you do it?"

Burrows looked at me for a while and shook his head a little. "It was over thirteen years, altogether, and my reasons were personal. Can you understand that?" he said, more tired than angry. "Look, if it's me you want to discuss, I'm sorry, the answer is no." He got up and carried his glass to the kitchen and returned with it filled.

"How did you know that I ran correspondent banking?" he asked.

"Research. That's what I do."

"And what has your research told you about Gerard so far?"

"Not a lot. That he was a big deal maker. That he was charming, and liked a party. That he liked women, and being seen with them," I answered.

Burrows snorted. "He liked to be seen with them, and he liked to fuck them, that's true. I don't know how much he actually liked them. In fact, I think he hated them." He stumbled a little over "fuck," as if he was out of practice with vulgarity. He drank some water. "Deal maker, charming, life of the party—you've been talking to people who didn't know him well."

Alan Burrows was a paradox. On the one hand, he kept proclaiming that he had nothing to tell me. And, so far, he hadn't told me much. On the other hand, he hadn't thrown me out yet. And he kept on talking. There was some heavy conflict there, and that was good news for me. "You know different?" I asked.

He ran a hand through his damp hair and looked into his glass. "Charming, a big deal maker, loved parties—that was the press he put out, and it was true, as far as it went. But there was another story, altogether different." He stopped and looked up at me again. "Your employer could write a book just on Gerard, but he'd have to do it as fiction, because nobody would believe it as fact." His voice quavered, like he'd run out of air. He took a noisy swallow from his glass and then was still.

"I'd like to hear that story, and you're the first person I've met who could tell it," I said.

Burrows shook his head, more vigorously this time. "Tell it . . . Jesus . . . I've spent fifteen years trying to forget it," he said, almost in a whisper.

"How's that going—the forgetting?" I asked softly.

"Not well," he said.

The lines seemed to deepen on Burrows's ruined, handsome face, and his eyes looked moist and more tired than ever. He gathered some breath and asked, "Are you really working for a writer?" So much for my decent story.

"No," I said after a while. "No, I'm not. I'm trying to help someone who did some business, legitimate business, with Nassouli a long time ago, and who's run into trouble because of it."

"Legitimate business—with Nassouli, I suppose that's theoretically possible," Burrows said with a small, harsh laugh. "But if your client did any kind of business with Gerard, he may need more help than you can give him. Tell him he should talk to a priest."

"I'll be sure to mention it. But right now, I'm all there is in the help department. Me, and maybe you."

"Is this usually an effective approach for you, Mr. March—lying to people, then asking for their help? Does it build a lot of trust?" Again, Burrows seemed unable to generate much anger. He seemed gripped, instead, by a powerful, bone-deep fatigue.

"I was acting in what I judged to be my client's best interests, Mr. Burrows. I thought you'd be more forthcoming talking to someone doing research for a book than you would someone pursuing an investigation. Maybe it was a bad call. I make them sometimes, and I correct them when I can. But I wasn't lying to you when I said this would be confidential."

Burrows waved his hand, like he was shooing a fly. "Being lied to doesn't bother me much, Mr. March. Maybe that comes from working for Nassouli for seven years, or maybe it just comes from working on Wall Street. Whatever—I've gotten comfortable with it. I've come to expect it."

He looked at me and looked away. He was poised on a precipice, balanced on the verge of something. His eyes were narrow and clouded, and they roamed aimlessly around the room. The conflict behind them was one I'd seen before. It took me back to cop days, to exhausted suspects caught between fear and the swelling need to speak and be understood . . . and maybe forgiven. I was wondering which way to push him, or if I should push at all, when he stiffened his shoulders and locked his eyes on mine.

He squinted and peered, like a man driving slowly through a fog—searching the opaque air for familiar shadows and looming hazards. He stared for a long time, and I held his gaze. I don't know exactly what Burrows sought in my eyes and face—some sign of shared knowledge, maybe. A common thread of loss or regret; or a mutual acquaintance with solitary rooms, and the tyranny of memory. Whatever it was, I guess he found it. He made his decision and spoke.

"I think it's hard for a lot of people to understand evil, believe the reality of it, unless they've experienced it firsthand, don't you? I know it was that way for me, before I met him. 'Evil' and 'corruption' were just words to me, before him. Gerard Nassouli was the worst man I've ever met, Mr. March. He was a fucking monster." The vulgarity gave him no trouble this time.

"Yes, he loved the deal making and the high life, and you must know from the papers what sorts of things he was engaged in at MWB. But his genius, and his true passion, was corruption. Corrupting people, and then collecting them, like some people collect bugs—pinned and mounted under glass. No deal was a complete success for him unless it involved adding somebody to his little collection. I think that's why MWB was so perfect for him. It let him marry his vocation with his avocation." He turned his glass slowly in his hands.

"It sounds strange, I know. It's hard to understand if you don't see it for yourself. I worked with the man almost every day for seven years, and I didn't see it at first. He was smart, and charming, but what he was best at was reading people. He could see into them, how they were put together, what they wanted, what drove them. And whatever it was, he would somehow arrange for them to have it—with no strings attached. Not at first, anyway." His voice was very soft now, and I was straining to hear. "In the end, it cost them everything."

When he paused, a palpable silence took hold of the apartment. There was no traffic noise, no whirring of the building's machinery, no humming of appliances. I kept very still and took slow breaths and focused my eyes on the wall behind Burrows, afraid that, like a deer, any stray motion or sound or even the force of my gaze might spook him and break the spell. Burrows leaned forward, his forearms resting on his thighs, the water glass still before him, held in both his hands. He peered inside, as if into a deep well.

"You'd think he was the best friend you'd ever had—smart, funny, worldly, and infinitely understanding of human failings. If you had a vice, a weakness, a little character tic, well, Gerard had plenty too. And whatever yours were, you'd never get even a raised eyebrow from him. Just a wink and a nod, as if to say 'It's no big deal. Go ahead. Enjoy. That's what men do.' And he'd sit back and wait and watch. To see the kind of women you liked, or men, to see what you envied, what made you bitter, to see what you liked and hated about yourself, to see what lies you told yourself, and, especially, to see what you most coveted. It could take months, years even. He didn't care. He was patient. It was like tending a garden, he used to say."

Burrows looked up, and the motion startled me. His eyes were red. "This is too vague, isn't it? You want to know what he was like, how he did business. You need specifics." Burrows's soft, deep voice was steady now, and it stayed that way through all the stories he told me.

Chapter Ten

"Larry—let's call him Larry—had just moved to town from somewhere in the Midwest, with his brand-new wife in tow. Larry was ambitious, and lucky. He had the world by the balls. And he had no clue at all of what was about to happen to him." Burrows found the rhythm of his narrative easily, and I got the feeling he'd waited a long time to tell his stories. His tone was ironical and detached. The irony seemed to come naturally to him. He had to work at the detachment.

"Larry had just landed a job trading currency for one of the biggest FX market-makers on the Street. He'd been a rising star at the regional bank that he'd come from, but, after all, it was just a regional bank—a farm team. This was the big league, and the FX market was hot back then. Larry was poised to make some real money. And that was a good thing, because Mrs. Larry, his pretty new wife, had pricey tastes, lofty social aspirations, and a grim resolve. Of the many things she wanted, at the top of her list was a place to live. But not just any place. Mrs. Larry imagined raising a towheaded brood in just the right sort of Manhattan apartment. Something on Park Ave., say, no higher than Eightieth Street, or maybe on Fifth, with a terrace and a nice view of the park.

"Now, Larry had come to town with what he'd thought was a tidy nest egg. But in New York City, in the midst of the real estate boom twenty years ago, it was chump change. Mrs. Larry had set her sights on only the toniest white-glove buildings, places with the pickiest boards . . . places that required that all apartments be purchased in cash. Much more cash than Larry had on hand, and more than he was likely to see—in the best of circumstances—for nearly a year, when his bonus would be paid. This did not please Mrs. Larry, whose strengths ran more to petulance and pouting than to patience. And Mrs. Larry was generous with her displeasure.

"Enter Nassouli. He had started cultivating Larry on the boy's first day at his new job. We were active in the FX markets, and Gerard made it a point to keep abreast of the comings and goings of traders at all the big market makers. He was especially interested in new, young traders. 'Fertile ground,' he called them.

"It took Nassouli all of a lunch with Larry, a dinner with him and the missus, and a boys' night out at a strip club to suss out the dynamics of Larry's domestic scene and the powerful forces at work on him there. Larry was a sitting duck. In short order, Nassouli had set himself up as the Larrys' Big Apple mentor, showing them the ropes, opening doors, introducing them to all the right people and all the right places. Within a week he'd delivered them into the clutches of a realtor friend of his, who proceeded to show Mrs. Larry only top-of-the-line apartments in top-of-the-line buildings, all of which—wonder of wonders—had strict, cash-only policies. Six weeks and a hundred or so apartments later, they had found *the* place—Seventy-fourth and Park, ten rooms, terraces, views—the whole ball of wax. Mrs. Larry would not be denied. Larry's problems came suddenly to a head.

"Ah, but there was his great, good friend Gerard, with such an easy solution to it all: a personal loan to the Larrys for the amount in question. And just to make sure that Larry's financial statements would pass muster before even the pickiest co-op board, Nassouli would pay the loan into an account—in Larry's name—at MWB. This account would have a very large balance and would appear, to whoever might ask, to have held this balance for quite some time. On top of all this, for good measure, Nassouli could arrange for some impressive letters of recommendation for the Larrys—from prominent people, famous people even, people who hadn't a clue as to who the Larrys were, but who owed Gerard some heavy favors.

"Larry offered only token resistance, and charming, affable, worldly, plugged-in Gerard blew through it like tissue paper. 'Not to worry, dear boy, really. You have a cash-flow problem—a timing issue. This is just a bridge loan. Happens all the time . . . this is how things get done here in the big city.' And as must happen in such cases, Larry was complicit in his own corruption. He believed what Nassouli told him—bought into it all—because Nassouli told him precisely what he'd wanted to hear. And that was all it took to make Larry a party to fraud and conspiracy and violations of who knows how many of his employer's rules of conduct.

"Two months later, the Larrys had closed on the place. Mrs. Larry was pleased, but it passed quickly. Now she had to grapple with renovation and decoration, and this left Larry, once again, to grapple with his lack of cash. But again, kindly Uncle Gerard came to the rescue. 'Remember that account at MWB—the one in your name? Just think of it as a credit line, dear boy, draw what you need . . . pay it back later . . . whenever you can.' Larry didn't muster even token resistance this time. Then *later* came.

"Bonus time eventually rolled around. Larry had had a great year, and the FX markets continued to be hot, so his bonus was a big one. But not big enough to settle accounts with Nassouli. Between the purchase of the apartment and his wife's many improvements, Larry was deep in the hole. But money wasn't what Gerard was looking for. What he had in mind instead was having a tame FX trader in his pocket, someone on a major market-making desk, someone who, every now and then, could do some little favors for him. Like providing some 'insight' into his bank's positions and trading strategies, or executing the occasional off-market trade. Nine months after his first lunch with Gerard Nassouli, that's what Larry became.

"He was one of maybe a dozen pet traders that Gerard had on file back then. Except in the particulars, the basic story was always the same. And with every 'favor' they did for Nassouli, they got in deeper and deeper, until they were completely his creatures." Burrows shook his head a little.

"Not one of them was particularly likeable. You couldn't really feel sorry for them. It was a simple quid pro quo. They'd made their deals with the devil, and they got what they'd deserved. A few of them seemed actually happy with the arrangement. But for most of them . . . it consumed them. You could see it happen over the course of months and years. It was like a cancer. At first it was a little secret thing, a small, dark corner, a little hunger that had to be fed, and not very often. But they'd get in deeper and the hunger would grow and grow and be more insistent, until the rest of their lives became irrelevant, and only the secret thing remained.

"Last I heard of Larry, he was living in Florida, working in boat sales, without Mrs. Larry. I heard she was still in New York, but somebody else's problem now." Burrows paused and took a small sip of water. My legs were stiff and I had a crick in my neck, but still I was reluctant to move. "Moe's story is a little different," Burrows continued in his soft rumble.

"Moe was a senior vice president at a prestigious investment bank, one of the last partnerships left on the Street. He had spent his whole career at the place, and he'd done well—by any standard other than Wall Street's. He'd made good—though not important—money. He'd gotten decent assignments, though not the choicest ones. But Moe had grown troubled. It had occurred to him one day as he sat in a meeting, the oldest by at least five years of everyone in the room, that his career had come quietly to a halt. People who'd been his peers two or three years before had gone on to make partner. Others whom he had recruited from business school were now sitting at the table with him, as equals. When confronted by Moe, in the oblique fashion that such things were discussed at his firm, his boss confirmed his fears. Yes, several of the partners felt that Moe was unready; some felt that he might be forever unready. They all acknowledged that he was superb at following someone else's lead, but wondered if he himself had a *strategic vision.* Could he *think outside the box*?

"Well, Moe started thinking, alright. About all of the years he had put in at the firm, about all the time he'd spent on the road, about how he'd uprooted his family with moves across the world, the havoc he had wreaked on his oldest son . . . pulling him out of high school just as he was entering senior year, how venomous his daughter had been. And, when he had a few drinks in him, and then a few more, he thought about some of the people who had made partner in recent years while he had languished. All that thinking left Moe a troubled man, a bitter man, an angry man. Nassouli was drawn to him like a fly to shit.

"Moe and Nassouli met while Moe was out following someone else's lead. In this case, it was prospecting for clients among some Latin American companies that ran big U.S. operations—part of his firm's strategy to build a franchise in the emerging markets. As it turned out, MWB handled a lot of meat-and-potatoes banking for these firms, at home and in the States. Nassouli caught the odor of discontent coming off Moe the first time they met, and a week later he took him to lunch. But Moe was no wet-behind-the-ears trader, and Nassouli saw that right away. His was an older and wiser head, and he would take a different kind of handling. No cramped, sweaty groping in the backseat for Moe, Nassouli understood, no quick feels in the cloakroom. No, Moe would need finesse. Moe would need romance.

"At first, Gerard was all business. 'Our clients were impressed by your firm's many capabilities . . .' and so forth. Of course, he seasoned it with some discreet flattery. 'They were quite pleased to have had access to so senior an executive as you, someone with such experience and insight into the markets . . .' Then, he dangled the hope that some actual business might be coming Moe's way. 'Yes, they are quite interested in talking further, but it would be important to them that they continue their discussions directly with you.' It was pure bullshit, of course, but it served Nassouli's purpose—Moe was hooked.

"Over the next several months, Nassouli arranged for Moe to have many quite promising—but ultimately inconclusive—meetings with MWB's Latin American clients. I don't know if it dawned on Moe that these sessions were all strangely similar: a room full of attentive, nodding heads, plenty of smiles, a few easy questions that he could hit out of the park, more nodding heads, but slowly and with great significance this time, like he had just explained quantum mechanics to them, then an expensive meal, more smiles, and then . . . nothing . . . nothing more firm than a promise to meet again. Interspersed with these elaborate teases were invitations to be Gerard's guest at some very high-end social functions—events that Moe had never been to before, but only heard about the day after, from the partners at his firm who regularly attended. Suddenly B-list Moe was on Gerard's A list. Cinderella was off to the ball.

"After months of courting, when the meetings with the Latins had gotten Moe all hot and bothered, and the mad social whirl had turned his head ever so slightly, it was time to get serious. Nassouli's pass at Moe took the form of a plea for Moe's sage advice. Gerard confided that MWB had been trying to build an investment banking business, but that it had become clear to them that they lacked talent at the top. Did Moe know of anyone with the experience, vision, and drive to build such a business? Moe's first thought was 'How about me?' And he said this— discreetly, of course. To which Gerard's response was to be stunned, even a bit embarrassed. 'Naturally, we would jump at the chance to get someone of your caliber and accomplishment, but it never occurred to us that you would walk away from a partnership.' He was quite the actor, that Gerard.

"It was Moe's turn to be embarrassed. After some stammering and stumbling, and aided by some single-malt lubrication deftly applied by Gerard, Moe revealed that partnership was not a certainty for him. Now Nassouli was even more stunned, and indignant on his friend's behalf. 'How can this be? To ignore a man of your keen intelligence, skill, insight—it's shameful!' Moe—who was quite well oiled by then—at first had no answer to these questions. 'Something to do with *visions* and *boxes*' was all he could say. But then it all came tumbling out—the damaged pride, the anger and bitterness, the sense of betrayal. It was music to Nassouli's ears.

"Now that he knew Moe's problem, Nassouli knew just what sweet nothings to whisper. The firm's gripe with Moe was lack of vision, that he didn't paint on a big enough canvas; the firm's strategy was to build an emerging markets franchise; MWB wanted to build an investment banking business. All well and good, said Gerard, here's a bold stroke for the partners. And he laid it all out for his good friend Moe: a strategic alliance between Moe's firm and MWB in the emerging markets, one that would let his firm tap into MWB's huge network and customer base in those markets—give them an instant presence—and an instant clientele.

"Moe didn't get it at first, and Gerard had to explain a few times. When it did sink in, Moe was flabbergasted, then leery. Did Nassouli really have the clout to strike this kind of deal? Gerard, reassuring but slightly bemused, explained that as head of New York, he was also head of the Americas for MWB, and one of the top five men in the bank— senior enough to make this happen. And what would MWB get out of this alliance? Again, Gerard had the ready answer: through Moe's firm, MWB would be able to offer their own clients investment banking services that would not otherwise be part of their repertoire. And all MWB would want would be to share some expenses and have a share in the revenues from the clients they brought to the table. What he didn't say, of course, was that this would give MWB another big, prestigious, squeaky-clean conduit for washing their clients' money.

"Then he whispered the sweetest nothing of all. 'Take this deal to your partners, take it to them as your brainchild, and we here at MWB will make it clear to them that without Moe—for whom we have the greatest respect, who has won our admiration, trust, and confidence—without Moe, there is no deal.' Moe must have pictured it happening—the meeting with the managing partners, himself making the presentation, the revenue projections sloping up and up, then the side conversations between Gerard and the senior partner. Moe knew, and Gerard saw the knowledge gleaming in Moe's grateful eyes, that this deal would be Moe's ticket to partnership." Burrows paused and drank a bit and shook his head a little.

"And if Gerard had just left it at that, as he easily could have, Moe would have been guilty of gullibility, stupidity perhaps, and, of course, vanity—but nothing more. He would not have been *complicit*. But that would not have satisfied Gerard. In the end, Gerard had his satisfaction.

"It happened the night before the alliance deal was to be signed. It had been a heady few months for Moe. The meeting with the partners had surpassed even his imaginings, and a few days later he'd been buttonholed by his boss, who confirmed what Moe had felt in his gut at the meeting: that he'd changed quite a few minds, that he'd made people sit up and take notice, that he'd be getting some very good news in a few months' time, when new partners were to be named. Moe called his friend Gerard to tell him about it, even before he'd called his wife. After that there had been a whirlwind of meetings, working sessions, a due diligence exercise that Moe—at Gerard's insistence—had run personally for his firm, and endless lunches and dinners. The next day was the signing, press briefings, interviews, and then off with the missus for a week at a spa. When he got back, the partnership announcements would be made. He had just one more dinner with his good friend Gerard, who had made it all happen.

"Dinner was in Nassouli's private conference room, adjoining his office. When the waiter had finished serving, it was just the two of them. Well, just the two of them and the state-of-the-art voice-recording system that Gerard had had installed in the room and that was operating flawlessly that night. Gerard got down to business quickly. They had two things to celebrate, he told Moe, not only the signing tomorrow, but also the first piece of business that MWB would bring to Moe's firm under the agreement. Gerard explained that this was a privately held firm in Colombia, a very old client of MWB, and that their chief executive was very influential with a large group of other MWB clients. They were looking for a capital infusion to finance new plants, new equipment, the development of new distribution channels. They were looking for someone to make an equity investment in their company, and were very excited by the idea of doing business with the venture capital arm of Moe's firm. Moe was surprised—and pleased. All of their plans had assumed a period of months to ramp up. He was also, naturally, full of questions: who are they, what business are they in, who are the principals?

"Gerard was smiling as he answered, you could hear it in his voice. And why not—it was the culmination of over a year's worth of patient gardening. 'Do you want the names we will give your partners, or the real names?' was his reply. Moe was confused. Gerard said it again, slowly, with no smile in his voice this time, as if Moe were a stupid child. Moe was still confused, but perhaps a little offended by Gerard's tone. Gerard cut him off. His voice was like a slap. 'Oh yes, you need things explained two or three times, don't you?' On the tape you could hear Moe gasp. But before he could say anything else, Gerard spelled it out for him. The names they'd give to Moe's firm would be that of a well-known Colombian coffee distributor and its nominal owner. The real principals—the actual owners of the coffee company—were an even better known cocaine cartel and its notoriously violent jefe.

"Moe laughed. His friend was making a joke—a bad joke. There's a long silence on the tape then, during which I picture Gerard gazing at Moe in a certain way that he had, as if at a turd that had turned up in his wineglass. Moe realized it was no joke. He sputtered, and stumbled for a while. 'This is ridiculous. You can't be serious. My firm will never be a party to this.' Gerard let him babble a bit, then cut him off. 'I assure you, the documentation on this company is ironclad. It will survive any due diligence, and the return on the investment will be very appealing. Your partners will not know. Unless, of course, you care to tell them. Perhaps you should tell them, Moe. As I think about it, I'm certain that you should. Would you like to do it tonight? Please, use my phone.' There's not much on the tape after that. Some sniffling and the sounds of Gerard finishing his meal, that's all.

"Of course, Moe didn't tell his partners that night, or ever. How could he? Two years after the deal had signed, he dropped dead of a massive coronary. The partnership agreements left his wife quite well off, from what I understand." Burrows paused and massaged his temples with his fingertips.

"Gerard took his time with Moe, played him very carefully. There were others who he played for even longer. But it wasn't all subtlety and craftsmanship with him. No, Gerard could be heavy-handed . . . brutal when he wanted." He paused again and rubbed his eyes beneath his glasses. "The last one is a short story.

"Nassouli went out with a lot of women . . . you know that. He seemed to have an endless string of them, would-be models, would-be actresses, some of them just girls, really, teenagers living away from home for the first time. He showed them all a fine time, at least at first. He was a charming person, very funny; he'd traveled all over the world. He would introduce them to people and places they'd read about in magazines, spend a lot of money on them . . . teach them all sorts of things. It's not a new story . . . it's a very old one, in fact. But if you were eighteen, and fresh from a South Florida trailer park, it was pretty intoxicating stuff.

"He would date a girl for three or four months, sometimes less, and then break it off—but always in an amicable way. 'Remember, I am your friend. If there's anything I can do to help you, in your career or in any way at all, please let me.' It was amazing, the number of girls who stayed friendly with him, and how many would show up at his parties. Amazing, too, the number of these women who—one way or another—wound up dating Gerard's clients, or colleagues, or other associates. Gerard called them 'party favors,' though he didn't let too many people hear him say that. After all, some of these girls ended up married to the men they'd met at Gerard's parties, and these men didn't think of their wives as party favors. They thought of them as trophies.

"He had another kind of party favor, too. When I knew him, Gerard frequented nearly every high-end strip club in Manhattan. And just as he collected models, he collected strippers, too—only for shorter times and in larger numbers. With those girls, the relationship was more straightforward. These party favors were handed out very freely, to people in Gerard's file—like Larry, for instance—if they got edgy and needed a little pacifying, or to clients who wanted an evening's entertainment, or to those Gerard was still cultivating, whose tastes were . . . a little grittier. But nothing from Gerard came free, and these party favors were no exception.

"You see, whenever he provided the party favors, Gerard would also provide the party space—one of MWB's corporate apartments, conveniently located, tastefully furnished, fully stocked, with maid and concierge service. And unbeknownst to the guests, fully wired for video in every room. So every favor done in the place was recorded, start to finish, in all its graphic details, for posterity. Gerard had an extensive collection of these videos, and each one was leverage, a chit, a marker that he held over the tape's featured players. And sometimes over people who weren't even there.

"He'd hold private screenings of these things sometimes, for a select few. They were incredible. Very clear pictures, even the audio was flawless. And every permutation you could imagine. . . . But I said this was a short story, didn't I?

"Well, Gerard had an associate who had run afoul of him . . . how is not important. This fellow, let's call him Curly Joe, had decided he was not going to do business with Gerard anymore. There was no threat of going to the authorities, never a question of that. Curly was sufficiently compromised himself to make that impractical, and besides, everyone was clear that that kind of decision would be . . . very unhealthy. But nonetheless, Gerard had a point to make.

"Curly Joe had been married for several years to a beautiful young woman, a former model, who he'd met at one of Nassouli's parties. She was a little wild back then, a little too fond of champagne, a little too eager for a few lines in the powder room. But when they'd met she'd been ready to settle down, and so too had Curly. They'd married, and had a baby less than a year later. Curly was by no means a saint, far from it, but he did love his wife, Mr. March. Everyone who knew him knew that about him.

"Well, Curly was determined to go his own way, and after much tension, Gerard seemed resigned to it. In fact, Gerard even invited him out—a combination reconciliation and farewell. It was a pleasant enough evening, they'd made the rounds of all their old haunts, and finally ended up at Nassouli's for a nightcap."

Burrows's voice was soft and rock steady, but his eyes were red and swollen-looking.

"He gave Curly some brandy and suggested, for old times' sake, a private screening. Curly balked—those things made him a little ill—but Gerard insisted. Besides, he said, he had a good one from the old days, one Curly hadn't seen before." Burrows stopped. He breathed deeply.

"I think you see where this is going, Mr. March." He was matter-of-fact now. "Suffice it to say, it was Curly's wife on the tape, the mother of his child. She was with two other women, two of Gerard's stripper friends, and a man. The man was someone Curly knew, another associate of Nassouli's, a particularly brutal person. Curly didn't watch much of it, but from what he saw they were drinking, and freebasing cocaine as well. There didn't seem to be any coercion involved. Though intoxicated, Curly's wife—actually his fiancée at the time, according to the time stamp on the video—was energetic and quite vocal, and she seemed to be the center of attention for the man and the other two women." Burrows paused and cleared his throat. "Gerard had a point to make—about having made Curly what he was, and that Curly should have no illusions about that, should have no illusions about himself or any of the things in his life that Gerard had given him. He made his point."

We were quiet for several minutes, while the world seemed to restart itself around us. Burrows looked up at me, a single tear track drying on his cheek. He didn't seem to notice or, if he did, to care. Finally, he spoke.

"I hope that's of some help to you and your client, Mr. March."

I nodded. I was full of questions, and I wasn't sure how much longer Burrows would be willing to provide answers. I plowed ahead. "Okay, Nassouli's game was to manipulate people into involving themselves in something illicit, and then use that involvement to blackmail them." Burrows nodded as I spoke. "But that would require that Nassouli have some incriminating evidence, some proof of each person's participation in whatever illicit thing had gone on." More nodding.

"Oh, yes," Burrows said, "Gerard was quite meticulous in his record-keeping. He maintained a file, a detailed audit trail, for every 'specimen' in his garden. Records of every meeting he'd had with a person, what was discussed, copies of documents, recordings, even videotapes—the whole history of their corruption. I think the cataloging was part of the pleasure for him."

He kept files. He kept files. He kept files. I took a moment to get my heart rate under control. I didn't want to pant.

"Wasn't that risky for him?" I asked. "Anything incriminating to his 'specimens' would be incriminating to Nassouli too, right? That taped conversation with Moe, for instance." Burrows nodded.

"Gerard was a huge risk-taker," he said. "And hugely arrogant. He'd take massive chances, as he did with Moe, but to him they were calculated. I'm sure there was no doubt in Gerard's mind about how Moe would react in the end, and he was right. He usually was about things like that. By the same token, he would never believe that his records would be in any hands but his own."

"Do you know where he kept them?"

"I know where he kept them fifteen years ago. In his office. There used to be a big credenza behind his desk, with lots of locking drawers. It was almost a safe."

"Who besides you knew the kinds of things Nassouli did, and knew about his files?"

"In New York, a very small circle—basically the rest of Gerard's management team—a handful of people."

"Who?"

He hesitated, then gave me three names. I recognized them all, and all, like Nassouli, were fugitives. "Those were the New York people. One or two people in London may have had some idea what he was up to, but they wouldn't have known the specifics. But bear in mind, my information is fifteen years old." Burrows paused again, as if deciding something. His face darkened. "There was another person, not an MWB employee technically, but someone very close to Gerard. Trautmann, Bernhard Trautmann. He and his company provided security for the New York branch, and anything that was rough around the edges—procuring girls from the strip clubs, for example, or the videotaping at the apartment—he took care of for Gerard. He knew a lot of what was going on. He probably knew some things that I didn't."

I read Burrows a list of company names, including Textiles Pan-Europa and Europa Mills U.S.A., the companies referred to in Pierro's fax, along with others mentioned in the *Economist* article.

"There were so many companies, Mr. March . . . they all run together. All nice businesses, with lots of receivables, and lots of invoices too—plenty of cash flowing across squeaky clean accounts, preferably in multiple currencies. Just right for bringing money into the system in nice, careful chunks, and just right for moving it all around afterward, through money transfers, loans, foreign exchange deals, what have you. *Placement* and *layering,* the authorities call it. The newspapers wrote a lot about it a while back." Burrows paused and looked beyond me, remembering. "Maybe those names are familiar . . . I just don't know. Frankly, my memories of that time are spotty and probably selective. I drank quite a bit then and for a long time afterward, and did other things too, none of which were very good for my gray cells." I wondered what his gray cells would do with my next question.

"Moe is dead, and you've said that Larry is in Florida, out of the business." I paused, and his eyes met mine, then slid away again. "Can you give me the names—the real names—of any other of Nassouli's 'specimens' from back then?" Burrows sat up straight and started to shake his head, started to withdraw. I hurried on. "Mr. Burrows, I don't want to know about their indiscretions. I could care less. But I need to talk to other people who Nassouli had on file. I need to know if they've had the same kind of trouble that my client is having."

Burrows pursed his lips and crossed his arms on his chest, still shaking his head. "I know the damage Nassouli did to these people, the hell he put them through—deservedly or otherwise. I had my own small part in that, and I have my own hell to deal with as a result. I'm not going to play a part in making them relive those nightmares."

"That's not what I'm trying to do, Mr. Burrows. Someone is putting my client through that same kind of hell. It's possible that whoever is victimizing my client is victimizing some of these people, too. It's possible they could use some help. I'll be discreet, I'll be quick, and I won't be heavy-handed, but I need to talk to some of these people."

"You'll forgive me if, at this point in my life, I find altruism slightly harder to believe in than the tooth fairy," Burrows said.

"I'm not claiming to be altruistic. I'm trying to act in my client's best interests. If I can establish that other people from Nassouli's files are being victimized too, it reduces considerably the avenues I need to pursue. If I find whoever is doing this, I will discourage him from bothering my client. If he is victimizing others, and I can offer a more general discouragement, I will." I paused for a bit and watched Burrows as he teetered again on some internal cliff edge. I said, softly, "If you're looking to make amends . . . to make something right . . . maybe this helps."

We stared at each other for what seemed like a long time. Burrows shook his head a little and rubbed his eyes. Then he gave me four names. I wrote them down.

"Thank you," I said. "This helps. I won't mention your name to any of these people."

Burrows shrugged, indifferent. He looked exhausted. I'd taken him about as far as I could, but I wanted to know one more thing. "Did you talk to the feds about any of this?" I asked.

"As I told you, the questions they asked had to do with Nassouli's whereabouts. They never asked anything else."

"And if they had?"

He shrugged. "I would probably have told them."

"No concern about legal action?"

He gave a little snort and shook his head. "According to my lawyer, the federal people are interested in what they can prosecute, which apparently means more recent events—those still within the statute of limitations. He tells me that the time has long since passed on activities they might have wished to discuss with me. Though I'm not sure I'd care in any event." Then he stood, and so did I, and I thought it was time to leave. But he had some questions of his own.

"Will you be looking for Nassouli, Mr. March?"

"I don't think so. A lot of people, with a lot more money and time than I've got, have spent nearly three years looking for him, with nothing to show for it. Right now, that doesn't look to be a productive use of my time."

"And Bernhard Trautmann . . . will you be speaking with him?"

"If I can find him, yes."

Burrows pursed his lips again. "I suspect you will. But be careful when you do, Mr. March. Be watchful. Trautmann is . . . a very brutal person, and violent—really quite the psychopath. But he is not stupid, not at all. I've seen him laughing and smiling with men who, the next moment, he was beating nearly to death. He seemed to enjoy putting them so at ease before almost killing them. He and Nassouli were well matched in that respect."

"I'll keep it in mind," I said, and I left Alan Burrows to his strange penance.

Chapter Eleven

" 'Satan is my banker.' It has a certain ring to it, don't you think? Get you noticed at a party," Mike said.

"Depends on the party," I said.

I was sitting in Mike's office at ten-thirty a.m. on the day before Thanksgiving, slouched in one of his sleek leather chairs, with my feet up on his sleek glass desk, drinking espresso from one of his demitasse cups. I'd just taken him through my meeting the night before with Burrows. Mike was cleaning off his desk, sifting through papers, tossing some, stacking the rest, and periodically calling his secretary, Fran, to carry off the stacks. She muttered darkly as she took them away. Like offices all over the city, Paley, Clay's were quiet and thinly staffed today, and a relaxed, preholiday mood prevailed. Even Mike had bowed to the informality of the day, wearing not a suit, but natty olive slacks and a tweed jacket. I was more casual still, in jeans and a gray turtleneck.

"But that's what Burrows was saying. That Nassouli was some sort of Mephistophelean mastermind sadist . . . ," Mike said.

"A *record-keeping* Mephistophelean mastermind sadist," I reminded him.

". . . a *record-keeping* Mephistophelean mastermind sadist," Mike continued, "who corrupted unsuspecting innocents in the worlds of finance and fashion . . ."

"I don't know how many actual innocents there were, at least among the financial types," I interrupted again.

"We can debate the fine points later. According to Burrows, the guy was the devil. And you found him credible?" I nodded yes.

"Why?" Mike asked. I thought about that. I was getting good at it by now, having spent much of last night mulling over what I'd seen and heard.

"It's a few things. First, I can't see what lying to me buys him. If he had something to hide, about his own participation in Nassouli's games, even—worst case—about involvement in squeezing Pierro, the simplest thing for him to do would be to brush me off. Just refuse to talk to me or, better still, talk to me but give me nothing. Bore me to death. But he didn't do that. Instead, he talked to me about bad acts that occurred fifteen, twenty years ago, and he implicated himself in those acts—at least to the extent that he was one of Nassouli's confidants. Unless he's a serious crazy, looking for attention, I don't see what he gets out of that.

"Second, he wanted to talk, he needed to. He gives off that vibe, like he's carrying some sort of heavy load. I don't know what it is—if it's about what he did while he was with Nassouli, or what happened with his wife, or something else—but whatever, he's working off a big karmic debt. Talking to me was part of that somehow.

"And there's that picture. The face I saw in Helene's photograph at MWB—that's the Gerard Nassouli that Burrows was describing."

Mike chewed on that for a while. "Any thoughts about the Pierros, in light of all of this?" he asked finally.

"No good ones," I answered. "Burrows said it was theoretically possible for someone to have done legitimate business with Nassouli, so I guess Pierro could be as clean as he claims to be. But my faith is being tested, Mike." He chuckled a little.

"As I've said, clients lie. Still, he is our client," Mike said.

"Yes, he is," I said. "And I need to talk to him again—to see if those names Burrows gave me ring any bells. I'd also like to know what he thinks about Burrows's portrait of his pal Gerry. And I've got to have that talk with Helene, too. What Burrows said about Nassouli and his string of girlfriends makes me wonder all the more about her." Mike nodded and added more papers to a growing stack.

"So now what?" he asked.

"Now I look for Trautmann, and for the four guys Burrows named. Shake the trees, see what falls out," I said.

"Trautmann sounds promising," Mike said. "Burrows said he was privy to Nassouli's doings, especially the seamy stuff. And it doesn't sound like blackmail would be an alien concept to him." I nodded.

"Of course," he continued, "the most promising person in all this might be Nassouli himself. Being on the run can get pretty expensive. And no one would know better how to use those files."

"He's hard to ignore," I said. "But it would be awfully risky, running a blackmail business while you're hiding out from the feds. And there's a local aspect to this thing that doesn't quite fit with that scenario. Pierro's fax was sent from Ninety-eighth Street, not Brazil. Somehow, I don't think of Gerard Nassouli as hiding out in the Bronx for the last three years."

"Maybe he has local help," Mike said. I shrugged.

"A partner can be a dangerous thing for a guy on the run," I said. "Anyway, the feds haven't found him in three years of looking. How much better am I going to do in four weeks?"

"That's a different issue. How about Trautmann as his local partner?" Mike asked, and dumped a pile of journals in the trash.

"Maybe. Could be Nassouli, Trautmann, Alger Hiss, and Gordon Liddy, all in it together," I observed.

"You know, I always thought that Tim Russert was a shifty-looking bastard too. Let's not forget about him," Mike said, smiling. He turned his attention to another pile of paper.

"What about Brill and Parsons—have you given up on the idea that this could be an inside job?" he asked. I shook my head.

"No, but without help from Neary, I can't go anyplace with it. And Neary's got no reason to do more than he already has, not unless I can convince him that something's going on in his shop. So far, I've got nothing to convince him with."

"You talk to him about Burrows?" he asked.

"Not yet. I called him this morning and offered to buy him lunch. Asked him for anything he had on Trautmann, too." I downed the last of my coffee and stood. Mike looked up from a pile of junk mail.

"Let me know how it goes," he said. "And, happy turkey."

It was a crisp day, in the middle forties. A few chunky white clouds slid across the dark blue sky and threw small, fast-moving shadows on the buildings and the quiet streets. I caught a cab in front of Lever House and headed downtown.

Another Green World is a high-end Chinese vegetarian place. It's all pale blues and greens and frosted glass and brushed steel—the trendiest thing on Mott Street. Downtown was even quieter than midtown had been, and Neary was one of only a handful of patrons.

"This is right up your alley," he said, and handed me a menu. "It's got about ten thousand kinds of tofu." We looked over the choices and agreed on dishes to share—noodles, dumplings, spring rolls, various veggies, and lots of tofu. After the waitress had come and gone, I took Neary through the highlights of my meeting the night before, omitting Burrows's name.

He listened in silence, and when I was finished he ran a hand through his short, wavy hair and was silent some more. Finally he spoke. "Nassouli was seriously bad. Okay. I've heard that before. He's a wanted man, after all. We knew about his conference room being wired for sound—almost all of them were at MWB. And we knew about the apartment playpen, too, though we hadn't come across any tapes."

"He was seriously bad, *and he kept detailed records*," I emphasized.

"Yeah, okay, he kept records. And from what your source had to say, it sounds like he'd have every reason to destroy those records before he split, either that or take them along," Neary said.

"And if he didn't do either?"

"Then that would be bad. And if I won the lottery, that would be good. But they're both big fucking 'ifs,' and right now I have no reason to believe in either one." Neary drank some tea and continued. "If I were you, I'd be looking to establish a pattern among Nassouli's other victims, and I'd be all over Trautmann."

"Gee, thanks for the pointers, Mr. Neary," I said testily.

"Hey—remember who's asking for the favors around here, and who's doing them, and don't get your drawers in a knot. I'm just saying, maybe you've got hold of something, maybe not. But even if you do, I haven't seen anything yet that connects it to my people. Show me that, and you'll have my undivided attention, believe me." Neary gestured toward the platters that had come. "Don't let this get cold." I started with noodles, Neary with spring rolls.

"I got some stuff on Trautmann for you," he said, after he'd had a couple rolls. "It came out of the file my predecessor put together when Brill took over security on MWB. There may be more, but it'll have to wait till Monday." He took a thick yellow envelope from his jacket pocket and handed it to me.

"This guy sounds like a real piece of work. He used to be on the job. Worked plainclothes, narcotics and vice, up in the Bronx, and he was a real comer for a couple of years. Lots of arrests, a bunch of commendations, everybody expected great things. But then he flamed out. A pimp and two of his girls got themselves beat nearly to death, and there was a big excessive-force complaint against Trautmann. And on the heels of it, a bunch of questions about some of his earlier cases. Allegations of coercion, evidence tampering, talk about protection payments. Ultimately, no charges were pressed—no one willing to testify, apparently—and Trautmann ended up resigning. That was twenty-five years ago.

"A couple of months after he leaves the force, he gets himself a PI license, starts working security at some clubs in Manhattan, basically a well-heeled bouncer. Then he opens a rent-a-cop outfit, Trident Security Consulting, doing more of the same—clubs, crowd control, that kind of stuff. After a while he moves up-market, starts specializing in security services for banks—specifically small branches of foreign banks. He got himself a handful of banks for clients, including MWB. As MWB New York grew, so did Trautmann's business with them. Eventually, he gave up the rest of his clients and worked exclusively for them."

"What's he been up to since they folded?" I asked.

"Trident Security is still around, but very small time. Back to the uniformed rent-a-cop business—a couple of fat old drunks, a couple of skinny kids—working mall security out in Queens and on the Island," Neary said.

"Feds didn't like him for anything in connection with MWB?"

"They took a long look, but ultimately, no. His story was that he was just a contractor, had nothing to do with the business, and I guess he sold them on it." Neary crunched some broccoli. "The guy must be fifty-something by now, but he's a serious hard case. Since he left the force, he's had ten complaints filed against him—assault, harassment, one rape, one attempted murder. The last one just four years ago. But the complainants always seem to change their minds or lose their memories, so nothing sticks." Neary paused to eat some fried tofu. "You look out for this guy."

I nodded. "You're not the first person to tell me that," I said. We ate in silence for a while, and I thought about Trautmann. "So . . . an ex-cop, around fifty years old, hard case—where have I heard a description like that before?" I asked innocently. "Oh, yeah, it was from Faith Herman, my fax-sending bag lady, whose testimony you dismissed with such contempt." Neary was wrestling a knot of cold noodles with his chopsticks, but he flipped me the bird with his free hand. He finished his noodles and closed in on the dumplings.

"What's up with the feds and Nassouli?" I asked. Neary shrugged and dipped a dumpling in soy sauce.

"You asked me that two days ago. Like I said, he used to be an obsession with them. Then five, six months ago it stops."

"Any theories?"

"There aren't too many possibilities. One: they've stopped looking 'cause they found him or they're damn sure they know where to find him. Two: they've stopped looking 'cause they've run out of places to look. Three: they haven't stopped looking, but they want to give the impression that they have. Don't ask me why they would do that."

I thought about that a little. "I agree. Three doesn't make sense to me, and I'm not sure two does either. If they really felt they'd crapped out on the search, I don't see them advertising it." Neary nodded agreement. "One is my favorite, then. I can see them being quiet if they'd found him but couldn't get at him." Neary nodded again. "But do you see them keeping quiet if they'd got him? That doesn't fit." Neary had another dumpling.

"Could be they're trying to work a deal," he said between chews. "Be pretty good for Shelly to have a guy like that as a cooperating witness, don't you think? And if they're still making the deal, or if they made it and have him on ice somewhere, I could see them being pretty fucking quiet about it."

"Anybody over there willing to whisper in your ear?"

Neary frowned. "Jesus, March. How much mileage do you think you get out of some free meals, anyway?"

"It's not like I'm asking for the keys to the Hoover Building or anything," I said. Neary's frown deepened, and he shook his head.

"Has it ever occurred to you that I actually *need* this job? This is not some little favor, you know? They take this shit pretty seriously." He pushed a big hand through his hair and was quiet for a while. "I can ask one or two questions—very carefully. And if I get any push back at all—that's it," he said finally.

"Thanks, Tom, I appreciate it," I said. Neary grunted and took the last two dumplings.

We walked over to Broadway and said our good-byes. Neary went south, and I headed north, toward home. I walked the whole way, stopping only at a toy store in Union Square to pick up some things for my nephews.

My building was still and empty-feeling. No neighbors to be seen or heard, all gone for the holiday, no doubt. I fired up my laptop and went online, to three of my preferred search services. I submitted to each of them the four names Burrows had given me—Kenneth Whelan, Michael Lenzi, Nicholas Welch, and Steven Bregman—and limited my initial searches to New York, New Jersey, and Connecticut. I logged off; the services would send me their results via e-mail.

I changed into running tights and a sweatshirt and went out. Being still full of tofu, and not wanting to puke all over my shoes, I set an easy pace—nine-minute miles—and wound my way through Washington Square, the Village, and SoHo for forty minutes. Afterward, I showered and changed and opened a can of tuna. Then I put on WFUV and read from a book of Carver stories until I fell asleep.

Chapter Twelve

The taxi dropped me in front of Ned's building at three in the afternoon on Thanksgiving—only an hour late, despite my best dilatory efforts. A guy I didn't know held the big bronze door for me. I crossed the vast lobby to the concierge's marble bunker, and another guy I didn't know. He rang upstairs to announce me. The elevator guy I knew. He nodded at me.

"Long time," he said. Not long enough.

The elevator door slid open, and I stepped into a foyer about a hundred feet square. The walls were cream colored, and the floor was black and white stone, set in a diamond pattern. A small, bronze chandelier hung from the high ceiling. There was an ebony table to my left, with some flowers on it, in a tall, glass vase. Straight ahead was a pair of glossy, black doors. I pressed the bell and heard a deep chime inside.

Meg answered. She's a jumpy girl from County Mayo, with lots of freckles and skittish blue eyes. I'd be jumpy too, I guess, if I were Ned and Janine's maid, and had to wear that silly getup. I heard music, something baroque, and voices and glassware.

"Hi, Meg," I said.

" 'Lo, Mr. March. Nice to see you," she answered in a soft brogue. I stepped inside, and she took my coat. I was in a much larger foyer, with pale gray walls and white molding. Some Dutch landscape sketches that

I'd always liked were hung on the walls, and a big Oriental carpet covered the floor.

My sister-in-law Janine inspected me from the opposite doorway. Dressed appropriately? Unexpected guests? Visible contusions? Weapons? I was wearing olive corduroys and a black sweater over a blue shirt, so the clothes passed muster. I was alone, wound-free, and if I was carrying it wasn't obvious. She smiled and crossed the foyer to greet me.

"Hello, stranger. It's been a while," she said. She patted my arms and made a kissing noise near my ear. Janine is forty-two, a year younger than Ned, but like Ned she looks and acts more like fifty. She's five and a half feet tall, with a long, fragile-looking neck, reedy arms and legs, and a body like a plank. Her hair is an expensive blond, worn in a rigid pageboy. Her nose is straight and narrow, and her mouth is small, with thin lips that are prone to pursing. Her eyes are a bright, cornflower blue, with aperture settings that range from large as saucers, as when Ned presents her with some expensive bauble, to narrow as knives, as when she flays an impertinent junior member of one of her charity boards. With me they were dialed to wary.

Janine wore tailored camel pants, a chocolate-colored cashmere twinset, and pearls. Her eyes flicked to my packages and grew quizzical.

"For the boys," I said.

"Oh, John, you didn't have to. They have too much as it is, really. What is it?"

"Puzzles for Alec and Legos for Derek." I gave her the packages, and she put them down in a corner.

"They'll love them, I'm sure. They've been asking every five minutes when Uncle Johnny will be here." She guided me across the foyer, to the left down a wide hallway, and finally to the living room. The music and the voices and the glassware sounds grew louder as we approached.

The living room, like the whole apartment, was large and formal. We stood at one end of the broad, high-ceilinged space. The walls were a green just darker than money, and the pilasters and molding and beamed ceiling were a crisp white. A white marble mantelpiece dominated one wall. The wall opposite us was mostly windows and French doors, framed in green and gold drapery. The doors opened onto a terrace that wrapped around much of the apartment. The waning sun filled the room with amber light.

The furniture was old and French, and though there was a lot of it, the room did not seem crowded. The ten or so people in it didn't come close to its capacity. Most of them turned to look as we entered. Some of them smiled. Ned was there, and so was Lauren, with her husband, Keith. Liz was there, talking to an older, dark-haired man I didn't know. My brother David was on the terrace, talking to someone I couldn't see. His wife, Stephanie, was sitting with some more people I didn't know. Ned crossed the room to greet me.

"We thought we'd have to start without you," he said, and clasped my shoulder. "Good to see you, Johnny. Let me get you something to drink." He led me to a large chrome drinks trolley. "Cranberry and soda still your choice?" I nodded, and he took a tumbler off the cart and started fishing for ice in a silver bucket.

Ned is a couple of inches shorter than I am, and broader. His gingery hair is short and wavy, and it was thinner and grayer than the last time I'd seen him. He has a ruddy complexion and a square face with blunt features. His gray eyes looked tired and distracted, and there were more lines than I remembered around his small mouth—the burdens of being the number two guy at Klein & Sons. He was wearing dark gray trousers and a navy blazer over a white shirt. Turkeys strutted over his red tie. He handed me my drink and looked like he was about to speak, but before he could, I felt a dig at my ribs and a kiss on my cheek. Liz.

"What happened, you forget how to tell time, or has it been so long you forgot the address?"

"Hey, yourself," I said, and kissed her cheek. She was wearing a black cashmere turtleneck over a short, plaid skirt. A matching plaid ribbon was tied in her thick, blond hair. Liz is rangy and tall, just my height in flat shoes. She's thirty-six and looks it. She has shrewd, green eyes, a strong nose, and a wide mouth, all set in a lean face. The effect is more handsome and smart than conventionally pretty.

The traders who work on the hugely profitable desk that Liz runs at Klein would probably use different words to describe her. "Scary bitch" would be the kindest of them, and they might have a point. Liz is handsome and smart, but she's also brutally impatient, utterly intolerant of mistakes, and merciless in her sarcasm.

Her companion was cut from the same cloth as all her men friends: older, European, attractive, and affluent looking. She introduced him as Marco. He smiled with a bemused detachment that I envied.

"Back in the bosom of your family. I knew you couldn't stay away," she said, looking me up and down. "You're too skinny, eat something."

Meg was walking around the room with a silver tray heaped with smoked salmon, pâté, shrimp, and a few things I didn't recognize. Liz hauled her over. I took some salmon and felt a hand on my shoulder.

"Lauren said she'd ground you down. It's nice when it happens to someone else. How you doing, John?" A wry smile lit Keith's narrow face. Lauren's husband is tall, around six foot four, and thin, with a thatch of unruly brown hair, piercing blue eyes, and a long, bumpy nose. He wore khakis, a tweed jacket, and a rumpled denim shirt, open at the collar. Keith has a Ph.D. in molecular biology, and he does things with DNA at Rockefeller University. I smiled and shook his hand. Lauren was behind him.

"See, it's not so bad," she said. "You're having a great time already, I can tell."

"Whee," I said.

"Come meet our strays." She and Keith led me to one of the large sofas and introduced me to a German couple and a young Italian man. They worked in Keith's lab, and they were all new arrivals to the city. Their English wasn't great, but they seemed pleasant enough, if a little nervous. Sitting next to Stephanie for too long can have that effect.

"You made it. David and I were betting that you wouldn't." Stephanie smiled thinly at me. She's thirty-four, the same age as David, and the two of them have been inseparable since b-school. It's no wonder. I can't imagine that either of them had ever encountered anyone as driven or abrasive as themselves before. It was either marry or kill each other. I guess they made the right choice.

Stephanie is five foot three and whippet thin, with wiry brown hair that she wrestles into strange shapes, darting brown eyes too big for her pinched face, and a bitter little mouth. She's an equity analyst for a big firm downtown, and a good one, from what I hear. But her real talent is scheming with David on how best to advance his career, and at whose expense. We were not close.

"Sorry to disappoint you," I said to her. I turned to Lauren. "Where are the boys?" My question was answered the next moment when two bundles of tousled energy exploded into the room.

"Uncle Johnny!" they both shouted. Derek, the elder at six, made a lame attempt to compose himself and shake my hand. His four-year-old brother, Alec, wrapped his arms around my legs and head-butted me in the knees. I lifted each one in turn for a hug and a kiss. My nephews have thick, gingery hair—in wild disarray, just then—and their dad's broad face and features. They'd doubled in size since the last time I'd seen them.

Janine had dressed them alike today, in khakis, blue oxford shirts, and loafers, but they were massively disheveled—faces red, shirttails out, sleeves up, trousers sagging. Alec had only one shoe. An amused-looking girl in a gray skirt and black sweater followed them in, holding the other one. Tyler is Ned and Janine's au pair, from somewhere in the Midwest. She's about twenty, with long blond hair and cool blue eyes. She smiled at me and knelt to help Alec with his shoe.

"You guys look like five miles of bad road," I said.

"You look like ten miles," Alec laughed, and whacked me in the thigh.

"Hey, we saw the stuff you got us. Want to build Legos?" Derek asked.

"Not now, sir," Janine said, coming up behind him. "We're about to eat, so you two get yourselves cleaned up. I don't know how you got into this state." She looked pointedly at Tyler, who seemed not to hear her.

"After dinner, guys," I said, as Tyler led them away.

"Here's David," Janine said to no one in particular. "Good. Let's go into the dining room, shall we?" David is about my height, and thin. He has the same ruddy coloring as Ned, and the same wavy, ginger hair, worn longer. His sharp features are gathered closely on his face, which seems always caught somewhere between a scowl and a sneer. He had on the same blue blazer–gray flannel rig as Ned, but with a blue-striped bow tie. He was coming in from the terrace, and someone was with him.

She was wearing little black shoes that had a strap over the top and a buckle on the side, forest green tights and a black pleated skirt that ended a few inches north of her knees, a wide suede belt with a buckle made of horn, and a close-fitting, high-collared tunic in a green that matched her tights. Sherwood Forest by way of SoHo. She wore no jewelry other than the one diamond and two emerald studs in her small ears. Her mouth was curved in a polite smile at something David was saying, but as she stepped into the room Jane Lu looked up and cocked one of her delicate brows at me.

I turned to Lauren, who wore a little smirk. "Another stray?" I asked.

"Yep. Her family is in Boston, and she's working tomorrow, and no one else she knew was in town. So I invited her. Didn't I mention it?"

"Must've slipped your mind." I followed her into the dining room. It was smaller than the living room, but not by much. It was painted a deep orange, and had its own set of French doors, with green drapes. An old tapestry depicting fruits and vegetables hung on one wall. The table was a long oval. Even with fifteen of us there was plenty of elbow room.

Ned and Janine had taken no liberties with tradition, but had attempted to cover all the bases. There were three kinds of stuffing with the immense turkey, cranberry in sauce and relish forms, potatoes mashed and sweet, peas, creamed onions, candied carrots, fresh-baked white bread and corn bread, pumpkin pie, apple pie, and Indian pudding.

There was a lot of shifting of seats as the meal progressed, and a lot of talk, as there always is when my family is together. Tablewide discourse was mainly about the financial markets and politics. The smaller conversations were more varied. Keith and Jane Lu discovered some mutual acquaintances in Cambridge and compared notes on a defunct biotech firm. Liz and Lauren traded stories about our cousins. Ned and Janine tried in vain to determine where in Europe Marco was from. Jane spoke for a while in rapid German to the German couple, who laughed and seemed not so lost afterward. Lauren and Liz and Jane talked about moving and decorating and laughed a lot. Tyler explained to Marco about the different Kansas Cities, and where exactly Missouri was. Janine and Stephanie spoke acidly about some parties they'd attended recently. Ned and David and Liz had a long conversation in low, serious tones about Klein matters. Their faces were grim and tired looking. The boys bent my ear about some cartoon where the heroes were cuddly bunnies that transformed into giant, war-waging robots.

It was a pleasant enough meal. The only hiccup in the conversation came when the German woman asked what line of work I was in. David and Stephanie gave little snorts, almost in unison, Lauren and Liz shot them both dirty looks, Ned coughed nervously, and Janine nearly spilled her wine. I told her, but English was a struggle for her, and she looked puzzled. Jane said something to her and she nodded.

"*Magnum, P.I., ja?*" she said, smiling.

It was after coffee that the inevitable happened. Ned buttonholed me as people were drifting out of the dining room. He looked like his collar was too tight. We sat back down. David lingered at the far end of the table and drained the last of the Chablis into his glass, a sour smile on his face.

"Why do you waste your time?" he said to Ned. "You know he's not interested. He never has been."

Ned frowned and cleared his throat. "I'd like to talk to John alone, if you don't mind," he said. David drank some wine, shook his head, and left.

"We contract all of our security work at Klein to Risk Management Associates—you probably know that," Ned began. I did know it. RMA was a competitor of Brill, a big international investigations outfit. "They've done a fine job for us, for over a decade, and we have no complaints. But they notified us recently that the partner who has handled all of our business, a fellow we have a lot of faith in, is retiring. This, combined with the fact that our security needs have become more complex and sensitive in the last few years, has led the management committee to decide that we need someone in-house to manage our relationship with RMA. To be the point man, so to speak, for all of our security issues. This is a senior role, an SVP slot. I'll cut to the chase, John—we think you'd be the right fellow for this." I shook my head.

"No," I said. "Thanks, Ned, but no. I could recommend some people who have much better backgrounds than I do for that sort of thing. But it's really not for me." Ned began to speak, to try and sell me, but David reappeared and cut him off.

"I told you it was pointless. Just like him—pointless—a waste. He doesn't want a real job, no matter how good it is or how much trouble you've gone through to create it for him. He'd rather keep doing whatever it is he does—peeping through keyholes, spying on people. He'd rather keep on being an embarrassment." Ned drew a sharp breath and his face darkened, but David turned to me and continued.

"And you—you're nothing if not predictable. Though I'm not sure why you bother; Mother's not around to be upset by you anymore, and Dad's not here to be amused. Who are you playing to now?"

"I didn't solicit your opinion, David," Ned said icily. "You're not on the management committee, and this has nothing to do with you. Now apologize and excuse yourself." But before David could say anything, I got up. We looked at each other for a long moment.

"Thanks anyway, Ned," I said. I walked down the long hallway, past the living room, where most people had congregated, through the den, where Keith was watching football and explaining it to Marco, and out the French doors to the terrace and the night air.

Windows were lit in the big buildings across Park Avenue, and people were moving in them. Parties, families. Between the buildings, I saw the dark mass of Central Park and the smaller, colder lights of the West

Side. From up here, the streets were silent. A chilly breeze carried some of the heat from my face. I leaned against the stone parapet and breathed out slowly.

Insufferable prick though he was, David had a point. But it wasn't just me that was predictable—it was that whole sorry fracas. My family and I have been having that argument, or something like it, for years.

There've been a few changes. Before career prospects, it had been about the company and the hours that I kept, and before that, about the probations and the suspensions from school. And before it was Ned, it had been my uncles offering the well-intentioned, sensible advice. Until her death, the kind words were spoken not by David, but by my mother, Elaine. And ever since my father, Philip, passed away, we'd been short one bemused, distracted spectator.

But the basic quarrel—about irresponsibility, expectations, and disappointment, about waste and embarrassment—endures. It's old business, and it goes all the way back to Philip and Elaine, and their larger struggle.

It wasn't outright war between them—there were no pitched battles, and it wasn't that well organized. It was more a simmering border feud, with fierce skirmishes, stretches of nervous quiet, and an endless tallying of encroachments. But as to who was defending what territories, and against whom, I couldn't say. Nor can I say how I became my father's proxy in these firefights—how I became a lightning rod for so much of my mother's disapproval and discontent. Maybe I was just less expert than my siblings at keeping out of the crossfire—at keeping my head down or choosing sides.

A door opened, and there were slow footsteps. Lauren stood next to me.

"Sorry," she said. She spoke softly. I laughed a little.

"I won't say *I told you so.*"

"Please don't. I feel lousy enough as it is. I dragged you here, and told you this wouldn't happen, and . . ."

"We've been at this a long time, Laurie. It's not your fault." She looked down at the street.

"Ned means well," she said after a while.

"And David?" I asked.

"David's a putz." She laughed, and I laughed with her.

"His Mom impression is coming along," I said. "Close your eyes, and you can't tell the difference."

Lauren turned to look at me. "She meant well, too, you know. Really."

"If you say so."

"It's just that . . . you were too much like Dad," Lauren said. "At least she thought you were." A cold gust blew across the terrace, and I felt her shiver beside me. She crossed her arms, hugging herself.

"And that was by definition a bad thing, right?" I asked. "She did marry the guy, after all." We were quiet, and watched a plane crawl across the sky.

"Ever wonder why?" she asked. "Ever wonder what the hell they saw in each other?" I chuckled.

"I don't give it a lot of thought," I said. "There's only so much you can know about people—and less still about marriages. And when it comes to your parents' marriage—forget it."

"Is that a professional opinion?"

"If you asked me professionally, I'd say what I say to people who want their spouses followed: *Are you sure you want to know?*" She laughed a little.

"Probably not. It's a little too close to thinking about them having sex—it'd cost me a fortune in therapy." The breeze picked up, and Lauren shivered again.

"Go in," I said. "You'll catch a chill."

"You come too." She rubbed her arms.

"In a minute," I said.

I watched Lauren go inside and stand by Keith and Marco in the den. In another incarnation, the room had been my father's study—the site of what my uncles called his very early retirement. It had been lined, floor to ceiling, with bookshelves then, and furnished with a broken-down leather sofa, a big leather chair, and a small writing table—all gone now. With its high windows and big view of sky, the room had seemed to me, at various times, like a treehouse, a lighthouse, and a sail-boat. He'd called it his duck blind.

It wasn't forbidden to us—we could go in when we liked. But I was the only one who ever did. I'd find him sprawled on the sofa, or in the chair, or sometimes writing or sketching at his small table, and I'd sprawl too, and read with him in silence. When I was older, he'd sometimes pull a volume off the shelf and toss it to me. He never said more than "You might like it," and he never asked afterward if I had. It was an eclectic list—poetry and fiction mostly—Rilke, Akhmatova, Borges, Raymond Chandler, Robertson Davies, John Fante, Philip Dick—and if there was a message there, I couldn't divine it.

He'd worked at Klein, in a job my grandfather made for him there, and one day, after twelve years, he'd stopped going—I never knew why. One of many things I never knew—about him, about them both.

I put my palms on the coping and felt the cold seep into my hands. I watched the figures move in the windows across the way. I thought about my words to Lauren and shook my head.

"Are you sure you want to know?"

"A fool for a client," I said to myself.

On paper, they had little in common. He was an only child, the end of an old WASP line whose money and distinction were spent before he was born. His legacy, he used to say, was a mildewed shack on Fisher's Island, a decent squash game, and a bulletproof liver. She was the youngest of four—the only daughter. Her family was old too, but not WASP. She didn't play squash, didn't drink much, and her inheritance was considerably bigger than a shack.

They met at a party in someone's apartment off Washington Square. They were married four months later in city hall. They flew to Italy that same day, and stayed there for over a year. It was, as far as I know, her only act of rebellion. She was four months' pregnant when they returned.

I don't know why they married, or why they left the country afterward, or why they stayed away so long, or why they came back. I don't know why Philip took the job at Klein in the first place, or why he stopped when he did, to spend his time in the study or on a squash court or with a pitcher of martinis. And while I can guess about Elaine's anger, I don't know why she married Philip to begin with, if what she wanted was the life she'd always had. What had she been looking for?

I never asked Philip about his work, and by the time I'd had my own brush with Wall Street, it was too late to compare notes. So I never knew what he'd made of it all—if his experience was anything like mine. Was he appalled by the greed and self-indulgence? Was he stunned by the bureaucracy and politicking? Was he bored silly? Was he able to find even a single thing there to care about? I never knew.

French doors opened from the living room, and Tyler stepped outside. "The boys are asking for you."

They were in Derek's room, doing something intricate with Legos. I got down on the floor and helped them do it.

"You okay, Uncle Johnny?" Alec asked. He peered at me over the lid of a toy chest.

"I'm fine, buddy. Pass those green pieces over, okay?"

After the Legos, we played with Hot Wheels for a while, and then we built an elaborate railroad out of wooden tracks. Then Derek tried to teach me to play something on his Game Boy, but the point of the thing eluded me, and I couldn't work the controls reliably. Then we played soccer with a Nerf ball, then I was a zombie, and then I tickled them both till they were sweaty and hoarse and threatening to barf. It was getting late for them by then, and they needed to catch their breath, and so did I, so we sprawled sideways on Derek's bed, with me in the middle, and I read six or eight stories to them.

After a while I realized that they'd fallen asleep. I sat there with them, quite still, and looked at the chaos of scattered toys on the floor, and at the darkness outside their windows. Alec sighed and shifted. I looked down at my nephews and thought about the protected, privileged world they lived in, and how far it was from where I lived these days. At some point I drifted off too, and when I opened my eyes I saw Jane Lu, leaning in the doorway, watching.

"Share a cab?" she whispered.

Chapter Thirteen

The restless gray skies and cold wind had kept all but the hardiest from the playground. Empty swings moved in small, noisy arcs, their metallic scraping like the call of distant birds. The sandbox was sodden from the weekend rain, and deserted. A few kids braved the slides. A few others clambered on an elaborate climbing structure that bristled with ramps and ladders and poles. A couple of nannies, a couple of moms, and some grandparents watched from the benches. I sat on one near the playground gate—just me and a stroller.

It was about one-thirty on Monday, and I was watching Alex Pierro and his mother on the climbing structure. The thing was intended for older kids, but he'd been insistent. He needed help on it, nonetheless. His mother held him gently at the waist as he negotiated a ladder to the second level. He pushed her away, indignant, when he made it to the top.

We'd met at one o'clock, on the corner of Fifth Avenue and 79th Street. Alex was in his stroller, wearing corduroy overalls, tiny workboots, and a fleece jacket against the cold. His cheeks and small hands were pink. He'd smiled at me briefly, but was more interested in his toy locomotives. I'd been surprised to see him.

"It's nearly his nap time," Helene had said, smiling. "He'll play around for a little, and he'll be out. We can talk then. I brought us some lunch." She'd tapped the large diaper bag that hung from the stroller. I'd followed her across Fifth, into Central Park, and down to the playground near 77th Street. Helene wore a bottle green sweater over a white turtleneck, snug jeans, and low-heeled, brown boots. Her hair was loose and parted in the middle, and her hair band matched her sweater.

"He won't last but a few minutes," she'd said when we got to the playground. She'd draped her coat on the stroller and followed after Alex. A half hour later, he showed no signs of flagging.

But it was pleasant there, watching the kids play, and I didn't mind the wait. I'd had a busy few days. On the Friday after Thanksgiving, I'd gotten results from the search services. Each one had returned several hits for each of the names I'd submitted. I compiled a list of all of the responses, eliminating the duplicates. For Kenneth Whelan and Steven Bregman I had five possibles each. I had eight for Nicholas Welch, and three for Michael Lenzi. I'd spent the weekend refining my list.

The search services had provided date-of-birth information for most of the names, along with last-known and previous addresses. Using the birth dates, I culled from my list anyone too old or too young to have dealt with MWB during the time that Alan Burrows was there. Ten names came off my list. That left me with two Whelans, three Bregmans, five Welches, and a single Michael Lenzi.

I then did an online search of publications for the four names, including in my survey the major dailies in the tristate area, a bunch of the suburban weeklies, several banking and finance trade rags, and *Who's Who*. I cross-referenced the results with my remaining list, and was able to pare it down some more. I turned up a two-year-old feature in a New Jersey paper about a Nick Welch who was a riding instructor, training aspiring Olympians out near Gladstone. According to the article, he was a Jersey boy, born and bred, and lived in the same house that he'd grown up in. There was a Nick Welch with a Gladstone address on my list, who seemed to have no prior addresses. I crossed him off. I was similarly able to eliminate another Welch, who'd been convicted of torching his tire business in Stamford, Connecticut, a year ago, and a Bregman, whose obituary three years back noted his long career with Con Ed.

I found some likely candidates this way, too. The latest *Who's Who* listed a Kenneth Whelan of Summit, New Jersey, who was a senior executive in corporate finance for a big Swiss bank. A brief piece in the *Wall Street Journal*, nearly three years ago, and a longer article in a trade rag from around the same time, reported that Steve Bregman was leaving his post at a big asset management firm to start his own hedge fund. The trade rag mentioned that Bregman made his home in Pound Ridge, New York. And Nick Welch of New Canaan, Connecticut, had received a two-paragraph obituary in his local paper eighteen months ago. He'd died in a boating accident on Long Island Sound, and had been head of fixed income sales at one of the largest broker-dealers on the Street. My list had a Whelan in Summit, a Bregman in Pound Ridge, and a Welch in New Canaan, and I'd put stars by each one.

First thing this morning I'd placed a call to the one Michael Lenzi left on my list, in Brooklyn Heights. A young-sounding woman had answered and given me an office number. I'd called it and found him. I'd told Lenzi the truth—or at least a version of it. His name had come up in the course of a confidential investigation, I'd said, and I wanted to meet with him. No, the investigation had nothing directly to do with him, but I was hoping that he could provide some background information. Lenzi had been wary, and curious. I'd cited my employer's concern with confidentiality and assured him that I could elaborate when we met. He'd finally agreed to fit me in tomorrow afternoon.

I'd taken a run at Kenneth Whelan of Summit, New Jersey, this morning too, but with less luck. None of the search services or online directories had a phone number for this Whelan, and the reverse directories showed someone else now living at the Summit address. I'd called the main New York number of the Swiss bank that *Who's Who* had given as Whelan's employer. I'd bounced between a dozen departments before finding a pleasant woman with a lilting Jamaican accent who'd informed me that Kenneth Whelan had relocated to the bank's Singapore office.

I'd called the other Kenneth Whelan on my list, in Rockland County, on the off chance that he too was a banker. No luck—he was in plumbing supplies. Singapore Whelan was likely my man. That was too bad, because I wanted to talk to these people face-to-face; I wanted to hear what they had to say, and to watch them as they said it. But for Whelan, the phone would have to do. Given the time difference, I'd try him tonight.

After my Whelan calls, I'd opened up the file Neary had given me on Trautmann, and dug out a phone number and an address for his company, Trident Security Consulting. Trautmann, it seemed, was running a new-economy outfit. The phone number got me an answering service, with an operator who could barely spell Trident. A reverse directory search revealed that the company's address belonged to a commercial mail drop on Hillside Avenue, in Bellerose, Queens. According to the file, Trautmann's home address was in Bellerose, too. A trip to Queens was in my future, then, but I wouldn't be calling for an appointment first. I'd surprise Trautmann—after I'd had a chance to look him over.

My last calls this morning were to Mr. and Mrs. Pierro. I'd found Rick in his office, and he'd squeezed me into his calendar for tomorrow morning. I'd found Helene at home. She hadn't seemed surprised by my call, or by my request to meet. She hadn't seemed concerned or curious, either. Her only question was if one o'clock this afternoon would do. I'd said that it would.

After that, I'd worked out the kinks with a quick four miles along the Hudson. Then I'd showered and shaved, dressed in black corduroys, a pale yellow turtleneck, and a black leather jacket, and headed uptown to meet Helene.

"He's on his last legs, really," Helene said as she trailed after Alex. He was headed for the slides now. "Could you catch him at the bottom?" The slides were for bigger kids too, but Alex was undaunted.

"Sure," I said, and followed. Helene spotted him on the ladder while I waited below. He made it to the top alright, but the slide was wet and slick, and his feet slipped out from under him as he was sitting down. He slid down fast on his back, with his feet in the air, and shot off the end of the slide. I caught him in midair and hoisted him up high, and he squealed with laughter. Helene came over, shaking her head.

"Thanks," she said to me. She took Alex from me. "That's enough for you, big man. You need a rest, right? How about a binky for you?" Alex rubbed his eyes.

"Binky," he agreed. In short order, Helene had him in the stroller, chewing on a pacifier. She slipped a cap on his head and mittens over his hands, and adjusted the seat so that he was lying flat. She put on her coat and took a pair of chocolate-colored gloves from her pocket.

"Let's walk a little, till he's asleep. Then we can eat," she said. We left the playground and followed a path south, toward the boat pond. By the time we got there, Alex was out cold.

The boat pond had been drained for the winter and there were plenty of empty benches around it to choose from. We picked a west-facing one. Helene opened the diaper bag and took out two paper-wrapped sandwiches on French bread, a couple of Granny Smith apples, a large bottle of water, paper cups and napkins. "I hope this is alright. I had some cookies in here, somewhere," she said, still digging in the bag. She looked up at me. "You didn't want a big sit-down lunch, did you?" I shook my head. "You pick—mozzarella with prosciutto or with tomato. Either one's okay with me." Her southern accent seemed more pronounced today.

"Tomato," I said. She handed me a sandwich and started unwrapping hers. It wasn't exactly the usual circumstance for conducting a sensitive interview: over a picnic lunch in the park, with the subject's toddler sleeping nearby. Not what I would've chosen. If Helene had meant to disarm me, she'd made a fine start of it. She opened the bottle of water and poured us each a cup. It was probably a good idea to cut to the chase, before she started knitting me socks.

"You know what I'm working on for your husband?" I asked.

"That fax he got. Somebody's trying to blackmail Rick because he did business with MWB way back when," she said, and handed me a cup. I nodded.

"Does he know you're talking to me today?" Her eyebrows went up.

"Of course. He told me to do all I could to help you." I nodded again.

"I was down at what's left of MWB last week, in Gerard Nassouli's old office. I saw a photo you'd taken of him, some years ago." She peeled off her gloves and took a bite of her sandwich. No response. Okay. "How long ago did you take it?"

"What did it look like?" she asked. I described it to her, and she nodded as I spoke. "That was a very long time ago. Let's see . . . it must be thirteen . . . no, fourteen years back." She took another bite of her sandwich.

"Before you'd met Rick?" She nodded. "When did you meet Nassouli?"

"Not long after I first came to town. About fifteen years ago."

"How did you meet him?" She thought for a moment.

"I'm not really sure. It was at a party, I know that. I think one of my roommates knew him. I was living with about a half-dozen girls back then, in a real ratty place in the East Village. Third-floor walk-up, bathroom in the kitchen, that kind of thing. The oldest girl was maybe twenty-two, and not a one of us had been in town longer than a year. I think one of them maybe dated him for a while."

"And you—did you date him too?" She looked up at me, with only the faintest smile on her face.

"Yes, I did. I dated him too, for a while."

"How long a while was that?"

"Three or four months, I think." We were quiet for a minute, working on our sandwiches. I drank some water. Alex sighed heavily and settled into some deeper level of sleep. The wind rippled puddles in the bottom of the boat pond and pushed some damp leaves around. Two pigeons landed near our bench and eyed our lunch.

"Did you sleep with him?" Helene was unfazed. If anything, she seemed vaguely amused. She chuckled softly and shook her head a little.

"'Dating'—is that term in style again? I'm too old to know. I guess it's not very clear as far as sex goes, is it?" She drank some water. "But to answer you—yes."

"Just during the three or four months that you were dating?" She nodded. "What happened with him? Why did it break off?" Helene shrugged a little.

"I don't know that there was a big reason. I don't think it was some deep romance for him. I know it wasn't for me. Probably, better things came along, one way or another."

"And after that three or four months, did you see much of him?"

"I did for a while. He'd invite me to parties and things. We'd have dinner every so often." She drank some water and looked at me, smiling a little. "Is this really part of your investigation, or are you just a gossip?" I ignored her question, and we both ate some more.

"How long did you stay in touch, after you'd stopped dating him?"

"Six or eight months, maybe a year." I did a little figuring and a little guessing.

"Until around the time that picture was taken?" Helene smiled again and nodded.

"Yes, around then."

"And then what happened? Why did you lose touch?"

"I guess I had better things to do with my time," she said, and took a bite of her apple.

"You part on good terms?"

"Oh, yes—very friendly." She chewed slowly, looking at me.

"What was he like?" I asked.

"Gerard? Well . . . he was charming, really. Old-fashioned good manners. Very generous, with gifts and favors and things. And quite the man of the world—at least to my eyes back then. Seemed like he'd been everywhere and knew everybody. Knew all the hot spots, and he could always get a table. Knew just what to order, the wines and everything. 'Course back then I still had hay in my hair, so I probably wasn't the best judge." She thought a little more. "And the man loved a party, that's for sure. Not that he was a big drinker or one of those guys who'd be dancing on the tables. That wasn't him. He just liked the feel of a party—the liquor flowing, the food, cigars, pretty women, music—he liked being right in the thick of the good life."

"What kinds of gifts and favors was he generous with?"

"Gifts? I don't remember, but he was always buying things out of the blue. Not huge things, not like a car or anything, but nice stuff. A Hermès scarf once, a camera—that kind of thing."

"And the favors?"

She ate some more of her apple. Her eyes skidded away from mine. "He helped me with a couple of jobs. My first catalogs. He knew the people who ran the company." Alex stirred a little, and Helene shushed him and rocked his stroller until he settled down.

"Did you meet Rick through Nassouli?" She shook her head.

"Indirectly. Rick had just moved to London. I was there working for a few weeks, with another girl who knew Gerry. Gerry had given Rick this girl's number. The three of us met for drinks; five months later, Rick and I got married. That was eleven years ago." She smiled again. The wind was picking up a little. Helene pulled a small, blue blanket out of the diaper bag and covered Alex.

"Last week, a guy told me some different things about Nassouli. Some very ugly things. That Nassouli used people, and corrupted them. That he went through women like candy, and that when he was done with them, he'd hand them out to friends, as gifts. He talked about other stuff too—videos, blackmail, things like that. Very dramatic, very nasty." I took another bite of the apple. It was good—tart and crisp. "You know anything about that?"

So far my questions hadn't seemed to trouble Helene much. She'd been matter-of-fact, vaguely amused even, and only a little evasive. If it wasn't genuine, it was an impressive facade. But now there were some cracks. Helene drank some water and coughed and studied the Alice in Wonderland statue that stood across the empty pond from us.

"I didn't know anything about his business. I met some of his business friends—I guess all his friends were business friends—but I didn't know any of them, except for Rick. So if this person was talking to you about business, I can't help you with that."

"It wasn't just about business, Helene." She drank some more water and chuckled ruefully to herself.

"Back then, Gerard had this whole . . . scene around him. Girls he'd dated who . . . hung around him—kept going to the dinners and the parties, kept taking the gifts and the favors. They had a good time doing it, from what I could tell." Her voice faded.

"He ever ask them for anything in return?" She was quiet for a while, looking at Alice, across the pond, thinking about rabbit holes, maybe.

"Not in so many words, but . . . yes, I think he did." Helene filled her cup and drank, and stared at the empty boat pond. Her face was still, and her skin seemed very smooth in the gray light. The wind ruffled her chestnut hair. She drew her coat a little closer around her.

"What kinds of things?" I asked. She shook her head. Didn't know, or wouldn't say. "Were you a part of that scene?" I asked, softly. Again it took her a while to answer.

"I drifted to the edge of it, I guess. I was new to New York then . . . new to everything. I didn't catch on right away. But eventually I did, and I knew it wasn't for me." She drank some water. "I suppose that's what the picture is about."

"But you parted on friendly terms, you said." She nodded.

"We did. Like I said, Gerard never asked in so many words. He was charming and polite, and also very slippery. He'd say things in a way that gave him an out if you called him on anything, and that gave you an out too—that let you say no, or ignore him or pretend to misunderstand him without having to be too blunt about it. It was a real talent he had."

"Rick know about this?" She nodded. "Is that why he didn't stay in touch with Nassouli?" A shrug. "And you guys never saw him when you moved back to New York?"

"No."

"Never even ran into him?" She shook her head. "Really? Isn't that a little odd? I mean, in certain circles, New York can be a pretty small town." She shrugged again. "When was the last time you saw him?" She stared at Alice and thought about it and shook her head some more.

"I don't really know. It was a long time ago . . . over a dozen years, I'd think." She picked at the remains of her sandwich, dissecting it, but she ate nothing more.

"Rick didn't tell me about any of this. How come?" Another shrug.

"I never knew anything about Gerard's business, and I hadn't even met Rick then. I guess he just didn't think it had anything to do with . . .

this fax thing." Her eyes met mine, and she smiled wryly. "And truth be told, John, my husband's pretty traditional—you know, a nice Italian boy from Long Island. I don't expect he'd be too comfortable discussing the history of my love life with many people."

I asked Helene if she'd ever heard of Michael Lenzi, Nick Welch, Kenneth Whelan, Steven Bregman, Bernhard Trautmann, or Al Burrows, and she shook her head no to each name. I thought she might have blanched when I mentioned Trautmann's, but I could have been mistaken. We were quiet for a time. The wind picked up some more, and every so often a cold raindrop fell. One landed on Alex's cheek, and he looked annoyed and rolled over. Helene pulled up the stroller's cloth canopy, and gathered up the lunch things.

"I should really be getting him back," she said, and stood. "It was nice seeing you, John. I hope I was some help—to you and to Rick. Let me know if there's anything else I can do." She handed me a small, round package. "We never got to the cookies. You take them home. They're really very good."

I rode the subway downtown, eating cookies and thinking about Helene. She'd confirmed her involvement with Nassouli, and explained some of it. In her own way, she'd validated Burrows's description of the man. She'd been uneasy at points, though that's often the case when people talk about their youthful indiscretions. And I'd gotten the sense of things left unsaid—again, not so unusual. I'd also gotten the sense that, when it came to appearing ingenuous, Helene Pierro was at least as good as her husband. By the time I got to my stop, the cookies were gone.

I had some time before I could try Kenneth Whelan in Singapore. I spent some of it calling Mike.

"No smoking gun, then? No prior career in adult video?" he asked, after listening to my report.

"Not that she admits to," I said. "She knew the guy, dated the guy, had sex with him, broke up with him."

". . . and declined to be a part of his little stable afterward," Mike added.

". . . and parted friends, and lived happily ever after. You know her socially—any of this surprise you?" I asked.

"Not really. She's never struck me as a shrinking violet, and she's never pretended she was raised in a convent. Anyone who came to New York on her own, to model, when she was barely old enough to vote, has probably been around the block a time or two."

"You don't think she was a bigger part of Nassouli's scene?"

"I don't think so," Mike said after a while. "From what I've seen, Helene's not the hanger-on type."

"So what type is she?"

"She's smart . . . a bit of a loner. She shows up at some social things— the fundraisers, mostly—and I think she's on the board at her daughters' school. But mostly she goes her own way." He paused. "Any of this help us with Pierro's problem?"

"Hell if I know," I admitted.

At around seven I placed a call to Singapore. All I had was the main number for the bank that employed Whelan, so that's what I dialed. A woman answered. She had a high, girlish voice with a faint English accent. The connection wasn't great, and there was a noticeable delay on the line. From the main receptionist I was passed to a couple of other people, and in the process I discovered that Whelan wasn't just another expat employee out there, he was the head guy for his bank in the whole Asia-Pacific region. I figured that would reduce my chances of reaching him, but I was wrong. After about ten minutes I found myself on the phone with Whelan's personal assistant, a Ms. Li, who asked in precise, unaccented English what I wished to discuss with Mr. Whelan.

"Tell him it's about MWB and Gerard Nassouli," I said. She put me on hold again. She was back in less than a minute.

"Hold, please, for Mr. Whelan," she said. And then Whelan came on.

"This is Kenneth Whelan. What can I do for you, Mr . . . Marsh, is it?" He had a deep voice, and even across the spotty connection he sounded like a radio announcer.

"It's March," I said. "I'm calling to ask you a few questions." And I told him my story. Whelan was quiet after I finished, for long enough that I wondered if we'd been cut off. But he was there.

"I don't know that I can help you much, Mr. Marsh. I dealt with Gerard Nassouli many years ago, when I was with another institution. We did some advisory work for an MWB client. They were looking to acquire a U.S. company . . . an automotive parts manufacturer, as I recall. They ended up not doing the deal—I can't remember why. It was all pretty straightforward. I never had much else to do with Mr. Nassouli after that, other than at some social events."

"It's March, Mr. Whelan, like the month. Do you recall the last time you saw Nassouli, or spoke with him?" Another pause.

"Not precisely, no. Certainly it was several years ago, long before the MWB blowup. Perhaps five or six years."

"And you've not seen him or spoken with him since?"

"No."

"Besides me, has anyone else contacted you regarding your dealings with Nassouli or MWB?" Whelan was quiet for a long while.

"No, no one, Mr. Marsh. No one but you has mentioned Nassouli to me in many years."

"My name is March, Mr. Whelan, like the March Hare. How long ago were you posted to Singapore?"

"It's been about three years, now," Whelan said, and then I heard Ms. Li's voice in the background. "I'm sorry, that's all the time I can give you. I hope this was useful. Good-bye, Mr. Marsh." There was a click, and all I heard was the hissing of the ether.

"It's March," I said to no one.

Chapter Fourteen

Rick Pierro's suit looked good. It was medium gray—darker than the cloud-filled sky, but lighter than the Town Car that idled at the curb—and it hung with an easy, liquid drape from its master's big frame. Though it was nearly noon, and had been raining hard since dawn, its trouser creases were sharp and supple. Pierro stepped briskly onto the pavement, into the café, and across the room to greet me.

He looked good, too, though perhaps not as good as his suit. His shiny black hair still held its obedient sweep back from his forehead, and his smile was still broad and bright and affable, but his dark eyes were tired and smudged-looking, and his olive skin was tinged with yellow. The flesh above the knot of his deep blue tie seemed to sag. Still a sleek bear, and still well dressed, but a little off his feed. The grip was as firm as ever, though.

"Good to see you, John," he said. Pierro sat and looked around the room. He had wanted to meet someplace out of the way, and I figured Black Cow fit the bill. It's in SoHo, just off Prince Street, a small place with a glass front, a high, tin ceiling, and some small black tables along one wall, opposite a massive ebony bar on the other. We were late for the breakfast crowd and early for lunch, and besides a pair of skinny women who'd come from the gallery next door, a bored waitress, and a guy behind the bar who looked like a junkie, we were alone in there. Pierro seemed satisfied with his anonymity, and turned to me, smiling.

"How was your Thanksgiving? Get your fill of turkey and ball games?" he asked. I made a noncommittal noise, and he continued. "I think it's my favorite holiday. I like having the whole family together, and my kids are still young enough to love the parade. My folks were up from Boca, and Helene's mom and sister were up too, and they went crazy in the kitchen." He patted his middle. "I got a little more here than I did last week," he said. In fact, it looked like he had a little less. The waitress wandered over, but Pierro raised a hand before she spoke.

"Nothing," he said. She shrugged and looked at me.

"More coffee, please." She wandered off to get some. Pierro looked at his watch.

"Sorry I don't have a lot of time, John. I'm on my way to a lunch uptown." I nodded.

"I won't keep you. I had a long talk with Al Burrows last week, and I got an earful about Gerard Nassouli. Maybe Helene mentioned it?" Pierro stared at a point around my left ear and nodded vaguely. "Burrows went into gruesome detail, but the long and short of his story was that Nassouli was the devil—not just a money launderer, but a corruptor and a blackmailer—and that you'd have to look hard to find someone he did a straight deal with." Pierro fixed his eyes on mine. He snorted.

"Is there a question there someplace—another version of *are you a crook,* maybe? I thought we'd settled this bullshit already." His voice was hoarse and rumbling. Mr. Nice-Bear was fast disappearing into the woods. I held his gaze but didn't speak. His big hands fiddled with the flatware.

"I guess you need to hear it again," he said. "Fine—my dealings with Gerry were legitimate. Okay? That do it for you? Can we get back to work on my problem now?" I looked at him some more.

"What do you make of what Burrows had to say?" I asked. He snorted again.

"How the hell should I know? How is it my place to make anything of it?" Pierro took a deep breath and forced a smile onto his face, but it was faint—a twitch away from a scowl. He sighed, and his shoulders sagged a little.

"I guess it's like what the government is saying about Gerry—I've got no reason to doubt it, but my dealings with him had nothing to do with any of that. So maybe Burrows is right—what the hell do I know?"

"Any reason why he would make up this kind of stuff?" I asked. Pierro turned a fork over and over. He shrugged.

"I barely knew the guy; I don't know what he'd do or wouldn't do," he said. I nodded, then I tried out the five names I'd gotten from Burrows: Whelan, Bregman, Welch, Lenzi, and Trautmann. He looked at the tabletop and listened to the names and said no five times.

Pierro checked his watch and looked up. He pinched the bridge of his nose and sighed again.

"I'm being a prick, aren't I?" he said. His voice was softer. "Sorry about that. I'm a little tired today. You get what you need here?"

"I asked my questions—you gave your answers." He made a sound that might have been a laugh.

"And my wife—you get what you need from her, too?" The edge was back in his voice. I nodded. "Did you really have to talk to her about all that . . . crap? It's ancient history, for chrissakes. How the hell does dredging that up help with anything?"

"I'm not sure it does," I said. "But I couldn't know unless I asked, and I had to ask. I'm sorry if it was uncomfortable for her."

"It bothered her a lot less than it did me," Pierro said. He shook his head. "I'm getting pissy again—sorry. It's just that . . . Helene's a good person, John . . . better than I deserve. She shouldn't have to air her dirty laundry for no reason."

"It wasn't for no reason, Rick. And as dirty laundry goes, I've heard a lot worse." Pierro's lips pursed.

"So now what?" he asked. I explained my plans to find the five people Burrows had named. He nodded.

"And if someone else has gotten a fax too, then we know something?" he asked.

"Then we know something." Pierro looked at his watch again, and I figured we were done. But we weren't.

"I didn't realize you were Ned March's brother," he said. I looked at him. "I know him by reputation, and I heard him speak at a conference a couple of years back—your brother David, too. Smart guys, the both of them. And Klein's a hell of a firm—one of the last of its kind." He chuckled. "I did a little research of my own," he said.

"So I gather." There was a trace of pleasure on Pierro's face, at having taken me by surprise. And there was something more—curiosity.

"Tell me if I'm out of line here, John, but I've got to ask—coming from a family like that, shouldn't you be running part of Klein or something? How the hell did you end up in this line of work?"

How did you end up in this line of work? Why do you do it? I've been asked those questions enough over the years that I should have some answers handy by now—but I don't. Instead, I've got some vague crap that I mutter about aversion to desk jobs and not being cut out for banking. I trotted a little of that out for Pierro. He smiled and shook his head, incredulous.

"Christ, if I'd had that kind of family juice when I was coming up, I'd have been CEO at French ten years ago." He looked at his watch and rose. "Got to get to getting, John. It was good to see you. And thanks, again, for everything you're doing," he said. And he and his good-looking suit strode out the door. I headed downtown.

"You're not in here," she said, and she stared deeply and with some consternation into the monitor that stood on her small metal desk. "If you're not in here, you don't have an appointment." She was maybe twenty, and had a gold stud in her nose and another in her tongue, and was made up like she'd just escaped from the road company of *Cats*. She was tiptoeing her fingers gingerly across the keyboard, careful that no harm should come to her immaculate French manicure, in an excruciating attempt to locate me in Michael Lenzi's appointment calendar. She wore one of those campy retro necklaces that had her name on it, rendered in gold-plated script. *Brie.* I stood a better chance with the cheese.

"Why don't I just rest here while you look," I said. She ignored me and continued her glacial typing. I sat down. I watched water drip from my umbrella. I looked at the wet leaf stuck to my boot. I listened as, every minute or so, Brie tapped a key. If she had to answer the phone, too, I'd be here till Christmas.

Arroyo Systems occupied part of a low floor in an anonymous building on Broadway, near Fulton Street. The reception area was windowless and small, furnished with a black leather chair, a matching love seat, a chrome and glass table, Brie's command center, and a dead plant in a large plastic pot. The sheetrock walls were scuffed, and the carpet was worn and stained. A couple of the fluorescent ceiling bulbs were out, and the working ones buzzed annoyingly. Some dusty photos of canyons hung on one wall. There were a half-dozen old banking and software trade magazines on the glass table, along with last Friday's *Post* and a few brochures about Arroyo Systems. These were filled with colorful but indecipherable diagrams, photos of smartly dressed people staring raptly at computer screens, and gobbledygook like "object-oriented n-tier message-based architecture." It was impossible to tell from them what Arroyo Systems did. I started reading the *Post*.

"You sure it was today—Tuesday?" Brie asked without looking up.

"I set it up with Mr. Lenzi yesterday morning—for one o'clock today. Why don't you just call him?" She looked at me like I was speaking Urdu, then turned back to the monitor. She was still delicately pressing keys and gazing uncomprehendingly at her screen when a wiry, intense-looking man opened the interior door and spoke to her.

"I'm expecting a guy around one." He paused and looked at me. "Maybe that's you. You March?" I nodded. "Mike Lenzi." He gave me a hard handshake. I followed him inside. Brie noticed none of this, and we left her pondering her screen, pristine nails poised above the keyboard.

"How long she keep you out there?" he asked.

"No more than a week," I said. He snorted.

"I don't know where we get them from—Mars, maybe. And we can't keep them longer than a month or two. We had one a while back—didn't make it through lunch. Went out on her break and that was it, never saw her again. Took a laptop and a couple of wallets with her."

I followed Lenzi down a short hall, past a conference room and a kitchen, to a warren of cubicles with shoulder-high partitions. We picked our way through them and headed for a row of offices along the back wall. The cubicles were densely packed with computer hardware and wild tangles of cabling, and every surface was covered with a thick, unstable sediment of paper, technical manuals, CDs, takeout food containers, candy wrappers, soda cans, coffee cups, and other stuff too deeply buried or decomposed to identify. The space was cramped and chaotic and smelled like a dorm room, or an airport transit lounge after a week of canceled flights.

I heard Russian being spoken, and another language that I didn't recognize. Most of the people I saw were young and male. Nearly all of them were casually dressed, some in suit pants and dress shirts, some in jeans and T-shirts, and others in what could have been pajamas.

Lenzi was the exception to the dress rule. He wore the pants to a navy suit, a blue-and-pink-striped shirt with cuff links, and a blue tie with a red geometric pattern. He was short, about five foot five, with dark, curly hair that had begun to gray and recede. His face was thin, and his dark eyes were deep-set. The skin beneath them looked soft and loose. He was clean-shaven, but the faint shadow on his jaw meant he had to work at it. I put his age at forty-five.

His office was small and had too much stuff in it. The grimy window, with its view of an airshaft, only made things worse. He ushered me into one of the guest chairs and shut the door. He edged around me and slid behind his big, dark desk.

"Lots of all-nighters?" I asked, gesturing out toward the cubicles.

"Programmers," he said, shaking his head. "Can't live with 'em, can't kill 'em. They're a fucking mess—excuse my French. If you were a client, I wouldn't take you past the conference room." Lenzi shifted restlessly in his seat. He picked up a paper clip and started playing with it.

"What kind of software do you guys make?" I asked.

"Trading systems. For FX, money markets, and derivatives. We do pricing, trade capture, position keeping, some risk. That probably doesn't make any sense to you." I shrugged.

"How big a company is it?"

"Small. We've been around almost two years, got sixty people or so, most of them out there," he cocked his thumb toward the door. "Couple of sales guys in London. But we're getting there." His optimism sounded more habitual than sincere.

"You've been here from the start?"

"Not from the start, but soon after."

"You're not a programmer, though," I said.

He snorted again. "Me? No, I do sales." He'd unbent the clip and wound it into a spring shape. Now he straightened it again. His hands were large and pale, with black hair and blue veins on the backs. His movements were quick and a little twitchy, like he'd had too much coffee.

"And before this—you were in banking?" I asked.

Lenzi bristled. "Whoa, buddy, before we start in on my résumé, how about you filling me in on what the hell this is about?"

"Fair enough," I said. "Ever hear of Merchant's Worldwide Bank?" Lenzi blanched, and paused in his torture of the paper clip.

"I've heard of it," he said.

"Your name came up in some work that I'm doing that's tangentially related to MWB—"

Lenzi cut me off. "Came up how?" He was quite still now.

"Only in the vaguest way. Just that you did some business with them a while back, maybe fifteen or twenty years ago." Lenzi placed his palms flat on the desk. His face was immobile except for a small, pulsing vein high on his forehead. I went on. "That you dealt with a guy there named Gerard Nassouli."

It was like I'd spit in his face. Lenzi pushed back from the desk and gripped the arms of his chair. His hands were white, and the veins in them stood out like blue wires. The skin of his face seemed to contract around the muscle and bone underneath, and two red patches flared at his cheeks. His mouth was a taut furrow, and his whole body seemed to coil. I had at least seven inches on him, and probably fifty pounds, but the guy was ready to come across the desk at me.

"Who are you, and what the fuck do you want?" The words came out in a dangerous hiss, like steam rushing from a valve. But he was fighting his rage, breathing deeply, flexing his fingers, trying to get the tiger back in the cage.

"I'm looking for some answers," I said evenly. "Nothing else. I just want to know if you knew Gerard Nassouli. And if anyone else has contacted you over the last few years about your dealings with him." Lenzi stared at me in silence, his chest rising and falling sharply. I kept going. "I don't care how you knew him, or what business you had with him. I don't want to know. All I want to know is if you were threatened on account of it. Were you squeezed because you had dealt with him?"

When he finally spoke, Lenzi's voice was a choked whisper. "You get the fuck out of here. Get out now, and if you ever come near me again, I'll fucking kill you—I swear it," he said.

This was not going well—death threats are always a sure sign. The rage that had overtaken him at the mention of Nassouli's name had made Lenzi deaf to everything else I'd said or might say. And my sitting here wasn't going to make it better. If I hung around any longer I was going to have to fight him or watch him have a stroke. I stood up and placed a card at the edge of his desk.

"I don't mean you any harm, Lenzi. If you decide you want to talk, give me a call." I left him alone with his tiger.

There was an espresso place around the corner from the Arroyo offices, and I went in and ordered a double and thought about Michael Lenzi. I was willing to bet I wasn't the first person to bring up the unwelcome subject of Gerard Nassouli with him. The indirect confirmation was useful, but I needed more. I finished my coffee, walked over to Fulton Street, and caught the subway.

Brooklyn Heights is at the western edge of the borough, across the East River from lower Manhattan and just south of the Brooklyn Bridge. It's an affluent, almost suburban neighborhood, and has more in common with Scarsdale than with Bay Ridge or Bensonhurst. Its quiet, leafy streets, meticulously maintained townhouses, and postcard views of the city skyline, along with its proximity to downtown offices, lure plenty of Wall Street types across the bridge. It was a ten-minute ride from downtown Manhattan to the heart of the Heights.

I took a slow elevator from the subway station to the street. It had stopped raining, but the sky was full of steely clouds and the wind was blowing in gusts off the river, shaking water from the bare trees. I walked down Clark Street a block and a half, to Willow Street. I took a left and walked nearly to the corner of Pierrepont. Lenzi's building was on the west side of the street. It was a wide, four-story, Federal-style townhouse in brick, with white trim and black shutters on its high, narrow windows. It was set a little back from the sidewalk and separated from it by a black wrought iron fence and some boxwood shrubs. A short flight of brick steps led to the entrance portico and a glass and wrought iron door. I went in.

I was in a small vestibule with a worn stone floor. In front of me was another glass door, this one locked. On the wall to my left was a video intercom and buttons for each apartment. Lenzi was in 4B. Through the inner door I saw a nicely decorated foyer with striped wallpaper, a small table, a couple of chairs, a bank of gleaming brass mailboxes, and an elevator. I pressed the intercom button for 4B.

"Yes?" she said. Her voice was tinny and remote through the little speaker, but it was the young-sounding woman. Now she sounded young and anxious. I looked into the camera lens and gave my best trustworthy smile.

"Mrs. Lenzi?" I said.

"Who are you?" Suspicious now, and scared. My trustworthy smile needed work.

"Mrs. Lenzi, my name is March. We spoke on the phone yesterday morning—"

She cut me off. "Oh Jesus, I don't believe it. I've got nothing to say to you. Nothing. You go away, or I'm calling the cops." She was scared and angry, but more scared.

"Mrs. Lenzi, please, I just want to talk to you—"

She cut me off again. "I mean it." She was getting shrill. "He said you might show up here. I thought he was being nuts, but . . . Jesus. I'm telling you, get out now or I'm calling 911." I heard a click from the speaker.

"Mrs. Lenzi? Mrs. Lenzi?" Nothing.

I went outside and stood on the steps. It was midafternoon, and the street was quiet. A few people came and went from houses up and down the block. A taxi rolled slowly by, dropped its fare at the corner of Pierrepont, and sped away. A few doors down, on my side of the street, a mailman brought his three-wheeled cart to a halt in front of a building much like Lenzi's. He went inside. I walked down the steps, down the block to Pierrepont Street, and around the corner. I pulled out my phone and called Lenzi's home number. I let it ring ten times. She wasn't picking up. On the next corner there was a newspaper box with the *Daily News* inside. I dug out some change and bought a copy.

I walked back to the corner of Willow to check on the mailman. He was working the building next door to Lenzi's now. It took him ten minutes. Then he was back at his cart for a moment, and then he was climbing the steps to Lenzi's building. I sprinted from the corner and went in behind him. I caught the inner door as it was closing. I walked through with my keys out, my umbrella hung on my arm, and my head buried in the sports page. The mailman turned to look at me.

"How's it going?" I asked, still in the paper. I pushed the elevator button. He grunted and kept looking at me. I turned to the funnies. The elevator came, and I got in and pressed 4. He was still looking at me as the door slid closed.

The door opened again on a small hallway with striped wallpaper like the lobby's. There were three apartments; 4B was opposite the elevator, its door a dark, shiny green with the apartment number in gold leaf, just above the peephole. I walked to the doors of the other apartments and listened. They were quiet. The whole building was quiet. I rang the doorbell. I heard footsteps from inside and someone at the peephole.

"Oh god," she gasped. "How did you get in here? Jesus . . . you broke in, you bastard. That's it, that's it, I'm calling 911, you son of a bitch." She was very scared now, getting frantic.

"Mrs. Lenzi, please calm down. I don't mean any harm to you or your husband. I just want to talk to you . . ."

"Talk? I talked to you for a minute on the phone, and now look. You fucking break in here . . . you have no idea . . ." She was crying now. The sound of her ragged breath got closer, as if she'd pressed her face against the door. She was pounding on it now. "Please, please, just go away. Please, you have no idea how he gets . . . how angry he is, just because I gave you his number. He's crazy. Please."

This was not going well, either. I didn't know what demons my questions had unleashed in the Lenzi household, but I thought of what Alan Burrows had said to me, about making people relive nightmares. And I thought, bitterly, of my reply. *I'll be discreet, I'll be quick, and I won't be heavy-handed.* Shit.

"Maybe I can help him, Mrs. Lenzi. I'll put my card under the door. Call me. Please."

"Help him? Help him?" She was hysterical, almost shrieking. Her voice was coming from lower down now, like she had sunk to the floor. "What the hell are you going to do? Get the bank to take him back? Make the fucking mortgage payment for him? Make him stop drinking?" Her words dissolved into sobbing and I thought I'd lost her, but she gulped some air and came back. "Please, just go away, please . . . we were hanging on, we were making it, and now . . . please, just leave him alone. If you want to help—let him be." And then her sobbing found a second wind, and I lost her completely.

I had a long wait for the subway at Clark Street, plenty of time to feel lousy about what I'd done to Lenzi and his wife, and to think about where to go from here. Something had happened to Lenzi, something bad enough that the mention of Nassouli's name made him crazy. Mrs. Lenzi might know what that something was, but if she did, she wasn't going to tell me. She was terrified of Lenzi's rage, and that their life was coming apart. Nothing good would come of pressing them any more.

I could make some guesses based on what little they had said. Lenzi had worked at a bank. And two years ago, maybe earlier, the bank had fired him. But which bank, and why was he fired? I thought about Arroyo Systems, and the kind of software they developed. *Trading systems. For FX, money markets, and derivatives.* Lenzi had come to Arroyo less than two years ago, having previously worked in banking. Maybe what qualified him to sell Arroyo's software was prior experience in those markets. It wasn't much of a theory, but it was one I could test.

Trading in over-the-counter instruments, like the ones Arroyo's system was meant to handle, is a person-to-person business. And working on a desk that trades in those markets is a little like living in a small town. Everyone knows everyone else, and, while they'll pretend otherwise, everyone gossips. If Lenzi worked in that world, as a trader or a salesman or a broker or in some other capacity, other players might know him. I had a player in mind.

It was just past four, things should be wrapping up. I got off the subway at the Wall Street stop and walked a couple of blocks east and a couple of blocks south. I called from outside the building.

"Klein. Liz March," she said brusquely.

"It's your brother."

"The embarrassing one?" she asked, laughing.

"That's me. Got a couple of minutes? I'm downstairs and I need a favor and I'll pay for it in coffee," I said.

"Hang on," she said, and put her hand over the phone and yelled something at someone. "I'll meet you at that place on William Street. Give me ten minutes."

I went around the corner and took a table and ordered a coffee and waited. Half an hour later she strode in. She was wearing a black pants suit, with a neon orange blouse underneath. Her hair was tied back with a band the same orange color.

"Wow," Liz said. "Twice in less than a week. This must signal something. Maybe the coming apocalypse. After Ned's go at career counseling, and David's kind words, I figured we wouldn't see you for another year or so." She ordered some complicated latte thing.

"You wouldn't have, except I need something from you," I said. She smiled. "You ever hear of a guy named Mike Lenzi?" Liz thought about it.

"Skinny, dark-haired guy? Thinks he's Joe Pesci in *Goodfellas*?" she asked after a while.

"That's him," I said. "Where do you know him from?"

"I don't, really. Just know of him. He ran the short-term interest rate desk at Plessey Guaranty for a bunch of years. Used to see him at the Robin Hood dinners. He'd always drink too much and chase anything in a skirt. Kind of an asshole."

"Know what happened to him?"

"I know he left Plessey a while back—couple of years ago. I don't know where he went."

"Know why he left?" Liz shook her head.

"I can probably find out. Want me to make a call?" I nodded. Liz took out her phone.

"This guy works for me," she said as she punched the number. "He's been around forever, and he knows everybody." She waited for the call to go through. "Bobby, it's me." She listened for a moment. "Yeah, yeah, that's right. No more than five hundred basis points." She listened some more. "That's bullshit. He's full of shit, and he's ripping us off, and you tell him I said so. And tell him he better think hard about this if he ever wants to deal with us again." She paused. "Fine, fine. Different topic. Remember Mike Lenzi, used to be over at Plessey? He left there, what, two years ago?" She looked at me and nodded her head as she listened. "Yeah, an asshole. You know what happened to him?" Bobby spoke for a while and Liz listened, nodding. "You're the best, Bobby. I'll be up in a couple. You want anything?" She hung up.

"Says Lenzi left there about two years ago, under a cloud. Some sort of malfeasance, but Plessey was very hush-hush about it. Of course, there were rumors. Bobby heard something to the effect that Lenzi had been giving away the store—disclosing position information— supposedly for years. Apparently Lenzi cut himself a deal so that he left all his stock and options on the table, and in return no charges were pressed. And neither side talks to anybody about anything 'cause it's too embarrassing all the way around. Bobby says Lenzi's not in the markets anymore. Thinks he's hawking some second-rate trading software. You owe Bobby a decaf skim latte, by the way." I paid up.

It was nearly six when I got off the subway at Fourteenth Street. The rain and wind had spent themselves, and in their wake the night was cold and clear. I was weary and stiff and wired from too much coffee, and, as I walked up Seventh Avenue, I couldn't shake the image of Lenzi's wife, a woman I'd never seen, crumpled by her front door, crying. I didn't tell myself that I'd had to do it, that trading her pain for information was part of the job, that I was acting in my client's best interest. Why bother, when it would lack all conviction? Shit.

But what I'd learned from her and her husband, and from Liz and Bobby, was enough to paint a picture. Michael Lenzi had been one of Nassouli's pet traders. He was in Nassouli's pocket fifteen or so years ago—that's how Burrows had known him—and he may have been doing favors for Nassouli right up until MWB closed. Around two years ago, somebody had tried to squeeze him. They'd had proof of his dealings with Nassouli, the sort of proof Nassouli kept in his personal files, and they'd threatened Lenzi with disclosure. Lenzi had said shove it, or something to that effect, after which a package had been delivered to his management at Plessey. Then it was good-bye, Mike, don't forget to leave your money at the door, and you'll never work in this business again.

My picture had lots of white space in it, though, and Lenzi was the only guy I knew who could fill in the gaps. Only he could tell me what they had on him, how they'd contacted him, and what they'd wanted. Only he could confirm that someone had, in fact, tried to squeeze him. Or, he could tell me that my picture was bullshit—that, after who knew how many years of favors for Nassouli, Lenzi's management had finally caught on and canned his ass.

I stripped off my clothes, changed into running stuff, and ran five miles in thirty-eight and a quarter minutes. After that, I went to the gym and pushed some steel around until my arms were quivering and I felt vaguely nauseated. Then I went home, showered, ate two cartons of yogurt, and fell into an empty sleep.

Chapter Fifteen

"Let me fill that," Lisa Welch said. She took my glass and moved serenely across the slate floor of her sunroom, into the adjoining kitchen.

She was a calm, almost ethereal woman with straight, straw-colored hair that fell halfway down her back. She had an open, fine-featured face and, though December was closing in, her prominent cheeks and broad forehead were tanned an attractive golden color. Her large eyes were an odd shade of blue that changed with the changing light—from gray to nearly violet. Her mouth was broad, and in repose fell into a faint, sad smile. She was five foot seven and maybe a hundred and twenty pounds, including the change in her pockets. She wore jeans and a sleeveless blue T-shirt that said "Sanibel Dive Shop" on the front. Her arms were firm and lightly tanned. She was about my age.

I heard her bare feet pad across the wide plank floors of her kitchen. I heard her open the fridge and pour water from a pitcher. I heard her open the oven to check the bread baking inside. The phone rang, and I heard her soft, even voice speaking, though I couldn't make out the words. An indolent chocolate Lab named Jesse slept near the wrought iron and glass table where I sat, and I heard him sigh heavily.

While I waited for Lisa, I watched her children play on the big back lawn, just beyond the stone patio that lay outside the sunroom. There were two of them—a boy and a girl, ages five and three, blond-haired, blue-eyed, broad-faced, long-limbed, like their mother. The girl seemed to have something of her mother's serenity. She was feeding two baby dolls in a toy stroller, and occasionally wheeling them around the patio. The little boy was more frenzied. He was climbing and jumping all over a backyard playground, doing imaginary battle with pirates, or robots, or robot pirates . . . it was hard to tell.

It was Thursday afternoon, and a warm day for late fall, in the low sixties. Birds twittered softly, and between their singing and the warmth of the sunroom, and the mild breeze through the open windows, and the muted sounds of the children's play, and Jesse's slow, heavy breathing, and the aroma of baking bread, and the gentle murmur of Lisa's voice, the whole place exerted a powerful soporific effect. Some cookies and milk, and I'd be ready for nap time. But that's not what I'd come for.

I'd spent yesterday morning winnowing down my list of names. Of the two Steven Bregmans left on my list, only the one in Pound Ridge was in finance. And of the three Nick Welches, only the departed Mr. Welch, late of New Canaan, fit the bill. I'd spent yesterday afternoon making contact with Steven Bregman and the widow Welch, and convincing them to see me.

My story to Bregman was the same as I'd used with Lenzi: his name had come up in connection with a confidential investigation, and I wanted to meet and ask some questions. He'd reacted predictably: wary silence, wary curiosity, a wary, grudging acquiescence. I'd told the same story to Lisa Welch, except with her husband's as the name that had come up. Her response surprised me.

"I thought this was over with," she'd said. "I got the check four months ago, and I thought that was it. My lawyer told me that was it." She wasn't nervous or upset, just puzzled. So was I.

"Mrs. Welch, I have no clue what you're talking about," I said.

"You're not from Connecticut Mutual?" she asked after a moment.

"No, ma'am."

"Oh . . . I apologize," she said, and agreed to see me.

New Canaan and Pound Ridge are neighboring towns, separated only by the state line, and I'd arranged my meetings for the same afternoon—Lisa at two, Bregman at five. I'd risen late this morning and gone for a run. Then, clean-shaven and breakfasted, and dressed in black pants, a maroon polo shirt, and a gray sweater, I'd picked up my rental car. It was 12:45 when my Taurus and I set off.

Getting out of the city was the usual hell—lunatic traffic, cratered streets, highways that ended without warning, road signs written by liars and idiots. I took 95 North, itself a nightmare of construction and careening trucks, and got off in Darien. Then I took 124 through the pristine, suburban splendor of Darien, and into the pristine, suburban splendor of New Canaan. The terrain grew hillier and the traffic lighter as I drove, and the houses and their properties grew larger.

The trees were bare in New Canaan, just as they were in New York—but they were much neater about it. Behind the artfully tumbled stone walls, the high-priced landscapes were brown and faded and buttoned up for winter. Leaves had been blown, bagged, and hauled away, perennials had been cut back and blanketed in straw, shrubs were swaddled in burlap, and deer fencing was strung. Lisa Welch lived off of 124, on a road that climbed up a ridge and went from hardtop to washboard about a mile before it got to her place.

The house was an old colonial with white clapboards, black shutters, and a shiny red door. It sat close to the road, on several acres of lawn, mature trees, and stone walls. It was not a huge house—four bedrooms, I guessed—but it had been meticulously renovated and updated. The double-hung windows were new and set with insulated glass. The plasterwork and wainscoting were unblemished. The floors were bird's-eye maple and perfectly laid. Halogen lights were mounted unobtrusively in the ceilings. The kitchen was outfitted with the latest high-end appliances—clad in the same cherry wood as the cabinets. And the security system was state of the art. The decor was simple, comfortable-looking, and expensive.

She'd told me to call her Lisa and ushered me through the kitchen and into the sunroom, where we'd watched her kids play outside and where she'd told me a little about Welch. He'd been fourteen years her senior. They'd met at a wedding—a cousin of hers had married a friend of his. They'd known each other less than a year when they'd gotten engaged. She'd quit her job as a preschool teacher, and they'd moved to Connecticut right after the honeymoon. They'd been married just six years when he died. He was, she said, a devoted father, and active in the church and local charities. It was a second marriage for him. The first had ended a decade before—no kids. Lisa had never met number one and didn't know where she lived. She glided across the sunroom and set the water glass down in front of me and folded herself back in her chair.

"I don't know how much I can tell you about Nick's business, John. He didn't bring it home with him. We didn't talk about it much, and I didn't know the people he worked with."

"No socializing?"

"No. Work just wasn't an all-consuming thing with him, not while I knew him."

"It used to be?"

"Oh, yes. When I first met him, it was his life. But his priorities changed."

"How so?" I asked. She smiled a little.

"He found other things. More important things. Like his family, like being a part of the community."

"Big change," I observed. She smiled again, but said nothing. She sat with one leg tucked beneath her, motionless except for her eyes, which followed her children.

"He'd been with his firm a long time?"

"Yes. He'd spent his professional life there. Over twenty years."

"Ever hear of MWB—Merchant's Worldwide Bank?" I asked. She shook her head. "How about Gerard Nassouli, or Bernhard Trautmann?" Lisa thought for a moment and shook her head again.

"As I said, I didn't know a lot about his work."

I drank some water. Outside, far away, a dog yipped. Jesse sighed, but did not stir. Lisa was perfectly still. The ball of her right foot rested lightly on the stone floor. It was a nice foot, tanned and high-arched, with well-kept toes. Silence settled over us like dust, and it was only with some effort that I spoke again.

"Lisa, forgive me for asking, but from what you said on the phone I wondered if there'd been problems with your husband's life insurance." She turned her head to look at me, her eyes a slate gray.

"We did have some, yes," she said.

"They paid off on the policy, what . . . four months ago, you said?" She nodded. "That's over a year after your husband passed away." Another nod. "That's a long time." She looked down at her long-fingered hands, resting lightly on the edge of the table.

"They had questions," she said, softly. "It took them a while to satisfy themselves."

"What kind of questions?" She pushed her hair back behind her ears and cleared her throat.

"They didn't come out and say it, not right away, but they wondered if Nick hadn't committed suicide," she said. She let out a deep breath.

"Why did they think that?"

"I really don't know, John. There was something about an exclusion period, and they said something about statistics, and the boat's service records . . . I don't know. Neither the police nor the Coast Guard shared their doubts." Jesse was dreaming, about chasing something or being chased. He growled and snuffled and whined, then settled back down. A slow, regular pulse beat in Lisa's long neck. She was otherwise motionless.

"What did you think?" I asked. She looked at me and then turned back to her children.

"I thought the suggestion was offensive and obscene, John," she said evenly. "My husband would never have taken his own life. Never." Her little girl pushed her stroller up to the French doors and waved at us. We waved back. "I don't know much about my husband's life in the time before we met. I never cared to. We were focused on the here and now, and on the future. I know he wasn't happy, back then. I know he was a . . . different person. Maybe not always a good person. But Nick changed his life when we met—for the better. He found his center, John, in being a husband and a father, in the church, in the volunteer work he did. He'd worked hard to find that. He would never have thrown it away."

"There'd been nothing odd in his mood, in how he behaved, in the days and weeks before his death? Nothing that had happened at work?"

"Nothing." She let out another sigh and looked up at the glass ceiling. "I can't tell you how many times I went over all this with the insurance people. Please don't ask me to go through it again with you." I nodded.

Jesse roused himself. He sniffed my shoes and circled the table and finally shambled over to the French doors. He looked back at Lisa and whined. She got up and let him out.

"Is any of this relevant to your case, John?" she asked. There was no reproach in her voice. She mostly sounded sleepy.

"I don't know," I said, and I meant it.

Lisa walked me to the door and gave me a warm, firm handshake. She stood, motionless, under a big, bare-limbed linden, and watched as I drove away.

I had two hours until my meeting with Bregman, time enough to grab some lunch and make some calls. I got back on 124 and continued north, over the state line. Pound Ridge is more serious money than New Canaan, and a lot of it is spent on privacy. The big houses and their parklike grounds are tucked far from the eyes of curious motorists, and all you see from the narrow, twisting roads are dense woods, empty fields, fences in studied disrepair, and, only occasionally, a nameless mailbox standing by an inconspicuous drive.

Pound Ridge doesn't have the same sort of Norman Rockwell Main Street as New Canaan. The closest it comes is Scott's Corners, a wide place on 124 with a firehouse, a high-end supermarket, and a surprising number of eateries. I parked my Taurus and went into a pizzeria. I got two slices and carried them outside and sat on a bench in the fading sunlight.

I spent the next half hour, and much of my cell phone battery, finding out that the senior claims investigator for Connecticut Mutual Insurance was one Stanislaus Kulpinski, that he had personally handled the investigation of the Welch claim, and that his office was in Stamford. Finally, I found Stan himself. He was hoarse and wheezy and old-sounding, and he chewed a lot of gum. I introduced myself and told him what I was interested in, but he wanted references before he would talk.

"Who do you know that I know? Anybody on the job in Connecticut?" he asked.

"No," I answered. "You know anybody in New York?"

"I know a lot of people," he said, and reeled off a bunch of names. None of them rang a bell, but I gave him the names of some guys I knew in the NYPD who didn't think I was something sticky on the sidewalk. "Give me your number, I'll call you in a half hour," he said. And he did, by which time I was back in my car, with my phone hooked up to the lighter.

"You want to know why I thought there was something funny with Welch? Okay. You know anything about boats?"

"Nothing," I said.

"You'll need some background, but I'll go light on the technical stuff," he said. He didn't go light enough. Twenty minutes later I knew more than I wanted to about the dangers of fire and explosion on boats with inboard, gasoline-powered engines, about how these boats were designed and equipped to ensure proper venting of volatile fumes, and about the safety practices employed by even the greenest power boater to prevent incineration. He told me about automatic sniffers, and exhaust blowers, and duct positioning, and rates of airflow through the engine compartment at various speeds. It was apparently a topic of great fascination to certain segments of the insurance industry.

"From which I gather that a boater blowing himself up in a power-boat is not a rare event," I said, when Stan had finished his discourse.

"No, not rare," he said, with a wet laugh.

"Which takes me back to my question. What got you interested in Welch?"

"Besides there being four months to go on his policy's suicide exclusion?"

"Besides that."

"Not much, at first," he began. "What happened with him wasn't so different from shit that happens every weekend. Guy took his boat out on a Saturday morning to fish. Went out real early, way before dawn. Topped off his tanks before he left. Stayed out a few hours. Then, just after sunrise, he starts up the engines to head back in and—*ka-boom.* Huge explosion. It's bad, but it happens. But you look a little closer, and you start to wonder." Stan paused to clear his throat. It sounded like a lung coming up.

"First, there were the stats. In insurance we keep statistics on all kinds of stuff, and the frequency of that kind of accident, on boats the same make, model, and age as Welch's, is low. Real low. I mean, besides Welch, it's never happened. The boat was designed so it wouldn't happen. By itself, it means nothing, but it's an attention-getter.

"Then, there was the service history. Welch took good care of that boat, and kept meticulous service records. A year before the accident, he'd had the engines overhauled, the fuel tanks checked, and the fuel lines replaced. He'd used the boat for the next year with no reported problems. Then, out of the blue, on his way back in . . . *boom.* That gets me wondering a little more.

"Next, there was Welch's experience with boats. This guy was no weekend skipper—he knew his way around, but good. This was the fifth boat he'd owned, and he'd worked in marinas from when he was twelve years old, all the way through college. Why is that important? Well, for his boat to go up like that, the buildup of fumes must've been intense. It's hard to believe he didn't smell anything topside, and impossible that he'd miss it when he checked below. Unless he didn't check below. Unless Mr. Experienced forgot the most basic safety precaution in a gas-powered boat and didn't check for fumes before he started up. Now I'm really getting curious.

"Finally, there was the fishing. Turns out that Saturday-morning fishing was a regular thing with him—spring, summer, and fall. He'd been out ten weeks in a row prior to the blast. Eight of those ten weeks, his fishing buddy—guy lives over in Wilton—went with him. In fact, best I could tell, this guy had gone with Welch twenty-one of his last twenty-five Saturday-morning trips. But the Wednesday before this last one, Welch calls his pal to cancel. Said something had come up. Still don't know what that 'something' was." Stan paused again. I heard gum wrappers crinkling, and his chewing got more vigorous. "Now I'm thinking so much, it makes my head hurt."

"Nobody else—the local cops, the Coast Guard—get a headache over this?" I asked. Stan chuckled a little. It turned into a wheeze.

"Just me. 'Course, the local cops got, what, fifteen guys on the force, oldest one has maybe a dozen years' experience. And I think one of 'em had actually been on a boat once. As for the Coasties . . . well, they know their shit, no question. But they're kind of jaded. They see so many people doing such incredibly stupid shit on the water, there's nothing they won't believe about how dumb a person can be. And to tell the truth, I didn't have much else to go on. To all appearances, the guy was happily married, in good health, had more money than God. No evidence of depression or mental instability. No sign that he or his wife was a cheater. And the wife—she had no interest in the claim. Didn't give a damn if she got paid or not."

"Any sign that somebody else was involved?" I asked.

"Not a one."

"You talk to the fishing buddy?"

"Till I was blue in the face. He said the same as everybody else—Welch was a happy guy with everything to live for."

"So, you finally convinced yourself it was accidental?" Stan laughed, more loudly this time.

"Hell no. After thirty years of this, I know the guy did himself in. I just got tired of trying to prove it." His laughter dissolved into a fit of coughing. It sounded like the other lung was coming up.

Steven Bregman lived a few miles from Scott's Corners, on a bumpy lane that ran off of Old Stone Hill Road. A pair of brick columns and a scuffed red mailbox marked the entrance to his property. It was almost five and dark out, and I passed by three times before I found it. The gravel drive was smooth and bordered by a line of tall firs. I followed it for half a mile, and then I saw a clearing, and light from spots mounted high in the trees.

The drive ended in a large, brick-paved circle. In the center was a stone fountain surrounded by curved stone benches and well-groomed shrubs. The main house was at twelve o'clock. It was a handsome, Italianate pile in brick and stone, two generous stories tall, with a slate roof and decorative brackets on the overhanging eaves. There were lots of windows, all tall and arched and framed in dressed stone. There was more stone along the foundation, and around the entrance portico too. A tower with four windows and a dangerous-looking finial rose above the roofline at one end of the house. At the other, there was a deep, arcaded porch that wrapped around to the back. The windows were dark.

At nine o'clock, set well back from the circle, was a carriage house. It was long and low and built in the same style as the residence, but with six pairs of wide, wooden doors dominating its facade. One pair was opened, and I saw a Bentley resting comfortably inside. There were lights on at the end of the building closest to the main house. I pulled the Taurus up to the opened bay. Someone called to me as I climbed out.

"You March?" I recognized Bregman's nasal voice and heavy New York accent from the telephone. He was standing in a narrow doorway at the lit-up end of the carriage house. "I'm in the office," he said. He made a "come on" gesture and went inside. I walked across the bricks and through the opened door.

The end of the carriage house had been partitioned off from the car bays to make Bregman's big office. The walls were brick, three of them broken up by tall windows. The long wall on my left was mostly high, built-in shelving, packed with glass bric-a-brac and with a wet bar at the far end. Bright lights hung amid the old beams and rafters.

There was a desk across the room, with a polished stone top. There were two flat-screened monitors on it, and two keyboards, and some neat stacks of paper next to an open metal briefcase. Bregman stood behind it.

He was a tall, skinny guy of about fifty who looked like a vulture. He had rounded shoulders and a long curved neck with lots of extra skin around his large Adam's apple. His head was narrow and topped with wiry black hair. His brows were black and wiry too, and his dark eyes were set deep and close to his bony nose. The shadow of a heavy beard darkened his sallow skin. His mouth was small and mean and lipless. He wore tan trousers, a green sweater over a blue shirt, and brown loafers. He sat, and eyed the inside of his briefcase as if it were a carcass.

Bregman didn't look up as I crossed the room, or offer me his hand to shake or a place to sit, either. I sat anyway, in one of the two yellow leather chairs that faced his desk.

"You said you had some questions. Go ahead and ask them. But make it quick; I'm pressed for time." He spoke fast and didn't look at me.

"I'll get to it, then," I said. "You know Gerard Nassouli?" Bregman was silent. He kept picking through his briefcase, and after a while I thought he hadn't heard me. I was about to repeat the question when he responded.

"Am I supposed to?" he said. He managed to make it sound bored, distracted, and snide, all at once. He was annoying me.

"Well, I suppose you do—that's why I'm here. But I wanted to hear you say it." He glanced up at me.

"Your tone's kind of arrogant for someone who's sitting in my house, asking for my time," he said, but there wasn't much force to it, and he seemed more interested in his briefcase. I didn't say anything. "Where am I supposed to know this guy from?" he asked.

"He ran MWB in New York, and maybe you did some business with him fifteen years ago or so." Bregman glanced over at me again, still distracted, and nodded a little—I wasn't sure at what.

"And if I did know the guy, so what?" he asked, his eyes flicking back to me again.

"Then I've got other things to talk to you about," I said.

"Other things like what?"

"Other things like blackmail."

He nodded to himself some more. He took a small stack of business cards from his briefcase, squared the edges, and put them next to a stack of papers on the desk. His long, pale hands were shaking a little. He pulled a few more papers from his case, put a few others in, closed the case, and stood it on the floor. Then he opened a drawer in the desk, and took out a slim, black semiautomatic pistol and pointed it at me.

"You greedy bastard," he said. His voice was quavering with rage and fear and a rush of adrenaline. "What's the matter, motherfucker, you didn't bleed me enough the first time? You want more?" His thin lips were white, and so were his nostrils and the fingers of his right hand around the pistol grip. It didn't look like he'd had a lot of experience shooting, but that didn't matter much. I'd be awfully hard to miss at this range. He was swallowing a lot and his big Adam's apple was jumping up and down. His hands shook more. Mine might too if I moved them, but I didn't. I kept them, and the rest of me, perfectly still.

"You've got the wrong guy, Bregman," I said slowly, but Bregman cut me off.

"*I* got the wrong guy? *You* got the wrong guy, motherfucker. *You* got the wrong guy." His voice was tight, like he was trying to yell but couldn't get enough air to do it. He got up and came around the desk. His movements were stiff and jerky, but he kept the gun on me the whole time, pointed mostly at my head. He stood in front of me.

"You think I'm going to take this shit? Get up, you cocksucker," he said. I started to rise, slowly, and as I did he backhanded me across the face with the gun. At least, he tried to. But I don't think he'd ever hit anyone before, and he didn't do it well or quickly. I sat back down as he pushed the gun at me. I drew my head back a little and with my left hand grabbed his wrist and the gun as they passed by my face. I twisted hard and felt something snap and Bregman screamed. I stood up and as I did I brought my right knee into his crotch. I got him dead on and with a lot of momentum behind me, and his scream turned into a weird bellow, like his intestines were going to come out of his mouth. He went down on his hands and knees, and then screamed again and collapsed on his right elbow, with his right hand out at an odd angle. Then he threw up.

My chair had tipped over, and Bregman's gun was underneath it. I righted the chair and picked up the gun. It was a Beretta. The new ones have this cool automatic safety that engages if you drop them, and it had worked as advertised. I set the manual safety too and slid the clip out. There was nothing in the chamber. I put the clip in my pocket and stuck the gun in my belt behind my back. My hands and knees were shaking now. I took some slow, deep breaths.

Bregman was in a fetal position and still retching. He was crying too. Shit. I got a glass of water from the wet bar and drank it. Then I drank another. I filled it again and got some ice from the little fridge and wrapped it in a bar towel and brought it and the water and some more bar towels to Bregman.

I got him into one of the yellow chairs and helped him clean himself up a little. When I was sure he wouldn't retch anymore, I gave him some water and wrapped his wrist in the bar towel with the ice. Then I pulled the other yellow chair over and sat down facing him.

"Now, would you care to tell me just what the fuck your problem is?" I asked.

Chapter Sixteen

I fished in my pockets for exact change, but all I had were bullets. They don't like ammo in the toll baskets at the Triboro Bridge, so I slowed and steered the Taurus into the single lane reserved for unfortunates with only paper money.

The bullets were from Steven Bregman's Beretta. I'd given the gun back to him, minus the clip, when we'd concluded our little chat. I'd left the empty clip in the mailbox at the top of his driveway, and kept the bullets. It wasn't that I didn't trust the guy . . . or maybe it was.

A sprained wrist and a kick in the balls had temporarily drained Bregman of his violence and galloping paranoia, but had left him by turns self-pitying, self-justifying, and conspiratorial. It was an unattractive mix. Still, Bregman was my pot of gold. When I'd got him calmed down, and explained why I was there—and convinced him that it wasn't to stick him up—he'd told all. Almost all, anyway.

The first fax had come to his office about a year ago, with a cover sheet that read: "We'll talk soon." The documents in it, according to Bregman, were a trumped-up, out-of-context misrepresentation of dealings he'd had with Nassouli, a long time before. The second fax had arrived a few days later. It had the same cover sheet as the first, but its contents were even more toxic. Bregman wouldn't tell me anything about his business with Nassouli, or anything specific about what had been sent to him in the faxes, but whatever it was had shaken him badly. And, he'd told me, it would've sent his investors running for the hills. So when the third one showed up, he'd been inclined to follow instructions.

It had come two weeks later, and it was short, just a single page. It named an amount—Bregman wouldn't say how much—that he was to have available in a week's time. He would receive transfer instructions then, and he would have to act on them immediately. Bregman did as he was told. A week later, in the early morning, the last fax came. It gave him four hours to wire the money to a numbered account at a bank in Luxembourg. Bregman had met the deadline, and hadn't heard a word since.

But from then on, he'd been brooding over what had happened, and been waiting for the other shoe to drop. It had driven him nuts. A few months after making the payment, Bregman's anger and fear had reached the boiling point. He couldn't take it anymore; he couldn't just sit there; he had to do something. What he did was hire himself a PI—he wouldn't tell me who—to identify the blackmailer. Though he never said, I got the feeling that for Bregman this was the first step in some dark revenge fantasy he'd been nurturing.

Bregman had hobbled his own efforts from the start, however. He hadn't told his investigator anything about the first two faxes, or given him any background on Nassouli or MWB, which had left the guy with nothing to go on besides the delivery instructions. After two months in Luxembourg, his investigator had mainly found out how seriously they take their banking secrecy over there. The funds had been transferred out moments after they'd come in, and the account had been closed the same day. Neither guile, nor threats, nor bribery had been sufficient to discover anything else.

Besides the story he'd had to tell, Bregman wasn't too helpful. He had no theories on who might've been behind the blackmail, beyond "Gerry, the motherfucker." And he recalled Trautmann only as "that psycho security guy."

His fretting and whining over his wrist and groin grew louder as our conversation wore on, but the thought that his blackmailer was victimizing other people had clearly cheered Bregman up. He couldn't keep the smile from his sour little mouth or the glint from his narrow eyes. He'd tried inexpertly but persistently to find out who my client was, and when that didn't pan out he'd tried to bribe me. I left before I kicked him in the nuts again.

I made it through the tolls and across the bridge and, finally, to the southbound FDR Drive. It was ten o'clock when I pulled the Taurus into a garage on Seventeenth Street. I gave the guy there something extra in his tip and told him to keep the car close. I'd be leaving early tomorrow.

Bellerose is a small, working-class neighborhood at the edge of Queens, hemmed in by parkways and right up against the Nassau County line. Belmont, where the horses run, is just next door. It's an old neighborhood, mostly Irish and Italian and German and Polish. Lots of cops, lots of firemen, lots of guys in the trades.

It's about fifteen miles east of Manhattan, and to get there you take the Midtown Tunnel to the Long Island Expressway. You stay on the LIE, past the crowded Calvary and Mt. Zion Cemeteries, through the blighted stretches of Rego Park, past Shea Stadium and the strange relics of the '64 World's Fair, out to exit 30. From there you pick up the Cross Island Parkway, and take it south a few exits, past a park and a golf course and the frightening hulk of Creedmore Psychiatric, to Hillside Avenue. That's where you get off.

It was 4:45 on Friday morning, overcast and still dark, with the temperature hovering near forty degrees, when I made the turn onto Hillside. I was in my Taurus, a thermos of coffee, a peanut butter sandwich, and a liter of water on the seat next to me, a pair of binoculars and a camera on the floor, and a Glock 30 digging into the small of my back.

I'd come to talk to Bernhard Trautmann. My story was going to be the same as the one I'd told to Al Burrows—that I was doing research for a writer interested in MWB. But I really didn't care if Trautmann bought it or not. Given what I'd heard about the guy, I wasn't expecting pleasant chitchat over tea and cakes. I was going to stir him up and see what happened. I'd come out here early in the hopes of getting a look at him before the stirring started.

Hillside Avenue is a gritty, commercial street. It runs east-west, with two lanes going in each direction, and a concrete strip in between and traffic lights every five paces. The buildings along it are small, low, flat-roofed, and ugly. They're faced in brick and fake stone and stuff that looks like roofing shingle, and they house a dense assortment of businesses. Mom-and-pop groceries, auto-body shops, hardware stores, diners, pizzerias, banks, pet stores, bars, and check-cashing places. Most of the storefronts were dark when I drove by, their steel security curtains still rolled down.

The residential streets run off of Hillside. The houses are a mix of one- and two-family units, 1950s-vintage, built shoulder to shoulder on tiny lots. They're small and boxy, and they look like little motels: one or two low stories; shallow, gabled roofs; cement steps from the street to the front doors; narrow, metal-railed porches; metal-framed windows looking out on swatches of lawn no bigger than a bathmat. Some of the houses are clad in brick, others in stucco or aluminum or an odd, wood-grained plastic. Some of them have ribbons of grass along the sides; others have strips of gravel or packed dirt. Some have small garages under the main floor; others have them out back, like big tool sheds in the tiny yards. Some have no garages at all. Otherwise, they look pretty much alike.

Most of the houses on Trautmann's street were already strung with Christmas lights, but not Trautmann's. His place was a neat, two-story box in beige stucco. It was on a corner lot, and had a short driveway on the side, leading to a small, detached garage in back. Apart from its lack of decoration, it didn't look too different from the rest of the houses on the block, but it had a shuttered, battened-down feel that the others didn't. Chest-high schoolyard fencing ran around the property, and a high, thick hedge filled the narrow gap between the fence and the house. The hedge ran along the fence in the back too, and screened the little yard from view. Shades were drawn over the windows, but light bled around the edges of one upstairs.

The place next door was a clone of Trautmann's, but in brick and without the fence or the hedge. There was a For Sale sign out front, and it looked vacant. The house behind his was another clone, with aluminum siding. It had a fenced backyard, where a hefty Rottweiler was bounding around and barking deeply.

The block was not ideal for parking and watching. There was almost no traffic at this hour, and even later in the day it wouldn't be heavy. What there was would mainly come from the locals. Even in my bland Taurus, I was going to stick out like a sore thumb to the residents, who would know their neighbors, and their cars, by sight.

I went around the block and parked on the cross street, about forty yards off the corner, behind a van and diagonally across the intersection from Trautmann's house. I killed my engine and cracked the windows to keep them from steaming up. His place was one of the few around with lights burning, and I hoped that meant I wouldn't have to wait long to get a glimpse of him. As it turned out, I didn't.

The Rottweiler's barking became louder and more insistent, and when I looked up the street I could see why. A man was running, headed in my direction. He was going at a good pace and had a fluid, efficient stride. He passed into the cone of light cast by a streetlamp, and I could see his breath condensing in front of him. He looked like a big guy, even at this distance, maybe two inches taller than me, and lean. He swung around the corner and pulled up at Trautmann's front stoop and checked his watch. Then he started to stretch. I picked up my binoculars.

He was wearing gray shorts and a gray sweatshirt with no sleeves, and the muscles in his broad shoulders and long arms and legs stood out like cables. His hands were like phonebooks. There was a faded tattoo of a scorpion on his right shoulder and a ropy, red scar down his left forearm. He did hamstring stretches, and then stretched his quads and his Achilles tendons. He stretched slowly and for a long time, and though he was big there was nothing awkward or abrupt in his movements. There was instead something serpentine.

His dark hair was brush-cut with some gray at the sides. His face was taut and narrow, with lots of planes and prominent bones—narrow, deep-set eyes, bony brow, small, sharp nose, high cheeks, and a thin mouth. His skin was the only thing that hinted at his fifty-three years. It was weathered and lined, as if he'd spent a lot of time in the wind or squinting at the sun. It made him look more like a cowboy in an advertisement than an ex-cop from Queens. I lowered my binoculars, picked up the camera, and took a half-dozen shots, full-face and profile.

He was doing hamstring stretches on the stairs when I realized that he was, unhurriedly and quite casually, checking out the street and the intersection—up and down and all around. I was on the shadowed side of the street and mostly hidden by the van, and the light was still pretty thin, so I didn't think he'd seen me. But I was impressed by whatever it was in his reptile brain that had told him to look around, and cautioned by how smoothly he'd done it. He did one more set of quad stretches, climbed the stairs, and went inside.

I didn't see him again for over an hour, during which time I drank my coffee, ate half my sandwich, and got suspicious looks from the few people who noticed me parked there. The neighborhood was waking and traffic had picked up, and I was thinking of moving to another street when a black Audi A8 backed out of Trautmann's driveway. Trautmann was at the wheel. I waited a bit, then pulled out after him. He was headed toward Hillside.

I let a few cars get between us, and a few more when we turned onto Hillside. Working solo, it's nearly impossible to tail anyone except a serious idiot for any length of time without being made. Trautmann was no idiot, and I knew he'd spot me sooner or later. I just wanted it to be later. There weren't too many A8s in this neck of the woods, so I could hang well back. He drove east for a couple of miles, into Nassau County, then pulled in at a diner. I drove past. It was a twenty-four-hour spot and looked busy. There was a doughnut place across the street, also doing good business. I circled the block and pulled into its side lot. I went inside, used the bathroom, filled my thermos with coffee, and bought three chocolate doughnuts. Then I went back to my Taurus. I had a partial view of the diner from there, of the door and the cash register. I waited and tried to make my doughnuts last.

Every so often, I took a discreet look with the binoculars. I couldn't see much—a piece of the counter, a tough-looking waitress working behind it, the cash register on a counter by the door, a big, friendly-looking, white-haired guy manning it, people entering, people paying up, people leaving. The big guy seemed to know most of the customers, and he laughed and chatted with nearly everyone who came and went.

I'd been out there long enough to finish my doughnuts and make a good dent in my coffee when, through the binoculars, I saw the big guy stiffen. His wide grin vanished and his whole face tightened, and he seemed suddenly very interested in his countertop. A second later, Trautmann strolled up to the register. He handed the big guy a check and a bill, and the big guy rang it up and gave him change. The whole time, Trautmann was Mr. Friendly—smiling, talking, laughing—but the big guy said not a word. Trautmann pocketed the change and clapped the big guy on the shoulder with one of his huge hands. The big guy flinched, and he watched Trautmann all the way out the door.

Trautmann walked across the diner lot. He was wearing a black leather field jacket over a gray shirt, well-tailored gray pants, and black cowboy boots. I took some more photos. He got into his car and pulled out, still headed east. I did the same. More businesses had opened and traffic had picked up considerably, and there were plenty of cars between us now. He stayed on Hillside through New Hyde Park and

Williston Park. When he got to East Williston he turned off, onto Roslyn Road, and headed north. After two miles he turned off Roslyn Road and pulled into the parking lot of a crappy-looking mall that called itself Roslyn Meadows.

It was a meadow of cracked asphalt, surrounding a corrugated metal heap that looked like the bad marriage of two airplane hangars. There was a discount electronics store at one end of the place and a down-market department store at the other, and lots of space for rent in between. It was still early, just after eight, and the lot was mostly empty. The few cars that were there were clustered around the ends.

I kept on going when Trautmann turned in. I saw his car cross the lot and disappear behind the building. I went down Roslyn Road another quarter mile, turned around at a Burger King, and drove back to the mall. I parked near the electronics store, next to a rusting pickup, and walked around back. Trautmann's Audi was parked about halfway down, near some dumpsters and a loading dock. There weren't many other cars there. There wasn't much at all besides chewed-up asphalt, a sagging metal fence, and a field of weeds beyond it. I went around to the front and went inside.

The holiday crowds hadn't turned up at Roslyn Meadows yet, and if they did, I suspected it would be to visit the OTB parlor. Still, the mall was ready for them, and decked out in its cheesy holiday best. Styrofoam candy canes and paper garland and mangy plastic trees abounded, and even the windows of the vacant stores—and there were quite a few of these—had been hung with paper reindeer. A fountain had been drained and transformed into something that was supposed to be Santa's workshop, though it looked more like Santa's grimy basement. Its centerpiece was a big wooden chair where Junior could be photo-graphed while he wailed and thrashed on Santa's lap. Neither Santa nor the elves were in yet. Probably still sleeping it off, or maybe down at the OTB. They did have the Christmas music cranking, though—"Santa Baby," one of my favorites. I was wearing a black sweatshirt and jeans and paddock boots, and a field jacket to cover my gun. I was overdressed for Roslyn Meadows.

A few food stalls were opened, including one that sold pretzels slathered in butter and cinnamon. A security guard leaned at the counter, eating one and dripping melted butter on his radio. He was maybe twenty-one, about five foot seven and a hundred and thirty pounds. His hair was already thinning, and he had bad skin and a ratty moustache. He wore a blue and gray uniform with Trident Metro Security patches on the shoulders and over the breast pocket. I saw a couple of his comrades as I strolled farther down the mall, but I didn't see Trautmann.

At the midpoint of the mall, a wide corridor branched off to the left, leading to more vacant storefronts, the mall offices, the loading dock, and the rear parking lot. Trautmann was at the far end, with a tall, stocky guy in a Trident uniform. Trautmann had his big hand on the guy's shoulder, and they were walking away from me, toward the doors to the loading dock. They went through, and the corridor was empty. I walked down. There was no one in the mall offices; the corridor was still empty. I walked farther down. The doors to the loading dock were ajar.

"I know how it is, Brian," I heard a voice say. It was a deep, friendly voice, with a heavy New York accent and wry, amused undertones. It was a voice you could have a couple of beers with, and a laugh about the general ridiculousness of things. "You need a little extra cash, a little more than I'm paying you, so you move a little weed, maybe some crank. I know how it goes, Brian, believe me—"

Brian cut him off. "I swear, Bernie, it was just the once. No shit, just one time." Brian was young and scared. "I got jammed up with this guy in Hempstead, and I had almost all the cash, and I went down to AC to get the rest, and nothing worked for me. I mean nothing. Not the craps, not the slots, not blackjack—I couldn't do nothing." Brian was practically wetting his pants. "And then the guy was really squeezing me, I mean bad, and I was scared and . . . I fucked up, Bernie, I know it. It was my bad, but it was just the once, I swear."

Trautmann was laughing. "AC? Jesus, Brian, how fucking stupid was that? And playing the slots? What were you thinking? Shit, you might as well take your money and burn it—save yourself the trip." He laughed some more, very relaxed. Mr. Friendly. "So, did it work—the dealing? Did you pay the guy off? He leaving you alone?" Mr. Friendly-Concerned now.

"Yeah, yeah he is." Brian was relaxing. "Jesus, what a fucking prick that guy is, too. A big fucking hard-on." Laughing now.

"Don't you hate that?" Trautmann asked, chuckling. "Don't you just fucking hate that?" And then there was a loud, wet, cracking sound—like a watermelon hitting pavement, and a startled cry and the sound of a body falling down.

"Gee, did that hurt, Bri? I guess that was my bad, huh?" Trautmann said, laughing. "Now don't go crying like some kind of pussy, Bri. Be a man, for chrissakes. Here . . . stuff this in your mouth if you can't fucking control yourself." And then there was another cracking sound and muffled sobbing.

"So, this Hempstead guy's a real hard-on, huh Bri, a real prick? Jeez, what does that make me? Fucking Mickey Mouse? Is that what I am, Brian?" Another crack, and then a bunch of dull thuds, like a sack of potatoes falling down stairs. More stifled sobs. "You think I give a shit what you do? You can fucking sell skag to babies for all I care. Just don't do it on my time, or at one of my places." A flurry of smacking sounds, like somebody pounding cutlets, and then some pleading words I couldn't make out.

"Shh . . . shh . . . take it easy, now, take it easy." Some shuffling and dragging sounds. "There you go, there you go . . . jeez, Brian, you fucking pissed yourself. Yuck." Trautmann was laughing harder. "Okay, okay. Give me your wallet. Fuck, I'm not going to touch it. Just take the money out." Trautmann chuckled. I heard bills folding. "You still driving that Camry? Yeah? Give me the keys. You're going to send me the title when you get home today, right?" I heard jingling, then a quick shuffling of feet and a loud smack and another desperate moan. "Just so you don't forget to send my title, yeah?" Then, the sounds of someone brushing off his hands and his clothes.

"Got to boogie, Bri, it's been a blast. You go clean yourself up and then you get the fuck out of here, 'cause if I see you again, you're going to think this was a walk in the park. *Capice,* buddy?" The outer door opened and closed, and then all I heard was Brian's exhausted sobbing, my own heart pounding, and "Rockin' Rudolf" playing through the loudspeakers.

The corridor was still empty. A ribbon of sweat slid down my spine. I headed back the way I'd come, at a jog. The mall was still pretty empty. I pushed through the doors to the parking lot and spotted my Taurus. The rusting pickup was gone, and in its place was a black Audi A8. I walked toward it. Trautmann got out and rested his forearms on the roof of the car and looked across at me.

"Do I know you?" he asked, smiling. "I mean, we've spent so much time together today, I feel like I should fucking know you." His smile was broad and a little ironic, and there was an amused look in his narrow blue eyes. His leather jacket hung open, and I saw an automatic holstered under his left arm. I looked at him a while. His smile never wavered.

"We don't know each other, Bernie, not yet. But I think maybe we should," I said.

"Ohhh . . . you know my name," he said in mock terror. "I got goose bumps all over." He was still smiling. "You have some business with me—need to hire on some security, maybe? Or maybe you got a crush on me, looking for a pair of my shorts to sniff?"

"I'm sure your underwear's really cool, but I just want to talk."

"Talk is great, I love it. Can't get enough talk. We can sit down and have some cocktails and talk our fucking heads off, just as soon as you tell me who you are and what you want and why you're following me all over the fucking place." He was still smiling, and his eyes hadn't left me.

"My name's March, and I want to talk to you about MWB and Gerard Nassouli," I said. I didn't expect he'd go pale and break out in a sweat and get weak in the knees and confess all—though it would've been nice. I didn't think he'd go for his gun and shout, "You'll never take me alive" and start blazing away, either. I wasn't expecting anything dramatic, and Trautmann didn't disappoint me. The smile stayed fixed, and so did the gaze. He didn't bat an eyelash. He just was quiet for a couple of beats.

"You're not a fed." It wasn't a question. He looked at me some more. "Not a cop. You private?" I nodded. His smile widened a little. "Maybe while we talk you want me to throw in some tips on running a tail, huh? I mean—no offense, buddy—but you were fucking terrible. You might as well have been riding in the car with me." I smiled but didn't say anything. Trautmann held his hands up. "Hey—I'm just busting balls. It's a bitch to do with just one guy, I know. Who'd you say you're working for?"

"I didn't," I answered and kept on smiling. Trautmann laughed. We stood there for a while, looking at each other and smiling, a couple of smart guys, wise to the world. Then I told him my story about the writer. He nodded while I told it, like it was the most reasonable thing he'd ever heard.

"A writer . . . that's cool. I'm a big reader—love reading the way I love talking. Maybe I read some of this guy's books. What's his name?"

"You'd probably know it, Bernie. He's a pretty well-known guy. And that's the thing—until he decides he's going to take on this project, he doesn't want his name mentioned. Afraid it might get too many other people interested—kind of muddy the waters." He nodded again, like this was just getting more and more reasonable.

"Muddy waters . . . yeah, I hate that shit too. And you want to talk about the bad old days, huh? Well, I'll tell you . . . you got a first name there, March?"

"John."

"I'll tell you, Johnny, I spent about a million hours under the hot lights, talking to Uncle about the bad old days—everything about 'em, down to what socks I wore and when—and I'm pretty fucking talked out on that subject. Know what I mean? But, shit, I tell you what—you go down to Federal Plaza, and tell the boys down there they have my okay to tell you everything I said to them. You tell 'em Bernie sent you. They'll fix you right up." He laughed deeply. Then he put his hands up again. "Hey—I'm just busting balls again, Johnny. I can't help myself, I swear. I need like a twelve-step or something. Seriously, you want to talk a little? You got some questions? I'll see if I can help you out." It was my turn to nod, like I believed every word. "Come on, let's go grab some coffee. Or you want something stronger?" he asked.

"Coffee's good," I said.

"There's a Starbucks up the street. Hop in; I'll bring you back here after."

I shook my head. "Right here is fine with me. I want to try one of those pretzel things."

"Whatever," Trautmann said, shrugging. He shut his car door and locked it with an electronic key. He walked around the car toward me. I stepped back a few paces and gestured for him to go first through the glass doors, into the mall. He smiled some more and walked ahead of me.

"Business must suck, huh, if the best you can do is that fucking rent-a-ride," he said, walking ahead of me and chuckling. "Shit, there I go again. I told you, I can't help it." He reached for the doors, and an alarm exploded behind me.

He was fast—very fast. I was looking for it—waiting for it—and all the same he nearly cleaned my clock. I started when the alarm blared—my eyes flickered involuntarily to the Audi, and my attention wavered for a half second—less. But it was enough for him. Trautmann pivoted into a high, fast, spinning kick, and if I hadn't been already tensed and waiting it would've taken my head clean off.

I leaned away and tried to block it with my right arm, but his boot tagged me on the shoulder and slid off and grazed my head above the ear. My arm went numb, and I heard the muffled *whump* before I felt the impact and saw the stars. I rolled with it, then bent and pivoted on my right foot and threw a kick backward at him with my left. I don't know what I was aiming at or if I was aiming, but I caught him on the hip as he was setting up another kick. It threw him off balance and sent him skidding backward into the doors. I followed fast and covered up with my right arm, which was still mostly useless, and caught him once with my left fist in the kidneys and again with my forearm in the face. It was like hitting a sandbag.

Trautmann grunted, and tagged me hard in the ribs with a short left. Then he grabbed a massive handful of my sweatshirt and dragged me in close and brought down two big, fast overhand rights. I caught some of them on my left arm, but not enough. His fist was like a sack full of cobblestones, and now my left arm was numb. A few more of those would send me down. I stepped in closer to him and jammed my left thumb at his eye. He saw it coming and turned his head, but he didn't see my right thumb. It caught him in the soft part of the throat, under his Adam's apple, and I dug in hard. He gagged and drew back a little, and when he did I slammed my head down on his nose. I heard a liquid crunch.

"Fuck!" he roared, and I pushed him away and my shirt tore and he stumbled backward, holding a hunk of it. "Motherfucker!" he yelled. He scrabbled upright and had his hand on his gun and stopped when he saw the Glock in mine.

He stood there, coiled in a half crouch, breathing hard, his hand on the butt of his gun, looking at me. His nose was bleeding and it was pulpy looking and might have been broken. There was an angry purple patch at the base of his throat, and a welt on his cheek. But there was no hatred in his eyes and no anger—no emotion at all—just cold appraisal.

My heart was pounding, and it was tough to hold the gun steady. Feeling was coming back in my right arm, but I didn't know how it'd take the recoil if I had to shoot him. Then he dropped his hand and put his palms out and stood up, relaxed and smiling. I took a deep breath and stepped back a couple of paces.

"I guess we're not going to have that talk, huh?" I said, after a while. Trautmann snorted.

"Oh, we'll talk, Johnny," he said, chuckling. His voice was raspy. "I'll do a little homework, and then we'll have a long talk. See, I know something about you now. I know you're not just a pussy PI like I thought. I know you're quick, and you take a punch pretty good. And next time we talk, I'll know even more. We'll have a great fucking conversation." He blew his nose onto the pavement, and a lot of blood came out. He looked at it and shook his head and smiled. "That's a promise," he said, and he went through the doors into the mall, laughing to himself.

I walked back to my Taurus and leaned against it and took some deep breaths. I looked around. The lot was quiet. The traffic on Roslyn Road was sparse and distant. It was a quiet, cold, gray day. It was barely nine-thirty. The adrenaline was starting to ebb, and my arms and legs were shaking. Pain was starting to register. The cut above my right ear was bleeding down the right side of my face. The other side was tender and starting to swell, and the inside of my mouth was cut. I was pretty sure I had a busted rib, and my arms would soon be a purple mess. I got in the car and drank some water and breathed some more. I put my gun on the seat next to me, and then I left Roslyn Meadows, and drove slowly and carefully back into the city.

Chapter Seventeen

"*Ai-yah*," Jane Lu gasped, "what happened to you?" She was getting off the elevator as I was getting on. She was dressed in an orange turtleneck, khaki pants, and a black leather jacket. Her perfect brow was knit with concern, and her mouth was set in a small frown.

"I'd smile insouciantly, but my face hurts too much. What are you doing home now? I thought you had a real job." It was Friday afternoon, and I was just back from the St. Vincent's emergency room, where I'd been poked, prodded, scanned, and pronounced more or less fit. Rest, ibuprofen, call if I started seeing things, lay off running for a couple of weeks. The pills they'd given me hadn't fully kicked in, and I was still enveloped in a thin haze of pain.

"I'm the boss, I just pretend to work," Jane said, distractedly. She was looking at the bruising along the side of my face and the cut above my ear. "Have you seen a doctor?"

"It's not as bad as it looks," I said.

"Have you seen a doctor?" she repeated.

"Yes, and I got a clean bill of health," I answered. "No broken bones, no concussion, didn't even need any stitches. Just a cracked rib. Not bad, all things considered."

"What happened?" she asked, still examining my face. She reached up and, very lightly, touched my left cheek. It was an unconscious gesture on her part and completely unexpected. I felt the delicate contact of her fingertips like an electrical surge, and I flinched in surprise. She withdrew them quickly. "Did I hurt you? I'm sorry."

"No . . . no, it's okay." I shook my head. *That* hurt.

"So, what happened?" she asked again.

"Workplace injury," I said

"Nice workplace. Do you need anything? From the drugstore, or the market?"

"Thanks, but I'm fine." She nodded but continued to frown.

"Well, if you do . . ." She reached into her tiny black purse and pulled out a business card and a pen and wrote quickly. "My office number is the same as Lauren's; my home number is on the back. Give a call." She handed me the card, and then she was gone. I got on the elevator and pushed 4. I looked at Jane's card on the way up. Her writing was precise and angular, like the writing on a blueprint. Her fragrance lingered faintly.

I hadn't seen Jane since Thanksgiving, when we'd shared the ride home. She'd sat wrapped in a big, black coat in the back of the cab, and I'd watched the play of light and shadow over her face as we rolled through the quiet streets. She hadn't said much, but when she did speak, her soft voice had sounded close, as if her lips were at my ear. Heat seemed to emanate from her, like a kind of perfume.

Jane's cell phone had chirped just as the cab slowed in front of our building, and it had startled us both. She'd answered, and listened in silence for a few moments. When she did speak, it was in Chinese. I didn't understand a word of it, but I saw tightness in her face and heard frustration and annoyance in her voice. She'd switched to English at the end.

"Look, I'm busy right now. And I don't know why we keep having this conversation—especially now that the day is over. I'll call you tomorrow." She'd snapped the phone shut. I'd seen her to her door, and there'd been a brief, confusing silence before we'd said good night.

I put her card on the kitchen counter, took off my jacket, and winced as muscles slid over my cracked rib. The pain was annoying, but, in truth, I'd gotten off easy. A couple of inches this way or that, a half step here, a half second there, and I would have gotten my ass severely kicked. I'd been lucky, and I knew it. But I wasn't up to deep contemplation of fate just then. What I needed was a soak, some food, and a lot of sleep.

I ran a bath and stripped off my clothes. My arms and shoulders were already looking like an LA sunset, and my side, around the busted rib, was a purple egg of pain. They'd look worse before they looked better. I eased myself into the tub, and sank down till just my head was above the water. I didn't come out until I was wrinkled and rubbery and my pain was at a respectable distance.

I pulled on sweatpants and a T-shirt and flicked on some lights against the fading day. A couple of calls had gone to voice mail while I was in the tub, and I retrieved the messages. One was from Mike's secretary, Fran. I'd left Mike a rambling message before I'd gone to St. Vincent's. Fran had called to tell me he was in court all day, but that he wanted me to meet him for lunch tomorrow, at his place.

The other message was from Clare. Her voice was nearly lost in the traffic sound. "Hi. I'll be down in your neck of the woods later on. Hope you're around." Great.

I made myself a couple of tuna sandwiches and brought them to the table, along with a quart of milk and what was left of a box of Oreos. I was just finishing the Oreos when the intercom squawked. Shit.

"Jesus—did you walk into a bus or something?" Clare stood in the doorway and looked me up and down with some shock. "Look at your arms—and your head." Her voice was scratchy, as it always was, like she'd just woken up and gargled with Scotch. She took off her long coat and sat on the sofa with her feet together and her coat across her knees. Her pale hair was loose and parted in the middle. It framed her narrow face and made her look more gaunt than usual—her gray eyes larger, and her cheekbones more pronounced. She had on a black sweater with a scooped neck, black jeans, and black brogues. She had diamonds at her ears and on her finger, and her big, steel watch on her wrist. She looked at me some more and winced.

"That is ugly. Does it hurt?"

"Only when I breathe." I lowered myself into a chair across from her. It was a deep one, and getting out would not be fun.

"It's nothing serious, right? You'll be okay?"

"I'm fine," I said. She shook her head slightly, then she looked away, out the windows. She fiddled with her watch, turning it around on her slim wrist. Her shoulders were stiff. She looked like she was waiting outside the principal's office.

"Haven't seen you in a while," she said, still looking out the windows.

"Couple of weeks," I said. Clare took a deep breath.

"Last time . . . Jesus . . . you really caught me off guard." I nodded a little, but didn't say anything. I had a sense of where this was going, and I didn't want to get in the way. Clare stumbled on. "I thought we were more or less on the same page, you know, and then . . ." Her voice trailed off, and she cleared her throat. "Anyway, you got me thinking about our . . . about this whole situation. That maybe it's not the healthiest thing in the world for me—or for you, either. You know what I mean?" She paused for a moment. Her eyes flicked back over my face and arms, and then to the windows again. "My timing's for shit, isn't it?" she said.

We were quiet for a while. It was nearly dark now, and the pinkish city glow was rising from the streets. Clare hadn't surprised me. Without knowing why, or thinking about it much, I'd breached the etiquette of adultery. And probably scared her into who knew what kind of paranoid imaginings. *Fatal Attraction* . . . boiled bunnies, maybe. If anything, I was surprised she'd come to say it in person. But I wasn't sure exactly how to respond. Expressing profound relief might be honest, but probably not polite. I decided less was more.

"I understand, Clare." I nodded. "And I think you're probably right." She relaxed visibly and smiled. It was easier for her to look at me now.

"I'm glad," she said with relief. Then she pursed her lips. "Don't get me wrong, it was flattering and all. But I don't think it had very much to do with me, you know?" I nodded. We were quiet again. Then Clare looked at her watch and sighed and stood up.

"I have this thing in the Village. I should get going," she said. "No, don't get up." She gave me a peck on the cheek. It didn't hurt much. "Take care of yourself, John. Maybe I'll see you around." She slipped on her coat. She was at the door when she stopped and turned, looking thoughtful again. "You know, you should maybe think about Prozac or something, Johnny. Seriously. I mean, you're a lot of fun in the sack but . . . you're not a lot of *fun*—you know? You should be a happier person." And then she left. It was the most intimate conversation we'd ever had.

I sat there, thinking about the drugs that might make me a happier person, until my eyes were closing and my chin was dropping on my chest.

It was late the next morning when I heaved myself out of bed and hobbled into the kitchen. I drank most of a quart of orange juice and leafed through the paper until I couldn't take it anymore. Then I hobbled into the shower and stayed there for a while. My bruises had darkened overnight, and the pain had localized around them and become more intense. The shower helped, but only a little. I shaved carefully, and then dressed slowly in jeans and a black corduroy shirt. It was nearly eleven when I pulled my jacket on and headed for the door. And then I stopped.

Pissing people off is part of the job, and so is all the jawing about payback. I'd heard it plenty of times before Trautmann's little speech. Usually, it was just talk. Usually. No matter how familiar, though, the feeling that someone might be out there nursing a grudge and making a plan was nasty all the same. Mostly, it's a background unease, like a low-grade hangover, or too much coffee, a prickly mix of skittish, wary, and angry. But a car backfiring, or glass breaking, or something moving too quick and too close, can bring it to the edge of your teeth, and set your heart pounding.

I was pretty certain that Trautmann was a psycho; but I was equally sure that he was not an idiot. I hoped that the not-idiot part would win out over the psycho part, and that Trautmann would lay low. But I couldn't count on it. I clipped the Glock in its holster behind my back and went out.

It was another cold, gray day, and the clouds looked heavy. I stood on the steps of my building and scanned the block. I saw nothing that made me nervous, but if Trautmann did things right, there wouldn't be anything to see. Better safe than sorry, I figured.

I wandered aimlessly for a few blocks, always against the flow of traffic, and still saw nothing. I headed for the subway station at Fourteenth Street and Seventh Avenue, where I caught a 3 train up to 42nd Street. I got on the shuttle at 42nd and rode it across to Grand Central. I walked upstairs, through the restored majesty of the train station, through crowds and noise that were nearly rush-hour strength, and down the long corridor to the north exit. At 48th and Park I hit daylight again. By then I was reasonably sure that only about a zillion Christmas shoppers accompanied me, and they were no more hostile than usual. I walked the rest of the way to Mike's place.

Mike's building is on East End Avenue, a broad, redbrick prewar that faces Carl Schurz Park and the East River. It has white stone trim, a long, green awning, and a wood-paneled lobby with a wide fireplace. A fire was burning briskly in it when I arrived. The doorman greeted me by name and tactfully ignored my damaged face. He called upstairs and sent me through to the elevators. I got out on eleven. Mike's door was ajar.

"In here," he called. I walked through the book-lined entrance foyer, down a book-lined hallway, and into the kitchen. It was a long room, with white cabinets, stone counters, and steel appliances. At the far end was a windowed breakfast nook with a steel-topped table and wooden chairs. Paula Metz sat at the table, drinking coffee and sorting through mail. She wore a black T-shirt, and snug jeans on her long legs. Her bare feet were propped on another chair, and her thick, dark blond hair was tied back. Mike stood at a counter, slicing bagels. He looked vaguely academic in khakis and a gray sweater.

"Jesus, Michael, he looks like shit. You didn't say he looked like shit." Paula brushed a ribbon of hair from her cheek with long fingers, and wrinkled her face in a sympathetic wince.

"He neglected to mention it in his message," Mike said. "How are you feeling?"

"Pretty much like shit," I said. I crossed the room, pecked Paula on the cheek, pulled off my jacket, and took a seat. Paula noticed the gun and raised her eyebrows.

"A little paranoid today?" she asked.

"Appropriately vigilant," I said.

At rest, Paula's face is too medieval looking to be usual-pretty— it's too pale and bony, and too long in the nose; the brown eyes are shadowed and too narrow, the brows too heavy, and the wide mouth is naturally downturned. But set in motion, animated by a keen interest in people, a wry sense of humor, and an intellect that made her the youngest name partner in the city's biggest patent law firm, her features lose their severity, and Paula is lovely. She sighed and drained her coffee mug.

"I hope he's giving you danger pay for this," she said.

"Danger pay? I'm just grateful he's feeding me lunch," I said. Paula rose and took a mug from a cabinet and filled it with coffee from a carafe on the counter. She passed it to me and leaned her hips against the counter next to Mike. He'd finished with the bagels and now was taking strips of smoked salmon from a white paper package and laying them on a platter.

"Well, he's good at that. And I hope you brought a few friends, 'cause there's enough here for ten," Paula said, and she was right. Besides the bagels and salmon, Mike had laid out a basket of muffins, a bowl of fruit salad, a plate of sliced onions and tomatoes, and a pitcher of orange juice.

"You always say John could use some meat on his bones," Mike said.

"You too," Paula said, and pinched him gently at the beltline. "I also say he could use a girlfriend. You got that covered yet?"

"First things first, honey," Mike said, and took some plates from a cabinet. Paula put some salmon and tomatoes on one and refilled her coffee mug.

"Well, much as I enjoy eavesdropping on your sordid business, I have to go into an actual courtroom next week, so I'm going down the hall to pretend to work. Eat hearty," she said, and she left.

Mike loaded up a plate. "Let's sit in the dining room," he said.

I took some of everything and followed him in. The dining room was square and cream colored, with wide windows that looked out onto the park and the river. The walls were hung with colored illustrations of fruits and vegetables, and in the center of the room was a round oak table covered with a white cloth.

I ate a little and talked a lot, about Kenneth Whelan, the Lenzis, Lisa Welch, Steven Bregman, and Bernhard Trautmann. Mike ate slowly and listened and did not interrupt. He was quiet when I finished, staring out the window.

"You think Lenzi was in the same boat as Bregman?" he asked, after a while.

"Pretty much. My guess is when the squeeze came he didn't pay, and he got burned because of it. Lost his job and a lot of money. But he's just as angry as Bregman, and just as scared. He's just as nuts, too." Mike nodded.

"And Welch? Did you buy the insurance guy's story?" he asked.

"Kulpinski. And I did buy it. It was pretty compelling, even if it was all circumstantial."

"Not compelling enough for the cops or the Coast Guard, though."

"Kulpinski couldn't come up with a motive for Welch's suicide."

"Blackmail's not a bad one," Mike said.

"A perennial favorite," I said. "According to his wife, Welch had turned his life around when they married. He'd left behind his wicked ways and discovered the virtues of hearth and home, and got reborn as Ozzie Nelson. In which case, it might've been pretty stressful to have his ugly past come up and bite the ass of his idyllic present. If that happened, in the form of blackmail, then staging an accident might've seemed like the best option to him. It put him beyond the reach of the blackmailer, left his family whole financially, and left them with untainted memories. It's more tenuous than Lenzi and Bregman, but my gut tells me Welch was squeezed too." Mike nodded again, slowly.

"And Whelan?" he asked.

"Hard to say. He took my call pretty quick, but we shouldn't read too much into that." Mike drank some coffee and looked out the window. I tore a corner off a bran muffin and ate it. Mike took a deep breath.

"A question mark by his name, then," he said. "But we know a few things now. We know this business with Rick isn't a one-shot deal. He seems to be the latest in a string of victims. How long a string, we don't know. And it looks like whoever is doing all this is using Nassouli's files." I nodded agreement.

"We know some other things, too," I said. "Whoever this is has been at it for a while now, a couple of years at least, and hasn't gotten caught. Which means he's not completely stupid. And he's had a chance to practice, a chance to get good at it." Mike grimaced.

"Which brings us to the question of who," he said.

"I know I'm not behind it, and I guess I'd be willing to vouch for you in a pinch, but beyond that, I'm not so sure," I said. Mike smiled a little.

"Trautmann's not at the top of your list?" he asked.

"I don't know. It's easy to like him for blackmail, or just about any other evil thing you can think of. But that has more to do with Trautmann being a psycho scumbag than with proof."

"How do you interpret yesterday's high jinks, then? You think he just attacks people for the fun of it, and yesterday was your lucky day?"

"It's fun for him, no question about it, but that's not the only reason he jumped me. He wanted to find out who my client was, and he wanted to scare me off."

"His methods were kind of extreme," Mike said.

" 'Extreme' is his style, I think. It's certainly a big part of his management technique."

"Wanting to scare you off would indicate he's got something to hide," Mike said. He went into the kitchen and came back with the coffee carafe. He filled my mug, and his too.

"I'm sure he's got a lot of things to hide, but nothing you can scare out of him. You come at this guy with anything less than rock-solid proof—smoking gun, pictures, and all—and he's going to file his nails and laugh in your face. He may be crazy, but he's not stupid. He's a genuine hard case."

"But is he a blackmailer?" Mike asked.

"He's capable of it, and from what Burrows said, he knew about Nassouli's files. He also fits Faith Herman's description of the guy who paid her to send the fax . . ."

"I'm waiting for the 'but' here."

". . . but there are pieces of this that I just don't think are his style," I said.

"For instance?"

"The handling of Bregman's payment, through the Luxembourg account. That's a big step up from kicking ass at the mall." Mike thought about it and shook his head.

"That doesn't convince me. You said Trautmann isn't dumb. He worked for Nassouli and MWB for a lot of years. You don't think he picked up any handy skills along the way?" he said.

"How about the way Bregman was played? One fax with bad news, the next one with worse news, then a couple of weeks to stew before the squeeze. To me that seems too subtle for Trautmann." Mike shook his head some more. His brow wrinkled.

"Or the items in Pierro's fax," I continued. "Would that stuff look incriminating to just anybody off the street? I don't think so. You need to know something about banking, about how credit is extended and how loans are arranged, for that stuff to mean anything. You think Trautmann picked that up hanging out with Nassouli?" Mike tapped his chin with a finger.

"Point taken," he said. "But if not Trautmann, who?"

"I keep coming back to Nassouli's files. They didn't make it into Brill's document system, and we're working under the assumption that they weren't shredded. That means someone walked off with them. Who was in a position to do that? And who had the expertise to use them?"

"You know my vote goes to Nassouli himself," Mike said.

"But there are other candidates—someone from the investigation, maybe, or from the liquidation team. They had access, and most of them would have the knowledge," I said. Mike shook his head.

"No one had easier access to those files than Nassouli, and no one would know better how to exploit them. And he could be very strapped for cash, out there on the road," he said. He looked at me. "You still have reservations?"

"Nassouli looks good on paper, but I just can't get over what a big fucking risk it would be for him."

"I go back to what I said last week—maybe he's got help. Maybe from Trautmann," Mike said.

"Maybe, but that's risky in a different way. A partner like Trautmann could be awfully dangerous for a guy on the run."

Mike thought about it for a while. "Everything we've heard about Nassouli says he was a risk taker. And how nervous would he really be about Trautmann? The guy did his dirty work for over twenty years. Trautmann already knows where all the bodies are buried. Why should Nassouli start worrying about him now?" I shrugged. Despite what my gut told me, Mike was right. A good case could be made for Trautmann and Nassouli as partners.

"Okay, it's a theory. But it's not one we can do much with. No one has seen Nassouli for nearly three years, and we've got no leverage on Traut-mann." We were quiet for a while, and I watched a barge move slowly down the river. It rode low in the water, and gulls wheeled above it.

"Maybe your friend in the park can ID Trautmann from the photos," Mike said.

"We'll see—assuming I can find her again. But even if she does, how much is that worth? She's not exactly unimpeachable."

"I wasn't planning on taking this to court, John."

"If Pierro is serious about negotiating, our evidence needs to be solid enough for court, even if we never go there."

Mike squeezed his eyes shut and ran his fingers through his thin hair. "What about Neary's source in the investigation? Anything come from that?" he asked.

"Not yet." Mike stared at a drawing hanging on the wall as if he'd never seen it before. He looked suddenly tired.

"We're fast running out of things to do," he said. I nodded. "We need to talk to Rick and set his expectations."

"By telling him what?" I asked.

"Beats the shit out of me," he said.

"That's a good line. Remember that for when we meet with Pierro. It's a confidence builder." Mike got up and moved restlessly around the room, looking out the window, staring at the pictures on his wall.

"How's he doing?" I asked.

"Not well," Mike said. "He can't ignore this anymore, or pretend it'll just work itself out. He can't keep it in its box much longer, and he's running out of steam trying." I nodded.

"It's about three weeks until the French executive committee meets," I said after a while. "We could try a brute-force approach. Blanket surveillance on Trautmann, smother him, and see what turns up. But even if Pierro wants to spring for the manpower, three weeks is not a lot of time. And if Trautmann is our guy, he'll be extra careful now." Mike looked at me, more tired. I went on. "If I find Faith Herman, and she makes Trautmann from the photos, we can try going at him full bore with that. Threaten to bring in cops, the feds, civil action, whatever. Maybe we'll get lucky and catch him on a day he's feeling jittery. Of course, he might get pissed off instead, and up the ante on Pierro—or burn him altogether."

"You're not helping," Mike said.

"I know," I said. "Look, if this works the way it worked with Bregman, Pierro should be getting another fax soon. Maybe we can get some play off of that." Mike gave me a skeptical look. I didn't do optimism well. He sat, and chewed distractedly on a bagel. Paula padded in from the hall, an empty coffee mug in her hand. She filled it and looked at Mike and put her hand on the back of his neck. He smiled up at her and leaned his head against her hip.

"You think Pierro could be more help to us than he has been?" he asked me.

"I wouldn't call either of them forthcoming, though they work hard at seeming to be," I said. I looked at Paula. "What do you make of them?" I asked her.

"Rick and Helene? They're the topic of the week, I guess." She smiled at Mike. "I don't know either of them well, and him less than her . . ."

"Don't let that stop you," I said. "We're at the point where baseless speculation looks like expert testimony to us." She smiled wider and nodded.

"Then I'll tell you the same thing I told him," she said, ruffling her fingers through Mike's thin hair. "I'd say Rick's a nice enough guy, in a salesman sort of way. He does the grip-and-grin with the best of them, but he manages to eke a little sincerity out of it. And he's smart—smarter than he pretends to be. I've got a client who was on the other side of an acquisition from him who can testify to that. He likes to be underestimated. But at least he's not the type to beat you over the head with how brilliant and successful he is." She swallowed some coffee. "I know he's into his kids, and I think he'd do pretty much anything for Helene."

"And Helene?"

"She's an interesting one, isn't she? Smart, great-looking, a sort of quirky take on things, also devoted to the kids . . . but kind of like a cat, don't you think? Very self-sufficient, very self-possessed—and tough when she needs to be."

"How so?" I asked. Paula smiled.

"A few years back, I ran into her and her girls one Saturday morning, at a doughnut shop out in East Hampton. There was a long line, and we were queued up behind these three body-builder types—real gym rats, giant arms and legs, crew cuts, lots of tattoos, the works. No one on line would look them in the eye. One of them had had a hot date the night before, and he was telling his pals about it—very loudly—grunt by grunt, with full anatomical detail.

"They were going on and on, and the line wasn't moving, and I was about to suggest we go elsewhere, when Helene just lit into them. Bawled them out, something fierce. She never cursed, or even raised her voice; she just got . . . all *southern* on them. Said how dare they ever talk about a woman that way, much less in the presence of children; and didn't their mommas raise them any better than that; and maybe they were afraid of women, and liked men better, and they were just too scared to admit it. She went on like that—nonstop—for five minutes, until these guys just went away. Everyone in the place gave her a round of applause."

"Tough," I said. Paula nodded.

"Like a cat—you get along with her, on her terms. Leave her—and her kittens—alone, and you can get along just fine."

"Otherwise?" I asked. Paula chuckled.

"Otherwise, she'll scratch the eyes right out of your head."

It was midafternoon when I left Mike and Paula. Behind the cloud cover, the sun was waning, and a raw wind was picking up off the river. It was gray and cold from sidewalk to sky. I was stiff and tired and overfed. Tomorrow I'd be looking for Faith Herman, and right now I just wanted to soak in my tub some more. I took a taxi home. It dropped me at the corner, and I stood there for a moment, looking around. No pedestrian traffic just then. No cars coming. Nothing much to see in the gathering twilight. Not at first, anyway.

I'd just started down the block when a panel truck pulled away from the curb in front of my building, revealing a dark sedan parked in the space behind it. Inside I saw the silhouettes of two big men. One of them was talking on a cell phone. Shit. I pulled the Glock from behind my back and held it down along my leg. I crossed the street and walked slowly, keeping close to the buildings, keeping parked cars and trucks between the sedan and me. I hadn't gone ten paces when I heard tires squeal at the corner. I turned to see an identical dark sedan driving the wrong way up the block. It pulled up a few feet behind me, and its doors popped open and two big guys in dark suits got out. I looked up the block at the first car. Its doors were open and two big guys were standing beside it. All the guys had guns, and all the guns were pointed at me.

Chapter Eighteen

"Federal agents," the biggest guy yelled. "Put your weapon on the ground. Put it on the ground now, and step back. Keep your hands visible. Do it now!"

"Fuck you, Pell. I'm putting it away. You want to have your own little Ruby Ridge here on Sixteenth Street, fine—tell your boys to blaze away." I kept my left hand up in the air, and slowly holstered the Glock with my right. My throat was tight, and I could feel my heart pounding in my chest. Tension ran through my arms and legs like electricity. Fred Pell lowered his gun and motioned to his men to do the same. What the hell was he doing here?

"Long time no see, Killer. A little jumpy today, are we?" Pell crossed the street, smiling. His companion from the car followed. At a gesture from Pell, the other two feds got back in their own car, drove the wrong way up the block, and pulled into the space in front of Pell's sedan.

I hadn't seen Fred Pell in over three years, and those years had not been kind to him. Not that he'd ever been a great beauty. He's a big guy, almost as tall as Tom Neary but a lot heavier. There were easily thirty more pounds of him now, most of it in his egg-shaped gut and wide hips. He had upgraded his tailor, though, and his navy suit provided effective camouflage.

The fringe of dark hair around his blunt, bald head was thinner than when I'd seen him last. The contours of his skull, the ridges and dips beneath the tight, bare skin, were more pronounced and Neanderthal. His face was still broad and bland, and pasty slabs of flesh still hid the bone structure. But now there were deep lines around the meaty nose and the large mouth. The skin around his black doll's eyes was pouched and shadowed. He smiled nastily and came toward me. I saw a lot of big, crooked teeth. Apparently no one had knocked any out in the last three years. Too bad. His chin and jaw disappeared into his fleshy neck. I knew Pell was in his mid-forties, but he looked much older.

"That's real nice, Killer," he said, pointing at the side of my face. "I like it. You been out making friends again, huh?" His laugh was wet. "See, Vincent," he said to the guy who was with him, "somebody's been whaling on Killer's head, here. Somebody beat us to it." Pell laughed some more. Vincent didn't say anything, but he moved behind me, close. "But, hey, that kind of thing happens," Pell said, "when you fuck around in a federal case." He tried to jab me in the shoulder with his thick finger. I swatted his hand away.

"Keep your hands off me, you fat shit, and tell your boyfriend to back off. He's making me nervous." Pell grinned wider. The other two feds had gotten out of their car and were crossing the street, headed toward us.

"Watch out, Vincent, Killer's getting all wound up, and he has a bad temper. It's like I told you up there in the woods, Killer. Remember? I said you're not cut out for this work. You think you're so much smarter than all us blue-collar types, but you get in over your head and get things all fucked up and, who knows, maybe get somebody killed." He paused for a moment and looked me in the eye. I felt the blood throbbing in my temples. "Even the shit-kickers up there were too much for you. You stick to finding those rich brats when they skip from rehab, or tracking down those lost polo ponies—that's about your speed."

Then he pushed me in the chest. Pell was faster and stronger than he looked, and I staggered back into Vincent, who had all the give of a brick wall. "And I'll put my hands on you any time I please, jerk-off, and don't you fucking forget it," he said.

Pell came up close and straightened the collar on my jacket. "Shit, he tagged you a couple of good ones, didn't he?" he said, looking at my face more closely. "But I hear you held your own. Busted his nose, I hear." Pell laughed. "See, Vincent, Killer here will fool you. You may think he's just a fucking arrogant rich kid, playing cops and robbers—and you'd be right. But he's a tougher monkey than you'd expect. Takes a serious whipping to get him to stay down, doesn't it, Killer?"

Pell wanted me to light the candle, and he was doing a good job of goading me into it. I was halfway there already. I needed to dial down my adrenaline some. I took a few slow breaths, and managed a laugh. "Is that why these guys are here? You needed a lot of help last time, too," I said. Pell's face darkened.

"When I come to kick your ass, motherfucker, I'll come alone, and you'll wish somebody else was around to pull me off."

"Come on, Freddy, you'll need somebody else just to help you carry that gut around." I heard Vincent snort a little behind me. Pell heard it too, and his face got darker. Poor Vincent. A career-limiting move on his part.

"You spend all these taxpayer dollars, staking out my place, two cars, four guys, who knows how much on doughnuts and coffee—all just to warn me off? You could've picked up the phone and called," I said. "Be a lot cheaper."

"For an old pal like you, Killer, I like the personal touch." He poked me lightly in the chest. "I want to know what the fuck you're doing, messing around in my case, you and your buddy Neary. And don't think I'm not going to tear him a new asshole, too. Boy Scout's not on the team anymore, and he's going to find out just how cold it is on the outside. Make him think twice about his choice of friends." He poked me in the chest again, harder this time. "So how about it, Killer, tell your old pal Special Agent Pell what's up. What's your interest in Gerard Nassouli?"

I laughed again and shook my head. "Sorry, Freddy, no can do. Attorney work-product, privileged communications—you know how it goes."

Pell smiled. "I know how it's going to go, Killer, and I can't wait to see it. Monday morning, nine o'clock sharp, you be at St. Andrews Plaza, Shelly DiPaolo's office. You bring your pal Neary, and you two can explain to Shelly just how it goes. She's kind of green—doesn't know much about how the world works. She'll love having you explain it all." One of the feds behind Pell snickered. "Oh yeah, you may want to bring some legal counsel along, just in case Shelly doesn't see things quite the same way you do." Shit.

Pell laughed, and so did the two suits behind him. "See you Monday,

Killer, you have yourself a great weekend," Pell said, and turned away. And then he pivoted and drove his fist into my ribs, just above the cracked one. There was white, searing pain, and I doubled over, gasping.

"Shit, Killer, after all that talk about you being so tough, don't make a liar of me. Straighten him up, Vincent."

Vincent took a step back. "Hey, Mr. Pell, sir—wait a minute. I . . . I didn't sign up for this kind of thing," he said. His voice was young-sounding and scared.

"You need a hand, sir?" one of the other suits piped in.

"Yeah," Pell said, "fucking Vincent's a little weak in the knees here." Someone grabbed me from behind and pulled me upright and locked my arms behind me. All the muscles in my side were in spasm. Pell's face was dark. His black eyes were even smaller now, and his nostrils flared. He looked like a demented pig. "This is for being such a fucking wise-ass," Pell said, and drew back his fist.

I stomped down on the instep of whoever was holding me and snapped my head back, into his face. He cursed and his grip loosened and I got off a kick that took Pell in the knee and crumpled him. But it put me off balance, and the guy behind me got his bearings back and jabbed me in the ribs. I doubled over, and he got a better grip on me and pulled me upright. Pell got up and dusted himself off. He looked down at his knee and the torn flap of fabric hanging from his pants. He had his gun out.

"Motherfucker," he said, softly, and hit me with the gun butt just above my right ear. I saw stars and felt blood down the side of my face. He wound up for another one.

"Hey! You get away from him. Leave him alone," yelled a voice from the corner. "I called 911. The police are on the way. You get away from him." It was an angry voice, and a scared one, but more angry than scared. It was a woman's voice. Jane Lu.

The guy behind me stepped away. I staggered a little but stayed upright. Pell's gun disappeared, and his ID came out.

"Federal agents, ma'am." He flashed his ID at Jane, and so did the rest of the suits. "Nothing to worry about here."

"Like hell there isn't." She walked quickly from the corner, carried by her anger. She was wearing jeans and a thick, black sweater and she was brandishing her opened cell phone like a weapon. "I saw what happened."

"What happened, ma'am, was this gentleman—who is armed, by the way—assaulted two federal agents who were questioning him in the course of a federal investigation." Pell puffed up into full, self-important government official mode. "What you saw was two federal agents using appropriate force to defend themselves." Jane ignored him. She took my arm and looked me over.

"Jesus Christ, John, look at you," she said.

"Jane," I said softly, "it's alright. Go inside now. The cops will be here in a minute. I'm fine. Go inside." She ignored me too.

"Jesus, look at your head," Jane said.

"You know this gentleman, ma'am?" Pell asked, sounding sly and more hostile now. I heard sirens approaching.

"He's my neighbor, Agent—what is your name? May I see that ID again?" It was Pell's turn to ignore her.

"Well, your *neighbor* is lucky we're not running him in for what he did. And by the way, what exactly is your relationship with your *neighbor*, Miss—what's your name?" Jane shook her head and looked at him like he was a new, but particularly disgusting, kind of cockroach. An NYPD blue-and-white rolled up the street, lights flashing. It stopped by the two fed sedans. Two uniforms got out, and one of Pell's boys flashed an ID and buttonholed them.

Pell grinned with his big, bad teeth. "I'll take care of these guys, Killer, unless you or your sweetie have something to say." Jane was about to speak, but I put my hand on hers and she stopped. "No? Okay, then, Killer, I'll see you bright and early Monday." Pell turned toward the police car but then turned back. "In case you are more than just a neighbor, honey, you might want to ask Killer here what happened to his wife. Word to the wise, babe." And he walked away, laughing.

"Christ, that hurts!"

"Hold still, I'm almost done," Jane said. We were in my apartment, sitting at the kitchen counter. Jane was washing the gash on my head with alcohol. "Just a little more. There you go. Now we'll put some of this stuff on." She tossed the damp gauze pad on the floor, on top of my bloodstained shirt, and took a tube of antiseptic ointment from my first aid kit. Her hands were strong and her movements quick and sure. "You should get that thing looked at," she said, as she daubed the ointment on. "That thing" was my side, which was more painful, swollen, and angry looking than ever. She was probably right.

"I will. But I've got to make some calls first."

"Go ahead and make them, and I'll make us some tea. Then I'll take you to the emergency room." I looked at her for a moment. She had insisted on coming in with me, and I hadn't put up much of a struggle. I was impressed by her composure and her competence, and by the ease with which she took charge. She hadn't yet asked a single question.

I walked back to my bedroom area and called Mike Metz. No one was home, and his cell phone was off. I left a message for him to call me ASAP. I tried Neary, but again I had no luck. I left him a message too. Neither of them would be happy with my news. Getting read the riot act by a cop—even an obnoxious federal one like Pell, who mauls you in the process—is one thing. It comes with the territory sometimes. Getting hauled in front of a federal prosecutor is another thing altogether.

U.S. attorneys on high-profile cases are dangerous beasts—ruthless and relentless, with broad investigative powers, and vast and scary resources at their disposal. Dealing with one is perilous and unpleasant at best; at worst, it's something like being smacked in the face with a two-by-four and dropped into a deep, dark pit. Shelly DiPaolo was rumored to be a particularly nasty example of the species. If she really wanted to know why we were interested in Nassouli, she had the where-withal to find out. This was one of the risks Mike and I had warned Pierro of, a risk I'd tried to avoid. Tried and failed, apparently.

I put on a clean shirt and sat on my bed and thought for a while about what Pell said. I'd known from the start that running afoul of the feds was a possibility. The surprise was that I'd been anywhere close to showing up on their radar. But Pell had known about my run-in with Trautmann, down to my bopping him in the nose. Had Trautmann dropped a dime on me? That didn't seem like his style. Did the feds have him under surveillance? Possible, I suppose. But Pell had known I'd been talking to Neary, too. How? Had Neary's source in the investigation been telling tales?

Fucking Pell. He was the same bastard he'd been three years ago, only more so. His feelings for me seemed as warm as ever, and he still knew which buttons to push. The bruises on the side of my face were throbbing, and I realized my jaw was clenched tight. I took a couple of slow breaths and worked it loose.

■

Jane Lu had found tea bags, mugs, milk, sugar, and chocolate chip cookies in my absence. She was at the kitchen counter, just pouring the water, when I came back in. It was fully dark outside, and she'd flicked on more lights. I took a seat at the counter.

"You make your calls?"

"Nobody home. I need to wait for calls back." She nodded and passed me a mug. She added milk to her tea, dipped a cookie in the mug, and took a small bite. She'd taken off her black sweater. Underneath she wore a gray MIT T-shirt with the sleeves cut off. I watched the muscles in her arms move as she fiddled with her tea bag. "How are you doing?" I asked. She thought about it for a minute.

"I'm alright. A little shaky, but alright. I haven't really seen anything like that before, much less been a part of it," she said. I nodded. She didn't seem shaky to me, not even a little.

"Calling 911 was the right thing to do. Wading in there to break things up with your cell phone wasn't. You were lucky—those guys are feds and more or less play by the rules—some rules anyway—but it wasn't smart. You yell, you scream, you shout 'Fire,' but you stay far away." She nodded and drank some tea. "But thanks—a lot. You saved me from what was shaping up to be a very bad evening." She looked at me and shook her head.

"Is this an everyday event with you—getting into fights, getting beat up?"

"Would you believe you caught me in a slow week?" She just looked at me. "Actually, I'm running my holiday special on beatings—goes on till Christmas." She looked some more. I looked back. "No, it's not an everyday thing. It happens sometimes, but not often," I said. "And I'm usually not the one who gets beat up," I added.

"That's good to hear," Jane said, smiling. "Are your relationships with the authorities all so friendly?"

"Some of them are good, and some are not so good. Pell is a special case," I said. Jane swirled tea around in her mug and said nothing.

"He didn't pique your curiosity?" I asked after a while.

She was quiet for a few moments and shook her head. "Lauren told me about what happened upstate. It . . . it must have been awful. I can't imagine." She shook her head a little more. I watched my tea darken in the mug.

"What else did Lauren have to say?" I asked.

Jane looked at me for a long minute. "She told me you went through a bad time afterward. Very bad." She sipped her tea. "She worries about you." She looked away, out the windows.

"Why does that man have it in for you?" Jane asked after a while.

"He thinks I ruined his shot at being the next FBI director." Jane gave me a quizzical look. "He thought the case was going to be a career maker for him. It was very high profile, a lot of media interest. The trial would've gotten a lot of coverage. And Pell was the special agent in charge. He would've been the star of the show, at least in his mind. But when the guy was killed . . . that was it. There was no big arrest, no perp to parade in front of the cameras, no trial, no CNN. There was barely a press conference. He blames me for that."

"Why? Because you . . . shot that man?" I nodded and finished my tea.

"What does Lauren worry about?" I asked. Jane thought about it before she answered.

"She worries that you're still going through a bad time, only now you keep it to yourself," she said. Her gaze shifted. "You're bleeding again." She tore open another gauze pad and came around the kitchen counter. She stood in front of me and pressed the pad on the cut, the palm of her hand resting on the side of my face. "You're going to ruin all your shirts if you keep on like this," she said softly. She was very close. Close enough, I was sure, to hear my heart hammering in my chest, and to feel its pounding through my skin. Her dark eyes were huge, and her scent seemed to fill my lungs. Her pulse was beating quickly at the side of her neck, and her face and neck were flushed.

We both jumped when the phone rang.

I took the call in my bedroom. It was Mike Metz. He was silent while I ran down what had happened with Pell, and he was silent for a while after.

"Fuck," he said finally.

"Well put," I said.

"This is bad, John. DiPaolo's a real piece of work, from what I hear."

"I've heard that too."

"She can make life very unpleasant for us if she's so inclined. We'll claim your case notes are attorney work-product, but she can push on that pretty hard if she wants to. Fuck." Mike sighed heavily. "Well, we knew this was a possibility. Nothing to do now but deal with it." I heard Mike pour something and swallow some of it. "But this came out of the blue. Pell knew about Trautmann and Neary, both, and he knew you were interested in Nassouli. How?"

"Hell if I know."

"You figure Trautmann called them?"

"I guess it's possible, but it doesn't seem like him. And I'm not sure why he'd do it."

"To get you off his back, I assume."

"Maybe. But it's a chancy thing for him to do. He risks drawing federal attention to himself, which is not something I'd think he'd be interested in. And he's also got to know that if I find out he's the one who called Pell, it's going to make me look at him all the harder. Trautmann's smart enough to figure that out."

"How would Pell find out, if not from him?"

"Could be the feds have Trautmann covered. I didn't see anybody, but that doesn't mean they weren't there."

"I thought Neary said they'd looked at Trautmann and decided to take a pass."

"That's what he said. But they could still have him staked out, maybe to get a line on Nassouli."

"If that's the case, it would make it hard for him to be our guy, no?"

"Harder, but not impossible."

"How do you figure they knew about Neary?"

"That's another puzzle. Neary has a source in the investigation that he was going to talk to. Maybe that source isn't so trustworthy. Maybe he went to Pell. Or maybe Pell connected the dots by himself once he heard I'd been talking to Trautmann. He knows Neary and I are friends."

"You talk to Neary yet?"

"I've got a call in to him."

"He won't be happy with this. He could be pretty exposed here, with his client and his management."

"I know, Mike, believe me, I know." Mike was quiet at the other end of the line.

"Does Neary know our client's name, John?"

"No. If he was inclined to, he could figure it out. But he didn't hear it from me."

"Well, that's something." I heard ice shifting in a glass at Mike's end. "Alright, I've got some calls to make. Meanwhile, prepare yourself for Monday—practice not talking."

"I know the drill, Mike."

"I don't care. I'm your lawyer, and I've got to say it. You say nothing unless you're asked a direct question, and even then you wait for me to give you the nod. If you have to talk, you answer only what was asked, and you do it briefly and politely. And, above all, you don't lose your temper and you don't act like a wiseass. Mostly, don't talk."

Jane Lu had gotten into my CDs, and Cassandra Wilson was playing when I came out. Jane was sitting on the sofa with her legs curled beneath her, reading the *Times*. Her loafers were on the floor. She'd made herself another cup of tea.

"Done?" she asked, looking up.

"One left. If you've got somewhere else you need to be, you don't need to wait. I'm fine, really." Jane smiled and shook her head.

"I don't mind. Besides, if I don't take you to the emergency room, I'm not sure you'll go." She held up her cell phone. "And I've already canceled."

"Nothing special, I hope." She smiled enigmatically and gave a little shrug.

"You should sit down, rest a little," she said. I nodded and settled at the other end of the sofa and about a half second later I was asleep. The next thing I knew, Jane was gently shaking my leg. It was nearly seven o'clock. "Telephone," she said. I dragged myself back to consciousness, off the sofa, and to my bedroom. It was Neary. I told him all.

"Fuck," he said, when I had finished.

"That seems to be the consensus."

"I'm glad you can be glib about this, March. But it's not that funny from where I sit. You don't know Shelly. She'll eat you alive, and have me for dessert. And in case you haven't noticed, my ass is hanging out here."

"I know that, Tom, and I'm sorry about it," I said.

"*Sorry?* A shitload of good *sorry* does me. *Sorry* doesn't pay my mortgage, or my kid's orthodontist, you know? It may not cost you much to dick around with these guys, March, but I'm in a different boat. There's no mattress full of family money just lying around my house."

"Tom, I got you jammed up here, I know. I didn't mean for it to happen, and I'm sorry that it did. But I—"

He cut me off. "Save your rationalizations—it's my own goddamn fault for not telling you to go to hell in the first place. You'd think I'd learn. I'll see you Monday," he said, and hung up. Shit. Shit. Shit.

Neary was pissed, and he had a right to be. Even if—best case—all DiPaolo did was rough us up, Tom could still have a big problem. His management and his clients were very sensitive about confidentiality. If they came to believe he'd breached theirs, his reputation would be fucked and he'd be out on his ass. Maybe even hauled into civil court.

"All set?" Jane asked. She had turned off the music and put her shoes and sweater back on. I nodded and grabbed a jacket. Jane looked at me. "Bad news?" she asked. I nodded again. I was reaching for the doorknob when the phone rang.

"I should take this," I said. It was Mike.

"I spoke to Pierro," he said.

"Let me guess—he wasn't happy. Well, he couldn't have been any worse than Neary."

"Oh, I wouldn't be too sure about that. I bet Tom didn't just get a fax demanding payment of five million dollars."

Chapter Nineteen

"Christ," Rick Pierro said hoarsely, "this just gets worse and worse." He rubbed his face with his big hands.

It was after ten on Saturday night, and Mike Metz and I were in Pierro's living room. Mike had been there for a while; I was fresh from St. Vincent's. It was a large room, done in earth tones. The deep sofas and chairs were upholstered in rust and ochre and sand-colored fabrics. The sage walls were hung with abstracts that went well with the carpet.

Pierro sat hunched on a large ottoman, his elbows resting on his knees. He was dressed in olive gabardine trousers, a yellow shirt, and a blue V-neck sweater. His shirttail had come out in back, and there was a smear of something, maybe mustard, on one of his sleeves. He pinched the bridge of his nose between his thumb and forefinger, and shut his eyes tightly. But when he opened them again, the fatigue and worry and anger were still there. His meaty shoulders drooped and his heavy features sagged. His hair was glossy and neat, and somehow out of place above his wrecked face.

Helene sat beside him. She placed a hand on his shoulder and kneaded it gently. She wore a black sweater and loose camel pants, and her chestnut hair was brushed straight back from her forehead and tied in a black ribbon. She was holding up better than her husband, but her face was pale and tense. Her gaze wandered around the room, occasionally resting on me, but if there was anything to read in it, it escaped me. Maybe I was just too tired.

Mike sat on a rust-colored sofa, reading the fax, looking placid. He was dressed as I'd seen him last, in khakis and a gray sweater. It was hard to believe that was only a few hours ago. He got up and walked to the doorway, where I was leaning. I was better at leaning now than at sitting, since the body blow from Pell had displaced my already fractured rib, and my pals at St. Vincent's had wrapped my midsection in a long elastic bandage. Mike handed me the fax. It was short and to the point:

$5 MILLION READY FOR WIRE TRANSFER BY 8AM EST THURSDAY. YOU WILL RECEIVE TRANSFER INSTRUCTIONS THEN. FUNDS MUST BE TRANSFERRED WITHIN 4 HOURS.

All in caps, all in bold type. The fax had come in on Pierro's home machine. It was like the message Bregman had received, though he'd been given a week to get his money together. Pierro had just four days. Like the first fax, this one had a phone number at the top of the page, a 718 area code this time.

"I'll check out this number tonight, and if I find an address for it, I'll go there tomorrow. But I'm not expecting much." Mike nodded and Helene looked at me. Pierro didn't stir.

"It's a lot of money, Rick," Mike observed.

Pierro shrugged. "Yeah, about thirty percent of my bonus last year," he said. "A lot" is a relative thing.

"It's a lot to pay for silence," I said, "especially for an innocent man."

Pierro lifted his big head and looked at me. "What the hell is that supposed to mean?" he said in a slow rumble.

Mike glanced at me and answered. His voice was low and even. "Only that making a payment may not be the wisest course, Rick. There's no way of knowing that this won't be just the first installment."

Pierro grimaced and pushed his fingertips into his temples. "Jesus . . . how many times have we been through this, Mike? I told you—guilty, innocent—in this climate, it doesn't matter a damn to my pals at French—or to anybody on the Street. I get a stink like this on me, and that's it—I'm done. All this—it's done." He held his hands out, gesturing at the room around us. "Well, that's not an option, okay? That's not an option for my family." He leaned forward again and let out a long breath. He rubbed the back of his neck.

"Besides, with what you tell me about this frigging prosecutor, it could be I'm hosed anyway. She can haul me in front of some frigging grand jury, drag my name through the papers . . ." He clenched his thick hands into fists. "How does she even know we exist, anyway? And why does she care? What the hell does she want from me?" He bounced the heel of his palm on his forehead. "How did things get so screwed up?" His voice was a harsh rasp. Mike sighed.

"This was always a risk, Rick," he said evenly. "We knew it could happen—we talked about it from the outset. But we didn't think we were fishing in their waters yet, so this was a surprise to us too." Mike paused and looked at Pierro, who stared down at his own big hands.

"Frankly, I have no idea how we came to Shelly DiPaolo's attention," Mike continued. "But as to why she cares—there's no mystery about that. The MWB case is a career maker for her, if it goes well—and a career breaker otherwise. From what John has heard, she needs a big win. Nassouli is one of her high-profile targets—one of her big fish—so it's no surprise she'd be interested in anyone even remotely connected with him. And no surprise she'd be hostile to anyone she thinks is making her job tougher. When she heard about John—snooping around the MWB offices, and asking questions about Nassouli—she probably thought he fell into both categories."

"So, she's interested and pissed off, and that's that? She says 'Drop your drawers,' and you just drop them?" Pierro asked. There was petulance mixed in with his frustration and fear. Mike ignored it.

"If it comes to that, yes. But it's never that simple. We don't know exactly what she wants yet, and we don't know how badly she wants it. It's true, she's got a lot of power. She can question John, and me, and make it hurt. And if Ms. DiPaolo really wants to know who we're working for, she can subpoena us, bring us in front of a grand jury, put us under oath, and ask—and have a judge jail us for contempt if we don't answer." Helene's eyes darted from Mike to me and back to her husband. Mike continued.

"But her powers aren't limitless, and they don't come free. She operates in a world of cost and benefit, just like everybody else. She can get us to drop our drawers, but it will cost her—in time, in money, in manpower. She's going to weigh those costs against what she thinks she can get out of this, and against all the other things she could be doing instead. We may not be able to stop her, but we can up the price—maybe to the point where it stops making sense to her. Ideally, though, it doesn't come to that. Ideally, we strike a bargain."

Pierro pinched the bridge of his nose again, and shook his head. Helene moved her hand to his neck, but he shrugged her off and stood. He thrust his hands in his pockets and walked to the windows and stared out.

"And if you do manage to deal with her, then what? Whoever this is wants his money in four days, and you guys haven't got jack for me." He moved back and forth in front of the window like a bear in a cage.

"We don't have hard and fast proof, it's true, but we have a theory . . ." Mike said, but Pierro cut him off.

"Yeah, yeah, Trautmann—you told me. But you don't have enough to negotiate with, so it doesn't do squat for me."

"We're still working on it, Rick. We have four days. It's not much time, but it's something, and John has accomplished a lot in the last couple of weeks." Pierro looked at me and gave a short, harsh laugh.

"Yeah, like getting the frigging FBI on my back," he said. Helene sighed and turned in her seat to look at him.

"That's enough, Rick," she said sharply. "You're being stupid, and you're saying things you don't mean. Haven't you been listening to Mike? He and John might get called before a grand jury because of us. And look at John's face, for Christ's sake. Look what he's been through for us. Now you apologize to him." Pierro shook his head and looked sheepish.

"Jeez, John, I don't know what I'm saying. I'm sorry—really. Helene is right, that was way out of line. It's just . . . hell, I don't know. This thing—it's making me nuts." I nodded at him. Mike continued.

"We have to take this one step at a time, Rick. First, we talk to the feds and see what they want and where that takes us. When we know that, we can make decisions about Thursday." Pierro nodded and turned away from us. We watched him pace by the windows for a while, and then Helene walked us to the door.

"Please forgive him," she said to both of us when we were in the foyer. "He's . . . well, you know the pressure he's under. It's making him crazy. But please, hang in there with us." She put her hand on my arm. Mike made reassuring noises. I had a question.

"That fax he got tonight—that's the only communication he's had since the first one? There's been nothing else?"

Helene looked at me impassively for a moment. No surprise, no confusion, no indignation, and no answer. "Please, John," she squeezed my arm, "just stick with us. Please."

"What the hell is going on?" I said to Mike when we were out on the street. "Is it me, or does it seem like all of a sudden we're just along for the ride?"

"It's not just you," he said, shaking his head. "The ground is definitely shifting. Yesterday, you talk to Trautmann, and then—*boom*—you get a visit from Pell, Pierro gets the squeeze, and on Thursday he's supposed to pay up. It feels like someone's nervous and in a big hurry."

"Trautmann didn't strike me as the nervous type. Impulsive, yes, but not the type to run scared," I said.

"If not him, then who?" Mike asked. I shook my head and scanned the street for a taxi.

"You really think you can work a deal with DiPaolo?" I asked. Mike snorted.

"Sure, we can deal. No problem. Something along the lines of us agreeing to answer all her questions and her agreeing not to jail us for contempt."

"You made it sound good upstairs."

"Rick needed something to get him through the night. After Monday we'll know better how to set his expectations." I spotted a cab. It cut across traffic and screeched to a halt nearby. "Call me tomorrow. Let me know how it goes," Mike said, and turned east, toward his home.

It didn't go well.

I traced the 718 number on Pierro's fax to a store in Brooklyn, on Atlantic Avenue, at the fringe of Boerum Hill. It was a tiny place, wedged between a hardware store and a pizza joint, and the only spot on the grimy, tired-looking block that was opened when I got there, early Sunday morning. The closest it had to a name was a plastic sign out front that read "Papers, Smokes, Lotto." Inside, there were a couple of inches of floor space, surrounded by high racks of periodicals in a dozen languages. Behind the counter was a dense mosaic of cigarettes, pornographic videos, and breath mints. A hand-printed sign taped to the register advertised phone cards and fax services.

The curly-haired kid who was minding the store was no help to me. He didn't glance up from his thick textbook when he told me that no, he hadn't worked yesterday. His cousin had been the only one there, all day long. The same cousin who'd left last night on a two-week trip to Florida. No, he didn't know where in Florida or how to contact him, or if he'd actually be back in two weeks' time.

I left him to his studies and rode the subway back into Manhattan, all the way to Lexington Avenue and 96th Street. Then, with photos of Trautmann in my pocket, I spent the next five hours wandering the northern reaches of Central Park, in search of Faith Herman. I worked the playgrounds and footpaths, the gardens and meadows, the rambles, the ponds, and the horse trails. I saw strollers and runners and power walkers, skaters and cyclists and horsemen—and women, too. I saw singles and couples and families, dog people, cat people, even a few ferret people. I saw winos and junkies, crazies and crooks, and lots of cops and tourists. I walked until my ribs were aching and it was time for lunch. Then I ate a hot dog and a pretzel on a bench in the sun, and when I was finished I walked some more. But I didn't see Faith Herman or anyone who looked like her.

It was oddly restful, all that fruitless walking around. The day was cold and clear, almost painfully bright, and I achieved a solitude and a detachment that I usually find only when I run. I thought about Pierro, and how the fear and anger had eroded him, and what he might be like after he'd lived with it for a year or two, the way Lenzi and Bregman had. I was pretty sure there'd be nothing left. I thought about Helene, too, and the steel she'd shown in managing her husband. Helene could take it. She could pay up and go on with life, and to hell with the other shoe. She was tough enough.

And I thought for a long time about Jane Lu. My run-in with Pell and my conversation with Neary had left me in a foul mood and full of dark thoughts, and I'd been bad company at the hospital, but Jane hadn't seemed to mind. The ER was busy, and we'd waited on plastic seats behind a gunshot leg, a taxi hit-and-run, and a subway stabbing. Along with the patients, doctors, nurses, and orderlies, a lot of cops, firemen, and EMS guys filtered in and out. They were heavily laden with equipment and fatigue, and Jane had watched them closely.

"Did you like being a policeman?" she'd asked.

"Most of the time."

"You don't seem very much like these guys."

"Not all cops are alike."

"Were you very much like any of them?"

"Not really." She'd turned to look at me.

"How did you get into it? Why do you like it?" she'd asked. Those questions again—both barrels. I'd been tired and irritated, and I'd started to give her some of the same bullshit I'd given Pierro when he had asked, but Jane cut me off. Annoyance flitted across her face, and she raised her hand.

"If you don't want to talk, just say so," she'd said, with a small laugh. "You don't have to placate me." I'd looked at her, surprised, and she'd looked steadily back, and I'd thought about her questions.

How? Why? There's no short answer to either one. *How* isn't a hard question, though; *how* is just a story—and it starts with Anne.

We met in our senior year of college, and I fell in love with her the way that I could back then—hungrily, drunkenly, and completely. And when graduation came, my only ideas about the future were that I didn't want to spend it at Klein & Sons, or apart from her. So when she went back to her hometown, to take a job on the local newspaper, I went with her.

Anne's father took me by surprise. Parents had never been my strong suit—especially not fathers—and I'd figured to do even worse with a county sheriff. But I was wrong. Donald Stennis was smart and well read, with a sneaky chess game, a dry, laconic wit, and an unsentimental but generous—and surprisingly liberal—view of life. The Adirondack Atticus Finch, Anne called him. More surprising still was Donald's trust in his only child, and his respect for her judgment. He made me welcome.

I lived in the apartment over the garage, cooking breakfast for Anne and Donald in the mornings, cleaning up when they'd gone to work, running and reading in the afternoons, playing chess with Donald in the evenings, and making love with Anne as quietly as we could after he'd turned in. It wasn't a bad time—it was nice—but after two months, I needed to do something with myself. I was bored, adrift, and getting antsy. Then Donald took me for a ride.

He called it the sheriff's tour of Burr County. We rode in his battered, unmarked Crown Victoria, across the length and breadth of his jurisdiction, down county roads and Main Streets and no-name washboard trails, through towns and hamlets and places that were little more than packed earth and rusted trailers. The air conditioning was broken, and we rolled down the windows. The car filled with the smell of pines and dirt, and with heavy midsummer heat. The whole time we drove, Donald talked.

His knowledge of the county, and the people in it, was vast. He knew where they lived and where they worked, where they went to church and where they went to drink, and if they drank too much, he knew that too. He knew who had married and who had divorced, who was cheating and who'd got caught, who'd beat his wife and whose wife was never coming home again. He knew the running buddies, and the ties of blood or marriage or schoolyards or jail yards that bound them together. He knew who'd gone to prison and who'd just gotten out, who'd gotten laid off and who'd come into sudden cash, who'd left town, and who would inevitably be back. He spoke of them with something close to affection.

It was a cop's-eye view—of greed, grievance, and rancor, of poverty, boozing, and rage, of just plain mean and just plain stupid—and how they came together and boiled over into crime and violence. It was a hard view, and often sad, he told me, but it had its humor, and, once in a while, a glimpse of redemption. It had fascinated Donald for nearly thirty years. He drove and talked for seven hours, and we were covered in sweat and dust when we pulled back into his driveway. It was there he'd made his simple pitch.

"Sometimes, you can't do much, and sometimes you can't do a damn thing at all. But now and then, you can make all the difference in the world. It's not for everybody, though. You can get used up—get sick from what you see, or angry, or sad about how little you can do. You can get tired, or mean, or, worse still, bored. It's not for everybody.

"All my guys are good guys; I get rid of the ones that aren't. But I haven't had a deputy with a college diploma for going on two years now. You're smart, you're curious, you're not a bully, and you don't scare easy. And I've got a uniform that's about your size. Give it a try. What the hell, if it's not for you, you got cooking to fall back on."

But it was for me.

Why is a tougher question. Some of my reasons were not so different from Donald's—a fascination with the whole strange pageant; a desire to help, to make a difference. I liked the chase, too, and the puzzles—the who and the how and the why, especially the why. But I also liked knowing, at the end of each day, what I'd been able to do and what I hadn't—and knowing it more certainly, more tangibly, than a P&L report could ever tell.

After Anne died, I quit this work, and a lot else besides. But after a while, I came back to it—for all those reasons, I guess, and for fear of that empty time when I'd stopped.

Jane had looked steadily back at me, silent amid the ER's buzz and hustle. I'd looked at her, and thought about the answers, and told her all of it.

It was after three when I made a last circuit of the East Meadow and the Conservatory Garden. Then I gave up on Faith Herman for the day and took a taxi home. The windows in my building were dark. It was quiet inside and empty feeling, and my apartment was filled with a cold, gray twilight. There were no messages. I sat at the kitchen counter, in my coat, in the gathering dusk.

I was tired and sore. My feeling of unassailable solitude had faded in the bleak, fading light, replaced by worries about Monday and the sense that the whole case had spun away from me. Maybe Shelly DiPaolo would take care of all that. Maybe after tomorrow there'd be no case. I shed my coat and flicked on some lights. I put a pot of coffee on and made myself a tuna sandwich. I called Mike Metz. No one was home, so I left him a message about coming up empty in Brooklyn and in the park. Then I pulled a volume of Andre Dubus stories from the shelf and read until the words stopped making sense.

Chapter Twenty

Sometime in the night a wind started to blow, clouds moved in, and a cold, slanting rain began to fall. It was falling hard by morning, overwhelming windshield wipers, coursing down gutters and over curbs, and washing the streets in reflected neon. It was falling harder still at nine o'clock, when Mike Metz, Tom Neary, and I walked into the sixth-floor conference room at One St. Andrews Plaza, the offices of the U.S. attorney for the southern district of New York. It was raw and miserable outside, but it was nothing compared to the weather in there.

The conference room was narrow and stark. There was a long window on one wall, covered with metal Venetian blinds. The center set was pulled up, giving a shadowy view onto the backside of One Police Plaza. Rain beat at the glass, and everything outside was the color of wet pavement. The other walls were dingy white, adorned only by framed color photos of the president and the attorney general. The metal and plastic conference table was surrounded by a dozen swivel chairs, covered in worn, brown tweed. They clashed violently with the powder blue carpet. Fluorescent lights flickered and buzzed overhead.

Three men sat facing the window. One of them was Fred Pell. The other two were strangers to me. They were laughing loudly when the receptionist opened the door, but went dead quiet when she ushered us in. We took seats opposite them, Mike in the center. All three of us were suited up today—in navy blue with white shirts and dark ties. We could've been IBM salesmen. Or feds.

Pell sat closest to the door. He was dressed in a double-breasted blue pinstripe, and his skin looked gray under the fluorescent light. Next to him was an empty chair, and on the other side of that was a big, doughy guy in shirtsleeves and a red bow tie. He was in his mid-thirties and had thinning blond hair, cut short, pink cheeks, and twinkling blue eyes. Next to him was a smaller, wiry guy, also in his thirties, with unruly black hair and dark, quick eyes set in a bony face. He was in shirtsleeves too, but his were blue and his tie wasn't bowed. In front of each of them were a yellow legal pad, a pen, and a cup of coffee. Pell had a small tape recorder, too. No one stood; no one shook hands. They gave us silence and cold, hard looks, and even Mr. Bow Tie did it pretty well.

Neary gave them back the dead-fish look—deader than any of them. I tried for boredom, and studied the president and the AG closely. Mike gave them a relaxed cordiality, introducing himself, handing out business cards, greeting Pell like this was a garden party and Mike was Martha Stewart.

"Special Agent Pell, it's been a long time since I saw you upstate. Three years ago or so, wasn't it? You're looking very well." Pell said nothing and tried to glare more. It made him look like he had gas. The other two identified themselves tersely. Mr. Bow Tie was Paul Conaway, and the wiry guy was Scott Katz, both assistant U.S. attorneys, working for Shelly DiPaolo. There were still no handshakes. Conaway told us that Shelly would be in momentarily. And then it was silent again.

I listened to the thin buzz of the lights and the muted sound of rain and wind outside. My hands felt cold, and my stomach was churning. It was nerves, the same kind of nerves I used to get at depositions or when I had to testify in court. I glanced at Mike. He had his game face on and looked a million miles away. Neary was looking more and more like a slab of granite. Then the door opened.

When I think "assistant U.S. attorney," I don't usually think "sexpot," so Shelly DiPaolo took me by surprise. She was short, no more than five foot one, though her frosted blond hair added three more inches, and her black, spike-heeled pumps another four. Her small, curvy body was packed tight into a steel gray suit with a short skirt. Under her jacket she wore a scoop-necked silk blouse in cherry red, the same color as her nail polish and her lipstick.

Her red lips were full—bee-stung—and her chin was sharp, with a little dimple in it. She had high cheeks, a small, sharp nose, and big, brown eyes, made bigger still by a lot of well-applied makeup. She wore heavy gold earrings, several gold chains around her neck, and a thin gold chain around her ankle. There was lots of jewelry on her hands and wrists, too, but no wedding ring. Her perfume was powerful and expensive. I put her age at around forty, but I had to look close to do it.

"Debby, get me a coffee, will you?" she called into the hall. Her accent was heavy Brooklyn. She turned into the conference room, ignoring us. "You guys need a refill?" she asked her people. They shook their heads. She glanced at us and called into the hall again. "Just the one, Deb, black with sugar. Thanks, hon." She shut the door and took the vacant seat next to Pell. Conaway whispered to her briefly, and she looked at us as she listened, then she nodded almost imperceptibly. Conaway spoke.

"We're pretty busy around here, gentlemen, as you might imagine. So we want to make this short. It has come to the attention of this office that you are making private inquiries"—he had a faint Boston accent, and he made "private inquiries" sound like "practicing necrophilia"—"into matters directly related to an active federal investigation. We are naturally quite concerned about this. It can't have escaped you that this office has a keen interest in Gerard Nassouli, and we take a dim view of anyone interfering with our witnesses, or potential witnesses. We've called you in today for two reasons: first, to ascertain your interest in this case, and second, to instruct you to cease your inquiries immediately." I wasn't sure if we were supposed to answer him or applaud his diction, but before we could do either, DiPaolo spoke.

"Let me offer you guys a little advice—no charge." She drummed her red nails on the tabletop. Her hands were small but strong looking. "What you just heard is as nice as we get here. You answer our questions, we stay nice. You don't," she shrugged, "we try something different.

"I've found out enough about you guys to know that that probably doesn't sit too well." She turned to Neary. "Tom, I've known you for a while, and I know how you get when you think you're right—how stubborn you can be." Pell snorted, and DiPaolo shot him a silencing look. She turned to Mike. "Counselor, you I don't know, but I asked around and learned a few things. Heard you were very smart, very . . . inventive, and that you hate to lose. Okay—you and me both." Then she turned to me. "And you, what can I say? You got great press, buddy. Depending on who I talk to, I hear that you're either a smart guy, a little arrogant maybe, but good at your work, or that you're some kind of fucked-up rich kid, couldn't cut it in the family biz, and now you're playing at detective, or that you're a cowboy, a showboat, and a screwup who should be doing time for murder-two." She shook her head.

"The point is, I understand that each of you, in your own special way, is a real hard-on. Victims of that old testosterone poisoning. Shit, I know how it is, boys. I know how it screws up your little brains. I've worked with guys like you so long, I sometimes think I picked up a case of it myself. But you got to get over it—here and now. Take a minute before you answer. Think it over."

We were all quiet for a while. Debby came in with coffee. DiPaolo blew on it and sipped some and looked at us. Mike spoke.

"We understand your concern, and we want to help you as much as we can. It's certainly not our wish or intent to have anything to do with an active investigation." Mike spoke softly and evenly. Except for DiPaolo, everyone on the other side of the table started taking notes. Katz looked at DiPaolo, and she nodded to him slightly.

"Yeah, that's nice. Why don't you start by telling us why you're asking around about Gerard Nassouli." Katz's accent was also heavy Brooklyn.

"Sure," Mike said. "Mr. March is conducting an investigation for me, as part of work that I'm performing for a client. In the course of this investigation we've come across what we believe may be a blackmail scheme, carried out by a person or persons, unknown. We think the scheme targets individuals who may have done business with Gerard Nassouli some time ago—fifteen years ago or longer—and that the perpetrators make use of documents that Nassouli would have had access to. Hence our interest in Nassouli."

The three federal prosecutors had pretty good poker faces, but Pell put it all out there. Surprise, puzzlement, and anger played across his fat face.

"You're making the right cooperative noises, counselor," Katz said, "but you're not actually telling us much. Let's get specific here, starting with the name of your client."

Mike smiled a genial, faraway smile. He looked at Katz and DiPaolo. "My client is very concerned with confidentiality. I'm sure you understand."

But Shelly DiPaolo did not look understanding. Her dark eyes got hard and narrow, and her full lips drew back over small, white teeth.

"Fine, counselor," she said, "you made your choice. You want to play it this way, that's okay." She turned to me. "You, you want to tell me who you're working for and who you've been talking to?"

I looked at Mike. He nodded. "I'm working for Mr. Metz, and I've been informed by him that everything I've done or discovered in the course of my investigation is considered attorney work-product, and is to be held in the strictest confidence."

Katz responded. "Did Mr. Metz tell you that the legal ground under that assertion is pretty fucking thin when it comes to keyhole peepers like you? That it might just open up under your feet and swallow you whole? How'd you like to add contempt or obstruction charges to your résumé?"

I looked at the president's photo. He had a nice tie on, and it went well with his suit. Mike answered for me. "I don't think the legal ground is all that shaky, Mr. Katz."

Katz looked pale, and his thin mouth was set in a hard frown. "Fine, we can roll the dice and see how a judge feels about it," Katz said, then he looked at me. "But you should know, March, it's your ass he's gambling with. Attorney-client confidentiality protects him just fine. You're the one that'll take the fall on this. Think about it."

"And perhaps Mr. Metz hasn't mentioned," Conaway chimed in, "that a client's name is not itself protected information under attorney work-product confidentiality. Indeed, counselor," he turned to Metz, "it's not covered under broader attorney-client protections, either."

Mike looked at DiPaolo without expression. DiPaolo turned to Neary. "Speaking of gambling . . . how're you doing in all this, Tom? As far as I can see, you've got no protection against anything. You know who this client is?"

"Nope," Neary said.

DiPaolo looked at him more and shook her head. "How about the blackmail victims—know any of them?"

"Nope."

"So what'd they want from you?"

"A look-see at procedures and systems—how documents get handled, how the liquidation teams work, a tour of the offices. We've done it before, for other Brill offices, outside investigators, even some government types—the standard busman's-holiday tour."

DiPaolo turned back to Mike. "What's your interest in that stuff?"

Mike smiled again. "Our working hypothesis is that the blackmailers are using documents that Nassouli would've had access to. But we believe it's possible that others may have had access to those documents. Someone on the liquidation team, for example, or someone in the investigation."

The prosecutors were stony faced, but Pell was looking apoplectic. He was sputtering, and his face was getting maroon, and he couldn't contain himself.

"What kind of crap . . ." DiPaolo gave him another icy look, and he shut up. She was quiet for a while.

"That's one hell of a theory, pal. Really great. It could call our whole chain of evidence into question. A fucking exculpatory wet dream for defense counsel. Maybe somebody thinks up a damages suit, too, and who knows what else. It's the kind of inflammatory, irresponsible crap that can trash an investigation. Do wonders for Brill's reputation, too." She looked at Tom. "That why you gave them the tour?" she asked him.

"Yep," he said.

"Find anything?"

Tom paused. "My understanding is they're looking for things from Nassouli's personal files. As far as I know, we've never had any of that stuff," he said. I thought a look of relief flitted over DiPaolo's face, but it was gone before I could be sure. If she was relieved, Mike quickly rained on her parade.

"We've discussed the possibility that someone on the liquidation team or in the investigation might have kept those documents out of the system altogether," he said.

"And your theory is based on . . . what?" she asked him.

Mike looked apologetic. "I'm sorry, but—"

Shelly cut him off. "Cut the crap, counselor. You're screwing with my witnesses, spouting this irresponsible shit that can fuck my investigation big time, then you and Bruce Wayne here," she gestured at me, "you hide behind attorney-client protections. Except you won't name your fucking client! You can't be this stupid, Metz. You must know the shit storm that's going to come down on you."

Mike was quiet for a while. "We have no desire to share our theories or discuss this case at all, with anyone, Ms. DiPaolo," he said evenly. "Frankly, we wouldn't be discussing it with you, if you hadn't invited us in. We're not talking to any defense counsel, we're not making statements or giving depositions, and if anyone asked us to, we'd claim attorney-client confidentiality. As I said, we have no wish to be involved in an active investigation."

"Then why are you messing with Trautmann?" Katz asked.

"Mr. Trautmann came to our attention as a close associate of Gerard Nassouli," Mike answered.

"Why did you assault Trautmann?" Katz asked me. I glanced at Mike. "Don't look at him, goddamn it, look at me. Answer my fucking question," Katz snarled. Mike nodded.

"Trautmann assaulted me. I defended myself."

"That's your story. Could be he'll want to press charges," Katz said.

"Could be I'll do the same—against him, and Slim there, too." I flicked a thumb at Pell. Pell's face clenched, and for a second he was going to come across the table, but DiPaolo put a hand on his arm. Mike gave me a warning look.

"Counselor," Shelly DiPaolo said, "we're reaching the end of useful conversation here. Paulie pointed out a few minutes ago that your client's name is not protected information. And since you didn't give him one of your slick, friendly answers, I assume you know it too. So, what's it going to be? You going to answer questions here, or in front of a grand jury?" Mike smiled at her.

"Mr. Conaway's point is well taken. But I'm sure you know that if you want to bring me before a grand jury, you'll need probable cause. From where I sit, I don't see that you have it."

Shelly DiPaolo was perfectly still, staring at Mike. Katz and Conaway shifted uncomfortably in their seats. Only Pell looked pleased—excited, in fact. When DiPaolo spoke, her voice was menacing.

" 'From where you sit,' huh? Then you must be sitting with your head up your ass, Metz. How about that your client has knowledge of criminal conduct material to this investigation? How about that you and March have knowledge of documents sought as evidence by this investigation? How about that you and March have conspired to tamper with evidence and witnesses? How about that the two of you are interfering with the conduct of a federal investigation? How's that for probable cause? How about I subpoena every fucking piece of paper you have on this case, and you spend the next six months Xeroxing and testifying? How does that look from where you sit, asshole?" Mike and DiPaolo looked at each other, without expression, for a long moment. Then Mike sighed.

"Frankly, I'm disappointed, Ms. DiPaolo. And I think, perhaps, I should be speaking to someone else."

The room was still and full of brittle silence. Everyone was looking at Shelly. She was pale, and her jaw was rigid. She stared at Mike, who seemed distant in the way that Pluto is distant. Then slowly and without rhythm, she began to drum her red nails on the tabletop. When she spoke, it was almost a whisper.

"I don't know what you think you're playing at, Metz, but it's a dangerous fucking game," she said.

"I'm not playing at anything," Mike said, his voice steady, but with an edge to it now. "And if I was, I wouldn't be playing with you. As you said, I'm not that stupid. I don't want much here, and mostly what I want is to keep my client out of your way. His dealings with Nassouli ended nearly two decades ago, and to the best of my knowledge he's done nothing that would warrant your attention.

"Our only interest in Nassouli—in the whole investigation—relates to Nassouli's personal files. And I'd think you'd be curious too. If Nassouli has the files, and you have Nassouli, then I'd think you'd want to know if he had a side business going. If he doesn't have the files, then I'd think you'd want to know if someone—maybe on your team, or on Neary's—had them and was up to no good. I'd like to work something out with you, Ms. DiPaolo, in a way that benefits us both, and protects my client. If you don't want to do that . . . well, that's unfortunate. But if that's the case, then maybe your colleague in San Diego, Mr. Perez, would be interested.

"So, if you think you can make probable cause out of all that smoke—fine, take your shot. But if you do, I think you'll be missing an opportunity. I think we both will. "

The rain was loud on the window. Conaway and Katz looked at Mike with disbelief, and maybe a little admiration. Pell looked impatient and a little confused, wondering when the blood was going to flow. Shelly looked down at her fingers, still drumming on the table. She shook her head in wonder and finally spoke, in low tones.

"I don't believe this. You son of a bitch, you're trying to strong-arm me. You've got nothing to trade with, and you're trying to strong-arm me. If nothing else, you've got balls, Metz." She laughed harshly. Then she leaned forward and pointed at Mike. "Well, enjoy them while you can, asshole, 'cause by the end of the day, they're going to be in my pocket. And you two," she pointed at Neary and me, "I'm going to see if I can't have your licenses tacked up on my wall by the end of the week—just for giggles." We didn't say anything. No one said anything, except Pell, who couldn't suppress a chuckle. "Now get out of here," DiPaolo said, "I've got work to do."

Chapter Twenty-one

"Very dramatic, that business with Perez," I said to Mike. He, Neary, and I were in the lobby of One St. Andrews. Mike shrugged.

"Clutching at straws," he said. We looked out at the rain and at the people crossing the plaza, leaning into the wind.

"I guess it could've been worse," I said, though I wasn't sure how. Neary helped me out.

"Yeah, there could've been gunfire."

"We won't know how bad it was until we see what DiPaolo does. It's her play to call," Mike said, buttoning his raincoat.

"She made her intentions pretty clear," Neary said.

Mike shrugged again. "Maybe. I've got a meeting uptown. If I hear anything, I'll let you know." Then he turned up his collar, opened his umbrella, and walked out into the rain. Neary and I looked at each other.

"You talk to your management?" I asked

"Yesterday," he said.

"How'd they take it?"

"The possibility that someone in our shop could be involved in a blackmail scheme scared the shit out of them. Enough so they actually stopped to think, and sort of understood why I'd let you in the door. But the jury's still out, and a lot will depend on how things go with DiPaolo."

"They tell Parsons about it?" I asked.

"Not yet. They want to see what happens here first." We were quiet.

"I'm sorry about all this, Tom," I said after a while.

He held up his hand and shook his head, smiling ruefully. "I got to get to the office," he said, and he belted his raincoat and walked out. I had no office, and at the moment I had no work, so I went home.

It was not quite eleven when I got back to my place. The shades were up on the tall windows, and as I stood before them the chill outside seemed to seep in through the glass, with the gray light and the boiling sound of the rain. My side ached terrifically under the elastic bandage.

The tension of the meeting had receded, and only weariness and an inchoate anger remained. I felt like someone had picked my pockets or slashed my tires. The case had been yanked out from under me, and I didn't know by whom. But maybe I was too tired to do anything with my anger, even if it had a direction. Right now, all I wanted was to wrap myself in my coat and sit down and close my eyes and listen to the rain. And if it never stopped pouring, that was okay with me.

I shook my head. I'd been spending altogether too much time sitting in the dark lately. I got rid of my suit and tie and put on jeans, a turtleneck, a warm sweater, and waterproof boots. I clipped the Glock behind my back, found a waterproof shell, a long-billed hat, and my photos of Trautmann. Sometimes futile activity beats no activity at all.

Central Park wasn't empty, but the people were few and far between, and most of them were walking unhappy-looking dogs. The trees were black and shiny, and the low spots had begun to flood. On the assumption that, if she were in the park, Faith Herman would've found some shelter on a day like today, I focused my search on places where a person could get in out of the rain. After two hours of squishing around, I found her.

The Delacorte Theatre is just south of the Great Lawn, right near the Turtle Pond—around where 81st Street would be if it kept on going through the park. The Delacorte is an outdoor venue, open only in summer, when the Public Theatre stages Shakespeare in the Park. I found Faith Herman, and her shopping cart, beneath the deep awning that shelters the Delacorte's ticket windows. She was sorting cans. Her hair was just as wild, her face just as wrinkled, her blue sneakers just as dirty as when I'd seen her last. She ignored my approach, but looked up apprehensively when I stopped under the awning. The rain was loud, and I was nearly shouting when I spoke.

"Faith, it's me—John March. Do you remember, we spoke in the park, a couple of weeks ago?" Her eyes darted around, and she looked scared and confused for a moment. Then recognition came.

"You're that guy who kicked the shit out of those prick kids," she said. She studied the side of my face. "Looks like somebody's been kicking the shit out of you."

"They've been trying, Faith," I said. "I need you to look at something for me." I took out three photos of Trautmann, two profiles and a full-face. "Have you seen this man before?" She was tentative, but she took them. She peered down at them for some time, then looked up and handed the photos back to me.

"That's him," she said.

"That's who?"

"The fax guy. The guy who paid me to send it."

"You're sure?"

"That's him, I tell you." I let out a deep breath I hadn't realized I'd been holding. She looked at me, expectantly.

"You need some cash?" I asked. She smiled. I gave her a hundred bucks. "Where can I reach you if I need to talk to you again? Where do you sleep?" She gave me the name of a shelter in the West 70s. She paused, and a shy look came across her face.

" 'Course, that's just where I leave my body at night," she said. I didn't speak, but I must have looked confused. She went on. "You know, when the nighttime comes, and I have to put my body someplace?" I must have looked stupid to her. "Jesus' car—I can't bring my body in Jesus' car. So every night when Jesus comes for me, I need to leave it someplace. Then I get in and we can drive all over the city, and over to Rome and Winnipeg, Boise too. All over. It's a real nice car—a big Lincoln, dark blue. Rides smooth. But you can't bring your body in. And no newspapers, either." She started sorting cans again. I stood there for a while, watching her, listening to water hit the awning, like a rain of stones.

It was nearly three when I got back home. I was cold and damp, despite my rain gear. I peeled off my clothes and unwound my bandage and stood under a hot shower for a long while. I thought about Faith Herman. The Lord giveth and the Lord taketh away—sometimes all at once. Faith was nuts, at least some of the time, but enough to make her ID of Trautmann pretty much worthless to anyone but me. But what the hell—more than likely, it was all beside the point. I let the hot water beat down on my neck and shoulders.

I was just winding the elastic bandage around my ribs when the phone rang. Metz, I thought, and I pulled on a T-shirt and picked up. But it wasn't Mike. It was a call from upstate. It was Donald Stennis.

"Get you in the middle of something?" he asked in his gravelly voice.

"No," I said.

We talked for a long time, as we always did—at first about Burr County, and the news and latest rumors. Donald shared them with me in his rough, rumbling bass. He told me about the three genius brothers who had torched their boss's car and blown up his gas grill—and video-taped themselves doing it; and the two kitchen chemists, just back from eighteen months of state hospitality, who were cooking up metham-phetamine again—Donald hadn't figured out where yet; and the bat-tling welder who had laid her husband out in the Tidy Shack parking lot last Friday, busting his nose for the fourth time that I could recall. He went on and on; I knew most of the players, even after three years. There were a few new actors—the ones driving around the county at night, dumping hospital waste from Buffalo by the roadsides, the guy poison-ing coyotes, and cutting off their paws and ears and tails—but not too many. And some things were immutable—like the announcement from the local Republicans, a year before the next election, that again they would have no candidate to run against Donald.

He told me how the fall had been for him. He talked about hunting in the bright woods and fishing in the icy streams and lakes, about the deer he had taken and the fish he hadn't, about the bear that was coming too close to the Green Gorge Trailer Court and the one that had nearly killed Van Adder's brown mutt, about the eagle found dead by the inter-state, and the first snowfall, four weeks ago.

Then he asked about me. As always I said little, and most of that was about work, the only story I knew how to tell—the only narrative that strung my days together and made any sense out of them.

And after that we spoke, as we always did, of Anne. Donald had been to the grave, there beside her mother's, just yesterday. Did I remember how pretty it was on that hillside? I remembered. That old oak was bare now, but for weeks it had been a fiery red. Anne loved that tree. She used to climb it when she was a kid, on the Sunday visits she and Donald made to her mother's grave. Did I remember that tree? I remembered.

Donald had brought a big bunch of orange mums. Mums were her favorite, orange mums and pink roses. I remembered. I remembered it all.

We were silent for a while, and then he asked, as he always did, if I was seeing anyone. I told him no.

"Takes time," he said. Then we wished each other well and said good-bye. I folded my arms on the counter and rested my head on them. My breathing was fast and ragged, but no tears would come.

Chapter Twenty-two

I was still sitting with my head on my arms when the phone rang again. It wasn't Mike this time, either. It was his secretary, Fran, asking me to come to Mike's office ASAP. She didn't know what for. I put on some more clothes and caught a cab uptown.

The evening rush was compounded by rain and holiday-season traffic, and it took me nearly an hour to get to the Paley, Clay offices. Fran was at her desk, busy with a stack of documents.

"Conference room," she said, barely glancing at me.

I went in to find Mike and Neary sitting side by side in silence, staring out at the nighttime cityscape. Neary was in shirtsleeves, his tie loose and his collar open. They were bleary-eyed and pale. There were coffee cups and a pitcher of water and glasses on the table in front of them. They looked like hell. I probably did too. It was that kind of day. Mike motioned for me to sit, and I did. Neary let out a deep breath and rubbed his face. Mike took a long pull on his water and set his glass down.

"DiPaolo called," Mike said, "with a take-it-or-leave-it-offer. We're going to take it."

"Do we draw straws to see who does the time, or is it rock-paper-scissors?" I asked. Mike smiled thinly. Neary didn't react.

"She wants three things from us," he said. "First, we agree to lay off

Nassouli. No more questions about him to anybody. We don't say his name; we don't even think about him too much. Second, anything we find—about who's behind this, Nassouli's files, anything—we turn over to her. Third, we say not a word about this to anyone or the whole deal is off—and that includes her pal Perez, out in San Diego."

"And in exchange for this . . . what?" I asked.

"She gives us a pass, and our client too," Mike said.

"That's pretty generous," I said, "especially considering the kind of hand we were playing. Why?" Mike and Neary traded looks.

"Apparently she's got an applecart that she doesn't want upset right now," Mike said.

"What, with Nassouli in it? Is she saying they've got him? Is she vouching for him—that he's not involved in any of this?" Mike was quiet. He looked at Neary. "What?" I asked, impatient.

"I suppose she is vouching for him," Mike said.

Neary scratched his chin. "Yeah, she's sort of giving him an alibi," he said, nodding at Mike. Then he looked at me, smiling. "I mean, being dead for nearly three years would pretty much rule him out of your case, don't you think?"

I sat back in my chair and shook my head while Neary and Metz were entertained by my surprise and confusion.

"What the hell is going on?" I asked.

"They found the body about six months ago," Neary said, "buried in some park, way out in Suffolk County. Best they can tell, he's been on the bench for around three years, since the time he dropped out of sight, they guess. One shot, a .32, in the head." I was quiet for a while.

"DiPaolo told you this?" I asked. Neary nodded.

"Reluctantly," he said. "But she told me." I shook my head some more.

"What's she up to? Why are they keeping such a tight lid on this?" I asked.

"That's the sixty-four-thousand-dollar question, isn't it?" Neary said, smiling. He looked at Mike.

"She didn't want to talk about any of this," Mike said. "And what little she did say was only to stop us pushing on Nassouli. But reading between the lines, and with what Tom has told me, my guess is that they're into heavy negotiations with people who're under indictment, or are about to be. I think they're trying real hard to create the impression with these guys that they've got Nassouli. And, while I imagine they're not lying about it outright, I'd say they'd very much like these folks to believe that Mr. Nassouli is being cooperative."

"Jesus," I said, shaking my head. "And DiPaolo was afraid we were going to screw up her little charade, asking questions about Nassouli?"

"That's my guess."

"She's skating on some thin ice," I said. Mike nodded.

"Makes you think they don't have as much as they'd like to on some of the big guys, if they're willing to take those kinds of risks," he said.

"Also makes you think they're under pressure to show something for the money they've spent, looking for Nassouli these past three years," Neary added.

"They came down on us pretty hard—and pretty fast," I said. Mike nodded.

"Which is what makes me think their negotiations must be going hot and heavy right now. Timing is everything," he said. I poured a glass of water and drank some, and then I sat back and shook my head some more.

"Don't get too comfortable there, buddy," Neary said to me. "And you may want to switch to coffee. We've got a long night ahead of us." I looked at him and then at Mike.

"I don't know if I can handle this much surprise at once," I said. "What's this 'we' business? Last time I checked you saw nothing in this that had anything to do with your shop. What happened? This Nassouli thing change your mind?"

"It's one of the things that did," Neary said.

"That and what else?" I asked.

"You wonder how Pell knew that I had helped you out?"

"I figured it was one of two things: your source in the investigation, whoever it was you asked about Nassouli, went crying to Freddy, or fat boy figured it out on his own after he found out I'd been talking to Trautmann."

"Well, you'd be wrong on both counts," Neary said. "Freddy didn't figure out jack shit on his own. And I never had a chance to talk to my guy; he's been away since Thanksgiving. According to Shelly, Pell got a message on his voice mail, around noon on Friday—an anonymous message from a pay phone in Brooklyn Heights. One call, telling him about you and Trautmann . . . and me."

My mind raced. The feds hadn't been watching Trautmann. Some-one had dropped a dime to Pell, about Trautmann and Neary both. That meant . . . "Trautmann," I said aloud, "working with somebody on the liquidation team."

Neary nodded and grinned nastily. "Someone from my team, or from Parsons. We're going to find out who."

Mike rounded up some coffee for me, and I told him and Neary about my conversation with Faith Herman. Neither of them was surprised by her identification of Trautmann or by her delusions of driving with Jesus, though the Lincoln got a little smile out of Neary. Then we talked names.

"It's not a long list," Neary said. "Basically, it's the people you met when you visited the MWB offices." I nodded.

Mike's brow furrowed. "Why just them? Why not look at anyone who's there now, and who's been on the job from the start?" he asked.

"The timing," Neary said. "Think about it—Trautmann and John trade punches on Friday morning; by Friday noon someone had called Pell. There wasn't much time between those events. The way I see it, Trautmann told our mole about his run-in with John, and the alarms went off immediately. The mole didn't have to play connect-the-dots, or go snooping around looking at visitor logs. Things happened too quickly for that. I think the mole recognized John from Trautmann's description right away, because he'd met John—with me." Mike nodded.

"But you're right about one thing," Neary continued. "We can pretty much discount anyone who hasn't been on the job from day one, or close to it."

We spent the next ten minutes in silence, as I recalled the people I'd encountered during my visit to MWB, and made a list: Chet, the guard with the scary eyes; smart, edgy Cheryl Compton; the other two Brill guys—Bobby Coe, who looked like a park ranger, and Mitch Vetter, who looked like a wiseguy wannabe; the fat uniform on the fourth floor— Tim; arrogant, sarcastic Evan Mills—an aging preppy, Neary had called him; Mills's three forensic accountants—Greer, the thin, fair-haired guy with glasses, Desai, the slender Indian, and Koch, the hefty Jets fan; the uniform on forty-four, whose name I never caught. Neary, independently, made his own list, and then we compared notes. They matched.

"Great minds think alike," I said. "You know how long all these people have been at MWB?"

"Not all of them." Neary checked his watch. It was close to eight. He pulled out his cell phone and made a call. "Hi, Kevin? It's Tom Neary." He listened for a moment and chuckled. "Yeah, yeah, it's still fucking miserable out there. Anybody working late tonight?" He listened some more. "None of the Parsons people either? Thanks, Kev. I'll be in later on." Neary looked at me. "We've got the place to ourselves."

"I've got to bring our client up to date," Mike said. "I only hope he hasn't unraveled completely."

It was still raining, and traffic in midtown was still a mess, so we got on the subway. It was damp and close and it smelled like a wet sock, but it was fast. We stood near the door and hung on as the train rumbled and swayed southward.

"Your management know the latest?" I asked Neary.

He nodded. "Yeah, and they're praying it's not one of our guys. They don't want to say anything to Parsons or the client until they know for sure. They'll let me play it out, as long as I do it quickly and, above all, quietly. Of course, they want me to check in every five minutes or so."

"Everyone wants quick and quiet," I said. "My client is up against a Thursday deadline, and I'm thinking these guys—the mole, at least—may want to close up shop soon."

He looked at me, puzzled. "Why?"

"For one thing, they seem to be in a big hurry. The day after my run-in with Trautmann, my client got hit up for cash—a nice chunk of change. They've given him only four days to collect it. In the other case I know about, they gave the guy a full week." Neary looked unconvinced. I continued. "And that call to Pell—it was panicky and way too cute—not the kind of thing Trautmann would do. He would know better; he'd know to lay low."

"You think the mole got jumpy and made the call on his own?" Neary asked. I nodded. "If that's the case, we better find him quick, or Trautmann may not leave us anything to find."

We rode the elevator to the third floor, where Neary stopped at the guard's desk. Kevin was a heavyset, fiftyish guy with a thick head of white hair and a beefy face. He was working his way through a fragrant pastrami sandwich and a copy of *Newsday*.

"We'll be on four. You've got my cell number. Give me a buzz if anyone comes in," Neary said. Kevin looked at him for a moment without expression, and nodded.

"Sure thing, Tom," he said. We didn't sign in.

The reception area on four was dimly lit and empty. Neary used his card key and held the metal door for me. The floor was in darkness except for the corridor that ran around the building's central core. Even on carpet, our footsteps seemed loud, and all the building noises, the clicks and whirrs and rumbles, were sudden and startling. I followed Neary around some corners to a locked door. He had the key. He flicked a wall switch, and lights blinked on overhead. We were in the small, windowless room, lined with shelves, that the Parsons people had called the project office. It smelled of dust and paper and the remains of someone's lunch. Neary disappeared for a moment and returned pushing a swivel chair. He took off his coat and suit jacket.

"It's a dirty job," he said, and he took a big white binder from a shelf.

We spent over two hours going through binders full of weekly time sheets, and when we'd finished we'd established starting dates for everyone on our list. Six names came off because they hadn't worked the job long enough, and there were four names left: Cheryl Compton and Mitchell Vetter, from Brill, and Evan Mills and Vijay Desai, from Parsons.

"Any of these names jump out at you as being more or less likely?" I asked him. He shook his head.

"Could be any of 'em," he said.

"Even Compton?" Neary shook his head again and ran a big hand over the back of his neck.

"I'd like to think otherwise, but I've been doing this long enough to know better." He put the last binder back on its shelf. "You have a plan in mind?"

"I have something. It might be reaching to call it a plan." Neary looked at his watch.

"Maybe some food will encourage it," he said.

And it did. I bought him dinner at After the Heat, an all-night barbecue place in the meatpacking district. We had ribs and potato salad and corn bread, some wicked pecan pie, and a lot of strong coffee. And while we ate, and afterward in the nearly empty restaurant, we developed something like a plan. It was not perfect, not by a long shot. It was inelegant and unsubtle and had no shortage of risk. But its faults were offset, at least in part, by the fact that it wouldn't take a lot of time to set up or carry out. Since time was something we had little of, that was a big plus.

"I'll talk to my management tonight. If they have no issues, I'll arrange what we need tomorrow morning. Assuming these four guys are in the office, we can do it tomorrow afternoon," Neary said.

I nodded. "The sooner the better."

It had stopped raining by the time we stepped outside, but the air had turned colder and the wind had stiffened. The streets were empty. It took a while for Neary to find a cab, and I waited with him in silence. When one finally came, he gave me a small nod, got in, and rode away. I looked at my watch. Five minutes till Tuesday.

I was at once exhausted and wired, drained by a day that seemed five days long, excited and anxious about tomorrow, and jumpy from too much coffee. I walked home, through the wet, quiet streets. Overhead, the thick mantle of cloud that had covered the city all day had been shattered by the wind. Now the pieces slid rapidly across the sky, and high above them I saw a pale moon floating, amid paler stars.

Chapter Twenty-three

I got little sleep that night, and none of it was good. Despite the late hour, I'd called Mike Metz when I got home. I'd told him about the list of names Neary and I had come up with, and about our plan. He'd told me about Pierro.

"He's on the ragged edge, John. If this doesn't end soon, he's going to come apart," Mike said.

"Things broke our way with DiPaolo. That was a piece of good news," I said.

"It helped. But he's desperate to get this behind him. He's got the money together already."

"And if this payment isn't the end of it—if it's just the beginning? He's flipping out after a few weeks. What's going to happen six months from now, or a year? It's not too late for him to go to the cops, or make a preemptive move with his management at French," I said.

"I pointed all that out to him, as I have a dozen times before. He doesn't want to hear it."

"You tell him about Nassouli?" I asked.

"Only some of it. I don't want to do anything to queer our deal with Shelly. But I told him that the feds had convinced us that Nassouli was not involved."

"How did he take it?"

"It didn't seem to register. He didn't ask any questions, didn't want to talk about it at all." I'd thought about that for a while. Mike's loud yawn had brought me back. "Call me when you confirm things with Neary," he'd said, and hung up.

It'd been one-thirty when I eased myself into bed. I'd spent the next four and a half hours trying in vain to find a comfortable position, while jumbled fragments of the day's events replayed themselves in my head. I awoke gritty-eyed and sore.

I took a long shower and shaved slowly. Then I wrapped up my ribs, and dressed in jeans and a black turtleneck. I went to the fridge and drank a quart of orange juice from the carton. I felt okay—clean, clear-headed, fit. But I was restless and impatient, anxious to hear from Neary, eager to get started. Tension hummed in the pit of my stomach. I kept moving back and forth in front of my windows.

The feeling of fitness, I knew, was illusory. I'd stiffen up again in an hour or so, and if I didn't get some sleep, I'd be stupid and shaky by noon. The impatience was dangerous, and I needed to tamp it down. Today, if we were good and we got lucky, we'd grab hold of something more than smoke and shadow. It was not a day to get edgy or overeager. It was a day to keep my head in the game. What I needed was a long run, but breakfast and a walk would have to suffice. After that, maybe, I could catch some decent sleep.

I forwarded my calls to my cell phone. I was putting on my jacket when I heard a familiar noise from upstairs. *Thump, thump—whump.* I hunted around my kitchen counter for the business card I knew was there. Her home number was on the back.

"Let me buy you breakfast," I said, when Jane Lu picked up, a little out of breath. There was a long moment of silence before she answered.

"I'll meet you downstairs in twenty minutes," she said.

Exactly twenty minutes later, Jane strode off the elevator. Her cropped black hair was still damp. She was wearing a silky purple turtleneck, well-cut black trousers, and black wing tip shoes. She had a long black coat on her arm and a black leather knapsack slung on her shoulder.

We walked around the corner to Rose Darling, a cozy, chintz-heavy place that stirs a mean bowl of oatmeal. We sat at a table near the front, in a large rectangle of sunlight. I ordered the oatmeal and a coffee. Jane ordered a muffin and tea. The waitress left, and we looked at each other for a while.

"No new injuries?" Jane asked.

I shook my head. "Same old ones, but they're more colorful now."
She smiled a little, and asked how my case was going. I told her about it,
omitting all the revealing specifics. She listened intently.

"With some luck, today could be the day," I said.

"With some luck, you won't collect any more bruises." The waitress
brought our drinks, and we sipped at them.

"Except for my sister reading me your résumé, I don't know much
about you," I said.

The little smile again, then she nodded. "Let's see. . . . My parents
came over from the mainland in the sixties. They were out west for a
while, then they moved to Boston. My dad's a computer scientist, my
mom's an M.D. I've got a sister, Barbara, and a brother, Joe—both older.
She's in the math department at MIT, he does software. We were all
born and raised in Cambridge. Just your typical overachieving Chinese
family."

"Lauren tells me you're some kind of genius. I think that was the
word she used."

She made a small, dismissive gesture with her hand. "That's a pretty
strong word. But I am good at what I do."

"How'd you end up in the CEO-for-hire business?"

She chuckled. "It was one of those right-place-at-the-right-time
things. I was a management consultant, working on a job for a company
that makes lasers. They were foundering and wanted someone to tell
them what to do. It was obvious to me what their problems were, and
what they had to do to fix them. But the partner I was working for
didn't see things the same way—and not for the first time. In fact, about
the only thing we ever agreed on was that we couldn't stand the sight of
one another. So when he ordered me not to discuss my assessment with
the client, I quit. Then I went to the company's chairman and gave him
my findings and my recommendations. And then I went home and
started looking into Ph.D. programs. Two days later the chairman called
me and made me an offer I couldn't refuse. The rest is history."

"Why do you like it?"

"I was in consulting, and before that in banking, and in both those
fields I found that, despite the happy talk about diversity and meritoc-
racy, it pays to be a white guy—especially if you've got your eye on the
executive suite. This work is different. The companies I deal with are
going under for the third time—usually bleeding cash, customers, and
employees. By then, their boards don't give a damn about your pedigree,

or whether or not you pee standing up or if you have two heads. They're not looking for love; they're looking for results. I like that kind of challenge. And I like being in charge." She drank some tea and grinned. "Of course, the money doesn't suck."

Our food came. I added sugar and milk to my oatmeal. Jane broke her muffin into large pieces. We ate.

"What else can I tell you?" she asked. I was quiet for a moment.

"That phone call you got, on Thanksgiving, as we were getting out of the cab—what was that about?" Jane's cheeks reddened, and she made a face somewhere between a smile and a wince.

"Would you believe that was my father? It must've been the tenth time he'd called, that week alone, to ask why I wasn't joining the family for Thanksgiving. What's worse is that he was still calling me about it on Sunday."

"Why such a big deal?" I asked. Jane toyed absently with the two studs in her right ear.

"It's a Chinese thing," she said. "My parents are very . . . traditional in certain ways. It doesn't matter to them that I'm thirty-one years old, or that I'm running my fourth company—it wouldn't matter if I were president of the United States. What they know is that I'm their youngest, a daughter, and unmarried—and by all rights I should still be living under their watchful eyes." She laughed a little, mostly to herself.

"The last company I ran was a little biotech up in Cambridge, and I bet I was the only CEO in town who was living in the same room she had in high school." Jane read the surprise in my face. "Like I said, it's a Chinese thing."

"All that . . . intrusion—it doesn't drive you crazy?" She shrugged.

"Less than it used to, but—sure—it makes me nuts sometimes. It's a lot of overhead. But it's what they need to do, and it's never kept me from doing what I've had to—so what the hell?" She smiled slyly. "Besides, I've been operating on a need-to-know basis since I was sixteen." She drank more of her tea. "More questions?" she asked.

"You haven't said anything about significant others."

"Nothing much to say."

"Nothing now, or nothing ever?"

"Nothing now."

"And before?"

She chuckled. "I guess history has proven them to be not so significant." Then her smile faded. For the first time since I'd known her, I saw a tentative look on her face. "And you? Anyone significant since . . . ?" I shook my head. She looked at me for a while, expressionless.

"Lauren says you spend a lot of time alone," she said.

"Lauren says quite a lot, apparently. Don't you ever need her to shut up and do some work?" Jane smiled a little, waiting for more of an answer. "It's something I know how to do," I said. "It works for me." Jane was silent, but she did small things with the curve of her mouth and the arch of her brow that managed to convey both deep skepticism and a little sadness. Her huge, black eyes held mine for what seemed a long time. Then her phone rang. Jane flipped it open and listened.

"Shit," she said after a while. "The meeting's not till tomorrow—what the hell is he doing here now?" She listened again. "I don't care what he's asking for—give him some coffee, put him in the conference room, tell him I'll be there in twenty minutes, and shut the door." She closed her phone. "Shit," she said softly.

"Not your father this time?" I asked. Her smile was tight and not happy. She shook her head.

"One of my board members, and biggest investors—but not my biggest fan. The board is meeting tomorrow, but he seems to want to get a head start on something." Her smile softened. "I've got to go," she said. She stood. "I'm sorry to run off. I liked this. Call me when you get your case wrapped up; I'll buy you dinner." She put on her coat and fiddled with the buttons and paused. Then she put her small, warm hand gently against the side of my face. And then she kissed me. "I hope you have some luck today," she said softly, and then she was gone.

I sat there, motionless, the blood rushing in my ears, the heat slowly fading on my lips. When my pulse was under 120 again, and I felt like I'd regained some control over my limbs, I gestured to the waitress for the check.

I was walking home when Neary called. We were on.

Chapter Twenty-four

My alarm went off at twelve-thirty. I had slept deeply and without dreaming for four hours. I splashed water on my face and ate a peanut butter and jelly sandwich and drank coffee while I watched the Weather Channel. The forecast called for temperatures to drop into the twenties that evening, and for snow to fall by dark. I didn't doubt it, judging from the heavy, pewter clouds that had moved in while I'd slept. I dug out a pair of flannel-lined jeans and some wool socks. I put on one of my miracle-fiber running shirts and pulled a black turtleneck over it. I checked my cell phone battery—fully charged. I checked the Glock—cleaned and loaded. I pulled on my black leather jacket and stuffed a pair of gloves into the pocket, and I was good to go.

I waited for Neary on the corner of Seventh Avenue and Sixteenth Street. At precisely two o'clock he rolled up, sitting in the passenger seat of a gray van. He looked tired, and so did his ride. It had dented fenders, a bad case of body rust, and some scarred black lettering on the driver's door that read "L&H Painting 1227–29 Myrtle Ave." The long side windows were thick with dirt, and the ones in the rear were even worse. But they were made of one-way glass. A rear door popped open, and I climbed inside. We pulled away, headed downtown.

There were two guys in the van with Neary. The driver was wiry, with unruly salt-and-pepper hair and a day's growth on his narrow face. His eyes were deep-set and pale blue. He wore a gray down jacket, and his hands were strong looking, with prominent veins. He had a small gold hoop in his right ear. He might have been thirty or fifty or anything in between.

"Eddie Sikes," he said in a scratchy whisper, as he eyed me in the rearview mirror. I nodded.

The guy in back with me was black, around my age and height, but bulkier. He had very short hair and an open, amiable face, with high cheekbones, a square chin, and a wide mouth that seemed on the verge of laughing. He wore horn-rimmed glasses and was dressed out of the Paul Stuart window: a brown checked blazer, brown woolen trousers, a blue button-down shirt, and a paisley tie. A brown topcoat was across his lap. He looked like a successful advertising executive, until you noticed the thin scar that ran from his left temple all the way down the side of his neck, and his enlarged, calloused knuckles, and his eyes—as warm and friendly as a pair of bullets. Of course, the matte black grip of a big automatic, visible on his hip where his jacket fell away, was also a good clue.

"Juan Pritchard," he said. His voice was pleasant, deep, and friendly sounding.

"Two men are in the building already," Neary told me. "They replaced two of the uniformed security people, walking the floors. They say all four of our guys are back from lunch. We've got a spot saved on Water that'll give us a view of everything."

I look around the van. It was the surveillance welcome wagon, a rolling smorgasbord of peeping gadgetry. High-powered binoculars, low-light scopes, digital cameras, video cameras, still cameras, an array of lenses, a half-dozen tripods, audio recorders, directional mikes, and a bunch of other stuff I couldn't identify, were racked up and down both sides of the van, nestled snugly in beds of custom-cut foam. It had all the creature comforts, too. At my feet was an ice chest filled with bottled water, and next to it a carton of some kind of high-protein energy bars. In the far corner, by one of the doors, there was even a little chemical toilet. It was the kind of deluxe stakeout rig only a firm like Brill could afford. We could live in here for a week if we had to. But we didn't have that kind of time, and we didn't need it, not for what we were up to.

At its most basic, our plan was to rattle cages—four of them, one at a time—and wait to see what happened. For it to work, I had to be right about two things: that our mole was an amateur, an otherwise straight citizen, except for this foray into serial blackmail; and that he or she was already spooked, maybe on the verge of running scared. The actual mechanics were simple. I would call one of our suspects. My speech would be short and threatening. Without identifying myself, and using a voice scrambler, I would tell him or her to be at the southeast corner of Broad and Pearl Streets in ten minutes' time. Otherwise, Nick Welch's suicide case would be reopened as a murder investigation. And then we would watch and wait. An innocent person might have any number of reactions to that kind of call: incomprehension, confusion, disbelief, anxiety. Our mole, on the other hand, inexperienced and already skittish, would—we hoped—do one of two things: show up at Broad and Pearl, or run. If that happened, we'd be watching and following. Then Neary and I would confront the guy and shake—hard.

It was simple, but not without risk. The biggest one, of course, was that I'd gotten it all wrong. Maybe our mole was no amateur, maybe Trautmann had trained him well, or maybe he had ice water in his veins. Maybe he'd take my call, and do absolutely nothing. If that was the case, our only alternative would be to mount close surveillance on Trautmann and all four of our suspects. That would be expensive and time consuming, and it would mean Pierro was shit-out-of-luck, for now at least.

There were other risks, and we'd tried to plan around them. But there'd be things we hadn't thought of. That was one of the truisms of this kind of work: nothing went according to plan. People did the unexpected, equipment broke, all luck was bad. Shit happens.

It was slow going downtown, but Sikes drove well. He knew the streets and was unruffled by the traffic. He and Pritchard made some desultory small talk about the Knicks, but mostly it was quiet in the van, with a faint undercurrent of tension. It wasn't obvious, or even unpleasant, just a low-level hum, like the cycling of a heating system. The sound of each of us getting his head in the game.

At three o'clock, a maroon Chrysler pulled out of a spot just off the southwest corner of Water and Broad, and our van pulled in. We had a view of the MWB offices, to the south, and the intersection of Broad and Pearl, to the north. An attractive woman with dark eyes and olive skin and lots of curly hair was behind the wheel of the Chrysler. There was a fine-featured Hispanic man in the passenger seat. Neary spoke to them.

"Thanks for keeping it warm. What's happening?" he asked.

"Nothing," the woman said. "Pressman and Sanchez were on the horn ten minutes ago. Said they were all at their desks."

"Okay. You and Victor head up Broad. Let me know your location," Neary said. The woman nodded, and they drove off.

"Let's do a radio check," Neary said to Sikes. Sikes reached into a compartment on the side of the driver's seat and took out a big radio in a black leather holster. He flicked a switch and static bloomed, then dwindled to a hiss.

"Unit One to all units, radio check," he said.

"Unit Two to Unit One, this is Pressman, on the third. I hear you, Eddie," said a voice.

"Three to One, Sanchez here, Sikes. I'm on four. You sound good," said another.

"Unit Four to Unit One. DiLillo here." It was the woman in the Chrysler. "Got a space on the west side of Broad, just south of Stone. Good view. Hear you fine. Victor's out walking."

"Unit Five to One. This is Victor, Eddie. It's freaking cold out," another voice said. Sikes looked at Neary, who nodded.

"Juan has your toy," Neary said to me. Pritchard pulled a black, plastic case from under his seat, opened it, and took out a black plastic box a little larger than a beeper. The voice scrambler. He handed it to me.

"Checked it out this morning. It works fine. Give it a try," he said. I spoke into it.

"Testing, testing, one, two, three. In brightest day, in blackest night, no evil shall escape my sight," I said. I sounded like a robot castrato. I flicked it off.

"I'll be outside the building," Pritchard said. He fixed a tiny earpiece in his left ear and went out the back door. A minute later he was on the radio, asking for a check. Sikes acknowledged him.

Neary reached back and handed me a sheet of paper. "Here's your cheat sheet," he said. On the page were the names, office numbers, and home addresses of each of our suspects, along with physical descriptions of each of them, and grainy headshots that looked like they were copied off ID photos. It also listed the cell numbers of everyone on our little team.

"Who first?" I asked. I thought I knew the answer. Neary's management wanted more than anything to know about the two Brill people on the list, and Neary wanted to know about Cheryl Compton.

"Compton," Neary said. Sikes picked up the radio.

"Unit One to Unit Two. Give me a location on Compton, Lenny," Sikes said. A couple of moments later a voice came back.

"Two to One. Give me a minute, Eddie," the voice said. There was silence for a while. "Two to One. She's not at her desk. She's . . . in the hallway. She's turning." There was another pause. "She's in the can, Eddie. Been in and out of there all day. Could be she's got her period, or the runs or something." Sikes rolled his eyes. Neary took the radio.

"One to Two. This is Neary. Spare me the health report, Len. Where's Vetter?"

"Two to One. Just passed him in his office, boss, working at his desk," Pressman answered. Neary looked at Sikes and me.

"Vetter first, then." He spoke into the radio. "Unit One to all units, we're live now with Mitch Vetter. Acknowledge." One by one Neary's people called in their acknowledgments. Neary handed me a cell phone. "Caller ID's blocked. It's all yours," he said. I punched in Vetter's number and switched on the voice scrambler.

"Mitchell Vetter speaking." I remembered the high-pitched voice and the New York accent.

"Listen to me. Unless you want to see the Nick Welch case reopened as a murder investigation, be at the corner of Broad Street and Pearl in ten minutes. Ten minutes, Vetter, or you'll be answering a lot of questions about Nick Welch." There was a long silence at the other end of the line. And then there was laughter.

"Sid? Fucking Sid, is that you?" Vetter was laughing hard. "Jesus, you are a sick puppy. The voice thing is a cute touch, though. But who the hell is Nick Whosis? Sid? Sid?" I hung up. Neary looked at me. I shook my head.

"He thought it was funny," I said. "Unless he is very slick, he didn't know who Nick Welch was. He thought I was somebody named Sid."

"Unit One to Unit Two. What's up, Lenny?" Neary said into the radio. Lenny's whispered voice came back quickly.

"Two here. He's at his desk, laughing and making a phone call. Now he's talking, still laughing. He's stopped laughing now, looks confused. Still talking, shaking his head. Now he's off the phone." Pressman paused for a moment. "He's just looking at the wall now, shaking his head. Now he's typing at his keyboard again."

"What do you think?" Neary asked me.

"I think he's not our guy, but give him a few minutes," I said. Neary nodded and called Pressman on the radio.

"One to Two. Lenny, stay close to Vetter for another fifteen." Pressman acknowledged. Neary handed the radio back to Sikes, who updated the other units. Then we waited. After about a day, fifteen minutes passed, during which time the most exciting thing Mr. Vetter did was to buy a soda. We agreed to move on. Neary looked at Sikes.

"Unit One to Unit Two. Where's Compton at, Lenny?" Sikes said. It took a couple of minutes for the answer to come back.

"Two here. She's at her desk, nobody else in the room." Neary nodded. Sikes got on the radio again and told all of Neary's people we were placing the call to Compton. They acknowledged, and Neary looked at me. I flicked on the voice box and punched her number.

"Cheryl Compton." She spoke quickly. I said my piece, and again there was a long silence, longer this time than with Vetter. But when Cheryl answered, it wasn't with laughter.

"Who is this?" she said in a low, tense voice.

"Ten minutes, Cheryl," I said. More silence.

"What the hell are you doing to me?" she hissed. I hung up. Neary looked at me.

"She wasn't laughing," I said. Sikes called Pressman.

"Talk to me, Lenny."

"She's just sitting there, holding on to the arms of her chair, looking at the walls. She looks . . . I don't know, real stiff." There was a pause. "Now she's picking up the phone. She's talking, now she's hanging up. Looks like maybe she left a message for somebody. Okay, she's getting up now. I'm moving." There was another pause, longer this time, then Pressman came back. "She's walking around the main corridor, to the north end of the building. She's going down one of the aisles. She's at a window, looking out. I got to keep moving, sorry."

We waited for Pressman to come back. Neary was pale and rigid with tension, and maybe anger. He looked exhausted. Sikes looked bored. Then Pressman spoke.

"Okay, she's back in her office now. She's on the phone again . . . talking . . . hanging up. Looks like another message. She's just sitting there again." Neary looked at me.

"I don't know, Tom," I said. "Give her some time." He looked at his watch. It was three-forty and getting dark out. It was also getting closer to rush hour, which mostly worked against us. The bigger crowds made it harder to spot a tail, but they also made it much easier to lose your subject.

"Twenty minutes," he said. Sikes spread the word. We waited. Pressman gave us reports every five minutes. He told us about Cheryl Compton sitting, staring at the walls, calling numbers that seemed not to answer, pacing around her desk, sitting back down, and staring some more. Twenty minutes came and went, and Neary gave it fifteen more. Five minutes before that deadline, Compton seemed to settle down and go back to work.

"Something's sure as hell bugging her," Neary said. "And I'd like to know who the fuck she's calling." His voice was tight with frustration. He shook his head. "It's getting late; let's move on. Where are Desai and Mills?"

"Keep an eye on her, Lenny," Sikes said into the radio. "We're moving to the fourth floor now. Unit One to Unit Three, where are your guys?" Sanchez's voice came over the radio, telling us that Mills and Desai were in their respective offices.

"Desai first," Neary said. Sikes nodded and picked up the radio.

"Unit One to Unit Three. We're going with Desai. Tell me what you see, Sanchez."

Sanchez's voice came back quickly. "I'm looking at him now, Eddie. He's working at his desk." Neary gave Sikes the nod, and Sikes notified all units that we were live with Desai. Neary looked at me. I picked up the cell phone and did my thing.

"What? Who . . . who is this?" Vijay Desai said. "Who are you calling for? Is this some kind of sales thing?"

"Ten minutes, Desai," I said.

"Ten minutes for what? Who is this?"

I hung up. I looked at Neary and shook my head.

"Either a great actor or completely clueless. My vote is clueless," I said.

Sikes got on the radio. "What's the haps, Sanchez?"

"He's just sitting there. Looks kind of confused."

"Give him ten," Neary said, but before Sikes could get back on the radio, Pressman's voice cut in.

"Unit Two to Unit One. Vetter is moving. He's got his coat on, headed for the elevators." He sounded out of breath.

Sikes spoke quickly. "Unit One to Unit Six. You hear that, Juan?"

"I heard," Pritchard said. "I'm by the doors. What's he wearing, Lenny?"

"Tan pants, brown leather coat, thigh length, blue-and-red-striped scarf," Pressman answered quickly.

"I'll let you know when I pick him up," Pritchard said. While we waited, Sikes spoke to Sanchez. Desai was apparently back at work. After a few minutes, Pritchard came back.

"Got him. He's headed up Water, toward William Street. I'm half a block back," Pritchard said. "Victor, you close by? Can you flank him?"

"Can do. I'm at Broad and Pearl, heading up Pearl to William," Victor said.

"Stay with him," Sikes said. The minutes passed slowly. It was nearly four-thirty, and night had all but fallen. The crowds were thicker on the sidewalks and the traffic heavier. It was going to be harder and harder to keep a tail. "Talk to me, Juan," Sikes said.

"Turning up William Street, now. It's getting crowded out here, Eddie," Pritchard said. Neary checked his watch. Desai's time was up. It was Mills's turn. Neary gave Sikes the nod.

"Sanchez, where's Mills?" Sikes asked.

"At his desk. I'm looking at him now." I flicked on the voice box, but before Sikes could notify the units, Pressman broke in again, breathless.

"Shit, Eddie, I lost her. I lost Compton. Goddamn, her coat's gone. Eddie, she's off the floor. She may be headed out. Shit." He was short of breath and sounded scared. Sikes's face furrowed in dismay. Neary let out a huge, disgusted breath.

"Un-fucking-believable," he said in a harsh whisper. He took the radio from Sikes. When he spoke, his voice was calm and level.

"Take it easy, Len. Check with the uniform at the desk. Lorna, you hearing this?"

The woman from the Chrysler answered. From the background noise, she was on the street. "Copy that. I'm headed toward the building now." Then Pressman came back.

"She signed out five minutes ago, boss. Shit." Lenny was not having a good day. I moved around the back of the van, peering out at the crowds streaming by. Neary stayed calm. He spoke into the radio.

"Lorna, keep your eyes open. She could be on the street, headed toward you. What's she wearing, Len?"

"Gray pants, some kind of parka, light gray and blue," Pressman answered. I looked out the rear windows. I caught a glimpse of a blue and gray jacket and a head of thick, brown hair.

"Got her!" I said. "On Water, headed toward Whitehall. Must've just passed us by." Neary got on the radio again.

"Where are you, Lorna?"

"I'm at the bank, boss. You guys are closer," she answered. Neary thought about it for a second, then reached into the back and came up with a tiny radio. He stuffed it in his pocket and plugged an earpiece in his ear. He handed Sikes the big radio.

"Eddie, you coordinate. Make sure everybody stays in touch. And keep that dork Pressman away from any sharp objects. I'll take Cheryl," Neary said. He looked at me. "You and Eddie do Mills. Fucking Murphy's Law." He smiled ironically, shook his head, and was gone. Sikes and I looked at each other.

"Call the ball, chief," he said. I nodded. He called Sanchez.

"Mills just went to the can, Eddie. I'll squawk you when he's back," Sanchez said. We waited and listened to the jumpy chatter on the radio. Pritchard and Victor were still on Vetter, in Hanover Square. Neary was on Compton, who'd turned up Whitehall. DiLillo was running up Broad Street, as best she could in the evening crush, trying to cut over to Whitehall and pick up Compton. Sanchez came on again, telling us Mills was back. I punched the number, and Mills picked up right away. I flicked on the voice box and spoke.

There was a sharp intake of breath on the other end of the line. Then silence. Then he hung up.

"What's up, Sanchez?" Sikes asked.

"You freaked him out. The guy is sitting there, white as a sheet, running his fingers through his hair." Sanchez paused. "He's got his cell phone out. He's getting up, now. Shit. He shut the office door, Eddie."

"Keep on him, Sanchez." We waited. Sikes checked status with the foot patrol. Pritchard and Victor were watching Vetter have coffee at a place off Hanover Square. They thought he might be waiting for someone. Neary was a block behind Compton, approaching Broadway. DiLillo was a block ahead of her. Sanchez cut in.

"He's leaving, Eddie. Repeat, Mills is leaving. Wearing black pants and a dark gray overcoat. Got a black leather briefcase on a shoulder strap. Guy doesn't look happy, Eddie." Sikes looked at me.

"Give me a radio," I said. Sikes reached around and grabbed one. I plugged the earpiece in and flicked the switch. Nothing. "Dead." I tossed it in his lap.

He swore colorfully. "That's the last one."

"You'd think an outfit like Brill could afford batteries," I said, laughing. "I'll use my phone." I climbed out of the van.

It was almost five, and the sidewalks were jammed. I nearly missed Mills as he came out of the building. He was walking quickly, but his gait was stiff. His long blond hair looked greasy, and his complexion was gray, though it could've been the streetlights. He was stabbing at his cell phone. He headed up Broad Street. I let him get a half block ahead of me before I followed. In these crowds, I was going to stay close. Mills turned on Water and passed the van without a glance. He took a right on White-hall, headed toward Bowling Green. I followed, struggling through the crowd. So far, it was the same route Cheryl Compton had taken.

It was much colder now, and the air felt like snow. The clouds, lit from below by the city, were heavy with it. Mills was still fiddling with his phone. The crowds grew thicker as we approached Bowling Green. The stream of people became a river, with tributaries and crosscurrents. One branch flowed north, up Broadway, another to the west, into the Bowling Green subway station, and there was a heavy press southbound, to the ferry terminal. People were bundled against the cold, and lost in the automatic routines of commuting. We were at the bottom of Bowling Green, just opposite the Custom House. Mills crossed Whitehall and headed for the subway. I was right behind him.

Chapter Twenty-five

I managed a quick call to Sikes before I descended beneath the river. I was on the 4 train, to Brooklyn, wedged between a musty-smelling man and a large woman whose breasts were mashed against my broken rib. I was riding at the front of the car, near the connecting door to the car ahead. Through its scratched glass I could just see Mills's arm and shoulder.

I knew from the sheet Neary had given me that Mills lived in Park Slope, and I figured we were headed there. That meant three stops to Atlantic Avenue, then a transfer, probably to the 1 train, and one more stop, maybe two. We rumbled along under the river, the lights in the car periodically winking out and fluttering back on. We slowed coming into the first stop in Brooklyn.

Borough Hall is a big transfer point, and lots of people got on and off the train. I got a momentary scare when I lost sight of Mills, but then he reappeared, having been hidden behind a man traveling with several large rugs. I shifted my position and saw him in profile. His narrow face was taut, and his lips had all but disappeared. So far he'd shown no signs of concern about being followed; no furtive glances, no sudden course changes. He seemed oblivious to what was going on around him, blinkered by tension and fear.

We went on, past Nevins Street, to Atlantic Avenue. Atlantic Avenue is a bigger transfer point than Borough Hall, linking more subway lines and connecting to the Long Island Rail Road's Flatbush Avenue station. If Mills were headed for Park Slope, he'd change here. He stirred as we approached the station. I wormed my way toward the doors. There was a rush of people when they opened, and in it I lost Mills. I scanned up and down the platform and saw nothing but a mass of shuffling bodies. The station was a maze of narrow passages and stairways. I was following signs to the 1 train when I saw a tall, thin figure jabbing at a cell phone. It was Mills, but he wasn't switching to another subway line. He was headed toward the LIRR station.

Flatbush Avenue is a small station, one end of a spur line that makes two other stops in Brooklyn and ends in Queens, at the LIRR's big hub in Jamaica. It's under perpetual renovation, but remains a ratty affair, with not much more to it than a couple of platforms, some ticket windows, an information booth, a decomposing newsstand, and a scabrous snack bar. At this hour it was packed. Up ahead, Mills moved with the crowd toward the platforms. I grabbed some schedules from the information booth and followed.

People were waiting four deep out there. It was easy to keep sight of Mills, but I was worried about losing him when the train came. I edged nearer, through a phalanx of heavy coats, and made no friends doing it. Mills was still working his cell phone, apparently without success. His face was waxen. The train came, and he pushed on. I did the same, at the opposite end of the car from Mills. It was standing room only and nearly as close as the subway. Something loud and garbled came from the PA system, and we lurched out of the station.

We rolled along at a good clip, first through tunnels, and then up on elevated tracks. I leaned near the door and looked out. There wasn't much to see through the Plexiglas: darkness, the smear of city lights, and my own face, white and tense. The conductor came by for tickets, and I bought one for Jamaica. We slowed coming into the East New York station. I pulled out my cell phone. The signal was spotty, but I tried Neary anyway. I heard his voice on the line, but between the weak signal and the train noise, I couldn't make out his words. I told him where I was and what I was doing, but I had no idea if he heard any of it. I looked down the car. Mills stood by the far doors, swaying as the car swayed.

I leafed through the schedules I'd grabbed and found the train we were on. The next stop would be Jamaica. It was the junction point for all the LIRR branch lines, and from there, Mills could go anyplace on a system that stretched from Manhattan to Montauk. After Jamaica, this particular train would go on to make the Hempstead branch run, stopping in several Queens neighborhoods on its way into Nassau County. One of those neighborhoods was Bellerose.

The platform was crowded when we pulled into Jamaica. There was a heavy flow of people on and off the train, but Mills didn't move and neither did I. After a few minutes, the doors closed and we pulled out again. The conductor came around for tickets, and I bought one for Bellerose.

I tried my cell again. The signal was still flaky. I punched Neary's number and this time heard him clearly. Unfortunately, I was hearing his voice mail greeting. I left a message, telling him where I thought I was headed. Then I tried Sikes. He answered right away. I could barely make out his words, but I heard urgency in his voice. I gave him my status quickly, and he started to tell me something about Compton when the signal cut out completely. I tried to get him back but couldn't.

The Hollis station came and went, and so did Queens Village, and then we were in Bellerose. Mills was standing by the door, ready to go. Lots of people got off at Bellerose; Mills was the first. He walked briskly, like he knew where he was going. I stayed well back. I wasn't worried about losing him now; I knew where he was going too. Mills walked out of the station onto Commonwealth Boulevard. I followed.

It was colder now, a wet, penetrating cold, and snow was coming down in big, ragged flakes that were too heavy to float. They melted on the pavement, and the streets around the station glistened under sodium lights. Mills walked north, toward Hillside Avenue. His stride was stiff and jerky, like he was fighting the urge to run. He never looked back.

He was two blocks ahead now. I remembered how the streets ran here, and I knew it wouldn't be long before Mills turned east off Commonwealth. He didn't disappoint me. When he turned, I did too, onto a parallel street. It was quieter back here, with little traffic and no pedestrians. Warm light spilled from the windows of the small houses, and it was easy to imagine dinner on the table and kids doing homework inside. A lot of the places were lit elaborately for Christmas, and the falling snow was painted in gaudy colors.

I could follow this street east for three blocks, then turn north again to get to Trautmann's house. If I was fast enough, I might even get there before Mills did. I broke into a run. It wasn't pleasant. There was a burst of pain with every footfall. It was work to get air into my lungs and work to get it out again, and each breath burned. After a block, the muscles in my side began to seize up. I slowed to a jog and then to a walk at Trautmann's street.

I stopped behind a parked panel truck. Trautmann's house was less than a block away, across the street. It was dark, and as shuttered and guarded looking as it had been the first time I'd seen it. My heart was pounding, and it wasn't from the run. I took some slow, deep breaths, trying to dissipate the building adrenaline.

I hadn't been there two minutes when Mills crossed the street and climbed the concrete steps to Trautmann's front door. He rang the bell and waited. He rang again, and waited, and rang again. He stepped away from the door and looked up and down the street and looked at his watch. Then he walked down the steps and up Trautmann's narrow driveway and disappeared around the side of the house. I stayed put. Nothing happened for a minute or two, and then I saw lights through the tall hedges at the back of the house.

I waited some more. The snow was falling faster now, in smaller flakes that stuck on the bushes and the tiny lawns. It was quiet, and the snow made it seem even quieter. I walked down the street at an even pace, past Trautmann's house on the opposite side. No car in the driveway. I kept on walking for another block. A station wagon drove by but did not pause. I crossed the street and turned back.

The For Sale sign was still up at the house next door to Trautmann's, and its windows were still dark and empty. I glanced around the street. No one. I walked quickly up the driveway and around to the back of the vacant house. The yard was a square of brown grass, now dusted in snow. It was bordered in the rear by a low cinderblock wall, and on the far side by a section of the fence that ran around Trautmann's property. I crossed to the far corner of the yard, where it abutted Trautmann's detached garage. There was a narrow strip of dirt between the rear of the garage and Trautmann's tall hedge. I scaled the fence and dropped quietly into the gap.

I crouched, listening, and a low growl came from the other side of the hedge. In the yard behind Trautmann's, the Rottweiler was running in agitated circles, snorting and grunting. His growls grew angrier, and his grunts became barks. Shit. I moved slowly along the back of the garage and then down the side. The dog quieted down. I stood in the shadows for a minute, getting my breathing under control, listening. Nothing moved. I peered into the small garage window. No car.

The rear of Trautmann's house was dark, except for some windows on the far side. I crossed the driveway and edged toward them, staying close to the back of the house. As I drew nearer, I saw that they were kitchen windows, set on either side of a metal storm door at the top of four concrete steps. I put my hand on the iron railing and my foot on the first step. I heard a scraping sound and a crackling noise.

And something white exploded behind my eyes, and swallowed me whole.

Chapter Twenty-six

Something cool was resting on the side of my face, pressing up against my cheek. It was smooth and flat. It was heavy. I opened an eye, and the world was dim and red and tilting away. I shut my eye, but things kept on tilting in the darkness.

Something cool was resting on the side of my face, pressing up . . . no. My face was resting on something cool. My cheek was pressed against something cool and smooth and flat. A floor. I was facedown on a floor. My body was loose and liquid and drifting, and I was tethered to the earth only by my face on the floor, and by my head, which was as dense as a crate of mud.

I heard sounds—murmuring, rising, falling, loud bursts. After a while, the sounds became words, many of them, coming rapidly, one after the other. I strained to catch them, but they were like live fish, slippery, wriggling, and I couldn't hang on. After a longer while, the words became speech.

"Stop whining, for chrissakes, and bring that box from the hall."

"You're sure he's not awake? His arms and legs keep moving."

"I told you, a jolt like he got, they twitch around. I gave him a pretty good boot in the head, too. He's not going anywhere. Just keep your pants dry."

"Shouldn't we put a plastic thing on his ankles too?"

"Go ahead, if you plan on carrying him around. Me, I'd rather he walk. Listen, take a deep breath and shut the fuck up for a couple of minutes, will you? Make yourself useful, bring that box in here."

"You fit it all in three boxes?"

"Everything we picked, videos and all."

"What about the rest?"

"Had a little bonfire on Sunday. Don't need any of that shit, and I sure as hell don't want it turning up around here. They'll be on our butts soon enough, thanks to you. Don't want to make it any easier for 'em than you already have, huh Millie?"

"I told you . . ."

"Now is not the time for you to talk. I don't give a shit what you told me. If you could've held your fucking water, none of this shit would be happening and I wouldn't be packing my fucking bags now."

"He knew . . ."

"Didn't they teach you English at prep school? What don't you understand about 'Shut the fuck up?' Christ . . . and this was such a sweet deal, too. Bought you that fucking hacienda down in Santa Whatever. Got me my place in the islands. And it had legs. We could've run this out for years. But you have to shit your pants the first time somebody asks a question. And calling the *Federales* . . . fucking incredible. Make us rush things with 'ole Ricky P. And now this."

"He knew about Welch . . ."

"How did you get this far, being so stupid, huh Millie? If he knew so much, he wouldn't be making phone calls, telling you to meet him on some street corner, you putz. He was fishing, and you were the fish. And he hooked you and gave you lots of line so you could fucking drag him here. And now what? Now I'm getting out of Dodge, thanks to you."

The voices approached and retreated, accompanied by footsteps, the hard sounds of heels on bare floors. The voices were familiar, but I couldn't find the names. A twitch shot through my shoulders and arms, and I realized my wrists were bound behind me. I tried opening my eyes. One was pressed against the floor and squeezed shut. The other was sticky, crusted with something. I worked it open, and when I did, the world began to spin and tip again, and I was sliding off the floor. I shut it quickly.

"I'm telling you, he's coming around. I just saw him blink," a voice said from close by. Footsteps approached.

"Yeah? Let's see," the other voice said, and something hard prodded my broken rib. I gasped involuntarily, and jerked away. "Shit, you're right, Millie. Get him up." They grabbed me roughly by the arms and hauled me into a chair. A spike of pain rode up my side, from hip to armpit. I opened my eyes, and the world started sliding. I squeezed them shut and opened them again. And again. Things steadied.

I was in a kitchen. It was a medium-sized, rectangular room, with a door and two windows at one end, a passage into a dark hallway at the other, and all the kitchen stuff massed on the long wall in between. The fittings were circa 1960-something: pea green cabinets, orange counter-tops, speckled linoleum floor, appliances the color of old mustard. Yellow roller shades covered the windows. A dim, ugly light came down from a fixture overhead.

I was sitting in a straight-backed wooden chair, near a square wooden table. Three cardboard boxes took up most of the tabletop. They were open, and I saw bulky manila envelopes inside. The counters were bare except for an uncapped gallon bottle of vodka, an ice tray, my gun, my cell phone, and some plastic handcuffs, the disposable kind they use for mass arrests. Mills's briefcase was resting against the dishwasher.

"Yo, earth to Johnny! You in there, pal?" Trautmann snapped his fingers in front of my nose. He was wearing jeans and a black Metallica T-shirt. He had a highball glass in his hand and a big automatic under his arm. His hands were huge, and the red scar on his forearm seemed to glow. There was tape across his nose and bruising under his eyes, and he made me think of the Vandals sacking Rome. He raised his glass and took a big swallow.

Mills stood behind him. He looked a thousand years older than the first time I'd seen him, and his steady stream of chatter had gone dry. His eyes were shadowed, and the bones of his face seemed very close to the surface. His lank hair fell forward over his forehead. He crossed his arms on his chest, hugging nothing. He looked at Trautmann and me like we were zoo animals out of our cages.

"How you feeling, Johnny? Not so hot, I bet." Trautmann chuckled and took a swig from his glass. He was right. Besides the pain in my side and the dizziness, twitches still jerked through my arms and legs, my eyes were jumping around in my head, and nausea was rippling through me in waves. Worst of all, my brains were Jell-O. My attention kept wandering, like an energetic drunk on a street full of bars.

"Got your wires all jangled up, huh? Sparky will do that." Trautmann picked something up off the kitchen table and flipped it end over end in the air. It looked like a long, black flashlight, but instead of a lamp at the end, it had a wide, flat head, tipped with two pairs of metal fangs. He caught it and pressed a button and a blue ribbon of electricity arced across two of the fangs. A stun gun.

"Not exactly street legal," he said. "It cranks way higher than what the cops can use. Really eats up the batteries, though. But don't worry, I got plenty on hand." Then he made a sudden, grunting noise and feinted at my chest with the stun gun. I didn't move, but only because I was processing things too slowly to be startled. Trautmann laughed massively.

"Who're you working for, anyway—the widow Welch, maybe? Pierro? I think it's Ricky, but Millie doesn't buy it. Tell me I'm right, Johnny." I looked at him but said nothing. Trautmann smiled. "Any friends of yours out there now?" he asked. "Your buddy, Neary, maybe? I'm betting no. I didn't see anybody, and I'm pretty careful. And you've been in here long enough that anybody outside would be good and worried by now. Would've come to take a look maybe, or called the cops. But it's all quiet out there. I figure you for the lone wolf type, anyway. Am I right?" I kept looking at him, and kept quiet.

"See," he turned to Mills, "you can take a lesson from this guy. He's a prep school faggot like you, but he doesn't piss his pants. In fact, I was reading up on Johnny, and it turns out he's a real trip." Trautmann drained his glass and went to the kitchen counter to fill it again. He poured liberally from the vodka bottle. He was putting it away pretty quick, and I thought maybe he was drunk, but he was such a head case it was hard to tell. Mills gnawed his lower lip and looked at Trautmann.

"You should see his press clippings, Millie. Next to naked pictures, it's some of the best shit I've found on the Internet—a fucking hoot. It turns out Johnny used to be a cop, somewhere up in North Bumfuck, New York. About three years back, he's carrying water for the feds and the state cops, who're in his neighborhood working a serial killer." Trautmann looked at me. "Dead broads in New York, Vermont, up in Canada. What, eight or ten stiffs in all?"

"Twelve," I said. Trautmann whistled. He flipped the stun gun and caught it one-handed.

"Busy boy. So, Washington's finest are on the job, sweating every fucking bear in the forest, I bet, and getting nowhere. But Johnny, here, he's got a theory—some local guy he likes for the killings. So, he goes to the feds and the state boys, and he tells them all about it. And what happens? They blow him off. Think he's full of shit, I guess, just some weird rich kid playing cops in the woods. Told him to shut up and stay out of the way. Which must've pissed Johnny off something fierce, 'cause he decided to become his own one-man task force, and he gets in this guy's shit in a big way." Trautmann swirled his drink around.

"But this woodchuck was even more of a psycho than anybody figured. After a couple months of having Johnny in his drawers, the guy flips out—flips out some more, I guess. And what does he do? He fucking offs Johnny's wife, for chrissakes!" He chuckled and took another swallow.

"It was real neat. No knives, no sex, nothing like his usual act, just one in the eye with a .22 target pistol. But he made damn sure Johnny knew who'd done it. Left a shell casing with a nice clean print, palm print on a window, tire tracks, everything. And then he goes home and writes it all down, full confession with names and dates and stuff nobody but him could've known. And then he sits and waits for the cops to come and take him away." Trautmann chuckled and went to the back door. He raised the shade and peered into the dark for a moment. Then he returned. He flipped the stun gun and caught it again.

"Except it didn't quite work out that way, 'cause the first cop on scene was Johnny." Trautmann laughed and emptied his glass. He set it on the kitchen counter. "I guess there were some . . . questions about what happened next. Some different versions of what went down. I know how that goes, pal, believe me. Anyway, the upshot is that when the cavalry arrives, they find Johnny and this crazy bastard. The guy's dead, of course. Got like ten holes blown in him, and he's got a gun in his hand, some cheap piece of shit with the numbers missing. Not too suspicious, huh?" Trautmann fished an ice cube out of his glass and put it in his mouth and crunched loudly.

"Johnny caught all kinds of shit for a while, most of it from that fat bastard Pell. Small world, ain't it? But did he get all jumpy and start crying like a baby? No. He just shut his mouth and toughed it out. Held his water, til it was declared a righteous shoot. See, that's a lesson for you, Millie. To keep your fucking mouth shut." Trautmann laughed again and punched Mills not so lightly on the shoulder. Mills rocked back and steadied himself on the refrigerator.

I didn't pay much attention to Trautmann's story; it was basically the official version, and I'd heard it all before. Instead, I watched Mills. He was shifting his weight from one foot to the other, making a distracted box step over a small parcel of floor, and staring at Trautmann. Fear, anger, and disgust played unhidden across his face. And something else was going on too, something concentrated and furious, as if he were working elaborate formulas in his head. Trautmann checked his watch.

"Time flies, Johnny, and I got a little more cleaning up to do before I split. But don't worry. We'll have plenty of time to talk once we're on the road." A chill ran through my belly. Going anywhere with Trautmann was a bad idea, fatally bad. I needed some time to clear my head, some time for Neary to get there.

"Where are you meeting him?" I asked. They looked at me, puzzled. "Where are you meeting Nassouli?" Mills's puzzled look grew. Trautmann smiled.

"What the fuck are you talking about? You think that rat bastard Gerry is in this?" he said, with a sour laugh.

"Everyone thinks he's pulling the strings," I said. My voice sounded brittle and unfamiliar in my ears. "And that you two are the errand boys." Trautmann guffawed.

"Hey, that's nice. I like that. That motherfucker skips on me, he ought to make up for it somehow. Let that prick do me some good for once—let him take the heat on this. But between you and me, I don't need fucking Gerry's help, not when I got my boy here." Trautmann laid a massive hand on Mills's shoulder and looked at him, smiling large.

"That's one thing about Mr. Mills, John, he does know his shit. Yep, it was a lucky fucking day when you found me going through those files, Evan." Mills shrank away, as if he didn't like being touched or having Trautmann say his name. Trautmann ignored him and looked at his watch again.

"You cool your jets, Johnny, I'll be back in a sec," Trautmann said, and he touched my arm with the stun gun.

Fireworks went off in my head, and my body wrenched fiercely, back and out of the chair. I was on the floor, twitching. There was blood in my mouth, and I realized I'd bitten my tongue. I was facedown again, but not out this time. Through half-closed, shaking eyes I saw Mills looking at me, expressionless.

"Come on, bud," Trautmann said, "I got one more thing in the basement you can help with." He guided Mills toward the hallway. Mr.

Friendly. His hand was on Mills's shoulder again, and I thought of Brian, the luckless guard at the Roslyn Meadows mall. And I knew suddenly that Mills was not coming out of that basement alive. Trautmann pulled open a door in the hallway and flicked a switch and a square of yellow light was thrown on the wall. He stood aside to let Mills pass and followed him down, closing the door behind him.

Shit. It was time to go. It was past time. I tried working my wrists around. I felt the hard bite of the plastic cuffs. They were cinched tight enough that my hands were cold and going numb. I got my knees under me and stood, too fast. The room took a tilt, and a heavy wave of nausea hit me. I squeezed my eyes shut until it passed. I went to the kitchen counter, moving quietly. My gun was gone, and so was my phone. Shit.

I went to the back door and turned around and worked the knob with clumsy fingers. I turned and pulled, but the door didn't move. I took a closer look and saw a heavy sliding bolt, mounted about a foot from the top of the door, out of reach. Shit. I went into the hallway, past the basement door, to the front of the house. I was in a small, wood-paneled foyer. There were dark rooms on either side, and a dark, narrow stairway up. Straight ahead was the front door—with another heavy bolt set up high.

I went back to the hallway, to the basement door. There was a sliding bolt on it, too, at the same impossible height, but there was no lock on the knob. I heard voices on the other side of the door, but I couldn't make out any words. I went to the kitchen, and, as quietly as I could, I slid my chair into the hallway, to the basement door. Working it with my feet and legs, I wedged it under the knob. It wouldn't stop him, but it might slow him down a little.

I twisted in the cuffs some more, but there was no play; they were too tight for me to work my arms out in front of me. I went into the kitchen and looked on the table. Nothing there but the boxes. I looked inside them and saw only the manila envelopes. Each one had a name written on it in heavy black marker. I saw one with Bregman's name on it. And I saw another with Pierro's. Shit.

I went to the stove. It was gas, an old one with four burners and pilot lights instead of electric igniters. The black knobs were worn. Time to go. Past time. My cold fingers found the knob for the right front burner. I turned it up all the way and heard the whispered *whump* as it ignited.

Then I clenched my teeth and reached back and put the plastic cuffs, and my wrists, into the flame.

I swallowed a scream and yanked them out again after a few seconds. I took a deep breath and caught a corner of my jacket between my teeth. I bit down hard and put my wrists back in. The pain was searing. I smelled burning plastic and something else I didn't want to think about. And then I heard a cry of surprise and two gunshots from the basement. Shit.

I worked my wrists again. There was a little give, but not enough, and they hurt like hell from the burns. I heard movement downstairs—footsteps. I took another mouthful of jacket and put my wrists back in the flame. My teeth ground into the leather. The plastic smell was stronger, and I heard a sizzling sound. The pain was huge, molten, growing like a fiery balloon. And then my wrists came free.

Blood flowed back into my hands and with it more pain. I knocked off the remains of the cuffs and the shards of melted plastic. I went to the boxes and from the middle one fished out Pierro's envelope. It was bulky, and there was something hard and plastic inside. I folded the envelope and shoved it under my belt, behind my back. I heard footsteps on the stairs. Shit.

I looked at the boxes and the forty or fifty yellow envelopes inside them, and the names written in black. I thought about Bregman and Lenzi and the poor bastards in Burrows's stories. I thought about Burrows himself, and Lenzi's wife, crumpled and crying by her front door. I grabbed the vodka bottle from the counter and emptied it on the boxes. The basement doorknob rattled and the door creaked. The chair slid a fraction of an inch and caught. There was a startled noise, a louder rattle, and a shove against the door. Shit.

I pulled an envelope, wet with vodka, from the nearest box and touched it to the lit stove. It burst into flame. An angry bellow came from behind the door, and something slammed against it. The door shuddered wildly, and I felt the impact through the floorboards, but the chair held. I ran the burning envelope over the boxes, and flames took hold immediately. The fire was smoky and had a chemical smell.

There was another noise from the basement, a shout, enraged and unintelligible, and then the sound of gunfire, roaring around the room. The vodka bottle exploded, one of the boxes jumped and fell, burning, to the floor, the stove shook, and flames leapt from a gash in its front. Something tore at my cheek and my neck. Light from the basement streamed through three ragged holes in the kitchen wall. Time to go. Way past time.

I fumbled with the bolt. There was another crash, and I looked back through the smoke to see the chair splinter and the basement door fly open, and then I was out—down the back stairs, across the yard, into the snow, gone.

Chapter Twenty-seven

It was a neighborhood of cops and firemen, and they knew the sound of gunshots and the smell of burning houses. They didn't like either in their own backyards. I'd gone maybe a block, toward Hillside Avenue, when a local guy stopped me. He was still in uniform and looked done in, like he had just gotten off a long shift. His service piece was still on his hip.

I moved slowly and kept my hands in plain sight. I told him that Trautmann's house was on fire and that there was someone in the basement, probably dead, and someone else inside or nearby, definitely armed. And I told him that if I didn't sit down soon I was going to fall down. He seemed to recognize Trautmann's name and did not seem shocked by the turn of events. He told me to sit on the curb. I was happy to do it. Windows and doorways all around had begun to fill with the curious, and a couple of big guys were approaching from down the block. I put my head down and thought about not puking, and tried not to shake. The snow began to cover me.

The night became a blur of flashing lights and squalling sirens. EMS arrived just behind the fire crew and three blue-and-whites. The techs shined lights in my eyes, picked the bigger splinters from my face, and dressed the wound on my head and the burns on my wrists. They said I

needed X rays and returned me to the cops, who offered me a squad car
to sit in. I got in back but left the door open, in case I had to throw up.

The smoke from Trautmann's house drifted down the block and into
the car and stung my eyes. I closed them and put my head back and listened to the squawks and chatter around me. From what the firemen
said, the blaze had stayed mostly in the kitchen. It hadn't taken long to
control, but the room was pretty much destroyed. No one had yet found
any bodies, alive or dead. At some point I dozed off.

The detectives woke me, two wrung-out looking guys in their early
fifties. They made me get out of the car and show ID, then they asked me
a lot of questions and got annoyed when I answered only a few of them.
They put on a little theater for my benefit: one guy was Menace, the
other was Earnest Concern. But they were tired, and it was a halfhearted
effort, and we all knew it. They were just wrapping up, thinking about
cuffing me, when Tom Neary arrived, picking his way through the crowd
of vehicles, uniforms, and onlookers. Eddie Sikes and Juan Pritchard
drifted in behind him. They looked like they'd been sleeping in their
clothes.

They all showed ID, and Neary spoke to the detectives while Sikes,
Pritchard, and I stood around. A wave of nausea and dizziness hit me
while we waited, and I listed heavily to port. Sikes and Pritchard steadied
me, and I sat back down in the squad car. Neary kept talking. The cops
listened in silence, and eventually everyone started to nod. Then we all
went to the station house. I rode with the cops; Neary and company followed. They didn't cuff me and they didn't search me, but there was
nothing to be found now. The manila envelope was safe with Juan
Pritchard, who'd tucked it deftly into the folds of his topcoat when I'd
passed it to him.

The station house was small and too warm and filled with the smell
of burnt coffee. We sat in a room of green painted cinderblock, in beige
metal chairs at a beige metal table, and we waited. I drank a Coke and
put my head down on the table. Neary shook me when the lawyers
came: Mike Metz and an attractive, fortyish, black woman I didn't
know—a Brill lawyer. A couple of feds were right behind them. I
didn't recognize them, but the Brill people did.

Neary explained our operation downtown, and Sikes told them how
I'd gone after Mills. I picked it up from there, telling them how I'd followed Mills to Trautmann's place, and what had happened inside. I took
them through it about ten times. I told them that I'd started the kitchen

fire while melting off the plastic cuffs, and that the shooting had made it worse. I kept the part about torching the boxes to myself. And I said not a word about Nassouli or Pierro. The Brill boys sang backup as necessary. They'd gotten my cell phone calls, and when they knew where I was going they'd headed for Bellerose. Once out of Manhattan, they'd run smack into a two-hour traffic jam.

The cops asked about my client. Mike answered for me, and they didn't ask again. After the sixth or seventh telling, the feds started to horn in with questions of their own. This ticked the cops off, and started them wondering aloud about the feds' interest in all of this. The feds didn't like that, and so began a major pissing contest. Somewhere in the third round, they decided we could go, with the usual warnings to stay available.

In the parking lot, I retrieved the envelope from Pritchard. Nobody asked any questions about it. Mike drove Neary and me into the city. I sat in back and put my head against the window and watched the snow come down and become a brown slurry on the road. They might have spoken to me from up front, but if they did I didn't answer.

They took me to the St. Vincent's ER, which would soon start awarding me frequent flyer miles. The people there checked my eyes, my reflexes, and my balance and took pictures of my head and my ribs. The attending looked at the films and told me that while I had no fractures, I did have a mild concussion. He changed the dressings on my wrists and said the scarring wouldn't be bad. He gave me some drugs and some ointment, and he cut me loose. Mike and Neary were waiting to take me home.

"No talking," I said.

"In the morning," Mike said. I nodded.

"Long day," Neary said. I nodded.

"Some nice work," he said.

"Not nice enough." The car pulled up in front of my building, and I went inside. It was just past midnight.

It was a sunny, breezy Wednesday morning, nearly forty degrees out, and all that was left of the snow in my neighborhood were wet streets and the brief, bright showers of melt that scattered from the buildings when the wind blew. It was ten o'clock, and I was sitting in a deep chair with my feet propped up, wearing jeans and a turtleneck, drinking coffee and watching the glittering drops fall past my window. Mike Metz had arrived thirty minutes before and Tom Neary a few minutes later. They were showered, shaved, and suited up, well groomed if not well rested. They sat at my table, drinking coffee and talking. I knew I should be paying attention, but it seemed like too much work. Finally, Neary dragged me into it.

"The MWB liquidation committee is in an uproar, and their lawyers are chomping at the bit. No big surprise. The folks at Parsons are shitting bricks and circling the wagons—rounding up as many lawyers of their own as they can find, and trying to figure out what their liability insurance covers. And they're mightily pissed at Brill, for not giving them a heads-up on this. My management could give a shit, though. We've come out of this heroes, for having uncovered the whole thing. Truth is, they're thanking god none of our people were involved," he said. He turned toward me. "By the way, they think we owe you one on this. I explained that this just put you slightly less in my debt."

"Good you're watching out for me," I said. "Speaking of your people, what was up with Compton? Why was she so jumpy? She was looking like our guy until Mills ran."

"Your call scared hell out of her, but not because of anything to do with this shit," Neary said. "She spotted the tail up by Wall Street, turned around, and walked right up to me—pissed as hell. I thought she was going to slug me. Wanted to know what the fuck was going on. I said I wanted to know the same thing. We jawed at each other for a while, and then she tells me she's going up to Fulton Street, to see her lawyer. Seems she got this weird phone call and she thinks it's her husband—estranged husband—harassing her again. Turns out she's been trying to divorce the guy for nearly a year and he's turned into a real creep. Calls her at all hours, heavy breathing, bizarre accusations, follows her around. She thought this was more of the same."

"You tell her what was up?" I asked.

"Some of it. At first she was happy it had nothing to do with her hubby. Then she got pissed at me all over again for suspecting her. I smoothed it over some, but I've still got work to do there. I don't want to lose her," Neary said.

"And Vetter?" I asked.

"Just a slacker, out for a long coffee break, best we could tell," Neary said. He yawned and rubbed his hands over his face.

"You hear anything from Queens?" I asked Mike.

"Not since last night. They said they'd call when they had a body or if there was any word on Trautmann, but I imagine I'm not first on their list," he answered. He got up and filled his coffee mug. "You doing okay?" he asked. "Ready for your guests?"

"Ready enough," I said, and it was true. The ache in my ribs had mostly subsided, as long as I didn't move too much or too quickly. Ditto the pain from my burnt wrists. The nausea was gone, the dizziness was on the wane, and my headache had dulled and shrunk. Best of all, I didn't feel quite as stupid as I had last night. But one night of sleep was just a down payment. I was still brutally tired, and anxious to get the parade of people in and out of here so I could get back to bed. The intercom buzzed. Neary went to the wall unit.

"They're here," he said.

Shelly DiPaolo was first through the door. She took off her coat and looked the place over like a realtor. She was wearing a snug black suit with a short skirt and high black pumps. Her nails and lips were plum colored. Her perfume made itself at home. She nodded her head and gave me a chilly smile.

"Nice bat cave," she said. I nodded back.

"Help yourself to coffee," I said.

Fred Pell was behind her. He took three unwilling steps inside and stopped, looking like he was trying to find a corner to piss in. His coat stayed on, and his hands stayed in his pockets. The closest he came to a greeting was: "I guess a trust fund comes in handy, huh?" I wasn't any happier having him at my place than he was being here, but I was too tired to do more than ignore him. DiPaolo perched herself on one of my kitchen stools and crossed her nice legs.

"We don't usually make house calls, except to bust people," she said, speaking to me. "But Mr. Metz here made a good point about press interest in what happened in Queens last night, and that maybe our office didn't want to be too directly associated with it right now. He also said you were kind of chewed up. That was an understatement. You look like shit."

"Thanks," I said.

"That's what happens when you get in over your head," Pell said, with a nasty grin. I looked at him, but DiPaolo jumped in before I could speak.

"Shut up, Freddy," she said. "You're in the man's house, for chrissakes." Pell began to purple. DiPaolo cleared her throat. She looked at me again.

"The counselor and I made a deal on Monday," she said. Christ, was it just two days ago? "I'm prepared to hold up my end of it. I want you to hold up yours. I've read the police report, and the report from our guys, so I know what happened last night. What you say happened, anyway." She paused for a moment. "You kept Nassouli's name out of it. That was part of the bargain, so you did good there. But the other part is giving us what you've got on this whole thing."

"Provided it doesn't compromise our client," Mike interrupted. DiPaolo looked annoyed, but she nodded agreement.

"Yeah, heaven forbid. So, March, the stage is yours. Hit it." I swallowed some coffee and began.

"We told you our theory on Monday—that somebody was running a blackmail business, using Nassouli's personal files, targeting his former business associates. Well, we were right. It was Trautmann and Mills, in it together, until last night.

"They must've grabbed Nassouli's files very early on, in the first days or weeks that Parsons was on the job, and before the Brill team came in with their document control system. That would've been just after Nassouli had dropped out of sight. I gather from what Trautmann said that Mills walked in on him while Trautmann was going after the files.

"Based on what I know of Trautmann, I'm surprised Mills didn't disappear then and there. But somehow he survived that encounter, and he and Trautmann partnered up. I don't know how he did it. Could be Mills had been going after the files, same as Trautmann was. Could be he'd already looked them over and figured out their value, to someone with the right background. Maybe he understood that he had some of the expertise, but not all of it. And when he stumbled on Trautmann maybe he saw someone who could fill in the gaps. Maybe he was able to sell Trautmann on all that before the psycho could whack him. Who knows? But one way or another, each of them saw in the other something that he needed.

"I'm not sure how they divided the labor, but I can guess. Mills was a forensic accountant. And he knew his way around finance and banking and funds transfer. I expect he would've analyzed the files and picked out the promising targets. Trautmann could've helped with that, since he'd actually known these people. Mills probably worked out the delivery instructions for the blackmail payments, so as not to trigger any suspicious activity reports. I'd guess he also took care of moving the money around, once they'd got hold of it.

"Wherever they kept their funds, I doubt it was under their own names. And from what I overheard, they had more than just offshore bank accounts. It sounded like they'd bought property, too. In which case, they'd have needed documentation—fake passports certainly, maybe bogus corporate documents too. I figure Trautmann would've handled that. He also took care of communicating with their victims." DiPaolo listened quietly, still except for one foot, which turned slow circles at the end of her crossed leg. Pell fidgeted.

"The earliest score I know about was two years ago. They were in the middle of their latest one when all this happened. The cases I know of—and I don't know them all—involved people who'd dealt with Nassouli a long time ago—ten years or more. Maybe that was by design. Sticking to people on the far side of the statute of limitations would've lessened the odds of running up against you guys. Or maybe they weren't that smart. I don't know.

"They'd had a couple of failures, but from what Trautmann said, they'd had enough successes to make it worthwhile. Between them, they'd moved the money where they wanted it, and figured out how to spend it without attracting attention. Everything was copacetic, until I came along." I paused and drank some more coffee.

"When I showed up at MWB with Tom, it primed the pump. Mills got jumpy. When Trautmann told him I'd paid him a visit too, Mills must've flipped. He must've recognized me right away from Trautmann's description, and gone into a panic. I'm not sure he ever came out of it. It was Mills who dimed me out to Pell. He thought it up all by himself, and it was just the kind of too-cute stunt that would occur to a smart amateur like him. I figure if he'd talked to Trautmann about it first, Bernie would've buried him on the spot. But you've got to give Mills some credit; his idea almost worked. It got you to haul us downtown and warn us off. We just put up more of a fight than he counted on." DiPaolo was expressionless, but in the corner of my eye I saw Mike shaking his head slowly. I didn't dwell.

"When Trautmann found out what Mills had done, he knew the clock was ticking. So things accelerated. They put the squeeze to their latest victim, to wrap him up this week, and they were packing up their shop. From what I heard, it sounded like they'd culled through the files to find the most promising prospects—I guess so they could start up again someplace else. The keepers were in the boxes. If I understood Trautmann right, he'd burned the rest." DiPaolo laughed, short and cold.

"And we know how the boxes ended up, don't we?" She looked at me. I looked back, blankly, and went on.

"I figure they were going to split after this last job. It could be that Trautmann was always planning to off Mills. He didn't strike me as the partnership type, and he was definitely seeing Mills as a liability. Or maybe it was yesterday's events—Mills's panic and his leading me to Trautmann—that decided him. Either way, Mills was going to disappear, and so was I, once Trautmann had found out what he wanted to know." I downed the last of my coffee. "I got lucky. Mills didn't."

Everyone was quiet. Neary got up and poured some coffee. Mike looked out the window. DiPaolo stretched her neck, like she was working out the kinks.

"That was nice, March. But it's full of 'could be,' and 'maybe,' and 'I guess,' and 'I figure.' You got anything firm to back this up?" she asked.

"I've got a bag lady who identified Trautmann as the guy who paid her to send a fax to one of the victims. But you should probably know, she talks to Jesus—and according to her, he talks back." Neary suppressed a snicker. DiPaolo shook her head.

"That's it? That's what you've got for me? A fucking fairy story, backed up by a schizo? That's great," she said. I shrugged.

"It's what I have. It fits what happened, what I saw and what I heard. I can't prove most of it—not the way you want it—and, yeah, there are parts I'm guessing at. But the big pieces fit." Pell snorted derisively and looked pleased. I thought he was going to say something, but he didn't.

DiPaolo played with a ringlet of her strange blond hair. "Tell me about the fire, and those boxes. I read the reports, but I want to hear you tell it," she said. I told her, just the way I'd told it to the cops last night. When I was done she looked at me without expression for a long time.

"The Queens arson guys are thinking maybe there was an accelerant used in the kitchen," she said.

I nodded. "There was. Like I said, there was most of a gallon of vodka that got shot. That stuff burns." She looked at me some more.

"Too bad for us. But pretty fucking lucky for your client, don't you think?" she said. I didn't respond. "What about other victims? Got any names for me?" I looked over at Mike, who was still looking out the window. I was about to speak when he broke the silence.

"I think that comes right up to the line of attorney work-product, Ms. DiPaolo," Mike said, and he said it so it sounded true. DiPaolo gave him a long look. I thought she was going to press the point, but I was wrong.

"You think either of those two had anything to do with Nassouli's death?" she asked me. The question took me by surprise. DiPaolo continued. "Agent Pell has advanced the theory that Trautmann did Nassouli. A falling-out among thieves. Trautmann finds out Nassouli is about to skip, gets a little miffed at being left high and dry, and airs him out. Then, along the lines of your story, he makes for the files, trying to get something out of the deal. What do you think about that?" I was quiet for a while.

Could be it was the hectoring and the innuendo, or having Pell in my face again, right here in my own apartment. Could be I thought they should do their own damn jobs and leave me out of it. Could be I was just cranky, or something else—I don't know. But whatever the reason, I didn't tell DiPaolo she was full of shit. I didn't tell her that Trautmann was still nursing a grudge against Nassouli—the kind you don't hang on to when you've already had your payback—and that he'd had no idea Nassouli was dead. I shrugged.

"It's a theory," I said. "Ask Trautmann when you find him." Again Pell snorted and looked happy with himself, but said nothing. DiPaolo looked at him.

"Tell him," she said. Pell darkened. "Stop dicking around, and tell him," she repeated.

"Okay, okay," Pell said, and he gave me a shit-eating grin. "We could ask Bernie, but we'd be waiting a long fucking time for his answer. NYPD took him out of that basement early this morning, two big holes in his chest, clean through to the other side. Dug a nine-millimeter slug out of the wall behind him. That's what you lost, isn't it, a nine?" Pell chuckled nastily. "What was that line of crap you were spouting—'the big pieces fit?' Big pieces of shit—you don't know who aced who, and you were in the house with them. Assuming you didn't do him yourself."

Mike, Neary, and I looked at each other. Neary looked surprised. Mike looked tense. It was quiet for a while, then Mike turned to DiPaolo and spoke slowly and softly.

"I'm going to take Agent Pell's comment as facetious, Ms. DiPaolo, since any suggestion that John played a role in Trautmann's death would require me to defend him vigorously. That would include voiding our agreement and talking openly about this case, and Gerard Nassouli, to a wide audience, including the NYPD and the press."

DiPaolo shot an annoyed look at Pell and waved her hand. "Relax, counselor. Nobody's making that noise. One of the guys out in Queens thought about it, but the physical evidence supports March's story. And, believe it or not, we even put in a good word for him. Said we didn't think he was bullshitting about the shooting." Mike relaxed visibly.

"Mills did Trautmann," Neary said, shaking his head. "I wouldn't have thought he had it in him. Go figure."

"Any line on him yet?" Mike asked Pell.

"Not yet. They've staked out his place in Brooklyn, and his parents' house in Jersey, too. They found a little burned-up hunk of his briefcase in the kitchen, had what was left of his passport in it, and info on air charters from Miami. Turns out he was booked on a late flight there last night. He wasn't on it, but they're looking out for him at the airports too. They'll find him." I didn't share his confidence, but I said nothing. I was still trying to get my head around Trautmann being dead, and Mills having killed him. Some part of me was relieved.

Pell turned to DiPaolo. "We done here?" he asked. She nodded, and Pell walked out, leaving the door open behind him. DiPaolo climbed down from her perch and pulled on her coat. Then she looked at all of us, but mainly at me. Her voice was just above a whisper.

"You got lucky here, you most of all, March. You fucked me on those files, and don't think I don't know it. But I've got enough agita right now; I don't need to go chasing twenty-year-old crimes, or newer ones where the victims only testify under subpoena. And I don't need to be dancing around with you and the counselor. You get a pass this time, but my hand to god, you'll never get another one from me." Then she left.

"Not a happy woman," Neary said.

"After chasing Nassouli for three years, and having him turn up dead, she's looking for some good news. She might've thought those files were going to be it—a shot in the arm to her prosecutions. That's not going to happen, so she's pissed. We should be very grateful that she's got a full plate," Mike said.

"I am," I said. "Any bets on them finding Mills?"

"I'd think the chances are good," Mike said, putting on his coat. "As you pointed out, he's mostly an amateur. Trautmann handled all the heavy lifting."

"I don't know. I wouldn't underestimate the guy," Neary said. "Bernie did, and look what happened to him." He had a point. Neary slung his coat over his arm and picked up his briefcase. I called to him before he reached the door.

"Where did you tell me they found Nassouli's body?" I asked him.

"Way out in Suffolk. A place called Cedar Point Park. It's on the South Fork; I don't know which town. Why?"

"Just curious," I said. He looked at me, shook his head, and left.

"What was that about?" Mike asked.

"Nothing. You find Pierro last night?"

"Late last night. He's in San Francisco. Ecstatic doesn't begin to describe him. Helene should be calling you."

"She already has. She's coming by this afternoon to pick it up," I said.

"You look inside?" he asked.

"No," I said. "You want to?"

Mike looked horrified. "Look inside? I don't even want to know it exists."

Chapter Twenty-eight

Helene wouldn't be over for a few hours. It was time enough. I poured myself some coffee and cranked up my laptop. I got online and found a map of Long Island, then one of Suffolk County and then one of East Hampton, where I found Cedar Point Park. It was on a knob of land that jutted into Gardiner's Bay and looked out over Shelter Island. I opened my address book and found Randy DiSilva's number.

Randy is a small, round, mostly bald man in his middle sixties. He has a bushy gray moustache and a perpetual tan, and looks like he should be fixing dog races in Florida instead of running a small detective agency with his two sons, out in Riverhead. But he was born and bred on eastern Long Island, and he knows his way around the potato farmers and fishermen, and the old- and new-money crowds, too. I use him whenever I've got divorce work out there. Usually when I call, it's a drop-everything, all-hands-on-deck kind of drill. And Randy is always happy to scramble the squadron on my behalf, and overcharge me wildly for it. But he's thorough and fast, and in two years, neither of us has had cause to complain.

I reached him on the first try. I told him what I wanted and when I needed it. He thought about it for a couple of minutes, and then quoted me a price. It was over twice what it ought to cost—just about right from Randy; I agreed. He told me he'd call in two hours, and I knew that he would.

I went into my bedroom, and from under a pile of clothes that smelled of smoke, I pulled the manila envelope. It was creased and torn in places, but still sealed. I could feel a thick sheaf of paper in there, but its bulk came from the videocassette. I sat on the bed and opened the little metal clasp.

I can't say I was surprised. I recognized some of the documents from Pierro's fax. There were others I hadn't seen before. I read through them. They all followed the same pattern. Six companies, introduced to Rick Pierro by Gerard Nassouli; six sets of faked loan applications, authored by Nassouli and Pierro; six hefty credit lines extended by French Samuelson; then a blizzard of transactions—dirty money to clean.

And, of course, there were pictures. There were eight of them, and they were grainy, like images transferred from video. But they were clear enough to see the players and follow the action. Everyone looked so young—Helene, Nassouli, Trautmann, and a blond girl who couldn't have been fifteen.

I took the package out to the living room and turned on the TV and the VCR. I didn't watch much, enough to know that the pictures came off the tape, enough to revise my estimate of the blond girl's age downward, and to wonder if she'd been there willingly, or if she'd even known where she was. Enough to see that Alan Burrows hadn't lied about the production values; even the sound quality was good. The dialogue was limited and repetitive, but the voices were distinct.

I hadn't heard Nassouli speak before, or seen him except in photographs. His voice was medium-deep, with a trace of an English accent, but it was otherwise unremarkable. The sleek, ursine look he had in photos was there on tape too, and so was his camera awareness. Here, he was less an active participant than a director, a manipulator, a watcher. Yet he was also aware of being watched, and he seemed to pose and preen for his unseen audience. Quite a piece of work. I stopped the tape and put everything back in the envelope and sat on my sofa, sick and tired. Disappointed, but somehow not surprised.

I wanted to go back to bed and pull the covers over my head and stay that way for a week or two. But I couldn't, not yet. I checked the time. I changed the dressings on my wrists. I made a tuna sandwich and heated some soup from a can and ate. I read the paper. I checked the time again. Finally, the phone rang. It was Randy, as good as his word.

"It'll be three years in April that the place changed hands," Randy told me. "April 10 was the closing date, in East Hampton. Buyers name of Dooley, from the city; local lawyers on both sides. Need the names?"

"No, that's okay," I said. "You know how long it was on the market before it sold?"

"Hang on a sec, I got that here." There was a ruffling of papers. "Here we go. It was fast. Went on the market March 14; they got an offer on the sixteenth and accepted it the same day. The way they priced it, I'm not surprised. It was an easy two hundred grand under market for back then. Like they say in the trade, it was priced to move. You need anything else?"

"Let me have the address again," I said, and he gave it to me. I thanked Randy and promised to put his check in the mail today. We said our good-byes.

I went to my laptop. I pulled up my case notes and read through them and looked at the date Randy had given me. I went back online. It didn't take long for me to find a detailed map of the area around the address I'd gotten from Randy. I sat there looking at it for a while, and then I pulled up driving instructions from that address to Cedar Point Park. The instructions were short and simple, and why not? The trip was barely half a mile. I pushed back from my table and looked out the windows at the bars of bright sunlight and blue shadow that fell on the buildings across the way. I rubbed my eyes.

It was wild conjecture and circumstantial bullshit, and I knew it—or at least a part of me did. No cop or prosecutor would waste a brain cell on it. Yeah, there was motive, more than enough. It was sitting in an envelope on my kitchen counter. It was easy to imagine a scene, three years back, of Gerard Nassouli waving a sample of that stuff in front of Pierro, in an attempt to finance the fugitive life he was about to embark on. And it was easy to imagine a murderous response. But that's all it was—imagination.

Pierro had a motive; Mrs. Pierro did too, for that matter. But so, it seemed, did virtually everyone who'd run across Gerard Nassouli. There were forty or fifty envelopes in those boxes back at Trautmann's place, and who knows how many more that went up in his bonfire. Forty or fifty people with motives, some perhaps better than Pierro's. But how many of them had had houses half a mile from where Nassouli's body was found? And how many of those had put their houses up for sale a week after Nassouli disappeared? How many of those houses had been priced to move so quickly?

"A fucking fairy story," I heard Shelly DiPaolo's voice say in my head. And she'd be right. I didn't even have a schizo to back me up on this one. But another part of me was unconvinced, troubled by the coincidences, and thinking about how one might trace the Pierros' movements on a March day nearly three years back.

"A fucking fairy story," I said aloud. And one that nobody cared about. Nobody mourned Gerard Nassouli; he'd left behind no family. And nobody would argue that the world wasn't a better place without him. I rubbed my eyes again and got up and drank a glass of water.

Maybe it was my own ruffled feathers fueling this. Maybe I was pissed off because they'd lied to me, both of them, from the get go—Pierro about being clean, Helene about everything else. But that wasn't a surprise, not really. Clients do it all the time, and I'd half-known that these clients were no different. Maybe it was because I'd thought better of Helene. I'd liked her. I'd liked the way she was with her kids, and I'd liked her photographs. I'd liked her style. I'd thought she was smart, and that she had better judgment than this, or at least better taste.

The intercom buzzed. She was right on time.

Helene walked in with her big shearling coat on her arm and her cheeks red from the chill outside. She wore snug, suede pants in a fawn color, a pink cashmere sweater, and low boots. A brown leather tote bag hung from her shoulder. She looked around.

"This is nice, John. Wonderful light, and great ceilings," she said. She was smiling and her brown eyes sparkled and her chestnut hair was loose and glossy. She looked brand-new. Her makeup was nearly invisible and a faint perfume moved around her, something with roses.

Helene focused on me, and her pretty smile faded, replaced by an equally pretty look of concern. "Oh lord, your wrists, your face—you've been hurt again, haven't you? It was over all this, wasn't it? Oh, John, I'm so sorry. Are you alright?"

"I'm fine. I just need some more sleep."

Her brow furrowed deeply. "This is too much, really. I . . . I'm so sorry, John."

I shook my head a little and told her to sit. I offered her a drink. She sat at the kitchen counter and asked for a seltzer. I poured two. She drank some of hers and set it down. She propped her elbows on the counter and rested her chin atop her clasped hands and looked at me. I looked back. The manila envelope was on her right, not three feet away. She never glanced at it.

"There's some news since we spoke this morning," I said. A frown moved quickly across her face and vanished, like a breeze rolling across a pond. She stared at me, waiting for it. I told her about Mills and Trautmann and who'd killed whom. She thought about it for a while, her face blank, then she gave a tiny shrug.

"I should think he'd be easier for the police to track down than that Trautmann," she said, without much concern. She sipped at her drink some more. I shrugged back at her.

"Maybe." Helene was quiet, watching the bubbles rise in her glass.

"We're so grateful, John, Rick and I both," she said, finally. I nodded.

"Is Rick still in San Francisco?" I asked.

"He's taking the red-eye home tonight. But he's so happy after talking to Mike, he could probably fly back under his own steam. Speaking of which . . . we wanted you to have this." She reached into her bag and drew out a small envelope. She handed it to me. It was heavy, ivory-colored stock. Inside was a check. It was a big one, and it was made out to me.

"What's this?"

"It's just a token, really," she said. "We're so lucky that we had you to stand by us. I don't know what we would've done otherwise." I handed the check back to her.

"Thanks, Helene, but no thanks," I said. She looked surprised and confused. "It's a nice gesture, but not a good idea. Technically, I work for Mike. He pays me well and passes along those costs to you, probably with a hefty markup. It's because I work for him, and not you, that what I do can stay confidential. Taking money from you complicates things." But Helene was insistent.

"But we want you to have something—a bonus—for everything you've done. We can give it to Mike, and he can pass it along to you. That's okay, right? Or do you want cash? We could do that too."

"You can do whatever the hell you please," I said, surprised by my own sudden anger. "It's your money. If you're determined to get rid of some, I can think of a dozen charities that could use it." Helene drew back, her face stiff. She was very still.

"I've offended you somehow, John," Helene said softly, the accent more distinct in her lowered voice. "I don't know how, but I must've, and I'm very sorry. It's the last thing I meant to do. If you'd like us to make a charitable donation, of course we will. Just tell me where to send it." I was quiet and so was she, for what seemed a long time. My eyes flickered down the counter to the manila envelope, and Helene's eyes followed.

"Jesus," she said, in a slow, tired sigh. She shook her head. She pressed her palms together in her lap and looked down at them and took a deep breath. When she spoke her voice was flat and exhausted.

"You looked. And now you're angry with us—angry with me. You, too? Why, because I lied? Because you saw the pictures and read the papers, and now you think that I'm a whore and Rick's a crook? Is that it? You're mad because you worked so hard, and got hurt, and it turned out to be all on account of a whore and a crook?" She ran out of breath and stopped. She shook her head a little.

"You're mad? How do you think we feel? All you did was work for a whore. It could've been worse. You could've woken up one morning to find you'd married one." She laughed, harsh and bitter. A tear rolled down her cheek, and then another, but she did not sob or sniffle.

"I was nineteen, for god's sake. I was a kid—too stupid, too full of myself. Were you never like that? Am I the only one?" A shudder ran through her and her shoulders shook but she bit back whatever was welling up. "And Rick—back then, he wasn't much more than a kid himself. He was finding his way, trying to make something out of his life. And the world he found himself in just didn't seem to want any part of him." The breath left her again and she paused, still shaking her head.

"You want an apology? Fine, we've got plenty of those—even more than we've got money. That's all we do now is say we're sorry. I say I'm sorry to Rick, for being . . . for not being what he thought I was. He says he's sorry to me for the mistakes he's made. He breaks down; I hold him together, and he says he's sorry for that too. We both say it, silently, to the children, and we pray they never know any of this." She stopped and held her glass, as if she was about to drink, but she didn't. Her voice was exhausted, too thin and strained to carry anger or sadness or anything other than her plain words.

"Jesus, I am just so tired of it all. I just want it to be over. But what's one more between friends, huh, John?" She straightened herself in her seat and put her hands in her lap. Tears were still rolling slowly down her cheeks. "I'm sorry, John. I'm sorry I lied. I'm sorry I let you down. I'm sorry you think I'm a whore. I'm sorry Rick and I weren't worthy of your efforts. There, does that about cover it?" She stood and pulled on her coat. She reached down the counter and took the envelope and tucked it in her bag. She chuckled ironically.

"Maybe you should have some kind of test for prospective clients; find out beforehand if they measure up to your moral standards. Find out if they're the kind of people who deserve your help. Then you could avoid these problems." She wiped her eyes and cheeks with the back of her hand, and drank some seltzer. Then she looked at me and shook her head. She put her hand lightly on my arm.

"I'm sorry, John. That was . . . that wasn't right. This has been so terrible. It's taken such a toll. I wish you could've known us before all this. This isn't us. We're . . . we're good people. I know that must sound stupid to you." She squeezed my arm gently and moved away, unhurried, to the door. I spoke as she reached for the knob.

"You ever go back to East Hampton?" I asked. She turned around.

"It was expensive to keep up, and there were vandalism problems, too, and it took so long to get out there, that's why we sold it," she said.

Her answer was matter-of-fact and mundane, low-key and unexceptional. It was delivered smoothly, but with pauses and stops in all the right places, so it didn't seem practiced. It was the best kind of lying. But it was the answer to a question I hadn't quite asked, and in the instant the words passed her lips, we both knew it. We looked at each other across a dense silence.

There was the briefest flash of something in Helene's eyes. Fear? Anger? It was gone too quickly to tell, replaced by a steely calculation, a quick, cold weighing of options and odds and possible outcomes. It reminded me, suddenly and vividly, of the look in Bernhard Trautmann's eyes when I'd stared at them over the barrel of my gun.

"Fuck you," she said, like she was spitting out a pit, and she left.

I stared at the door for a long time, until the hairs on the back of my neck relaxed and my spine warmed up. Helene Pierro was a scary person, less obviously so than someone like Trautmann, but all the more dangerous because of that. Her perfume still hung in the air, more like a threat than a promise now.

I rinsed Helene's glass and my own and put them in the dishwasher. Then I wrote out a check to Randy DiSilva, slipped it in an envelope, and went out to mail it. The temperature was dropping with the sun, and a chill ran through me as I stood in the doorway of my building. I found myself checking the street, as I had when I'd thought Trautmann might be around, looking for payback, and realized I had that same creepy, watch-your-back feeling. I shook my head. Helene was scary, I told myself, but a drive-by wasn't her style. I dropped the letter in the box on the corner and went back home. I was hurting in many different places, and my bed was calling.

I pulled the shades and kicked off my shoes and stretched out. I thought some more about my conversation with Helene, and about calling Mike, and somewhere in there I drifted off. Despite my weariness, or maybe because of it, my sleep was tiring and fevered. I tossed and turned and got tangled in the sheets and pillows. I came near to waking several times, and when I did I was sweating. My eyes were hot, and my throat felt parched and dusty. I willed myself back down. At some point I had the dream again, or a version of it. It was by the lake and Anne was there, but so was Helene Pierro and someone else, whose face I couldn't see. I was calling out to . . . someone, when the doorbell woke me.

It was dark out, just six p.m., according to my clock. I rubbed my face and my head. I went into the bathroom and drank cold water from the tap. The bell rang again. I splashed water on my face and took some deep breaths. Then I went to the door, flicking on lights as I walked. I looked through the peephole. Jane Lu. I opened the door and Jane smiled at me, but her smile turned into a frown as she surveyed the latest damage.

"This is ridiculous," she said. "How can you get any health insurance?" She wore a charcoal gray pants suit with a bolero jacket, and underneath it a square-necked blouse in pearl gray. Her boots were black suede with a square heel. She held two paper bags in her arms. The delicious smell of Chinese food hit me, and my stomach made a longing noise. Hunger chased away my grogginess.

"Come in," I yawned. "We can talk about my health plan after we eat." I turned into the apartment, and as I did there were fast footsteps in the hallway. I turned back and saw a dark figure there, and Jane lurched forward and staggered into my arms. Her packages scattered. Evan Mills locked the door and pointed my gun at my face.

Chapter Twenty-nine

Mills may have been an amateur when he started with Trautmann, but he'd been an apt pupil. He made us turn around, and then he grabbed a handful of Jane's hair and screwed the gun barrel up under her chin. He made me lie on the floor, with my hands behind me. He made Jane put the cuffs on me. They were plastic again, thumb cuffs this time. Jane knelt by me, and I could hear her ragged breathing, and smell her perfume, and feel the heat coming off of her. She was trembling badly. When she finished, he made her lie on the floor too. Then he tightened my cuffs and cuffed her. Then he sat us both on the sofa. He worked quickly and said maybe ten words the whole time.

We sprawled uncomfortably back on the sofa and he stood before us and we all looked at each other. The air was thick with fear, adrenaline, and the sound of hard breathing. My heart was hammering, shaking my body, and my ears were full of pounding blood. I concentrated on breathing slowly and deeply, on driving my heart rate down, and I saw that Mills was doing the same. Jane's eyes were large, and they darted back and forth between Mills and me. She was still shaking, though not as much now. Her body was rigid, and her mouth was a tight, angry line. But I saw that she, too, had wrestled her breathing under control—slow, deep, in through the nose, out through the mouth.

Mills wore the same clothes as he had yesterday—the black slacks, the navy sweater over a yellow shirt—but the overcoat was gone, replaced by a bulky black parka. The look was less aging preppy now than speed freak, amped out and coming down off a weeklong jag. He was wrinkled and sodden and grimy—like he'd slept in an ashtray, though he probably hadn't slept at all. His face was skeletal and unshaven, and there was lots of gray in the stubble around his chin. His hair was dark and matted. There were burns on his dirty hands and a strong smell of smoke around him.

The skin under his eyes was gray with fatigue, but the eyes themselves were wired and scary. They roiled with a crazy mix of fear, anger, brutal exhaustion, some of the furious calculation I'd seen last night, and . . . something else. Something that was over the edge and around the bend, something that had slipped its moorings and drifted way out of the harbor. Something that came from putting two bullets in a man and finding that you liked it and that you were looking for a chance to do it again. When I spoke, I did it softly and slowly.

"They've got nothing on you. Zero. Trautmann was self-defense, and no one will say anything different. He was going to do you; that was clear to me, and it's what I told the cops. They were surprised to find him in that basement instead of you. As for the blackmail—that's up in smoke. There's no proof, and none of the victims will say a word. Get yourself the right lawyer and you walk away clean on this," I said.

Mills looked at me and smiled a little. He took a deep breath and walked into my kitchen. He put the gun down on the counter and peeled off his parka and tossed it on the counter too. He worked his neck and stretched his arms and shook them out, like a broad jumper limbering up. He ran his hands through his dirty hair, pushing it back behind his ears. He unbuttoned his shirt cuffs and pushed his sleeves up over his wiry forearms and washed his hands and face in my sink. He dried them with a paper towel that he balled up and tossed on the counter. He took another deep breath and looked around the place and nodded appreciatively. Then he picked up the gun and came around the counter and hit me two times in the face with it.

He was strong, but he was sloppy and not that fast, so I could roll a little with the blows. On the other hand, I was bound and lying nearly prone, so I couldn't roll much. It hurt like hell. The barrel raked my cheek and my ear, and my head somehow ended up in Jane's lap. I heard her cry out and felt her start to shake again. I knew I was bleeding on her. Mills grabbed my shoulder and hoisted me back up and started talking.

"Do you know how long I put up with that Neanderthal? How long I had to listen to his ravings and his insults and his bullying and his stupid fucking nicknames? Almost three years, John. Almost three years of that shit. And do you know how hard I worked? I mean, it's not like it was all laid out for us. It took research. I had to study those files, figure out what scam Nassouli had going with each of those people, figure out where they all were today, how much they were worth, how much they had at stake. And all the while listening to that ape-man grunting in the background."

He paced slowly in front of me, gesturing casually with the gun. His voice was calm, almost distracted, but his eyes were weird and frantic. He'd liked hitting me, and a part of him was thinking about that.

"I worked hard, and I put up with a lot of crap, and that's not even counting my day job. But all that's behind me, now. I'm a rich man, John. You don't know what it feels like, becoming rich, do you? From what Bernie said, you've always been rich. But I'll tell you, it's very . . . liberating. You think I'm going to give that up? Your bullshit isn't even convincing." He paused and wiped his mouth with the back of his hand.

"I know DiPaolo, and I know Pell. I know how hungry they are. And even if they did let go of this, you think my masters at Parsons and Perkins would? Not likely. Best case, I'm stuck in civil court for the rest of my life, hocking my underwear to pay the lawyers. No thanks." He thought for a moment, and gave us a conspiratorial look.

"Besides, the cops will eventually find a delivery guy in Cobble Hill with no coat and a hole in his head, and the bullet they dig out of him will match what they pull out of Bernie. And after that they'll have something on me, don't you think?" I heard Jane inhale sharply, and then there was quiet. Shit.

"Why aren't you on your way out of town?" I asked after a while. Mills looked at me sharply, less distracted now.

"Well, you're kind of the reason for that, John. You kind of fucked that up for me, big time. When you torched Bernie's place, you torched my plane tickets and all my traveling cash too. And what do I find when I go back to my apartment? Why, cops, of course. And at my garage too, so I can't even get my goddamned car out. And I can't very well use my credit cards, now can I? Even I know that. So I figured you could help me out a little, John. I figured you could make up for all the trouble you caused and give me a hand getting to Miami. We can start with the couple of thousand that went up the chimney, and a change of clothes and the keys to your car and . . ."—he looked at Jane and wiggled his eyebrows theatrically—"and then we'll see what else comes to mind." Shit. Shit. Shit. Mills went to the kitchen counter and took a seat, the same one Helene had used. He hitched his arm over the back and crossed his legs, gesturing with the gun in his hand.

"Yes, I could use a little R and R before I run down south. I did a lot of wandering last night, all over town—Queens, Brooklyn, Manhattan. Quite a journey—very gritty, very noir, very Charles Bukowski. A real dark night of the soul. I never realized how busy the subway is, even late at night. But I was surprised, how little cash people carry these days—or maybe it was just my bad luck. That delivery guy was my best, and he had maybe three hundred bucks, plus the coat. Of course, he made me work for it. He . . ."

The telephone rang like a grenade, once, twice, three times before it went to voice mail. Mills looked at me, more figuring going on in his head. Who was it? Would they call again? How long before they got worried? How long before someone knocked on the door? He got up and flexed his shoulders.

"First things first," he said.

He made us lie on the bathroom floor while he took a leak and showered and shaved. My bathroom isn't small, but even so it was cramped with the three of us in there, and the forced intimacy with Mills—the proximity of his white, hairless body, and his smell, and the sounds he made—was bizarre and repellent. I was filled with a sudden rage when he picked through my medicine cabinet, and I had to stop myself straining at the cuffs. Jane had grown very still. Her body was relaxed and her breathing was like clockwork, but her face was immobile and her eyes remote. I spoke to her softly while Mills was in the shower and we lay on the floor, our faces against the tile.

"I'm glad I had the cleaning lady in this week," I said. She looked at me, but before she could speak, Mills kicked me in the head with a wet foot.

"Shut the fuck up, John."

He made us lie on the floor in my bedroom while he rifled my closets. He put on a pair of corduroys and a button-down shirt. He was taller than me, and skinny, but they fit well enough. The shower and the fresh clothes made him look cleaner but not better. Staring out from his shaven face, his eyes looked somehow more crazy. He marched us out to the sofa and pushed us down on it again. He stood before us, tapping his bare foot.

"Cash," he said. He looked at me, expectantly.

"There's a hundred or so in my wallet, on the counter, and maybe three hundred in my top dresser drawer. If you want more than that, we need to go to a cash machine," I said.

"I'm sure you'd love to make that trip, huh?" He looked at Jane. "What about you?" She turned toward him, but seemed to look right through him.

"There are two hundred dollars in my bag," she said. Her voice was dead flat. He looked at her a while and nodded. He picked up her purse and looked through it. He pocketed the cash and put her cell phone on the counter. He looked at her driver's license photo and back at Jane.

"It doesn't do you justice," he said. Shit. Then he went into the bedroom and came back quickly with a wad of cash.

"Six hundred twenty-seven dollars total. Not great, but a start," he said. He looked at me. "Car keys."

"I don't own a car," I said slowly. Mills's pale face grew paler, and his wide, thin mouth twitched. He backhanded me with the gun. I saw it coming and flicked my head back, but not far enough. He caught me on the eyebrow. It started to bleed.

"You just keep fucking me up here, John. How can you not own a car? It's not like you can't afford to keep one. What are you, too fucking cheap?" He shook his head and said something to himself. He turned to Jane. "How about you?" She looked through him and shook her head. Mills looked at her, and for a moment I thought he was going to hit her too, and my whole body tensed. But he relaxed.

"Fuck it," he said. "A car would've been nice, but it could've been a hassle too. What I'm thinking now is maybe a bus. What do you think, John? I take the PATH to Jersey City, hop on a Jersey Transit train to Trenton, connect over to the Philly commuter line, and catch a bus from Philly to Miami. And once I'm in Miami, John, I am gone, gone, gone." He liked the story he was telling, and he liked telling it to us. He knew the implications, and knew that we did too. He smiled, and his eyes were shiny.

"So, good company, a good night's sleep, and an early start in the morning. That sounds like a plan to me. But first, some dinner." He went into the kitchen and started rummaging through the refrigerator and the cabinets. He muttered to himself about the pitiful state of my larder.

I looked at Jane and smiled what I hoped was a comforting smile. She stared back at me, uncomforted. Mills was crazy, and he was getting crazier by the minute, and we both knew it. He wasn't pretending that we could walk away from this if we just cooperated; I wouldn't have believed him if he had. He'd killed twice and liked it, and he was going to do it again. The only questions were when, and what would come first, and would he give me any opening at all.

He took his head out of the refrigerator suddenly, as if a thought had occurred to him, and he looked over at the paper bags near the front door. White cardboard containers had spilled out of them. One had burst open, and a pile of cold sesame noodles was growing colder on the wood floor. He walked over, knelt down, picked up a few noodles in his fingers, and ate them.

"Now, this is more like it. A little dusty, but definitely more like it," he said, chuckling.

He sat at the kitchen counter, eating from the containers with the complimentary chopsticks. He ate quickly, but he was messy. He worked his way through the food in silence, staring at us—mostly at Jane—as he ate. He wiped his mouth and threw the napkin on the counter and sighed.

"That was good. A little cold, but excellent choices. My compliments." He nodded to Jane. She was still and distant. "Now, shall we see what the future holds?" He broke open a fortune cookie and looked at the strip of paper inside and began laughing wildly. "Oh, this is priceless—really priceless," he cackled. He held the fortune up. "You will receive an unexpected visit," he read. His shoulders shook and his face reddened and little tears formed in his eyes. He was becoming hysterical, and he fought to control it. After a while he won. He took a deep breath and wiped his forehead with the back of his hand.

"Must be the MSG; goes right to my head." He focused on us again, and then on Jane. She was motionless and far, far away. "Hey, pearl of the Orient, do you ever talk? I know you're miffed because I fucked up your cozy little evening with John-boy. Well, your honey fucked me out of a few million dollars, so you tell me, who's worse off? But hey, maybe later we can make it up to one another, huh?" Jane gave him no reaction. He picked the gun off the counter and started tossing it lightly from one hand to the other. He was working himself up to it now. He looked at me.

"You like the inscrutable types, John? Is she a change of pace after the late Mrs. March? Hope to change your luck by changing models, maybe?" Mills paused, and said in a stage whisper, "I got a newsflash for you, pal, it's not working." He laughed wildly at his joke, and his laughter threatened to go over the edge again, but he pulled it back. Shit.

"It's a pity Bernie can't join us tonight. I know he would've loved this. And you made a real impression on him, John. I mean, he had a serious hard-on for you, and it just got worse when he read all that stuff about you. And of course, he always loved the ladies." He looked at Jane, but she gave him nothing. He moved closer to her.

"And speaking of ladies, I saw the lovely and talented Helene Pierro come in and out of here this afternoon. First time I've seen her with clothes on; almost didn't recognize her. Frankly, I like her better without. Very limber, and such a nice way with the language. I guess Bernie was right after all, about you working for Pierro." He stood in front of Jane and put his hand on her shoulder, and my stomach lurched. Jane was perfectly still, her gaze beyond the horizon. He was getting to it now.

"Poor Bernie. I'll miss him in a way. He wasn't dumb, just a little crass. But he was inventive. And let me tell you, he could've had quite a career in adult entertainment. Did you ever get to see his work, John? Maybe with Jane's help I could re-create some of his more memorable moments. For your viewing pleasure, and as a sort of memorial to Bernie. I know . . ."

I didn't see it coming, and neither did Mills. Jane was fast. Her square boot heels hammered his bare feet like pile drivers, and while the scream was still forming in his throat, she twisted back and kicked up at his crotch. The angle wasn't great and the sofa slid, and she caught him high, just at the beltline. Mills staggered backward, his feet bloody. He brought the gun up, and I launched myself low off the sofa. I caught him in the knees and he fell back against the kitchen counter and bounced off and scrabbled out from under me. Jane did some scissor thing with her legs and flipped herself off the sofa, coming up lightly on two feet.

Mills was screaming and scrambling to his feet. He squeezed off a shot and something hot roared past my ear and whanged into an iron column behind me. I got my legs under me, and to my right I saw Jane square herself, take a half step, and launch a kick. Mills raised the gun, and I drove up and forward with everything I had and he fired. I buried my head in his sternum and felt the breath leave him and felt his feet come off the ground and I kept going—forward, forward, until I heard glass shattering, heard Mills cry out, and felt the cold night air on my face.

I leaned on my shoulder against the empty window frame. Below me, the street was still, a tableau of frozen traffic, upturned faces, and the body of Evan Mills, broken in a sea of broken glass. The only movement was the tattered window shade, brushing against my face; the only sound I heard was my own gasping. I eased myself carefully back inside.

I remember trying to think of something clever to say, something understated and ironic. Maybe something about first dates or lousy houseguests, I don't know. I remember turning around. And then I saw her there, on her back, her hands still bound, one leg out, the other bent beneath her, her head resting at an odd angle in a spray of blood.

Chapter Thirty

They kept me overnight, for observation, they said. They inventoried the new damage and declared me lucky—cuts, abrasions, and bruises only. Nothing broken, nothing shot. I was the lucky one. But I was still getting over a head injury, and someone thought I was displaying a strange lack of affect, and they had the beds available, so what the hell?

From time to time there were a lot of people in my hospital room, but I don't remember much of what they said. The Manhattan cops came first, and then the feds; the Queens cops were close behind. Fred Pell was there; Shelly DiPaolo sent Conaway in her stead. Mike stood in the doorway while they asked questions and I gave answers, and when I got tired of repeating myself, he made them leave. They seemed satisfied, he said. I didn't care if they were or not. When the cops were gone, the nurse gave me something for pain. It worked well, but left me feeling like my brain was hovering high above the rest of me.

After that, Tom Neary stopped by, and so did my brother Ned and both my sisters. Even though I was the lucky one, they all seemed very grave. Maybe it was just me; maybe it was the drugs. They came and spoke and left quickly, until only Mike remained. I was getting tired.

"Where is she?" I asked. He told me. I closed my eyes.

When I opened them again, the room was mostly dark and Mike was gone. I looked at the clock. It was past midnight, and quiet. I heard voices speaking far away, I heard the distant whoosh of traffic, and I heard my own breathing, still slow and regular from sleep. Beyond my small table lamp, the only light came from the blue glow of a television, playing to an empty bed across the hall.

I hauled myself up to a sitting position. The world stayed on its axis and my brain was back home in my skull. I lowered the railing and swung my legs over and stood. The floor was cold, and I felt a draft creep in behind me. I stepped into the hallway. It was empty and dark. The nurses' station was a long way off and lit up like a cruise ship on a night-time sea. I walked quietly across the hall and down two doors. The door to room 420 was open. It was a double room, but there was no other occupant than Jane, asleep like a child atop the high bed.

They'd told me she would be fine. Yes, it looked bad; head wounds often do, they'd said. But this was a graze and a mild concussion and nothing more. Not even a scar would remain. She'd be out in two days' time. She would be fine, they'd promised, and though I believed them, I needed to see. I walked slowly to her bed.

She was on her side, turned toward me, and in repose her face looked very young and impossibly beautiful. Her cropped black hair was like ink on the pillow, and in the glow of a nightlight I could see the bandage on the side of her head and the bruising around it like a shadow. Even amid the hospital odors, I caught a hint of her perfume.

There was a chair against the wall that was light enough for me to lift without screaming. I carried it to the bed and sat. When I looked up, Jane was looking back at me. She smiled a tired, sort of goofy smile and murmured something I couldn't make out. I leaned in closer.

"Stay," she whispered. Then she reached a small hand out from under her blanket and took hold of mine and closed her dark eyes and slept. I put my head back and shut my eyes too, and it was well after dawn when human voices woke us.

Acknowledgments

Thanks are due many people for their support while I was writing this book. To my early readers, Nina Spiegelman, Barbara Wang, and John Spiegelman, for their advice and awesome tolerance for pestering. To Joe Toto, for his tour of the old neighborhood. To the first pros that read this, Rod Huntress, Chris Niles, and Susan Schwartz, for the kind of feedback that can only come from people unrelated to the author by blood or marriage. To my agent, Denise Marcil, and her team at The Marcil Agency, for all of their efforts on my behalf. To Sonny Mehta, at Knopf, for making the editorial process so thoroughly entertaining. And to Alice Wang, for more than I can possibly say.

A NOTE ABOUT THE AUTHOR

Peter Spiegelman is a veteran of more than twenty years in the financial services and software industries, and has worked with leading financial institutions in major markets around the globe. Mr. Spiegelman retired in 2001 to devote himself to writing. *Black Maps* is his first novel. He lives in Connecticut.

A NOTE ON THE TYPE

This book was set in Minion, a typeface produced by the Adobe Corporation specifically for the Macintosh personal computer and released in 1990. Designed by Robert Slimbach, Minion combines the classic characteristics of old-style faces with the full complement of weights required for modern typesetting.

Composed by Creative Graphics,
Allentown, Pennsylvania
Printed and bound by Berryville Graphics,
Berryville, Virginia
Designed by Virginia Tan